ECHOES

ECHOES

ALICE REEDS

Entangled Publishing, LLC
2614 South Timberline Road
Suite 105, PMB 159
Fort Collins, CO 80525
rights@entangledpublishing.com

Entangled Teen is an imprint of Entangled Publishing, LLC.

Visit our website at www.entangledpublishing.com.

Edited by Lydia Sharp and Stephen Morgan
Cover design by Fiona Jayde
Cover image by Sundarananda/iStock
Interior design by Toni Kerr

ISBN 978-1-64063-247-9
Ebook ISBN 978-1-64063-248-6

Manufactured in the United States of America

First Edition August 2018

10 9 8 7 6 5 4 3 2 1

an imprint of Entangled Publishing LLC

To seventeen-year-old me, who was sure her idea would never amount to much of anything:
You've made it.

CHAPTER ONE
THE ISLAND

We *are going to die.*

That was the first thought that shot through my mind. *Maybe it's just a dream* was my second, but then the plane dipped down again, shaking and rattling. I gripped the armrests like my life depended on it. Maybe it did.

Movement to my left told me Miles was awake, too. His eyes were wide, like mine. Normally, I'd have delighted in seeing him shook for once. But thinking you're about to die has a weird way of bringing people together.

"What the hell is going on?" he said.

"I don't know…turbulence?"

At the front of the plane, the door to the cockpit was open. The pilot looked back at us, his expression tense.

He yelled, "You kids, hold on—"

The plane plummeted, and my stomach shot into my chest. A scream got stuck in my throat. Air punched out of my lungs. The ceiling screeched and tore and buckled and peeled away, exposing the sky —

Darkness. *Am I alive? Dead?*

My mind swam toward the surface of an endless black ocean. When I opened my eyes, a blinding light stung my vision. The feeling of falling was gone. We'd stopped.

Blinking against the pain, the first thing I could make out was the shattered TV screen dangling from the back of the seat in front of me. The same TV I'd watched only a few hours ago. *Was* it hours ago? A minute? A day? I had no idea. I touched my face and head — no blood, at least. *How is that possible?*

Beyond the broken TV, where a wall and cockpit door had once been, was nothing but a hole with frayed metal edges digging into the ground. Where was the front of the plane? Outside, where the wing used to be, were shrubs and broken trees, dirt and sand. And out past the sand, endless water. The ocean.

Holy hell.

Panic tightened my throat and my hands shook.

We crashed.

I had to calm down. Deep breaths in and out. Own the moment, own your fear. Don't let it own you. That was my mantra in moments like this, thanks to years of kickboxing, and it worked. A little. My hands weren't trembling anymore.

I was okay. I'd survived. Which meant anyone else on the plane —

Oh no.

Miles.

When I looked from the window to my other side, I was

sure there would be a bloody corpse. But no. No blood on his white button-down shirt that I could see. But there had to be some injuries below the surface. And he wasn't moving.

"Miles?" I croaked, my throat raw, as if I hadn't spoken in days. No answer. "Miles?" I tried again, louder this time.

Still nothing.

I pushed up and out of the seat, my legs unsteady. I willed them to walk the few steps toward him while I held on to the backrests of my seat and the one opposite him.

I might not have liked him, not even the smallest bit, but I didn't want him *dead*. He was spoiled. The personification of everything I grew up hating. Arrogant, rich, and egocentric, all of it bundled up into a single person. Hell, my family could probably pay rent and buy a month's worth of food using the money he spent on a jacket or shoes.

But wishing him dead? I wouldn't go that far.

His eyes were closed. And his chest... If it was moving, I couldn't tell.

"Miles," I said firmly.

Still no sound or movement. My heart constricted, and my throat closed. It was too quiet. Just the awful sound of waves crashing against the beach. I put my ear to his chest. Okay, he was breathing. But unconscious.

"Miles!" I shouted.

Nothing. Now what?

Standing in front of him, I raised my hand then smacked him across the cheek, the loud *crack* breaking the staticy sounding repetition of waves slapping against sand. My palm stung, yet *still* no movement from him.

Dammit. I raised my hand to hit him again—

His light brown eyes flew open, locking on to me. In another second, they flitted with recognition.

"Oh, thank God," I breathed.

"Did you just hit me?" His forehead wrinkled, and his fists clenched white. Whatever. At least he wasn't dead. "What is *wrong* with you, Fiona?"

"Nothing." I backed away, glad to give him space. "And we have bigger problems than—"

He stood up, swaying, a challenging glare in his eyes. "Than what?" he snapped. "Teaching you to keep your hands to yourself?"

Still alive and still an asshole. "I'm sorry for making sure you were alive. Next time, I'll just leave you to die and take care of myself." No, I wouldn't. But let him think it.

He grunted, took a step away, and almost fell over. Quickly, I reached out and grabbed his arm, held it just long enough to keep him from falling. He scowled at me, but then he looked around, and something else flashed behind his eyes. Like the reality of our situation was settling in. He swayed again and leaned against the back of a seat.

"You okay?" It was out of my mouth before I could stop it.

"I'm super. Just fantastic." Was his speech a little slurred, or was my brain jumbled from the crash?

Pull yourself together.

I watched him for a moment longer, made sure he remained standing and wouldn't fall over, and then headed to the exit door in the back. Summoning all those countless hours at the gym, I shoved it open. The metal swung aside, and the stairs unfolded and buried themselves in the sand.

"Can you walk?" I asked.

He didn't answer, and instead tried to take a step on his own. But he swayed again like he was drunk. I held out my hand, but he growled and waved me off. Using the seats to hold himself up, he walked the few steps toward the exit. Twenty-four hours ago, I'd have pushed him and then beat myself up for stooping to his level. Now, I had to force myself not to help. Somehow, he managed to get down the stairs without landing face first in the sand.

As I came out and got my first look at the plane from the outside, my legs turned to jelly. My heart beat as hard as a jackhammer, and my entire body trembled. The plane, if one could even still call it that, had crashed with the front half of the tail section slightly digging into the ground, trees, and shrubs. Half of the windows were broken. Cracks ran all over them like spider webs, and some were completely shattered. And the gaping hole in the side of the plane where the wing used to be... *So screwed.*

Backing away a little farther, closer toward the ocean, I could just make out a column of smoke rising from the jungle. Was that where the rest of our plane was? How far away was that? A mile? It had to be at least that, and I couldn't see anything between us and the smoke but trees. We were isolated. Alone.

Except we hadn't been the only people on the plane.

"We have to find the pilot," I said. "He'll know what to do."

"Assuming the pilot is even alive."

Shit. "But he's got to be. *We're* okay."

"Maybe we were just lucky," he said. "What we really

need is the plane's computer. It's got an SOS signal. It's how anyone will be able to find us."

Someone could be dying, and he was thinking about an SOS? Only thinking about us. But on our own, we wouldn't be able to use the plane's computer. "We need that pilot, need to make sure he's okay, if we want to survive."

"Survival won't mean shit if we don't get off the island."

"Getting off the island won't mean shit if we're *dead*."

He took a deep breath. "Listen. It doesn't matter. The computer was in the cockpit. So, we find the pilot, we find the computer. Okay?"

"Okay," I said. "Let's go."

He stood up and started toward the jungle, but he was still shaky on his feet. Another second and he'd probably fall over.

I took his arm and lowered him to sit on the sand. "Easy."

"Must have hit my head," he murmured. "You'll have to go alone."

"What? *No*." Going together, that I could do, but on my own? Not happening. "Forget about it."

"You have to," Miles argued. "Please? I can't…"He looked pale and sick, and were it anyone else, I would've felt bad for him, maybe even asked if there was anything I could do to help him feel better, but he wasn't anyone else. He was the person I liked least out of our entire class and had the misfortune of being sent on this trip with.

"What if you get worse? Who'll help you?"

I had exactly zero medical knowledge beyond what to do when you get punched a little too hard during a fight or training, so it wasn't like I was in any way useful, but pretending I cared about his well-being was easier than having to admit that I didn't want to go into that jungle alone. For all I knew there could be wild animals or other kinds of predators hiding in there, just waiting to pounce.

"The smoke is right there, I can see it," he said, his speech wobbly. "Just follow it and *voila*."

"That easy, huh?" In theory, I knew it was nothing more than that. We'd survived a plane crash without much harm compared to what could've happened, and I wasn't willing to get myself killed in a jungle five minutes later. Even if there wasn't anything evil in there, I could still get lost, and then what?

"Come on, you're the one with the bad-girl reputation, this amazing and brave fighter you supposedly are, something title here and something trophy there—or was all of that just made up?"

I resisted the urge to kick him. Who did he think he was? I'd fought for those awards, very much literally, and I surely wasn't going to let some rich, snobby asshole question my achievements.

"One more word and I'll throw you in the ocean," I threatened, my voice the closest thing to cold I could muster.

"You're awfully stubborn. Has anyone ever told you that?"

I smirked. "Says the donkey."

Even as I argued, I knew I'd lost. He wasn't in any shape to do anything. He probably couldn't even make it to the edge of the jungle, even if he crawled, let alone wander through it for possibly hours.

Hours of wandering alone…

But what choice did I have?

"Fine," I conceded. "I'll go, and you get in the fuselage. Stay out of the sun."

I tried to help him, but he shrugged me off. To his credit, he got to his feet and made it to our broken half of the plane with me just following. Good, he wasn't totally helpless.

Once he was sitting inside, I turned toward the jungle. Cracked my neck. Quietly sighed.

I so didn't sign up for any of this.

"Just do it," he said. "The quicker you go, the sooner you'll find the pilot, radio for help, and we'll be out of here. I'll be fine." Groan. "Just get it done."

Gut punch.

He sounded straight up like my father—the sort of person who never really cared about fears or why something frightened me. No. According to him, I was simply supposed to do it and that would teach me that there was no reason for me to be afraid, because obviously that was a much better way to go about these things than taking two minutes to talk to me and tell me that it would be okay.

No, that was Mom's job. Dad pushed me. Mom consoled me.

Push. Pull.

Rinse. Repeat.

Miles was right, though. I had to go in there. I had to pull myself together. It was just trees. Walls of giant plants, hot and dank and teeming with danger and death and horrors I didn't want to imagine. I shivered. I needed a distraction. Something to focus on. Something. Anything else.

Normally, I'd focus on my opponent, whoever was in front of me in the ring. But here?

Miles. I could focus on how much I hated him. How much I hated that he was right.

Yeah, that was better. I clenched my fists—my palms were unusually dry for how anxious I was—and took a deep breath. All I could hear was the rush and yawn of the ocean behind me. Within a minute, I was focused. Calm. Serene.

"Fiona," Miles pressed. "Sometime today, please? Before it gets dark."

I exhaled sharply. "Try not to piss anything off while I'm gone."

Before he could snap a retort, I headed for the jungle.

CHAPTER TWO
17 HOURS EARLIER

This couldn't be the right terminal.

Our school must've made a mistake. Star Aviation Support MIA didn't look big enough for international flights. Not that I would know for sure — I'd never been on an international flight — but those planes have to be huge.

As my cab came to a halt, I paid the driver, grabbed my black wheelie bag from the trunk — it was the same one I always took with me to kickboxing competitions, the sheer number of stickers on it making it unmistakably mine — and made my way to the terminal. The air was cool with a note of pine and bleach, and…white marble flooring at an airport? It was spotless. The floors. The windows. Even the pretty red-haired woman behind the ticket counter with her toothpaste-commercial–worthy smile.

"Am I in the right place?" I asked, handing over my ticket, passport, and luggage.

After checking the paperwork, she said, "Yes, Ms. Wolf.

Down the hallway to your left."

As I stepped between the metal detectors, the TSA agent eyed me like he was confused. Or maybe suspicious. I'd gone with a simple outfit today, nothing flashy or extravagant. Light blue ripped jeans, Chuck Taylor's in black, a cut-out sleeveless black Royal Blood shirt with an unbuttoned light gray flannel over it, and a dark gray hoodie. Considering that and my blue hair, well, he wasn't the first person to give me that kind of look. But also, seeing as we were the only people here, maybe he was just doing his job.

The lounge was lined with windows and a swarm of modern-art-looking armchairs. I never realized a room could try so hard. The mouth-watering scent of freshly brewed coffee and pastries filled the air. This was way nicer than other airports I'd been to, with their cheap plastic seating, screaming children, and the dingy smell of McDonald's. I'd never left the U.S. before. I never would've even dreamed about going to Germany, seeing a place like Berlin, somewhere I'd only heard about during history classes or seen in movies. I'd been so excited last night that I'd struggled to fall asleep, even after my father chased me through what felt like a million drills during training.

For a moment, I just looked around...and then I spotted him. Miles Echo, his body lazily sprawled over an armchair, his legs hanging off of one of the armrests like he owned this place. He was tall, but I was pretty sure he could've sat normally if he weren't so damn extra. His head was a wild mess of raven hair. A pair of Ray-Ban Wayfarer sunglasses hid his eyes. His clothes—black jeans, some pretentious white button-down shirt, and a black jacket—were probably worth more than a small country. His skin had a naturally sun-kissed tone. I bet he never got sunburn. Lucky jerk.

"It's impolite to stare," he said.

"So is being an ass." I sat in the seat farthest from him.

He pulled his sunglasses down and looked me over.

Was he...checking me out?

No. He wouldn't. I wasn't his type, and vice versa.

Miles was hot, no question. And when I first met him, I'd thought *what if*. But then he'd opened his mouth.

It was pure luck that we'd been thrown into this thing together. The pharmaceutical internship had picked us out of thousands of candidates after evaluating us through personal essays and aptitude tests. Our grades and school performance were meaningless, they'd said. The tests showed our aptitude for pharmaceutical chemistry made us the most promising of the students who'd applied.

How exactly that was true, I wasn't sure, since my best grade in chemistry last year had been a C, though I could understand why they picked Miles. Straight As across the board and a handsome face. Too bad he was a dick hiding behind expensive clothes, but Briola Bio Tech didn't know that.

As if to prove my point, he started taking selfies. On a next-year's iPhone. He scrolled through them quickly before choosing one to post on Instagram.

"Really, Miles? Would it hurt you to post something other than your own face for once?"

"Not my fault I have almost two hundred and seventy thousand followers who love my face," he said without taking his eyes off his phone. "You, on the other hand…"

If he had even an ounce of humility, his popularity might have been attractive. Or if he posted something more than selfies with captions stupid enough to decrease my IQ just from reading them.

I only had about forty thousand followers, steadily built over a period of years rather than instant fame, but they had more to say than heart-eyes emojis. Some of the best kickboxing and martial arts discussions happened in the comments of my competition pics. I'd take that over a brainless feed any day.

"Mr. Echo, Ms. Wolf." A woman in a blue, white, and yellow uniform, topped off with a tiny striped hat and matching neckerchief, approached us. "I'm Stephany," she said. "And I'll be your flight attendant. If you'll follow me, please, your plane is ready."

My palms were sweating again. There were literally no other passengers around. Just Miles and me. Something about the situation felt really off.

I caught up to the attendant, with Miles somewhere behind me. Stephany led us through a set of sliding glass doors. Outside, we were met by a blast of suffocating heat—even by Miami standards—and blinding sunlight. No wonder Miles had left his sunglasses on.

And was that…? Holy crap. A private jet. It looked like the one I'd seen Adam Lambert fly in during his tour with Queen. A set of stairs opened up in front of us, leading inside.

It didn't make any sense. Sure, our school—the Academy for Fine Education, what preposterous and pompous nonsense—was full of rich kids like Miles. They looked at me the same way he did. Oh, *she's* here on a scholarship. I was sure they could have flown everyone out in their own jets, but why Briola Bio Tech would treat two interns with such style was baffling.

"Stephany, are you sure this is our flight?"

"Yes," she assured me, the smile on her face kind, understanding. "Everything is correct. Your luggage is already stowed away, and the pilot merely waiting for you to settle in."

I was flying to Germany. In a private jet with flat-screen TVs. And internet. This was a once-in-a-lifetime luxury.

As I found a seat, Miles flopped down across the aisle from me. The plane could fit up to eight passengers, but it was just the two of us. I set my luggage on the next seat over, buckled up, and pulled my book out.

Anne of Green Gables.

One of my best friends was an old homeless guy named Joe. Calling him "out there" was a bit of an understatement. Conspiracy theories are legit. Microwaves cause cancer. The government is watching everyone. The Mandela effect is totally a thing.

Sometimes, I saw him playing chess at the park — sometimes alone and other times with whoever felt up to the challenge of playing against him — and it took him ten minutes just to make his move and notice I was standing behind him. But then he'd smile, and we'd talk about books until it was time for him to make his next move on the chess board.

Every week, I bought a new book at the used bookstore. He was even poorer than me, though, so I always gave it to him when I was done.

I'd mentioned to him that I would be gone for three weeks during the summer. It wouldn't have bothered me if he hadn't remembered, because he wasn't always with it. Sometimes I thought I was just a welcome distraction for him. But he'd surprised me with this book about Anne, and a bracelet he'd made himself. Nothing extravagant, yet so special. He owned next to nothing, but still, he'd found a way to give me something.

"Anne's a fighter," he'd said. "Just like you."

Joe could be strange at times—weren't we all—but he genuinely cared. This book was proof.

I'd barely gotten through a page when the plane rolled to the runway.

Stephany moved my bag into the overhead compartment then eyed my book but didn't take it. Miles had made himself comfortable, stretching his legs across a seat opposite him.

"You don't happen to have some Aquadeco on board?" he asked, and I wondered if he made that up. But the flight attendant nodded and went to retrieve what was likely just tap water in a fancy bottle.

This luxe was standard for him. I wouldn't be surprised if Daddy Dearest always let him fly in private jets. Who decided it was fair to hand out that much privilege to only a chosen few?

Takeoff was smoother than any other I remembered. I could be privileged, too, even if only for this flight. So there. I leaned against the cubby window and watched as Miami grew smaller and smaller until it was nothing but ocean and clouds.

Once I plugged my headphones into my armrest, I

turned on the touchscreen TV—more like an oversized iPad, really—in front of me. It welcomed me with a map that showed our location, time, date, and how much time was left until we reached Berlin. The movies available weren't even remotely interesting, though, so I turned the TV off and picked up my book again.

A few more chapters in, I felt my eyes growing heavy. With a ten-hour flight ahead of us, crossing the Atlantic and into Europe, I might as well sleep.

The engine erupts into flames. Oxygen masks drop from above. The plane dips and takes my heart with it.

Falling. Falling. Falling—

"Wake up," Miles said. "Fiona, we're—"

My eyes flew open, heart racing. Pounding so hard my chest ached.

"What happened?" I looked out the window. Sunrise. Clouds. Airplane wing intact. "What's"—my throat caught—"what's wrong?"

The front half of the plane breaks off. Open air. The ocean. And coming closer, too fast, we're going to crash, an island—

"It's the pilot," Miles said, eyes wide. He swallowed and clutched his armrests. "He—he says we're...*oh God.*" My stomach jumped hot into my throat. Then a smile spread across his stupid chiseled face as his body relaxed. "He says we're landing in five. Just thought you'd want to know."

Jerk.

"Not funny." I wiped my sweaty palms on my pant legs and tried to banish the remaining flashes of my nightmare. Unfortunately, the same technique wouldn't get rid of Miles. "What would it take for you to never speak to me again?"

"A billion bucks."

Asshole. I turned away from him.

When we dipped beneath the clouds, I looked out the window and saw a sea of light: Berlin. The sky was slowly transforming from night to day. It was around five a.m. Germany time.

When the plane began its descent, I felt that earlier sense of darkness, of plummeting to the ground, the strange dream of a crash, a dead pilot, panic and dread... But touchdown was smooth and standard. We taxied and then stopped a little way from a building.

I'd slept during the better part of the flight but didn't feel rested. My nervousness over the day ahead of us crept up on me. Was this jet lag? I took my bag from the compartment, getting my feet used to solid ground again, trying not to sway. Outside, the air was different from the humidity back home in Florida. This air was dry. Crackling. Charged.

Stephany led us to the small building. The inside of this airport wasn't as fancy as the one we left in Miami, a single open space instead of a couple of rooms and sections, but it had similar glass doors with STAR AVIATION SUPPORT TXL written on them. The walls and stone flooring were white with a deep burgundy carpet running through the middle like a runway. The employees took forever checking our passports then finally handed over our luggage.

As I zipped up my hoodie, Miles primped, pulling and smoothing his clothes back into position. He checked his hair in a window reflection.

Even more unsettling than his ridiculous vanity was the fact we were alone. "Isn't someone supposed to come around and get us? One of the emails said a Briola rep would take us to our hotel…I thought."

Miles shrugged.

Guess we'd have to wait a little more. Annoying, but it gave me time to text my parents that we'd landed—Mom worried herself sick about me whenever I was away from home.

When I'd first told my parents about the trip, about how I'd been chosen for this Berlinternship, my father had been less than impressed. Not unusual. If it wasn't a gold kickboxing medal, what did it matter?

Dear old Dad.

With a stone-faced expression, he'd complained how going would mean me missing three weeks of practice, how I needed that time if I wanted to succeed at Nationals. But in the end, with a bit of talking to Mom, he caved. At least Mom was on my side. My biggest cheerleader.

I pulled out my phone and took it off airplane mode. Getting a reply from them any time soon, considering it was almost midnight back home, was unlikely. Once I was done, I closed my message app then scrolled through Instagram and liked a selfie my best friend, Melany, had posted. It was of her and her internship partner at LAX. They were pretending to drink out of a water-cooler spigot in what looked like a break room. Cute.

Just as I was about to put my phone away, I saw it. The

little red bubble.

Ding.

A voicemail?

My parents never called me without texting first. Who…?

I looked up. Miles was typing away on his own phone, absorbed by his different universe from mine. The Briola representative was still nowhere to be seen.

So I hit play and raised the phone to my ear. A familiar male voice floated out from the speaker. My homeless, chess-playing friend.

"Fiona, it's Joe." There was a pause so long I thought the voicemail had ended, then he said, "There's something you have to know. They're watching you. They're behind this." Another pause. "Trust no one."

CHAPTER THREE
THE ISLAND

When I was five years old and still living in New York, I went to Central Park for the first time. A group of parents had decided to take my friends and me there so we could play. See something more of the city. It'd taken a while to get there, or at least it felt that way to us, since we were possibly the least patient children ever. But in the end, it had been so worth it. The park was magic with all the trees and green and critters. I saw a real live squirrel. Not at all like my part of the city.

At some point, on a sugar high from way too much ice cream, we'd decided to play hide and seek. I wanted to find the best place to hide. And I did—in the heart of some trees. Once I realized I was lost, it was too late.

First I cried, then I screamed. When my dad found me, I learned my first big lesson.

"You're not strong enough to handle this much fear," he said. "No one is."

The answer was to disconnect from it. To numb it. I had to be brave.

Twelve years later, I still heard those words every time I went into a kickboxing match. And times like now, when my heart sped up at the thought of going into the jungle alone.

We need to find the pilot.

He could be dying, and here I was hesitating. I should have been easier on myself. More forgiving. But I wasn't the forgiving type. If I wanted to get out of this alive, I couldn't afford to be.

So I rolled my shoulders, calmed my breath and my wildly beating heart, and stepped into the jungle.

Humanity explored jungles and forests for centuries, wrote tales of adventures and songs about the thrill of discovering new places. Maybe that was how I should've looked at it. Who knew? Maybe we were the first people to ever be wherever we were. Maybe I was the first person to ever step into this particular jungle.

Which meant only wildlife lived here. Not a comforting thought after all.

Palm trees rose high toward the sky, their leaves big and offering shade. The ground was soft and easy to walk on. Columns of sunlight slipped through the gaps between leaves. The farther I went, the denser the trees became. Colorful flowers in blues, pinks, and hues of orange dotted some of the bushes and plants closer to the ground.

I pulled out my phone. Silly, but I had to know, and yep, there was no cell signal or wifi. Which made sense. If we were on a deserted island, the phones were useless. And then, without a warning or goodbye, it died on me altogether. The battery must have drained during the long flight.

The snap of a branch made my heart drop into my stomach. I stopped, crouched, and went into a fighting stance. My eyes darted over everything around me. Up every trunk, across every bush and rock, over the ground. But there was nothing unusual. Maybe I'd been the one to snap the branch. Maybe it was just some bird. Something harmless. Or maybe I'd imagined it.

Be fearless. Wouldn't be the first time my dad insisted it was all in my head.

I continued on, my steps much more cautious now. I'd been taught to tread lightly on quick feet, a feather in the ring. I could hesitate on the inside, but I couldn't let my opponents see me flinch.

The wind rustled through the leaves above me. The chirp of a bird off in the distance, the crunch of a dry leaf— anything my ears could pick up on. The more I focused on those noises, the more distant the sound of my heart and breathing became in my own ears. Good. I needed to be in control of the situation, of my own fear.

Stepping out into a small clearing, I looked toward the sky. It was much harder to see the smoke from there than from the beach, but I could just make it out. It seemed weaker, the color fainter, the plume thinner. Time to pick up the pace. If the smoke died out, I might never find the plane.

Assuming the pilot was even still alive. If he was, if he could do anything, wouldn't he have already sent an SOS signal? Alerted anyone and everyone that we were here? Who knew, maybe we were lucky, and he'd done it, but it would simply take a while for anyone to come.

Unless he was unconscious.

I had to hold on to the thought, cling to it as though my life depended on it. My mom always used to tell me that I could do anything I wanted to if I just worked for it. If I tried hard enough. *Wanted* it enough. I hoped she would be right this time. I had no idea if our parents knew what had happened to us, if *anyone* did, and I didn't even want to imagine how worried Mom would be once she found out.

The foliage became absurdly thick, some leaves bigger than an iPad, others thin and long like tall grass, and the occasional ferns in between. The air felt heavy, moist almost, with a hint of smoke the farther I went—a good sign. Pushing through it was like pushing through water. Slow. Exhausting. Suffocating. But a tree had fallen over and crushed a small path forward. If I could get higher, maybe I could see better.

With both hands, I pulled myself up onto the tree. One end was propped between two other trees, and the other dug into the ground. Its bark was partially covered by soft moss, but really, it was pretty smooth, barely any texture. My shoes slipped as I climbed onto it, but I grabbed a branch, my knuckles turning white—

Somewhere in front of me, between the branches of a couple of trees, I saw…something. The thick branches, leaves, and bushes obscured it, but not entirely. I could see pieces of something bulky, brown, and furry, and it seemed big. Really big.

Slowly, quietly, I lowered myself back down the tree. The last thing I wanted was to invade some animal's territory.

Too late. It let out a loud roar like thunder, a blend of different animal noises like some kind of pissed off lion and a hungry bear. *What the hell is that thing?* Branches and leaves leaned away and shivered as the animal moved toward me.

Whatever that animal was, it wasn't friendly, and I didn't care if it was trying to drive me off or wanted to eat me.

As soon as my feet hit the ground, I swallowed hard and took off in a random direction, not thinking where I was going besides *away*. Faster and faster, I ran past trees and jumped over branches here and avoided running into something there. My breathing became labored too quickly, quicker than it had in years. My legs, already exhausted from walking and climbing, ached and burned, like someone had set them on fire.

Branches tore at my sleeves, scratched my skin, but I pushed on. Part of me wanted to turn around just long enough to see how close it was, *what* it was, but that would be stupid. *Duck and weave, dodge and feint.*

Could I climb a tree and hide? No. I'd still be scaling it when the beast snatched me out of the air. But maybe something to hide *behind*?

Yes, there. A dip in the ground surrounded by taller bushes, ferns, and some rocks. And those exotic flowers. Those gorgeous colors. Who would have thought my blue hair would one day work like camouflage?

Ignoring the poke of branches sticking out of the bushes, I dove into them and made myself as tiny as possible. I closed my eyes, calmed my breathing, and listened. *Crunch. Thud.* The beast was close. But then, silence.

I had no idea how far I'd run, how close I'd been to the other half of the plane before I'd had to turn around, how far I would have to go to get back to that place. But in that moment, all that mattered was I was still alive, and the sounds of the beast didn't seem to be getting closer anymore. I couldn't see it. Couldn't even see branches bending away from its body. But I still heard it. Deep, wet breaths.

I held my hand over my mouth. *Quiet. Stay quiet.*

After a few moments, the branches bent again, but farther away from me. The deep breaths continued but grew more distant. It was leaving! It had given up.

Letting out a sigh of relief, I relaxed, at least somewhat. I'd been lucky this time, somehow, but my body had surprised me, let me down in a way it hadn't in a long time. I wouldn't be able to fight that thing if I had to, at least not today. Hopefully I wouldn't need to any time soon, though. I just wanted to get off this island, which meant getting back up and continuing to look for that damn plane.

I stood up and tried to orientate myself, trace back my steps, which turned out to be futile, so instead I looked for a clearing. It took a handful of minutes, but I finally found one. Looking up at the sky and above the tree line, I could just make out the smoke column way more to my left than it should be, but at least now I knew where I had to go and more or less which way led back to the beach.

But just as I began to walk again, the beast roared once more, though not anywhere close to me, and then...the sound of it moving away. Instinctively, I started to duck back into my hiding place, just to be sure, but as I listened to it go, I realized where it was headed. Toward the beach.

Shit.

Straight toward Miles.

CHAPTER FOUR
BERLIN

*T*rust no one.

I stood there with my phone glued to my ear, my body frozen. I'd heard of red flags, but this was insane. As far as I knew, Joe didn't even have a cell phone. And while I didn't want to give too much credibility to a guy who took seriously whatever conspiracy theories were in the latest Dan Brown book, I couldn't just ignore his warning.

This wasn't the first time Joe had said some version of this. But the guy believed cell phones—or any phone, really—caused cancer. Which meant that in his mind, he'd risked his life to call me. It didn't matter if he was crazy. He believed what he'd said.

So, if something was wrong, how did he know about it? And how was he involved?

If it had been a message from Miles, I'd have laughed. What a stupid prank. But I'd known Joe for a while. He was one of the few decent people in my life. Whatever his reason for leaving that message, he believed it was real. I wanted to talk to someone about it, but there was only Miles. This might affect him, too, though. Could I tell him, show him, ask him what he thought without him laughing at me? Maybe I just misunderstood, maybe things weren't as bad as they seemed. If we were both caught in some sort of trouble, though, he deserved to know. But Joe hadn't said "trust no one except Miles." He'd said "trust no one," period.

Just as I looked up, Miles pulled out a slick black credit card from his wallet. "Don't know about you, but I'm sick of waiting around. Follow me."

Normally, I'd have said something snarky. But if he was a part of whatever was going on, I needed to play along, act like I knew nothing. For now. So I followed him. We found a cream-colored Mercedes cab waiting outside. The driver exited and greeted us in German, but his accent didn't match. He was tall and kind of chubby, with black hair, an even blacker beard, and dark eyes.

"Uh…" I floundered for the words I'd practiced over and over. "*Hallo. Wir müssen…* Um—"

Miles pointed at himself. "*Ich bin Miles.*" Then he pointed at me. "*Das ist Fiona.*"

The driver nodded. "Memet."

"*Wir müssen zu dieser Adresse.*" Miles handed him a piece of paper. The driver looked it over and nodded.

Of course Mr. Perfect spoke fluent German. Was there anything he couldn't do?

"I didn't know you spoke German." At least I knew I could kick his ass if it came to it.

He flashed that thousand-watt smile at me. "There's

lots of things you don't know about me."

The driver took our luggage and placed it in the trunk while asking us questions in German. At one point, after he asked something, Miles glanced at me in response.

"No." Miles shrugged. "But maybe."

"But maybe what?" I asked, annoyed.

"But maybe I'm growing on you."

"Yeah. Like a fungus."

We took off toward our hotel, but the traffic in Berlin was a lot like traffic back home. The closer we got to the city center, the thicker the cars and crowds got. Wanting to distract myself from Joe's message, I watched the city pass us by. The buildings had fancy facades with all sorts of different ornaments and decorations, big windows, and old, heavy-looking wooden doors. My shoulders relaxed. We also passed new, modern buildings and some that were shabby, rundown, and probably abandoned.

Later we went through a tunnel that seemed to span several miles, and once we emerged from the other side, the scenery was completely different. Everywhere I looked there were high-rises with glass facades, hotels, and a casino. The houses looked richer, well maintained, and the stores more expensive. A couple of high-end cars were parked along the streets. Definitely the hub of the city.

Joe's message nagged at me. I looked at my phone and worried my lower lip.

"You okay?" Miles asked.

I flinched then tried to cover it by slipping on a sweet yet annoyed smile and said, "Mind your own damn business."

Surprisingly, he did.

The cab halted in front of a gorgeous brick monstrosity. The hotel was seven stories high. Inside, the marble floor was dotted with potted plants, and the walls were covered in warm white, almost a little yellow, velvety-looking wallpaper.

First a private jet, and now this? What had we done to receive this royal treatment? Not that I was complaining.

"*Guten Morgen*," the receptionist greeted us.

"Good morning," I said. "I'm Fiona Wolf. There should be a reservation."

She switched to English and told me she needed a reservation number, which I pulled up on my phone.

"Great." She typed away on her keyboard. "Miss Wolf and Mr. Echo, right?"

"Yes," Miles said, flashing that irresistible smile that usually charmed everyone. Except the receptionist ignored him, and when his smile promptly dropped, I did what I could to cover my laugh with a cough.

"Fourth floor. Room 269. Enjoy your stay." She nodded and handed me a key. *One* key.

Umm…no. I looked at her, frowning. "Are you sure that it's only one room?"

"Let's see…" She clicked away at her console. "Reservations for M. Echo and F. Wolf. One room. Enjoy your stay."

This so couldn't be happening. I already didn't like the idea of sharing this internship with Miles, and now I had to share a room with him? And what about Joe's message? What if this was all a setup so "they" could "watch" me? Whatever that meant.

The elevator opened to a long hallway with gray walls

and wine-colored carpet. We found room 269, and I slipped the key over the door's electronic lock — *whirr, click* —

Whoa.

Before we'd flown to Berlin, I'd looked up this hotel online. I was sure Briola would book us two of the cheapest rooms, which I'd checked out and was prepared for. This was anything but. The room was generously sized, with a king-size four-post bed in a vintage Biedermeier style. The frame was painted in whites and grays that matched the rest of the furniture, which was a similar style.

This couldn't be right. We were high school students, not honeymooning celebrities.

Wordlessly, I dropped my suitcase and marched out of the room then back into the elevator. Miles stayed behind.

Downstairs, I returned to the receptionist. The lobby wasn't empty anymore. Two figures were sitting on one of the sofas in the lounge, their backs turned toward me. "Sorry, I think there must be a mistake."

"Is the key not working?" she asked, concerned. "Or are there any damages to the room?"

"No, no. That's not it." I shook my head lightly. This entire situation was simply ridiculous. "There's only one bed. So, like, that cannot be right. We need two. Is there another room we could get, additionally? Or two completely different rooms, ideally."

She looked at her monitor and typed. "Unfortunately, we are completely booked. I'm very sorry."

"How is that even possible? This place is huge!"

"We are in an exclusive and much requested location, Miss Wolf. As I said, I'm very sorry for the inconvenience, but there isn't anything I can do for you."

What even, honestly? Ugh.

Defeated, I turned to the elevators but then stopped. "I do have another question," I said, trying to keep my voice as calm as possible.

"Yes?"

"Who made that reservation?"

She looked at her monitor and typed something again, her frown deepening.

I wiped my hands on my sides. *Please say Briola, please say Briola, please say Briola.*

"I'm terribly sorry, Miss Wolf, but there's no record here. Odd. Is there anything el—"

"What do you mean no record? Who booked that room?"

"Miss—"

"No. Don't 'Miss Wolf' me. Something—"

My voice had risen enough that the two men in the lobby were watching me, annoyance written across Buzz Cut and Blondie's faces as though I disturbed their peaceful time of staring at the wall or something, but I didn't care.

"Miss Wolf, please calm down. We will sort this out."

"Sure you will." I walked away, already so done with this trip. This whole hotel situation was absurd in every way.

Blood pounded in my ears like I was about to enter a fight. Okay, just keep it cool, relax. We'd go to the Briola headquarters, and everything would be fine. They'd explain why the hotel couldn't find the information. *Everything would be fine.* It had to be.

In the elevator, I sent a collective prayer to every God

and superhero I could think of, wishing and hoping for things to right themselves.

Back in our room, I dropped the key card onto the small table by the door and set my bag next to the sofa.

"No luck?" Miles was lying on the bed, his legs hanging off the end.

I shook my head, a fog over my mind. "Nope." This didn't make any sense.

He shrugged. "Oh well. At least there's more than enough space to sleep." He glanced at me, then at the open space beside him on the bed.

"You can sleep on the sofa."

"*You* can sleep on the sofa," he quipped.

I knew he was just trying to mess with me, but that didn't change the fact that I *really* needed to kick something.

Or someone.

Him.

"I'm not opposed to sharing," he offered, something lingering at the edge of his voice that I couldn't quite identify. Really, I didn't have another choice. I mean, sure, I could have slept on the sofa or argued with him all day, but that wasn't productive or helpful.

"Just don't get any ideas," I hissed.

Thankfully, sleep was still hours away, so I didn't have to worry about it just yet.

As I started to unpack, there was a knock at the door.

"Wonder who that is?" Miles said and slipped off the bed. His tone conveyed he knew exactly who it was. Guess he had done something useful while I was gone, because when he opened the door, I smelled food.

"*Guten Morgen. Ich bringe Ihr Frühstück*," the guy on the other side said. Miles said something to him and then stepped aside, letting him walk in. The bellboy didn't seem much older than us, his hair a silvery shade of blond. He was tall and really thin, skinny enough that his uniform hung loosely off of his body.

"Do you prefer to eat inside or on the balcony?" he said in English. Miles must've told him to switch languages.

"Balcony?" I asked.

The bellboy stopped in front of the curtains. Pushing them aside, he revealed two windows with a glass balcony door between them, which he opened with a quiet *click* and then pushed the cart outside.

Wow. A balcony. I just assumed there would be windows and nothing more.

It was beautiful. The view was amazing, the sun rising on a cloudless blue sky and the TV Tower peaking just over the building opposite ours. The balcony itself was light gray stone with sleek metal and frosted glass fencing, two potted plants standing in either corner, and in the middle of it all a metal table with two chairs.

Miles and I sat down on the chairs while the bellboy parked the cart next to the table.

"I hope the meal will be to your liking," he said, and folded his hands behind his back.

"I'm sure it will be fine." I smiled. Better than fine. I felt like royalty.

Miles tipped him, and the bellboy disappeared out of our room while Miles opened the first silver box on the cart. Inside, we found two plates of pancakes and a steaming pot of coffee. I went for the porcelain coffee pot, placed one of the mugs in front of me, and poured some java. The heavenly smell of freshly made coffee surrounded us, mixing with the smell of pancakes.

"This is insane," I said after a couple of silent minutes of eating. I looked up from my mug at Miles, who wore an amused expression. His hair was a complete mess now from the breeze, and some of it hung over his forehead, almost into his eyes, though he didn't brush it away.

"Makes you feel like a celebrity," he said. "Doesn't it?"

"And how would I know what that feels like? Not everybody grows up wiping their ass with hundred-dollar bills."

"You know that's not what I meant. Come on, just admit it. This room is great."

I wanted to say no. But even I couldn't say that with a straight face. This *was* amazing. I wouldn't admit it, though. Not to him.

The food was gone in a flash, one incredible flavor after the next. My God. Sure, we'd scored high on those aptitude tests, or whatever, but I didn't know what we'd done to deserve this kind of special treatment.

As Miles set the cart in the hall, I snatched a new outfit from my suitcase and slipped into the bathroom to change before we left for Briola headquarters. A dark pair of jeans, a white dress shirt, and my favorite black jacket with silver studs all over the shoulders. My father hated it, tried to force me to take a different one, but Mom had switched it last minute without him noticing. In one of the pockets, I found a hair tie and pulled my hair into a high ponytail.

"Our cab is waiting," Miles called. "If you're not out here in sixty seconds, I'm leaving without you."

I rolled my eyes and finished applying a bit of eyeliner, and some warm-toned nude shadow. For a moment, I eyed one of my dark liquid lipsticks, which of course belonged on the long list of things my father hated, but went with a light gloss instead. Nothing too dark or heavy, just a classy extra touch. I was probably already pushing the envelope with my "unprofessional" hair color; no need to give Briola another reason to reconsider their decision.

Part of me wished Miles would leave without me. But when I came back out, he was still waiting. And the look on his face when he saw me…

"What's wrong?" I said.

He coughed. "Nothing. You…" He coughed again. "You look good."

I turned away so he wouldn't see the heat flushing my face. Of course, I knew he was just saying that because now I looked more like all the girls he ever dated, thanks to the makeup, but getting a compliment was still nice, even if it was from him. "Did you write down the address?"

"Yeah."

I grabbed my purse, and we made our way downstairs then through the lobby. Just like Miles said, there was a cab waiting for us outside. We got in and left the city center behind. We passed factories, some new, and others that looked like they'd been standing there since the beginning of the previous century. Occasional buses and gigantic trucks passed us. There were far fewer pedestrians out here and way more fenced-off areas with CCTV cameras and metal gates. A patrolling police car crossed the street in front of us while we waited for the light to change.

We came to a halt outside a tall, gated entrance. The

wall surrounding the property, even the gate itself, was overgrown with vines and leaves. We'd have to go inside to see the actual building. Given the ridiculously expensive services Briola had already offered, I expected nothing short of a palace.

"You want me to wait?" the driver asked.

"Yeah, if you don't mind," Miles said. "Will this cover it?" He pulled out a few Euro bills, paid the driver, and got out.

I got out, too, and then followed him to the front of the gate.

At the side of the gate, there was an intercom box. I pressed the button…and got nothing. Which, upon closer inspection, wasn't a total surprise. The intercom was as neglected as the rusted gate; what was once white and shiny silver was now dirty and somewhat dusty, the button hanging on for dear life.

"Box is busted," I said. "How do we get inside?"

Miles went back to the gate and pushed one side. It budged, but just a little.

"Come help me," he said.

I joined him, and we pushed it together until it was open just enough for us to slip inside, but as soon as we did, I wished we hadn't.

Miles froze. "Wait… What?"

"This can't be it," I said.

Instead of the shiny new headquarters of Briola, we found an old, broke-down factory that seemed barely still standing. It wasn't just the missing windows and gaping holes where doors should be. Something was very wrong. A tree grew half inside the building and half out of the window. If this place had ever been a pharmaceutical factory, that had to be several decades ago, if not longer.

"We have a problem," Miles said.

I glanced back at where the cab had dropped us off. It was long gone. "No shit, Sherlock."

CHAPTER FIVE
THE ISLAND

I'd been raised to be brave and not shy away from challenges, but chasing a beast and hoping I could catch it wasn't quite what my father meant. Yet I took off running as fast as my legs could carry me, ignoring my exhaustion and how much my body screamed at me to stop. I wasn't entirely sure I went the right way, but I had to trust myself. And I didn't like playing savior to Miles, no way, but the idea of being on the island on my own scared me more than I disliked being stranded with him in the first place.

The air was too hot, too humid. My lungs burned, screamed. But I couldn't slow down. This thing, whatever it was, was far larger than I was, faster, so my hopes of making it to the beach first were already abysmal.

I blasted through a wall of branches and leaves—

Then practically stumbled out onto the beach, my feet slipping in the sand despite my best efforts not to lose my balance. Looking around, I tried to orientate myself, see if I was in the right spot, or if our half of the plane was anywhere close to me.

There, not too far off in the distance I spotted the plane and Miles still sitting on the steps like he had been when I left. The beast was nowhere to be seen, though that didn't mean it wasn't close.

Miles looked up and spotted me running, my expression enough to force him up. I never thought I'd feel such relief at seeing him, a realization so strange I could barely comprehend it. In ten out of ten cases at school, just seeing him annoyed me, yet here I was racing toward him as quickly as the sand allowed, and as soon as I could, I threw my arms around him and pulled him into a hug.

I shocked myself with that gesture, coming seemingly out of nowhere. It was a miracle he even managed to remain standing, considering the sheer force with which I'd run into him. I tried to suck more air into my burning lungs, my heart beating hard enough that even he could probably feel it, my legs shaking with exhaustion. He was alive, unharmed. I wasn't alone.

"What happened? You okay?" Miles's voice sounded equal parts confusion, surprise, and concern.

Was I okay? I was the girl who two weeks ago had written "asshole" on his locker with red lipstick, yet now stood here hugging him in relief. My vote went to *losing my mind*.

I pulled away, waited for him to laugh or make some snide remark. But he didn't. He looked genuinely concerned…and maybe something else. Something I couldn't quite identify. My cheeks turned warm, stupidly blushing, and as much as I wanted to, I couldn't blame it on the run. Honestly, what had I been thinking?

Oh right, now I remembered. I'd been thinking he was about to die.

"There's a beast in the jungle," I managed to say through a wheeze, still trying to catch my breath. "It came after me, but I hid and lost it somehow. But then it changed direction and went this way instead, after you. I thought. And now it's…I don't know."

"So you do care about me, after all," Miles said, that stupid smirk on his face.

"Don't get your hopes up," I said, trying to sound as unimpressed and indifferent as I wished I felt. Why didn't I just let the thing make a snack out of him?

He raised his brow a tiny bit, and that said more than enough. I did care. And he knew. Damn him.

"Where is this 'beast' now?" he finally asked.

"I don't know, but we have to hurry before it comes back." My body screamed in protest at the mere prospect of running again. Luckily, I was used to pushing myself, exhaustion a close acquaintance of mine.

"Fiona."

"What?"

He looked down at me. "You can't be serious."

"About what?"

"Come on." He shook his head. "A beast?"

Of all the… "You don't believe me."

He held up his hands in mock defeat. "I believe you saw something. But are you sure it wasn't a wild boar or something?"

"It wasn't a boar. It was—"

A thunderous lion, bear, elephant hybrid-like roar

ripped through the jungle, close but not right by us. We still had some time. Or at least I hoped we did. I whipped my head around, scanning the branches and shrubs, trying to look as far into the jungle as I could, which wasn't nearly far enough for my liking. Time was ticking.

I looked back at Miles, who had gone pale again but wasn't backing away. He attempted to walk on his own, but he was still swaying, a little less than before but still noticeably. If the beast came for us, running wouldn't be an option.

"Put your arm over me," I said.

"I'm flattered, really, and I don't dislike the idea, but is now the right time for that?" Same snark, but now his voice contained an edge of worry.

"Miles, stop joking and think for a second. If that thing comes back for us, we need to be ready to run. And I'm not leaving you again—"

The beast roared again in the distance. Except the sound wasn't as loud anymore. Definitely much farther away. Had it changed direction? Lost interest in us?

We stood perfectly still, listening, waiting. Afraid to move. Part of me expected the beast to just burst out of the jungle right in front of us, all teeth and claws—did it even have any? Thinking back...I didn't know, didn't *want* to know. But nothing happened. The only things I heard were my labored breathing and the ocean.

Relief washed over me like a waterfall, my muscles relaxing. I was okay; we were okay. No one hurt. No one killed. I closed my eyes and took a deep, shaky breath, and let myself sink down onto the sand.

"I guess it must've gone back to wherever it came from,"

I finally said. The adrenaline rush was over. My eyelids felt like lead. Like I'd just finished a fight.

"Maybe you went through its territory," Miles suggested. "We can go around it to get to the plane."

I didn't want to admit out loud that he was probably right. Maybe I'd been close to its nest or something.

My hair was stuck to my neck and the sides of my face, and I regretted not putting it into a ponytail before our flight. The sleeves of my flannel were a series of rips and slashes from branches. The skin on my arms was scratched, angry red welts that were just shallow enough not to bleed. My jeans were stained with mud and grass, and I wished I had worn something different today. Something thinner, better suited for this kind of heat, though I supposed the thick material had been the only thing keeping my legs from matching my arms. Fine. I guess when you're stranded, you may as well look the part.

Finally, I picked myself up off of the ground. This felt like when I'd first started to train for competitions. My training had gotten harder overnight. I'd felt like giving up then. But I'd made it. One fight at a time. I couldn't let this be any different.

Miles tapped my shoulder with something. A bottle of water. "Found it in some cupboard in the plane," he said. "Got one for you, thought you could use it."

"I…" After a second, I took the bottle. "Thank you."

For a short while we just stood there, my breathing returning to normal along with my heartbeat. Going back into the jungle still wasn't something I was particularly looking forward to, but what had to be done, had to be done.

Looking at the sky, I saw the sun was still high, past its zenith, so we had maybe a few hours left until sunset. I wondered what time it was, but with my phone dead, I had no way of knowing.

"Will you even be able to go?" Miles didn't look as awfully pale as he did before, and he also wasn't swaying anymore.

He shrugged. "That break while you were gone helped. No more dizziness or anything. I'm fine, no need to worry."

"If you're sure."

"I'm sure," he said.

"Then let's go."

CHAPTER SIX
BERLIN

"This can't be the right place," I said.

"Of course it's the right place. It's just...not there."

"But..." The road to the building, the building that should be Briola Bio Tech's state-of-the-art headquarters, was cracked. Old. Overgrown with weeds sprouting through the fractured concrete. "This doesn't make sense. It has to be the wrong address. You must have made a mistake."

"My father always says that," Miles said quietly, a flash of something rushing across his eyes. A shadow gone so quickly I barely caught it.

I guess we have something *in common.*

"We need to think about what we should do next," he said.

"What we need to do next is confront whoever brought us here."

He held up his hands in mock defeat. "Okay, but how? There isn't exactly a receptionist here to tell us who to talk to at Briola."

I looked back at the building and then at Miles. His right hand was tangled in his hair. He seemed confused and determined at the same time; his brows pulled together, and his eyes closed for the briefest of moments before he let out a sigh. Was he just acting or was his reaction genuine? I still wasn't sure if I could trust him—or anyone.

"Let's go around the block," I suggested. "Maybe you were right, and it was just the wrong number. Maybe it's... down the road or something."

I prayed that was the case. But I had a piece of information he didn't have. One that, if true, meant I had to question everything.

Trust no one.

Joe...what the hell is going on?

Most of the buildings along the road looked similar. Old, kind of run down. Some of them were still in use. Trucks stood next to the buildings while workers carried their loads into them. Two men stood near the gate of a factory and looked our way. I could only imagine how out of place we seemed. They seemed familiar, or at least the one with the buzz cut did. But I couldn't remember from where.

We took a right at the next intersection and another right into the parallel road. My hands turned clammy. We walked and walked but found nothing at all. No sign of this being the place where we needed to be. No trace of the company that flew us in.

"Well, that was a waste of time," Miles noted with a

hint of frustration in his voice. We arrived back where we'd started.

A rush of fury overcame me. I walked up to the brick pillar at the left of the gate and gave it a nice kick, imagining it was whoever was behind this. The pillar shook from the force. My shoe, and my now aching foot, didn't appreciate this treatment, though.

"Well, I know not to piss you off too much," Miles said, sounding impressed. "Wouldn't want to be on the receiving end of a kick like that."

I shook my head, amused. "Listen, I just thought of something," I said. "I saw an internet café on our way here. We could go there and check the address for Briola on their website."

"Good idea."

Within fifteen or twenty minutes of walking, we found the internet café. It was a small shop squeezed between two bigger ones selling used computers and junk.

We walked inside, where we were met with the rather uninviting smell of old air, a hint of sweat, and tea. The man behind the counter reminded me of our first cab driver visually, similar skin tone and curly black hair. He greeted us with a smile that faded the second he noticed my blue hair and wary gaze.

"*Zwei Colas*," Miles said.

At hearing Miles speak German, the man behind the counter relaxed, but he still looked us up and down as he retrieved two glass bottles of Coke. In moments like this I was grateful that Miles spoke German.

"Americans?" the man asked.

Miles nodded. "Students."

"We'd like to use one of your computers," I said.

"Of course," the man said.

Miles gave him money for the drinks and then handed me one.

"Thank you," I murmured, then we looked for a place to sit.

"What did you say? Was that an actual *thank you*?"

"You heard me."

And Miles had the nerve to smile. "Yeah. I did."

The computers looked like they'd seen better days. The monitors weren't even flat-screens. The keyboards were dusty, and the keys were loud and sticky in a few places.

When I logged on, a timer started in the top right corner and displayed the total price.

I pulled up my email inbox while Miles dragged a chair over. The email from Briola should have their address and everything in it. After clicking on it, it took another minute for everything to load. The connection speed here must be set at turtle.

The email finally opened fully, and I scrolled down to the address.

"Bloody…"

"Since when are you British?" Miles said, amused.

"Stop joking for a second and look at this." I pointed at the screen.

He leaned closer and then sucked in a sharp breath. The address we'd gone to was correct. A moment later, he gave me one of those "told you so" looks.

"Check their website," Miles said, and leaned back in his chair.

I scrolled down until I found the link. A new window

popped up and began to load. An information banner appeared.

The website you are trying to access isn't currently in use.

The hairs on my neck stood up. It was impossible and crazy. It must have been some really mean prank or something, because it just couldn't be real.

I jumped onto Google next. Maybe it could tell me where to find that stupid company. Google knew everything, didn't it? But—

"Miles."

"I see it."

We both stared dumbfounded at the search results. Nothing. Even typing in Briola BIO TECH only brought up links to other bio tech companies. As far as Google was concerned, Briola didn't exist.

Ludicrous. The website had existed. At least, it had before today. I'd literally looked at it with my father after they made me the offer. If it was going to take precious time away from my training, it had to meet his standards.

My father had talked to someone representing Briola over the phone a week or two ago to ask them about what they did, how this entire thing would go down, about the hotel, how much money we should bring along.

And what about the company itself? They'd offered this opportunity through our school. Hell, was my school in on this, too? Everyone?

Trust no one.

"I'm done with this bullshit," Miles said, and stood up. "I'm calling my father."

He walked to the counter and asked for a key to the phone booths. Making an international call that way was definitely cheaper than using a cell phone, though I didn't understand why Miles, of all people, would care about the cost of anything.

Had he just wanted to be away from me? Or was he calling someone other than his father? Was he giving *them* a report on me?

I went back to the original email and inspected the address and link once more. Then I studied the email address itself. No obvious indication of it being fake. But of course, they wouldn't make it obvious.

Except for bringing us all the way here and putting us in a hotel, only to let us then find an abandoned building instead of a bio tech facility, for their website to just disappear...

Yeah. Nothing obvious or suspicious about that at all.

Miles came back, cursing. "Of course his cell phone isn't on. So typical," he muttered as he sat back down in his chair, his arms crossed over his chest. "The idiot probably never plugged it back into the charger. Moron." He seemed angry. Really angry. But there was something in his voice, in his eyes, that bordered on disappointment.

Lucky him. My dad wouldn't disappear. Not even if I wanted him to.

Last year I heard a story of how Miles supposedly spent an hour with a freshman girl who was crying outside our school as she waited for her ride. Apparently, her father never showed up, so Miles offered to drive her home. The knight in shiny armor or whatever. Her father had simply forgotten to pick her up. He'd been in a *very* important business meeting, so of course had turned off his phone. Because a meeting like that is more important than your kid.

I'd always assumed the story was fake, the kind of rumor Miles probably started himself so everyone would think better of him. But now, going by his reaction? I wasn't so sure.

Unless this was all part of an act.

I took the phone key from him and called my parents. Maybe they would be more helpful. The booth was pretty small and didn't smell much better than the entire café itself.

After a couple beeps, our answering machine picked up, and my mother's happy voice said, "Hello, this is the Wolf family. We are currently on a cruise through the Caribbean. If you leave a message and your number, we will call you back when we return. Thank you!"

A cruise?

My parents hadn't gone on a vacation in years. Vacations were, according to my father, a waste of money and time. Besides, he had to be there to support me. My training.

But that wasn't even the strangest thing about the message. No. What was far more astonishing was my parents, who were usually so private and careful, recording that message in the first place, letting anyone who'd call know that they weren't home. It was the perfect way to just have someone break into our house, like an invitation between the lines or whatever. They'd never do something stupid like that. So why did they?

"No luck?" Miles asked upon my return.

"They said they're on a cruise," I said, sounding dazed.

"Yours are MIA, too? I guess that could be a

coincidence…maybe."

We both turned silent. The situation was insane and impossible, yet it was real. We were sitting here, thousands of miles away from home, in a foreign county and continent, all on our own. There was no one around to help us.

"Shit," I said quietly, over and over.

"We should go back to the hotel and think this through, look at our options," Miles suggested. "And we need to get as much cash off of our cards as we can. In case they get blocked for whatever reasons."

I hadn't even thought of that. "You really think that will happen?"

"At this point?" he said. "I think anything can happen."

The hotel room looked the same way we'd left it, with our luggage and travel clothes lying around. The cart holding our breakfast was gone, though. I took off my jacket, which joined the rest of my clothes on the sofa, and then flopped onto the bed.

A moment later, Miles joined me with his laptop. A brand-new MacBook Pro, of course. I moved farther onto the bed and sat opposite to him.

"Okay, what we know is that supposedly, this pharmaceutical company, Briola Bio Tech, booked us a privet jet from the U.S. to Germany. They gave us their address and website link. Until today, that all seemed fine."

"Right," I said. "I checked their website a couple of minutes before I drove to the airport. It was there. Which means it disappeared over the last twenty-four hours."

"Hold on a second," Miles said, and looked up at me. "Let's say this company isn't real. Who arranged all this? Who's paying for the room?" He paused. "And why?"

I knew a clue to at least one of those questions. Should I tell him?

"Actually..." I started.

"Yeah?"

Paranoia aside, this was a crucial part of the puzzle. "I asked the receptionist about who booked our room earlier today," I said and then sighed. "You won't like the answer, though."

"Tell me."

"They don't know who booked the room."

He frowned. "This isn't funny."

"Do I look like I'm joking? I wasn't sure if I believed it, either, but after this, Briola just vanishing somehow, it kind of makes sense."

"Fiona, none of this makes sense. At all."

If he was only acting a part in this, he deserved an Oscar for his performance. "Check the price of the room."

Miles tapped his keyboard, looking all focused and stern. I controlled my breathing the way they'd taught me in kickboxing class in an effort to stay calm. Wanting to distract myself if only for a moment, I concentrated on the sun outside our window behind Miles, on the blue of the sky and the fluffy clouds moving along slowly. The change of his facial expression caught my eye.

"Three hundred and fifty euros per night," he said, his voice completely flat.

"Are you serious?" Stupid question. Looking at this

room, I could totally see why it would be that expensive. It was a great room with vintage furniture, free internet, a flat-screen TV, and even a damn balcony with a brilliant view. And that breakfast we were served…everything screamed money.

Miles pushed the laptop aside and then backed off the bed. "Get the money you took from the ATM." Slightly confused, I followed his order and got my wallet.

We threw together our cash in the center of the bed, then Miles took it all and began counting. European money looked so different from U.S. dollars, was far more colorful, making differentiating between the bills easier, though I was confused by the lack of one-euro bills.

"Eighteen hundred euros," he concluded.

"That's a lot, isn't it?" At least to me it was. For him, that was probably his weekly allowance or something.

"It is a lot. But for a bio tech company? Pocket change."

I could hear my father now. How dumb I'd been to come here. To neglect my training. Well, he'd have to accept that getting through whatever this mess was would only make me stronger in the end.

"What if we try to call them?" Our parents had spoken with Briola. So there was at least a tiny chance that someone would pick up, possibly have answers, anything at all.

"Judging by the address and website, chances aren't good."

"We could still try. Damn it, we have to do *something*."

He nodded and pulled out his phone, dialed the number from the email, and put the call on speaker.

"The number you have reached has been disconnected,"

a monotone voice said. A sudden *click* indicated the call had ended. I'd known it wouldn't work, yet somehow, I still felt disappointed.

"You know what I think?" Miles asked while putting his phone down next to his laptop.

Something told me I didn't want to. "What?"

"I think we should get out of here, go to the airport, and try to get the quickest plane back home."

Fair point. Briola was gone. The room had been booked for us seemingly by no one. And there was no guarantee that what money we had would last long enough to figure out this mystery.

What if this was the moment when Miles would lead me into some kind of trap? But how could he? There was no chance of anyone at the airport being in on whatever was going on. That just seemed too out there even for this, or so I hoped. Also, if I fought him on this, who knew if it would make things worse for me, or if it would clue him in on the fact that I was suspicious of him.

Besides, if we went home, I could confront Joe. Demand he explain that cryptic warning.

"What about the room?"

"To hell with the room," he said and threw his hands in the air. "I don't plan on paying for it, do you?"

Now *that* confused me. "What are you talking about? You are aware that rooms get paid for beforehand, right?"

"Not in Europe. Here, you pay afterward, not before."

"Okay. But what if we get caught?" Breaking rules, going against authority. That never went over well—not with my father, anyway.

"Easy," Miles said. "We just don't get caught."

I frowned. "And how are we supposed to do that?"

"Don't you watch spy movies?" He ran his hands over his face and into his hair. "When the night shift starts, only one person is down there, right? One of us will start a conversation with them and the other will sneak past with our stuff. And then we'll disappear."

"Really?" I wasn't convinced at all.

Miles gave me a challenging look. "You have a better idea?"

Joe had said I shouldn't trust anyone. But right now, I didn't have a better option. And maybe Miles was just that good at playing me, but what if I was wrong and he was a victim here, too?

"Fine," I said. "Let's do this."

CHAPTER SEVEN
THE ISLAND

"**D**o you remember which way you went?" Miles asked.

Everything in the jungle looked like more of the same again and again, like someone had lazily designed a *Minecraft* biome where you'd get lost without a compass in two minutes flat.

But some things stood out to me. Odd-shaped trees with strangely growing branches. I'd passed those before. A splintered bark that looked like it might've been struck by lightning at some point. A cluster of bushes dotted with blue flowers.

"That way." I pointed in that direction and up to where we would have seen the smoke if not for the heavy foliage.

"You sure?"

He didn't know I'd taught myself to remember my surroundings since that awful day at the park when I was five. I couldn't get lost again. Not like that.

"Yeah. I'm sure."

"Well then, lead the way," Miles said, and made a sweeping motion with his arm.

We didn't talk much, besides the repeated question from Miles whether I was sure we were headed in the right direction. But still, it felt nice having him with me. An extra pair of eyes and ears. If something came for us, two were better than one.

At first he'd been wobbly on his legs, the two of us starting out much slower than I had on my own, but the longer we walked the surer he seemed to get. Maybe he really did feel better like he said back at the beach. Not that it would matter much, depending on the success, or lack thereof, of our search.

About halfway, or what I thought was halfway, we came across a banana tree. I'd never really been the biggest fan of bananas, hated them as a kid, but right about now I didn't even care. It was something to eat, and in our situation, I didn't have the luxury of being picky. Getting them off the tree required me having to actually climb it under Miles's watchful, and just a little doubtful, eye, but I got it done.

With a bunch of bananas in hand and squished into our pockets—skinny jeans with shallow pockets really sucked—we continued on our way. After eating I immediately felt better, stronger, and ready to face whatever waited for us at the cockpit. Miles's face also had its normal color back, and his steps seemed surer, stronger.

"That's where I saw it earlier," I said, and pointed toward the fallen tree I'd climbed on. We'd made great progress.

"Which means we must be close to that animal's territory," he said, looking around. So far, we hadn't seen anything. No signs of the beast, nothing that would indicate that this was part of its territory, no traces on the ground, no scratches on the trees like the ones boars left. Then again, it wasn't like a beast could just pull a metal fence around what it thought belonged to it and put a KEEP OUT sign on it.

"Let's give this area a wide berth," I said. "Just in case."

So we made a circle around the tree. Of course, there was no guarantee that we were avoiding anything.

But the farther we went, the more I felt hopeful that maybe we'd be lucky this time. Maybe I'd just been unlucky before, and by now it had forgotten I'd even been there, or maybe it deemed me not an easy enough source of food, too tricky to catch to be worth it or something. Still, I paid attention to every snap of a branch, every rustling of leaves, paid attention where I stepped and reminded Miles to do the same a few times.

"There," Miles said after what felt like hours more of walking. He stopped mid-step and grabbed my arm, then he raised his other hand and pointed at something through the leaves. I followed his finger, tried to make out what he thought he could see, and suddenly I saw it, too.

A large object reflecting the sunlight. Something white and metallic. We pushed through the branches and saw it clearly. The front of the plane and the cockpit.

We actually found it!

Turning my head, I looked up at Miles. Our eyes met, and both of us smiled at each other for a moment. We'd made it, somehow. After the hell of the rest of the day, this one small victory felt huge.

"I'm pleasantly surprised," Miles admitted. "I would've put my money on you not having a single clue where we were going."

"Thanks for the vote of confidence."

"You're very welcome."

"Goes to show that you shouldn't underestimate me," I said instead of agreeing with him. I hadn't believed I would find the plane, either. Technically I hadn't, he did. But we weren't lost, thanks to me, and that had to count for something. "Let's find the pilot."

Slowly we approached the plane, the eerie quiet around us making me nervous. It didn't necessarily mean the pilot was dead or had moved on. Maybe he was hiding, worried that the beast would come for him if he made any noise. I had to believe he was okay. He had to be okay.

"Hello?" I called out. "Anybody here?"

No response.

The walls that connected the cockpit to our part of the plane were just as jagged and frayed as ours, small pieces of metal littering the ground around it, but the door was still closed. I pulled on it with no result. Miles joined me, but even working together, it wouldn't budge. The only option was the front, the nose slightly sticking up off of the ground, the ripped end digging into the ground the way our front part was.

Even as tall as Miles was, it was clear that he couldn't reach high enough to get in on his own. "Help me up onto the front of the plane," he said.

He put one foot in my clasped hands, and I held him up and steady while he grabbed whatever he could and pulled himself up.

"I see him," Miles said. "He's in the cockpit!"

"Yes!" Yes. Yes. Yes—

"Oh…*shit*. Fiona…"

My fragile hope cracked like a piece of glass. Miles slowly turned his head and looked down at me, his eyes sad and apologetic.

"He's dead."

CHAPTER EIGHT
BERLIN

"I still think this is a horrible idea," I said while we stood in the elevator going down to the lobby.

"I blend in," Miles said. "One cannot *not* notice you with that hair of yours, which means you have to take her attention off of the lobby so I can sneak past. Just accept that." He looked down at me. Each time I stood next to him I was reminded of just how tall he was, surely over six feet. He'd changed back into a pair of dark jeans, dark shoes, a light gray shirt and black jacket, while his obsidian-colored hair was still a mess that almost seemed like it was planned to look that way.

Miles and I couldn't have looked more different. My blue hair fell over my shoulders, and I was back in my comfy jeans, T-shirt, and hoodie. The last thing I wanted was for people to think we might be related—or worse, in a relationship.

The door slid open, and Miles whispered, "Show

time." I took a deep breath and stepped forward with my small bag hanging off my shoulder, leaving Miles behind with our two suitcases, both small enough that he could make it through the lobby without drawing attention. He stacked mine onto his to make it even easier. For others it hopefully looked like I was just about to leave for the city, for a party or something, not like I was planning on sneaking out of the country.

Miles nudged me out of the elevator because I wasn't fast enough, it seemed, and I made my way toward reception. The same woman sat behind the desk as before. Her eyes were fixed on the monitor to her right and underlined with dark circles. I guessed she was exhausted after working all day. Maybe the fact that she was tired would help us, somehow.

"Good evening," I said, slightly nervous, leaning against the desk with my elbows.

The woman looked up from her monitor at me. She seemed almost surprised that I was standing in front of her, like she hadn't even noticed me before I spoke.

"Good evening," she replied. "How can I help you?"

"Well, I was wondering where in the area I could get a bite to eat, nothing too fancy, rather something more…" I stopped for a moment to come up with a fitting word. "Unique, perhaps?"

She looked at the watch on her right wrist. "At past nine p.m.?"

"I know it's a totally weird time but, you know, with the jet lag and all, I'm just craving food right now." I tried to sound convincing, as far as that was even possible with a stupid story like that, and the fact that the hotel offered room service. I was glad she was the one I was talking to and not some guy. Though, lying to her face and just this entire shitty plan in general were hard enough to go through with.

"Of course." For a moment she stayed silent, maybe thinking about places to eat. "Do you happen to have a map or phone?"

I looked around and noticed a bunch of tourist type maps of Berlin laying on the other end of the desk. Those would take up more of her field of vision than my phone. I picked up one of them, unfolded it, and placed the map between us while positioning myself a bit closer in hopes of obscuring her view of the lobby behind me.

She took a pen and started to point at different locations on the map, drawing a circle or two in several places while explaining what each of them was. I pretended to listen while I looked over my shoulder as inconspicuously as I could and spotted Miles making his way across the lobby. It wasn't that big of a distance, forty feet at most, doable.

The receptionist looked up, noticing me look at something and turning in her chair just a bit. Hastily I asked her to clarify some directions I certainly hadn't actually listened to, and moved a little toward her, my arms spread out a little more, hopefully blocking her view.

"Are you sure you're okay?" she asked, possibly, or rather definitely, noticing my strange behavior. Damn it.

"Definitely, just really hungry."

She looked at me for a moment longer and then pointed at something more on the map. I looked over my shoulder again. Just in that moment Miles finally made it to the door and slipped outside.

"Fabulous," I said through a fake smile. "Thank you so much. I really appreciate it."

"I hope you'll find your way and that those places are really open at this time. I'm not entirely sure, unfortunately."

"I'm sure it'll be okay. Thank you again."

"Didn't you arrive with a boy?" she asked and looked around as though she expected to see Miles somewhere waiting for me.

"Yes, but he isn't feeling too great, so he stayed in the room, already asleep like a rock, so it's just me." I hoped she wouldn't send anyone up to our room to check on Miles. Did hotels even do something like that?

"Be careful. Berlin is a dangerous city at night, even more so depending on where you go."

"I will. Thanks again and good night," I said, smiled again, and folded the map.

I tried to walk out of the hotel looking as casual as possible, not suspicious like someone who was just about to flee without paying. Miles truly had the ability to bring out the worst version of me. Away from home for only a day and I was already turning into a lying criminal, even if Miles was trying his best to help. Or maybe it was part of some plan to get me into trouble, so whoever the bad guys were would have an easier time doing whatever they planned on doing, whatever Joe knew and made them a danger to me. All of this just sucked so hard.

"That was awful," I said once I caught up with Miles outside.

"Now that's what I call teamwork. See, it wasn't that bad," he said with a smug smile that I would have loved to slap away. I rolled my eyes instead.

"Let's get going before they smell the lie and come after us." I took my bag and suitcase from him. He just shook his head with that smile still way too present.

The thing about Berlin was that they had a lot of different types of public transportation. They had buses and metro buses, trams and metro trams, and something called S- and U-Bahn, which were basically under and over ground trains. And they also had normal trains. How did the people of Berlin not get lost in all of that? According to the internet, we had to take the S-Bahn and a bus in order to get to the airport, one of two that Berlin offered.

Briefly I wondered what we'd say or do if someone stopped us to ask why we were out so late at night, but all I could do was hope that we were inconspicuous enough that no one would notice. It wasn't like "we committed a crime" was written on our foreheads or anything, and Berlin was a tourist city, after all, so hopefully we'd look like any other tourists to onlookers.

After a handful of minutes of nothing but walking, we reached the Potsdamer Platz, from where we had to take said S-Bahn. At the station, we followed signs that directed us to where the S1 stopped. On the way, we stumbled across one of their ticket machines, which luckily had the option of changing the language to English. We bought two normal AB zone tickets and made our way over to the platform.

"Everything about Briola is absolutely insane," I said quietly, while we sat in the back of the bus that would take us from the S1 to the Berlin Tegel airport. "I mean who does something like this, and why?"

"At this point I don't care anymore. Are they real, are

they just some elaborate fake, it's irrelevant, no? Personally, I don't want to have anything to do with this anymore."

"Same. I wish we could just be home already." Depending on what flight we ended up with, it would take a long time to get home, possibly up to thirty-one hours, even though it had only taken like nine or so to get to Berlin. No private jet and direct route this time. "Do you think our school was scammed somehow?"

"Academy of Fine Education…with a name like that you'd think they'd know how not to be scammed, but alas, here we are. I should have my father sue them for putting us into this kind of danger. Hell knows what else could've happened."

I tried not to look too much into the fact that he said *us* instead of *me*. It was probably just something he said without consciously realizing it.

"Can't sue something that isn't there," I pointed out.

"Briola might not be. Our school is, though, and with how much cash they've gotten from my family over the years, I expected better." Was it me or did he just sound truly entitled? It was Miles, so of course he did; hell, he *was* entitled, a first-class citizen, while I was a mere peasant. No matter how many competitions I'd won so far, that simple fact would likely never change. I doubted anyone in my sport ever managed to win enough money, and get it through sponsorships, to match the Echo fortune. "Also," he continued, "if a guy can sue Red Bull for not giving him wings, I can sue Briola or whoever approached our school for this project."

We finally arrived and got off the bus. This airport was much smaller than MIA, though it seemed just as confusing. Inside, the lights were bright, the floors and walls white, and it was full of people pushing carts or pulling their suitcases.

Miles and I made our way to the counters. I sighed with relief, my body relaxing at the thought of just how close we were to getting tickets and going home. Usually I enjoyed being away from home, catching a break from my father, but now I couldn't imagine a place that would make me happier, even though I'd be alone while I waited for my parents to return. It still made no sense to me that they had just left without telling me anything, without texting. They hadn't even bothered to read the text I'd sent them earlier today. Did they not care about me at all?

When our turn came, Miles's expression changed back into the one he usually wore, the flirty, charming smile and eyes, and he postured as if he simply owned this place, like there was nothing he couldn't get or do.

The lady behind the counter greeted us with a small smile. The moment she noticed Miles, she lit up even more. As much as I wanted to make some snarky remark, if his usual self would get us home, I was willing to let it slide.

Miles asked her for two tickets to Miami, no matter which class. All that mattered was that we get there. The lady looked at her monitor and typed something into the system.

"Unfortunately, all the flights are already booked," she informed us.

"How about tomorrow, then?"

"The same. The system tells me that all the flights going to your destination are booked until next Monday. It's high season for these flights right now, which is why people usually reserve their tickets weeks in advance." She looked like she was genuinely sorry for not being able to help us, her eyes soft and a tiny frown on her lips.

"Are you completely sure? Not even with a transfer?" I sounded way too desperate for my own liking.

"I'm afraid it looks the same," she said after checking the system again. "I'm really sorry. But you could come back in a couple days, and maybe then the situation will look different. Seats could open up for any of the booked-out flights in the next week and a half."

"Okay, well, thank you for your help anyway," Miles said, the happy, flirty tone gone and replaced by disappointment. The smile disappeared from his face; even his shoulders seemed to sag a little.

We made our way to a small waiting area. It was crowded with other passengers waiting for check-ins or arrivals, faces of different nationalities, ages and genders. Some sat with their eyes glued to their phones, others were having conversations or checking the signs far more frequently than necessary. Among them I thought I could see those two men that I'd noticed had watched us at Siemensstadt, but they couldn't be the same ones. The chances were tiny, barely even a thing. They probably just looked similar to them.

We flopped down on two chairs and just sat there. This was bad, really bad. I let my head fall into my open palms, my elbows resting on my knees.

The more we tried, the more absurd everything became. None of it made any sense—the jet, the hotel, the abandoned factory, Briola disappearing, my parents gone, and Miles's father not answering his phone, either, and now the sold-out tickets. And Joe's voicemail.

Trust no one.

Disliking Miles was so much easier than this. Distrust was so much harder to deal with than his snarky comments and our usual back and forth. He was an ass, but at least before this trip I knew what I was getting, knew what I could expect from him. Now, I had mixed signals.

Regardless of whether or not Miles was on my side, we needed a plan and a way to make it through the next couple of days until we'd be able to go home. And I had to stop wondering if those two guys from Siemensstadt were suspiciously watching us, because it wasn't helping me think.

With a heavy sigh, I looked up and noticed Miles playing around with his phone. His brows were slightly pulled together, his expression focused on the screen. I ran my hands over my face and hair and straightened my back.

"What are you doing?" *Please don't let it be another selfie.*

He gave me that cocksure smirk, the one his Instagram followers couldn't seem to get enough of, and said, "Getting us out of here."

CHAPTER NINE
THE ISLAND

I sank to my knees and grabbed fistfuls of grass.

The pilot was dead. Hopelessness licked at the edges of my sanity, dug its claws into my mind. I wanted to beg anyone I could think of to help us, save us, but the Marvel heroes weren't real, couldn't do anything for us.

"Fiona," Miles said cautiously. "There's another chance, even without him."

"What's that? Unless you found another plane and another pilot, we're done."

"No, we're not."

At that I finally looked up, met his eyes, and found a strange type of confidence in them. "What are you talking about?"

"The plane's computer board," he said and smiled a little.

"And you think it's that damn easy to use?" Did he actually think that could work? It took pilots months to learn how to control planes, how to even as much as have a basic understanding of the computers they ran with, why did he think he'd be able to just wing it with no prior knowledge whatsoever. If he said he actually took lessons, I would punch him in the face, except if he managed to get that computer board thing, then maybe I would do it only very lightly.

"Not everything has to be complicated."

"Spare me your Zen Yoda philosophy," I said and got back up onto my feet.

"If I get it running, I can access its flight records and find out exactly what happened." He paused, and I could hear the inevitable *but*.

"What's the problem?"

"But first we have to get the body out so I have room to work."

Touching a dead body was better than being dead, but that didn't make the idea any less appalling. I went back to the side of the plane and held out my hands toward him. His grip was confident and strong, two things I wished I felt inside myself, and he pulled me up.

My nose was assaulted by the stench of dried blood and dead human the second I got close to the shattered front windows. It was like a mix of salt and metal, sugary sweetness, a strong note of cigarette smoke and dog shit that'd been lying in the blazing sun all day long.

"You still think that it's a good idea?" I asked Miles, whose face had gone green. I had a feeling mine didn't look much better. Not with the somersaults my stomach was doing.

"We don't have a choice, not if we want that computer."

I braced myself for the view that would meet me. I'd never seen a corpse outside of books and movies.

The pilot was still in his seat, his head thrown back, eyes toward the ceiling, and his white dress shirt stained in dried red. Something was sticking out of his chest. Glass? Metal? My heart raced and slammed against my chest. I cursed again. *Own your fear; don't let it own you.*

"For me to get at the computer, we have to take him out," Miles said. "One of us has to go in and take off his seat belt, push him toward the window, and the other has to pull him out. Which job do you want?"

I was going to let him be the brave one and go inside, but his face was paler than when we'd first crashed. No matter how much he always played the brave one, I was the stronger one. Much as I hated how my dad pushed me, the years of training had taught me to keep my cool. Ignore pain, push through, and still win.

"I'll go in," I said. "You pull him out." My stomach flipped at the prospect of getting closer to the pilot, but I'd made my choice.

"You don't have to do that," Miles said.

"Too late."

Before he could stop me, I took in one last breath and went in. The smell inside was ten times worse than outside. I used all my mental strength not to throw up while I moved past the second seat. Glass crunched underneath my feet, and I was thankful I'd chosen to wear relatively thick-soled Chuck Taylors for our flight. Not really ideal for any of our activities so far, but at least they were comfortable.

From behind, I unfastened the pilot's seat belt and let

out a small yelp as I noticed his wide-open eyes staring at me—well, technically the ceiling. Was he…? No. He was dead. A quick gulp of air corrupted my nose with a fresh wave of stench. I swallowed. Definitely dead.

"You all right?" Miles called.

"Yes." I pushed the pilot's eyes shut, which wasn't as easy as they made it seem on TV, though I cringed at the feeling of his skin against mine. It felt oddly greasy, an inexplicable shade of cold despite the temperature around us, and stiff, as though the pilot's body had turned into something like stone.

I held his legs while Miles held his arms. God, the smell was even worse now. I'd noticed it before, but the longer I was there, the more intense the smell of cigarettes seemed to be, like the stench of death wasn't bad enough itself. My chest clenched. The guy must have smoked like a chimney.

We left the plane with the dead man hanging between us. He was awfully heavy. But I'd powered through worse, and I wasn't about to let Miles see me slow down. We carried the pilot across the clearing and then an additional couple of feet into the jungle.

Miles wiped his forehead with his right arm and leaned against a tree. My breathing was going fast and heavy, my muscles impossibly sore. That smell. I'd thought it would get better outside the plane, but it was just as bad.

"We need to bury him," I finally said between two gasps of breath.

"Are you crazy? We need to get back up there and get the computer."

"We can't just leave him like this. No one deserves to just be left to get eaten by that beast or some other animal,"

I argued. "You go work your magic, and I'll do this."

"Are you sure?"

"We don't have much time. Just go. I'll be fine."

For a moment he didn't move, but then he finally nodded and walked off. In some twisted way, I wished he'd stayed.

I wasn't a weak girl. I trained for years in hellholes worse than this, but moving even a single muscle right now was the hardest thing I had done in my entire life. Each movement sent a wave of pain through me.

The pilot's grave wouldn't be six feet deep. No way would I manage to do that with my bare hands. It would be shallow and pathetic. I wished I could do more. No one deserved this, any of it.

I walked over to the plane and searched for a metal piece of a good size that I could use to dig. I found one half sticking out of the ground, then pulled it out, walked back to the pilot, and began to dig.

The hole wasn't nearly deep enough, but it was the best I could do. I needed to leave myself enough energy to run if that thing came after us again. I was thankful for those bananas we'd eaten on our way, though thinking about food made me feel sicker than I already did. I put the metal aside and pulled the pilot into the grave. His body was stiff. Rigor mortis had already kicked in. It only made everything so much harder. I slipped twice, once landing on my ass and then almost inside the hole along with the body. Once I finally managed to get it inside without accidentally joining it, I covered it with dirt as fast as I could.

After everything was done, I jogged back to the bottom

of the plane to check on Miles. I wondered if he truly had any kind of computer knowledge to get this task done, or if he'd just said it to give us hope. I couldn't hate him if he had.

"Did you find it?" I asked, looking up.

Miles poked his head out of the broken cockpit. He opened his mouth to speak, and I held on to a little piece of hope that he'd say he had good news.

"I've got it. But there's no power. And it looks like it might have been damaged in the crash."

"Well, can you fix it?"

"Yeah, I think so. But it'll take—"

A roar shook the plane. Hell, it shook me.

The beast was close, way too close. We looked at each other, wide eyed.

"That sound like a boar to you?" I challenged.

"Shit," he muttered, and disappeared back into the cockpit.

"Miles, what the hell? We have to go!"

But he didn't come back out. Seconds passed that felt like an eternity. The beast wasn't here. Not yet. But if we didn't run…

Miles finally exited the cockpit and jumped back down beside me. The computer board was in his hands now, a strange piece of tech I'd never seen before, not much bigger than the palm of my hand.

"We leave without this," he said, "and that whole thing was a waste. Now, let's go!"

CHAPTER TEN
BERLIN

"**W**hat do you mean you're getting us out of here?" I said, not even hiding my suspicion.

He went back to his phone. "I'm booking us a hotel room—with two beds this time." I was about to argue, simply because I was so used to it, but he spoke again before I could. "It'll be less expensive than taking two separate rooms." Of course he was right. I hated that. "The place isn't anything fancy. But it's pretty cheap and near the airport."

When we arrived, the hotel, or rather *motel*, wasn't anything special. The building was a couple stories high and kind of washed out and dirty on the outside, nothing like our previous hotel, the facade seemingly made up of rectangular concrete plates with ridges between them. Inside, the lobby had odd-colored walls, something between white, cream, and gray, and cheap laminate flooring. I wondered how Miles would survive this.

Our room was on the third floor. The elevator squeaked louder the higher it went, and the flooring was soft, almost squishy. I got out the second the doors slid open.

The room was tiny, despite the fact that it was a double. The floor was covered by worn carpet, the walls a weird cream color, and the furniture cheap. There were two beds on opposite sides of the room, with two small tables next to them. The only window was between our beds.

I placed my suitcase and bag against the foot of a bed and sat down on it. The mattress must have been made of stone.

"We should try contacting our school and friends... anyone, really," I suggested sometime later. Someone was bound to answer. They had to.

"Good idea," Miles said, and actually sounded like he meant it.

I called home first but got the same message as before, then I tried my father's and my mom's cell phones. Both went straight to voicemail. I listened to both, even if only to hear their voices for a moment, my mom's cheerful instruction for people to leave their number and reason for calling after the beep, and my father's stern tone that almost seemed annoyed.

Next, I tried Melany. She'd been my best friend ever since I moved to Miami. On my first day of freshman year, our English teacher had Melany and me work on something together and we just *clicked*, inseparable ever since. She was completely different than the people I grew up with, or my kickboxing friends and acquaintances — cute and sweet, funny, kind, and just the best friend I could ever imagine having. Could anyone blame me for totally having something like a crush on her during the summer that we'd spent at her aunt's in Palm Beach between sophomore and junior year? It had taken me until about half a year later to ever bring it up—my crush on her long gone by that time, even more so since I'd realized we were way better off as friends.

I closed my eyes as I listened to the rings and waited for her to pick up her cell, calculating the time difference in my head. She was in L.A. for her internship. If I remembered correctly L.A. was nine hours behind Berlin, so she had to be awake and able to pick up. But she didn't. My heart sunk, squeezed painfully. I tried again but got the same result. Then I tried Jacky, Melany's internship partner, but she didn't pick up, either. Maybe they were somewhere that required them to silence their phones.

My hands lightly trembled as I typed a text, asked Melany to get back to me, telling her that things were bad, that I needed to talk to her, hoping that the urgency of the situation would show through my words. I tapped send and then texted Jacky, asking her to tell Melany to text me.

After a while, both texts remained delivered but unread. Come *on*.

It didn't seem like Miles was having much success, either, his mouth a pressed, straight line, a frown crinkling his forehead, his eyes staring daggers at his phone. He swiped and tapped around on his screen, then typed something, swiped again, and then held the phone to his ear. The look of frustration and annoyance on his face only deepened the longer I watched him.

"No luck?" I eventually asked.

"What are these asses even doing?" he said without

looking up. "It's the middle of the day in the States. Usually everyone clings to their phones like they need them to survive, yet this one time it actually matters, nothing. My father the moron still hasn't turned his phone back on, and no one at his office is picking up, either. What does he even pay them for?"

I didn't say anything to that, just wondered if his emotions were real, whether he really had called anyone or if it was just part of the act. But it seemed authentic.

"Last one to try is our school," he said, and did just that. I was glad he didn't ask me to do it. My father would already kill me for this phone bill. But even before Miles made the call and turned on the speaker, I already had a feeling it wouldn't work out. Nothing seemed to be on our side, everyone just magically gone, unreachable. I had no idea how it was possible, how any of this was possible, yet it was happening. In the end, Miles groaned, cut the call, and threw his phone onto his bedside table before leaving the room to change.

While I waited for him to return so I could do the same, I went back to my phone and clicked on the photos app. Scrolling through the nearly two thousand pictures I had saved, I stopped on one of my parents I'd taken last Christmas. They were sitting on the sofa in our living room, my father with his arm around my mother's shoulders, the smile on her face happy and bright, brighter than the lights on our tree. My father was smiling, too, though much more subtly. According to my mom, I had his eyes, the same light shades of blue and the same shape, my skin just as untypically fair for someone living in Florida, my face more of a heart shape like my mom's, though her nose was a little thinner, pointier than mine. Whose genes had given me my relatively full lips, I didn't know, though Mom always argued that it came from my grandmother. She hated the scar I had above my left eye, but I thought it looked pretty badass.

It'd only been a day, yet I missed them. I missed the way my mom asked me about school the same way every single day, the way my father made me do drills during warm up, the dinners we ate together in the evening, the occasional movie nights my mom forced my father to participate in even if both she and I knew he would absolutely hate the one we'd picked.

We really were on our own.

I woke with a scream stuck in my throat. My eyes flew open as I sat up. There was nothing but darkness around me. Still night. My heart raced, and my breathing was wild, irregular, and shaky. I got rid of my blanket, threw it onto the foot of the bed, leaned my back against the wall, and pulled my knees up.

My body shook while tears streamed down my cheeks. I hugged my knees and placed my head on them. I felt so lost and alone, even though Miles was sleeping in the same room. I had no idea what to do. I didn't understand any of it, nothing, not a single thing made sense.

A weird, strangled noise escaped my lips before I could stop it. I kept my eyes closed and tried to shut the world out, pretend I wasn't here. Pretend this wasn't happening.

This wasn't me. I didn't behave like this, ever. I was stronger than this, yet here I was, unable to pull myself together. I could win fights and medals at a state level, but this situation I couldn't deal with.

"Fiona?" Miles's sleep-filled voice asked quietly. I didn't answer, stayed the way I was. "Fiona?" he tried again.

I thought he moved. *Stay away*, I wanted to say, but I remained silent instead.

"What's wrong?"

Sheets rustled, and the floor creaked ever so quietly as Miles moved, came closer. Maybe he even crouched down in front of me to be on my level. I wasn't sure, though, because my eyes were still closed, my face hidden by the curtain of my hair.

I heard him move again. Maybe he was going back to bed; maybe he couldn't be bothered enough to deal with me. But I was wrong. He sat down right there next to me. I felt the warmth of his body, so close.

"Hey," he said softly. "We'll be okay." A moment later his hand was on my back. He pulled me toward him, his arm around my shoulders and my body leaning against his. His warmth on my skin, his smell in my nose, something citrusy with an underlying warm note that I couldn't quite pinpoint. Something woodsy. For a few seconds I allowed it, let myself be in that position.

I thought about why people felt drawn to him, could almost understand it, the way he pretended to care, pretended to calm me like I mattered somehow. He'd never failed to let me know that he cared about everyone but me, but in this moment, I let myself think that things were different. That I mattered to him. That I was as special to him as he seemed to make everyone else feel. That opening myself up to him, even if only for this moment, wouldn't just get me hurt.

"We are completely fucked," I said, nothing more than a whisper. "No one will help us; no one can get us back home."

"Don't worry," he said, his voice velvet. "We'll find a way to get home, I promise." For once, he didn't sound cold or amused, flirty, or angry, just genuine. He sounded like someone I could like if things had been different. Sure, he looked good as hell, he was smart and more cultured than I'd thought, spoke German to a degree, which had been a huge perk so far, and now he was trying to console me. But really, that didn't change anything, did it? That didn't change what he'd done in the past.

I pulled myself together. I remembered who he was and why we disliked each other in the first place, that moment during my first week at our school that started it all.

After class, our calculus teacher, Mathersen, had pulled me aside and started reprimanding me for supposedly breaking some kind of rule and demanding an explanation I didn't have. I hadn't done anything, didn't even know what he was talking about, but I felt like my body had frozen. I couldn't speak no matter how much I wanted to explain that this was a mistake, that I wasn't guilty of anything. I couldn't do it. All I could think of in that moment was how afraid I was of that teacher, even though he wasn't actually doing anything to me, wasn't even shouting, of his threat to call my parents to tell them about it. If he were to do it, my father would get angry, would shout, would punish me for breaking rules, for acting out of line. The truth wouldn't matter. Only what people believed.

But then, suddenly, Miles was there next to me. He stopped the teacher, told him that it hadn't been me because it had been one of his friends who'd done it. I didn't know if it was true or if Miles threw one of his friends under the bus, but I was grateful. Without being asked to, he helped me, even though he didn't even know me. *He's a good guy*, I'd thought, *someone I could be friends with*. So, once the teacher dismissed me, I wanted to thank Miles for it. I caught up with him in the hallway, but he spoke up before I could.

"That was kind of pathetic," he said, killing anything I wanted to say just moments prior. "You should stand up for yourself instead of letting him talk to you like that. Mathersen is all bark and no bite. Next time, don't be afraid of him. He really wouldn't do anything."

His tone had been amused, nonchalant even, like I was just some kind of entertainment, my fear something for him to laugh at, a child he was chastising for doing something silly. He didn't sound mean, not outright, but it didn't change what he'd called me.

Pathetic.

And then he walked away, just like that.

He wasn't a good guy, I realized. He wasn't even nice. He was an asshole, and who was he to speak to me like that? I wasn't pathetic or weak. But somehow his words had stunned me enough that I couldn't even tell him that, too shocked to say anything at all. A shade of disliking that very closely resembled hate bloomed inside my chest and only grew stronger as the years passed.

But what if, maybe, things had changed since then? Despite Joe's warning, I hadn't noticed Miles do anything suspicious, so what if I could trust him, if I could at least try to let him in? Even if that was the case, I had to think about it some more and the middle of the night wasn't the right time for it.

"Whatever," I finally said. "As much as I appreciate this gesture of yours, you should go to bed and back to sleep, Miles." I pushed him away with both hands.

"Now you just sound straight up like the nanny Leon and I used to have as kids," he said and moved away, though only a bit, his tone light. Leon? Did Miles have a brother? "You sure you're good?"

"Yes!" That came out snappier than I intended it to.

"Okay," he said, his tone sounding strangely close to disappointed or something like it, and finally got up. Halfway across the room he stopped and turned back toward me. "Just remember, we're not screwed, okay? If we're going to make it back home, I need you to not give up."

How lucky for the both of us that I was raised to not even consider giving up as an option.

CHAPTER ELEVEN
THE ISLAND

As we ran back to the beach, I gauged Miles's expressions, his pacing and breathing. He'd already surprised me more than once, and it seemed he wasn't done. He kept up with me. And to be honest, I was surprising myself, the fact that I could still keep going after all the running I'd already done that day and recovering from the crash. But we were both excited with the computer board in hand. If he could get it working, we could get off this damn island.

At the same time, I wondered what would happen if his body would turn out to be weaker than his mentality, exhaustion stronger than the fear and adrenaline, and force him to stop. I didn't know if we had time for a break, or if a break would equal being caught and torn apart by the beast. I simply didn't know how many more punches his body would be able to take. It was already a miracle that he'd made it this far, considering he could barely stand earlier today.

I only knew my body was approaching its limits.

I didn't want to lose him, didn't want to consider what would happen if he gave up, if he stopped. It was an odd feeling, worrying about him, of all people. But on this island, he was all I had. Without him, I didn't know if I'd be able to continue on. If I could bury another person. Burying the pilot, a complete stranger, had already been hard enough.

We made it back to the beach as the sun was going down. Drained and feeling like I was already asleep, I sank down into the sand. Its warmth bit into the exposed skin on my legs. I dug my hands into the sand until I reached the cool layer, anything to get my body to relax, to make the struggle smaller. It didn't quite seem like my heart and lungs were getting the memo.

Miles took deep breaths and coughed next to me. I heard his steps moving away, the sand crunching as he went, the sound mixing with the waves, until he came back a moment later. He held out another bottle of water he'd taken from the plane. I opened it with unsteady hands, but the water was like healing magic on my dry throat. Already, I felt refreshed.

I had no idea how much longer I could last like this. But the simple answer was that I had to last until it was over. At least now we had the hope of the computer.

"What now?" I asked once my breathing evened out.

"With what?"

"That thing." I nodded toward the tech in his hand, the odd cables and pieces attached to some green piece of plastic or something like it. "What do you need to get it to work?"

"My laptop and some tools."

Quickly we got up and crossed the remaining distance to the plane. The only logical place for his laptop to be was the cargo area, in the back of our half of the plane, since he didn't have any carry-on with him as far as I could remember. I would've been way too worried about something as valuable and expensive as a laptop to be handled by airport staff, but I guessed he didn't care much. He could easily buy a new one if it disappeared. It took us a moment to figure out that the hatch in the rearmost wall of the passenger cabin would lead exactly there.

It took some fiddling with two relatively small silver handles to get it open. The inside was dark, just enough light coming in through the now-opened hatch for me to make out what I assumed were our suitcases and some empty cargo net hanging off of the wall. Nothing more. Shouldn't there have been more? Life rafts? Supplies?

"What is that thing, actually?" Miles asked. It took me a moment to figure out what he was talking about. The beast.

"I have no idea. I only saw it off in the distance, pieces of it through the branches, nothing more. But it's definitely something big, heavy, furry, and brown. I don't know enough about animals to make any good guesses at what it could be."

Miles nodded but didn't say or ask anything more. Part of me wanted to know what it was, too. Maybe I'd be less afraid if it wasn't this big mysterious thing anymore. But another part of me knew it would make no difference. My only hope was that it would stay in the jungle, that it wouldn't come for us in the night and kill us in our sleep—if I'd even be able to sleep for as much as a minute.

Miles went in and dug out his laptop, briefly opening it, his face going hauntingly white in its bright glow. He rummaged a moment more, pulled out some other cable and a notebook, but it seemed like he was just making sure it was there, since he didn't pull it out completely. He pushed it back between his clothes, got up, and then we went back outside to use what was left of the daylight.

We sat down in the sand, and Miles hooked everything up and balanced it on his knees. I wasn't surprised that he seemed to have the newest MacBook Pro model, nor that it seemed to be gigantic, but if it would get the job done, it could be made of pure gold and decorated with Swarovski crystals for all I cared.

Slowly the sun disappeared behind the horizon, drowned in the ocean, and the night began around us. What time was it? Ten? Eleven? I guessed it didn't make much of a difference.

It was getting cooler, at least in comparison to the oppressive heat of the day, a welcome change. I was glad we'd managed to take a few of those bananas with us, even if they were squished. It was still food. Slipping a few feet into the jungle to pee in the bushes, though, was about as awkward as I'd imagined it would be.

As the sunlight faded, the stars slowly turned brighter, and a quarter moon rose. Despite the waning light, Miles seemed determined to get this done, though I could see him struggle now.

He was still an asshole and an idiot. That hadn't changed in the slightest. But he'd also shown he was more than that. And at least I wasn't alone in this. Tom Hanks had Wilson; I had Miles. Hopefully he'd prove more helpful than a volleyball with a handprint on it.

I still couldn't figure him out. He'd done so much for the both of us on the island. But then again, his own survival depended on it. I couldn't forget that. Over the years he'd never helped me in any kind of way—well, at least not without making some kind of joke out of it first.

Case in point? Last year, one of our classmates had needed help. Nothing big, just a simple explanation to properly understand a chemistry assignment. Since I wasn't nearly good enough to do it—my skills were less than stellar, no matter what those Briola aptitude tests said—I'd put aside my pride, told my friend to wait a minute, and asked Miles. He was, without a doubt, the best in our class. So why not ask him? Because that's what people do for each other, right? Put aside their differences.

Not him. He'd flat out told me no.

I'd gotten annoyed—because, honestly, what even was his problem—flipped him off, and watched as he smiled, self-satisfied at my reaction, only throwing me off so much more. He laughed just a little, claimed he was just joking and that of course he'd help, then he got up and walked over to my friend.

With a muted *thwap* Miles closed his laptop, the sound pulling me back to the present. I turned to look at him, part of me hoping he would declare that he managed to get in a signal and send an SOS, that help was coming, but I quickly knew it wasn't the case.

"Without a lamp, or sunlight, I won't be able to fix anything and get everything running," he said. "I'll have to hope the battery will still have enough power tomorrow."

I nodded at that but didn't say anything. I'd hoped we'd

have answers today, as soon as possible, but I should've known that it wouldn't be quite that easy. Besides, I'd rather wait a night to get answers than not have any at all.

"Do you remember anything about the crash?" I asked.

"I fell asleep pretty early into the flight," he said. "Any ideas as to what even happened? Like, what caused the plane to go down in the first place?"

"Your guess is as good as mine. Could've been anything. Failed engine, bad weather." And now we wouldn't be able to ask the pilot.

"We'll find out in the morning," he said. "As soon as I can access the board."

"Where the hell do you think we are?"

"Do I look like I know?" Frustration marked his words. "Listen, the board will tell us that, too. Why we crashed, where we are. It records everything. One thing I'm sure of, we're nowhere close to Germany."

"How do you know?"

He pointed at the ocean. "The water, it doesn't look right." The moonlight glittered across the steadily incoming waves like a sea of little mirrors. "I've seen pictures of beaches in Europe, and the water didn't look like that, I think. It's too turquoise, too light somehow."

I raised a doubtful brow. "That doesn't make sense. We were flying to Europe."

"If you don't like my theory, what's yours?" he challenged.

I didn't have one. I didn't take geography and I certainly hadn't looked up pictures of European beaches while doing research for this trip. The only ocean I'd ever seen was the Atlantic, from the shores of the U.S., and that definitely wasn't where we were now.

Finally, I shook my head. I was tired and simply done with this day. Tomorrow wouldn't necessarily be much better, but at least it would be a new day, a new chance, and if Miles could do what he claimed he could, maybe we'd find a way to get rescued tomorrow, would send some SOS and this awful nightmare would be over.

"We should go to sleep," Miles said before I could and stood up, his things gathered in his arms.

"Yeah."

Luckily, we didn't have to sleep outside on the sand but instead could stretch out on the seats inside. They were comfortable, though I could already imagine my skin sticking to the pale leather uncomfortably at some point in the night, but I wasn't about to complain. Besides, Miles was the only one who would be sleeping tonight. One of us had to stay awake and on guard. We already knew there was at least one deadly animal on the island, and I wasn't interested in waking up to it chewing on my body.

Miles must have been truly exhausted. Only a few minutes had passed when I heard his breathing get deeper, slower. He was asleep.

Would I ever see my home again? My parents and friends? Did they know by now what had happened? They must have. Our plane hadn't arrived, so they'd know we'd gotten lost somewhere along the way. Crashed.

Were my parents worried? Had my mother cried? I wanted to believe my father would console her. But he'd been so angry when I left. Angry that I'd insisted on going. He'd tell me this was my fault. If I'd never gone, this never would have happened.

I doubted anyone would come looking for a teenage kickboxer, but they wouldn't give up on Miles. The son of seriously rich parents, someone valuable. His family had the resources to keep searching, no matter how long it took.

A branch snapped in the jungle. I sat up, alert, sleep, for just a moment, not the biggest thing on my mind. But no other sound came. Just the wind. The water. Miles. And the relentless wait for morning.

Truth is built on lies.

First with my father sitting with me on the side of the ring. The biggest fight of my career is tomorrow. Losing isn't an option. Not tomorrow. Not today.

My trainer is in the middle of the ring, waiting for us. He's older. Wiser. Patient. But this is also his job. My jaw still aches from his punch to my face, like my teeth got knocked loose.

"You get back in there and you beat him," Dad says. "Do that for me today so I know you'll do it tomorrow."

My mouth aches. My hands ache. I won the last fight. And the one before that. And the one before that. I won all of them. But that doesn't matter. I have to win tomorrow. I know what happens if I don't win. Punishment. Career over. Grounded. Life over. If I ever want to get out of here, if I ever want something for myself, I have to keep going.

"Okay," I say, and I start to stand.

But Dad stops me. "I know what you're doing," he says.

"I'm not doing anything."

"I know you're not. That's the problem. You think I can't see you holding back?" He taps the top of my head. "You think I don't know what's going on in there?"

"Hey, maybe we should call it a day," the trainer says.

My dad glares at him. "What do we pay you for?"

He looks at me with more pain in his eyes than I've ever felt in my body. "She's just a kid, man."

"She's my kid." He shakes his head. "You want something done right, you have to do it yourself." He removes a pair of gloves from my gym bag. The gloves he brings with him every time but never puts on. And he starts to lace them around his hands.

I shot up as though someone had poured freezing water onto me.

Oh no. I'd fallen asleep, let my guard down. Had anything happened? Were we still safe? How could I be so—

"Morning, sunshine," Miles said. He was sitting a few feet from me, his laptop open and connected to the computer board. His hair was a mess, strands sticking up in odd directions. "Want some breakfast?"

"But what about the beast? What about—"

"Fiona." He waited for me to meet his eyes. "We're okay."

I closed my eyes and swallowed, flopped back into my seat. We were okay. Much as my racing heart insisted otherwise. "Wait," I said. "You made breakfast?"

"Well…not exactly." He held out a plastic plate of crackers, cheese, and a soda. "From the serving cart."

"What, no pancakes and strawberries?"

He paused for a second, then laughed. "What do you think this is? A five-star hotel?"

When I took the plate, a silly warmth spread up my body. I turned away from him in case it showed on my face.

After a few bites, I said, "How's the computer board coming?"

He tapped away. "Only a few hours of laptop battery life left." He let that hang there, ominous, before he smiled. "But I've almost got it. I brought in our suitcases if you want a change of clothes while you wait."

Wow. I certainly hadn't expected that.

"I…thank you."

In the end, most of my clothes were anything but suitable for an island. But then, we'd been on the way to Germany. Not a tropical hellhole.

The best solution I could come up with was just another band T-shirt—Placebo give me strength—with cutouts on the sides, similar to the one I'd worn for the flight, and some shorts my mom argued I should take with me in case I had free time on a warm day during the internship. They'd be the worst when running through the jungle, but while I was on the beach, at least I wouldn't feel like I was melting the entire day.

With my clothes, a towel, and my bag of toiletries, I made my way over to the exit, opened the door, and went outside, leaving Miles behind tapping up a storm on his laptop. I dumped my stuff onto the sand near the shore and then took off my pants, throwing them onto my pile as well. The waves weren't particularly high today, the sun only halfway up toward its zenith, and a light breeze caressed my skin. Bracing myself for the cold, I stepped into the water, one foot after the other. The water was freezing, but I welcomed the sensation. It would wake me up faster than a Red Bull.

Oh, what I'd give for an energy drink and a pair of wings to fly off the island and sue Briola to hell and back.

Before I could change my mind, I took a deep breath and sank into the water until it swallowed me whole. I knew my hair would lose its color more quickly this way—salty ocean water not the dye's best friend, especially not blue dye—but it was so worth it. It was cold but felt so good. I pulled my old shirt off once I stood again and then used it like a washcloth to get rid of yesterday's dried sweat and dirt a little more thoroughly.

Turning around, I was just in time to see Miles come out of the plane, his shirt off, stretching his arms high and yawning.

I probably shouldn't have stared, but I couldn't help myself. He looked good. Distractingly so. His chest and stomach were toned, and he wore some kind of necklace I'd never noticed before. The silver stood out against his tan skin and reflected the sunlight.

Focusing back on what I'd been doing, I could practically feel Miles's eyes on me, but I didn't turn around, and I wouldn't start playing coy. I'd spent ages in changing rooms across the years, fought competition after competition in revealing kickboxing gear. I didn't feel ashamed of how I looked. In fact, I knew I looked pretty damn amazing. And if he didn't think so, whatever.

Besides, bikinis and underwear were practically the same thing. The former sometimes exposing far *more* skin. So why should I feel fine wearing one in front of people but not the other?

Finally, once I was done, mostly all the sweat gone from my skin and replaced by traces of salt, I turned around and looked at Miles properly this time, his expression something like a mixture of confusion and intrigue.

"Why that face?" I asked, amused by his expression and feeling smug about how he quickly tried to pretend he hadn't watched me. "Most girls don't wear Victoria's Secret on the daily, especially not when there's no one around they'd want to impress."

I walked back out of the water, dried myself off and slipped into my new set of clothes. Then I picked up my brush to untangle the nest on my head, but the knots were tight, even worse now that my hair was wet. This would take all morning.

"Done?" I asked and nodded toward the plane so he'd understand what I meant. Seeing as how he was creeping on me outside instead of working inside, that seemed like the only likely answer.

"Two minutes. It's pulling the data from the board."

I gathered my stuff. "Then what are we waiting for? Let's get some answers."

I went with him back into the plane. A loading bar slowly processed on the screen. A minute and a half until completion. We were close. To information. To answers. Hopefully, to escape.

The bar finished, and a blast of text and code came

up on the screen.

"Did you do it?" I asked, hopefully, almost desperately, my voice hoarse. I was desperate, no need to pretend I wasn't. This was our last option, the last straw. If it didn't work, I had no idea what we'd do.

Miles's eyes went wide. "Not exactly."

"What's that supposed to mean?"

"I don't… This doesn't make any sense."

I sat down next to him and looked at the screen. None of the pieces of text or code made sense to me. "Where are we? Can you send a signal?"

"Hang on for a second and just let me look at this. Please?"

I nodded, stunned by his use of the word *please*. "Fine." I sat there and watched as he did whatever it was he was doing, more text and code spreading across the screen and then disappearing again.

"I'd love to give you a good-news type of answer to those questions, but, well, I can't."

No. "But…?"

Miles turned his head and looked at me, really looked at me for the first time since we got back onto the beach. He was completely serious. Maybe even a bit scared. "Fiona, this plane never actually flew."

My stomach sank, and I sat up straight. "What?"

"It's brand new." He pulled up the relevant information on the screen. "The system isn't even fully set up and configured. I don't know how we ended up here, but it wasn't in this plane." A certain shade of horror clouded his eyes. Their usual light honey color seemed obscured, darker, and filled with terror. My stomach lurched and ached like someone had pulled the ground away from under my feet.

"But that doesn't make any sense. I *remember* the crash." At least the moments leading up to it.

I slumped back against my seat, my body caving in as though it were a balloon someone let the air out of. I closed my eyes like that could somehow block out reality. What had we done to deserve this? Why this was happening? "I mean, this makes no sense at all. Did you see the outside of this thing? If it never flew, how the hell did it crash?"

He shook his head. "I don't know."

My body felt like it was suspended in midair, and every cell of me refused to acknowledge this piece of information. It was too shocking, too crazy, too impossible. I couldn't breathe. It was as if someone had just cut the connection between my brain and my body and left me hanging like that, unable to understand. I waited for an error message to pop up saying that Fiona.exe crashed and needed to be restarted or something. But how could you restart a human?

"What about sending a signal?" I asked.

"I tried to force the system into finishing the setup process so that we could access the GPS and send for help. But there's literally no program on the board."

"Can't you just plug into the plane and hack something?" I was grasping at any straw I could think of, though those words sounded stupid even to me. At that moment, all I wanted and cared about was a way to escape, but all I got was more hopelessness and a smack across the head with something that couldn't be true, no way.

"I wish this was an episode of *Crime Scenes* where I

could just yell 'Enhance!' and voila, we're saved! But no. Without the board already tracking, there's no information to send."

I had to gather all my strength to not break down in tears. But then I remembered how my father always reminded me that there was no room for failure. Even if there was no way to win.

I forced myself to sit up. I was stronger than this. Burying my head in the sand wouldn't change anything.

"Why would anyone stage this?" I asked. "I mean, that's what this is. Just a staged scene with us as involuntary actors."

"Except that dead pilot."

True. I still remembered the stench, could barely believe I'd actually buried him just yesterday, that all of that really happened.

In a surprising angry fit, Miles detached the board thing from his laptop and threw it across the plane. It didn't break, just ricocheted off of the wall and fell to the floor with a quiet, unsatisfying clatter. He didn't really seem like the person to throw stuff, but the annoyance and anger, disappointment and confusion at our general situation was evident on his face—his brows drawn together, creasing his forehead, his eyes dark.

"Something else is strange."

"What *isn't* strange?" He slouched back in his seat and sighed.

"Think about it. This entire thing is staged, right, so how is it possible that I can remember the moment we started crashing?" When I closed my eyes, I could still see the roof of the plane peeling away, could feel the ice-cold fear gripping my body, but none of that really happened, supposedly. "If that crash never happened, how does you feeling dizzy and stuff after we woke up make any sort of sense?"

"It doesn't. No matter how you look at it, how you'd try and make sense of it, piece it all together. What use and purpose would it even serve?"

"Whatever reason stands behind this, it means that the island is even more dangerous than we thought." Chills ran down my spine at that realization. "The beast isn't our only enemy. It's the smaller of two evils. Something — someone — bigger must be behind this."

"Who knows, maybe we're part of some survival TV show without knowing it," Miles suggested, in what I assumed was an attempt to be funny, lighten the mood, a futile distraction. "Two teens alone on an island fighting to survive against a beast. Who will win, who will die, call and vote now for a chance to win a brand-new Audi."

"The ironic thing is that it's the sort of trash Melany and I would totally watch and then rant about on Twitter."

"Of course you would," he said, and looked at me from the corner of his eye, the tiniest of smiles pulling up one corner of his mouth.

"I'll have you know our *Drag Race* season finale Twitter commentary was very popular."

"I know."

"You don't follow me, or Melany for that matter."

"Interesting that you know that," he pointed out. "It's true, but if half our class liked or retweeted it, it was bound to show up on my timeline."

"Anyway," I said, wanting to lead the conversation back

to what actually mattered, though I very much appreciated his comedic relief. Miles had his moments, even I had to admit that, ones in which he wasn't annoying or awful, but actually kind of a nice person to be around. Who would've thought? "We should see what else is on the island. The pilot and plane can't help us, but maybe there is something else out there. Plus, we should find more food and figure out if this really is an island. Right?"

He sighed a little. "Right."

I already hated everything about this plan, even if it was the only one that made sense. I didn't want to think about seeing the beast again, but I liked thinking about who had put us on the island and for what reason even less. A crash was one thing, but knowing that this had nothing to do with an accident, that whoever killed the pilot to make this stage more believable could come back and do the same to us? That was something else entirely.

CHAPTER TWELVE
BERLIN

At the airport once more, without our luggage this time—bringing it along would mean checking out of the motel and paying for the room, spending money we couldn't spare until we knew for sure we had a flight—we waited in line for what seemed like hours. A middle-aged man stood behind the counter, his hair combed back and a full moustache under his nose.

"What can I do for you?" he asked with a heavy German accent.

"We need two tickets to Miami," Miles said.

"Let me check." He typed something, and his eyes flew over the monitor, up and down. As his face lit up slightly, hope swelled in my chest. "Today must be your lucky day. Just two hours ago, it seems two tickets were returned for a flight later today. Is economy okay?"

"Yes," I said, probably a little too eagerly. I would've even taken a spot in a cage with the dogs if it meant I'd get to go home, and, looking at the smile pulling up the corners of Miles's mouth, it seemed he shared my notion.

"That'll be one thousand eight hundred eighty-nine euro for two tickets, one way."

That was more than we had, if I remembered correctly, at least in cash. We had to pay for public transport and food, and had spent too much. Without a moment of hesitation, Miles pulled out his wallet and handed over his card, a move that looked so natural on him, like it was no big deal to him. I couldn't even imagine what it felt like to pay that much money for anything all at once, but to him it was normal. His clothes and Instagram posts showed as much, along with the way he carried himself and even how he handed over his card. In a way it was fascinating, and I was grateful that he did it, that he didn't tell the guy that he'd just take one ticket and leave me behind. Maybe he wasn't so bad after all? Could that be?

"I'm very sorry, Mr. Echo," the man said, "but your card has been declined."

"That's impossible," Miles said, sounding as though he wanted to call the man a moron. "Try again."

So he did. The outcome stayed the same. *Fuck*. We'd taken precautions for a situation like this, taken out as much money as we could to avoid it, but of course it didn't work out. Nothing worked in our favor; how could I even hope it would? Miles looked furious, his eyes dark and sharp, staring at the man who just handed him back his card and said there was nothing he could do for us. This couldn't be happening. Not again.

Someone next to us coughed. A man in a dark uniform. The word "security" was stitched above his breast pocket.

"If you could follow me, please," he said, his voice heavy and deep. He was tall, taller than Miles even, his shoulders broad and his body seemingly made of bulky muscles and nothing else. I was almost sure he could crack open my skull with his bare hands. Even with my years of fighting experience, I definitely stood no chance against him.

Afraid to argue with him, we stayed silent and did as we were told. In a way, I was surprised by Miles's compliance. Usually he was the first to ask questions and demand explanation. Maybe he was just as taken aback by the whole thing as I was. I held my bag closer to my body as we walked away from the counters, away from the masses of faceless tourists and business people waiting for their flights. The man opened a door in front of us and motioned for us to walk in. The words STAFF ONLY were written in bold black letters on the door.

The hallway was completely nondescript—white walls, white floor, and a couple of doors, also white, along the walls. There were no windows, though there were CCTV cameras hanging on the ceiling at regular intervals. My skin was crawling at the mere thought of people watching us, tracing our every step, analyzing. A shiver ran down my spine, and I wrapped my arms around my body. Everything about this situation seemed off. I wasn't a stranger to being watched, to having pictures taken of me, or people analyzing my footwork and technique, but this didn't feel right, felt off and bad in every way I could think of. Completely wrong.

He opened another door and led us into a characterless room furnished with a couple of chairs on one side, a window on the wall opposite to us, and another room behind it with a desk and a guard. It reminded me of interrogation rooms I'd seen in TV shows, though it was too big, and the window wasn't a one-way mirror. And we hadn't done anything.

"Sit down. Someone will come and talk to you in a moment," Mr. Bulky Muscles said, and then he left and closed the door behind him with a *click*.

I looked at Miles. He shrugged and seemed as confused as I felt. The guard on the other side of the window glanced at us as if to make sure we weren't up to no good, like setting the chairs on fire, trying to kill each other, or plotting how to kill him.

No one came, no one told us why we'd been pulled aside at all, let alone why we'd been placed in this room and treated like criminals. We had done nothing wrong. We hadn't screamed at the guy behind the counter, we'd merely asked for tickets home, and as far as I knew, having your card declined wasn't a crime. They couldn't think that Miles stole it, could they? His name was on it, matched his ID and passport. Maybe this was all just some kind of misunderstanding?

The door finally opened, and a different security guy came inside.

"Hello," he said and came to a halt in front of us. His expression was blank, his eyes dark brown, and his hair shaved short. "I am sure you have many questions. For now, I cannot answer them, but I need you to give me your passports. We just need them for a checkup, nothing bad, everything is okay. I will give them right back to you once we are done."

What was wrong with these people? They weren't willing to tell us what was going on but made demands? They asked us for the only thing that we definitely couldn't give away? This was crazy.

"What kind of checkup? What did we do?" Miles's voice might have seemed normal to someone who didn't know him, but I knew he was trying to keep it together. I'd heard him use it once before, when he'd defended one of his rich buddies against a teacher. Apparently the teacher hadn't been fair toward his buddy, and Miles wasn't having any of it.

I'd just waited for him to say something that would cross a line with the teacher so he'd get detention, but it unfortunately hadn't happened. Because people like him never got detention.

"You've done nothing wrong. As I've said, this is merely a routine checkup," he assured us. Like this was normal. Except nothing that had happened since we'd landed in this damn city was normal.

The guy didn't say more, just stood there and looked at us expectantly, his hand stretched out, palm up. Reluctantly, we reached for our passports. I looked at mine for a moment before giving it to him, scared that this was an awful mistake, but it wasn't like we actually had a choice.

With our passports, he turned around and left. We were alone once more under the watchful eyes of the guy next door and the CCTV cameras. Worried, and a tiny bit panicked, I looked around for something to occupy my mind. I started to count the chairs.

One…two…three…

There were seven of them in total, which was a useless

piece of information. Next, I looked at the ceiling above us, counted the tiles and then the lamps until there was nothing left to count, and I felt not even a tiny bit less anxious and confused. Even waiting for my turn at competitions, local or State, felt less nerve-racking than this.

Miles pulled out his phone but then put it away quickly. I guessed there was no signal in the room. One of the ceiling lamps started to flicker every once in a while.

For some reason, this reminded me of the first time I'd waited outside the principal's office while he talked to my parents. The school bully had taken it upon himself to bully a new freshman, a girl who looked scared and hid her head, like she just wanted it to be over. My old kickboxing teacher had taught me that we learned how to fight so that we wouldn't have to, but what about the people who couldn't stand up for themselves?

So yes. I'd told the bully to back off. And yes, when he took a swing at me, I put him on the ground. I'd been bullied plenty of times. And maybe I wasn't strong enough to save myself back then, but I sure as hell wasn't going to let someone else suffer the same fate.

With a huff I got up from my chair and walked around in circles, my mind buzzing, until I suddenly stopped again, a switch turning on a light in my mind.

"I am done with this nonsense," I announced with clenched fists. My voice was drenched in anger. I usually wasn't the type to stand up like this against authority, especially male authority, but even I had limits, and this had crossed all lines. We were already screwed, it couldn't get any worse, so whatever. I pushed my fears aside, pulled myself together like my father always said I was supposed to do, and decided that I didn't feel like being meek anymore. We weren't just some pawns for these people to play with. "I have no idea what game they think they're playing, but I'm done with it." My voice echoed off of the walls. I walked closer to the window, looked at the guy in the other room, who very pointedly ignored me, and yelled: "Hey, asshole, we demand answers, immediately. You can't do this. We have a right to know why we are here!"

"Fiona, calm down," Miles said behind me, then got up from his chair and took a step toward me. The conflict on his face and in his voice was clear, like he was torn between agreeing and disagreeing. Normally he was the one who'd have acted the way I did, so why didn't he now? "You'll only make things worse."

"Worse? How could any of it be worse?"

"Screaming won't help us, either. It'll just get us into more trouble."

"Maybe it will, but maybe then they'll actually explain this to us and not just treat us like we're a couple of kids needing a time out!"

Looking at him, I wanted to ask him what his problem was, why he was acting this way, why he wasn't as upset by all of this as I was, why he didn't show it. All I could see was confusion—whether at the way I behaved or our general situation, I didn't know—but it wasn't the expression I hoped to see.

Did that mean he was pretending, that maybe somehow this was part of a grander plan, him pretending to be complacent so they could take away my passport, take away the thing I needed to board any plane or train or boat or whatever? Or was his reaction genuine? Did he really not know how to handle this situation, was the confusion real, was he really afraid of getting into even more trouble than this? I didn't know, desperately wanted the answer to be the latter option, wanted him to just, for once, be feeling the way I usually did when standing at the crossroad between opposing authority and hoping it would all pass and go away if I cooperated, did as I was told.

"What do you suggest?" he asked, surprising me. I turned and looked at him, my brain experiencing some form of whiplash from his sudden change of heart.

"We should trick them."

"And why and how, exactly, would we do that without getting into trouble?"

"Doesn't really look like they'll just let us go easily, even if I don't understand what their problem is, so our only option is tricking our way out of this situation so we can escape." He didn't seem quite convinced by my suggestion, and raised a questioning brow. "You made me follow your crazy plan at the first hotel. Now you'll have to trust me. It'll be easy. All you have to do is pretend to faint and *voila*."

It was a stupid idea, I was aware of it, the likeliness of it actually working abysmal. I was sure these people dealt with actual criminals and people causing trouble on a daily basis, so probably no trick we'd come up with would be something they hadn't dealt with before. But we had to try, right?

"Let's do it."

Just as instructed, Miles pretended to faint somewhere behind me, while I banged my fist against the glass. Once, twice. "Help," I yelled, again and again, feeling more and more stupid with each time. The plan was stupid as hell, but this was what we had, our only chance to get out relying on them buying the act and only one guy coming to check on us. "We need help," I repeated. For a while, the guy behind the glass didn't do anything, didn't even look in our direction, as if he couldn't hear the banging and my yelling. But then, suddenly, he got up and walked out of his room.

"What are you doing?" he asked, standing in the door, his expression stoic, authoritative, channeling just how much he was above us, how much power he had, and how much he didn't care about what was happening.

"He just fainted. You have to help him," I said, walking up to him and trying to sound panicked, worried, convincing enough. For a moment the man didn't move, just stood there looking at me and then across the room at Miles. "*Please*," I begged.

Gears turned in his eyes as he tried to decide if helping us was worth it, if he even believed that Miles actually needed help. I held my breath, tried to stay calm no matter what, and repeated *let this work* over and over in my mind.

I was the distraction last time, Miles this time. But this would get us into exponentially more trouble if it didn't work out.

Finally, he moved, let go of the door and started walking toward Miles. Slowly the door fell closed behind him, so I advanced and caught it before it could click shut again, held it open, watched the man walk around the chairs from the right. Good. Miles had strategically chosen a place behind the chairs with only two ways leading around it and none straight through.

"Run!" I shouted just as the guy was a handful of feet away from Miles, the distance hopefully giving Miles enough time.

On command, Miles got to his feet and circled the chairs the other way, toward me. The security guy started yelling, telling us to stop right there, cursing in German, running after Miles, but he wasn't quick enough.

I ripped open the door far enough for us to slip through and waited for Miles to make it out into the hallway before pulling the door shut, hoping to buy us a few seconds, however long it would take the guy to unlock the door. I hoped he hadn't alerted his friends yet, that we would make it, that we hadn't pulled that stunt for nothing.

To my surprise, taking me completely aback, Miles took my hand and pulled. I tried my best to ignore how my heart skipped a beat, my mind zeroed in on that point of contact for just a moment, and a strange electric current raced through me, warm and nice. Now wasn't the time for this.

Together we ran down the hallways and crashed through a door, back into the public part of the airport. We continued out of the building as fast as we could, as if a pack of rabid, bloodthirsty dogs were chasing after us. A few times I looked behind us, checking if they were following, but didn't see anyone. That, of course, didn't mean they wouldn't catch up in seconds, other security guards possibly appearing just around the next corner, alerted by the one we'd shut in.

We reached the bus stop just as a bus pulled into it. We didn't check if it was the one that would get us back to the motel, we just jumped in and sat down all the way in the back. Miles didn't let go of my hand, as if he was looking for security in it, as if it was the only thing keeping him sane. Maybe he was the only thing keeping me sane, too.

Without exchanging a single word, we made it back to the motel, skipped the elevator, and raced up the stairs, taking two at a time. It was only when we reached our room that Miles let go of my hand. I closed the door behind us, leaned against it, and slowly sank down onto the floor.

I rested my head against the door, my mind a stormy mess that couldn't be tamed by anything I did, or anything I tried to think of. Everything got sucked into this hurricane that left nothing but horror behind, devastated landscapes and broken homes.

Miles walked in circles, as much as that was even possible in this small room, while I just tried to not fall apart. As I looked up at him, realization slowly hit me, crept up on me. No matter how much I tried to fight it, hold on to what Joe said, the warning he'd given me, a subconscious part of me knew that all the hate I felt for Miles, all the distrust I accumulated across the years, that it was all slowly falling apart and away, like paint being chipped away over time. I didn't want it to happen, didn't know if I could trust my gut feeling, could trust *him*. But I also knew I didn't think of him the way I used to anymore.

Miles had so many chances to throw me under the bus, leave me behind, reveal himself as the bad guy, but he hadn't. Instead he helped me, *us*, every time. And sure, he could've feigned surprise at the Briola HQ being nothing but shambles, or only said that his father didn't pick up, but everything else? I simply couldn't imagine how the airport thing could've just been some elaborately planned stunt. I could see how torn he'd been when I suggested my plan, and even if he could act well, everything he'd done, his reactions and words, it all seemed too genuine. Besides, he didn't have to, but ultimately, he trusted me, went along with my plan.

No matter how I looked at everything that happened, no matter how much I tried to find explanations, even the dumbest ones I could think of, none of it made sense. I had to admit the one single truth I couldn't pretend wasn't there: I was at wits' end, easy as that. I was out of tricks, arguments, ideas, energy, everything and anything.

I had to tell him.

CHAPTER THIRTEEN
THE ISLAND

"Let's avoid the beast's territory."

That seemed like a good idea, a great one, but I quickly realized that it was hard to avoid something when you had no idea where that something actually was. We knew the beast guarded an area around the crashed front of the plane but didn't know how far it reached.

Exploring the jungle, seeing what else there was, if anything at all, was our objective for the day. It was a good plan, something that needed to be done, but it didn't make it any less scary. Not necessarily because of the beast, but rather because of what it would mean if this really was an island, if we ended up not finding anything at all. What would we do then? Or what if we stumbled upon whoever put us on the island?

I pushed that thought aside. I'd worry about that once the moment came, though I wished it simply wouldn't. Hopefully coming across food wouldn't be an issue. If we'd found bananas yesterday, chances were we'd be able to do it again, and who knew what other fruit we might find.

Anxious energy circulated through my entire body the farther we went. We were relatively lucky so far, but who knew how much longer things would stay that way? My hands trembled, my heart beating faster than it should, my breathing shakier than I wanted it to be. I tried to push all of that aside, focus on the path ahead of us instead.

"How about we play a game to pass the time?" Miles asked.

I raised a questioning eyebrow. "A game?"

"Yes, a game. I don't know about you, but I don't think it's all too healthy to think about the million ways we might die."

For a moment I stared at him, baffled by his words, which carried way too much truth for my liking. "Are you afraid?"

"As if you're not."

"I'm fine." And I totally was fine, even if his serious side-eye told me he didn't believe me. He didn't have to. He'd admitted *he* was afraid. Miles Echo. I always thought it'd be reassuring to know that despite his wealth and high-end clothing, he was just as human as everybody else. My father would've said he was weak. Yet I thought it was kind of nice, seeing this raw side of him without any of his usual theatrics and swagger.

"What kind of game?" I said.

"Ever heard of favorite five things?"

"Favorite car, color, animal, body part, and time." I smirked. I didn't have many friends at school. I'd always been an outsider. First the poor girl. Then the kickboxer.

Always the weird girl. But the few friends I did have, like Melany, were friends for life. We'd played our own version of this game.

"Audi, green, dog, boobs, and two p.m.," Miles answered, and looked at me from the corner of his eye while he said the body part. I was so not surprised, and I rolled my eyes and shook my head. What an idiot.

"I don't care about cars, prefer motorbikes, blue, cat, eyes, and three thirty-three a.m." Carefully I sidestepped some kind of rock sticking out of the ground, which I almost missed because of the tall grass growing around it.

"How can you not care about cars?"

"Not everybody feels the need to show off how much money they have."

Especially if they didn't have any.

"Maybe not, but you can't deny that driving an expensive car is kind of amazing. Feeling the speed. The roar of the engine. The power." A shade of passion colored his voice.

Maybe he was right, but I'd never even sat in an expensive car.

"Wait," Miles suddenly said and grabbed my arm, his touch feeling much too welcome, a fact I refused to think about, especially at that moment. We both came to an immediate halt. "I think I heard something," he whispered almost inaudibly. I looked around while my heart picked up speed, and I held my breath. "Okay, no, it's nothing, must have been my imagination."

"You sure?"

He nodded, and we started walking again. My steps turned more cautious, softer and planned. I tried not to step on every breaking twig that was in my way, tried to avoid crunching leaves, though it wasn't always possible.

"Word, city, height, book, and band," Miles said. The game, I already forgot all about it.

"Illusive, New York City, five eight, *Fight Club*, and Kaleo."

Their concert had been incredible. My mom had bought me the tickets for my last birthday. One of those rare times when my dad was out of town on business. I'd gone wild with ten thousand strangers. The lights had flown all around us, sweeping over the crowd, and the adrenaline pumping through our veins had turned us into one collective body.

I wouldn't let that be the last birthday I spent with my mom.

"Illusive? Sounds like a word you'd like," he said.

"And you think you're competent enough to judge that?"

"Yes, I think so." He looked pretty sure of himself. Even his half smirk, half smile made its way back onto his face. Although I would never admit it to him, barely even to myself, I actually liked that smile of his.

"You have my tentative interest," I said.

He raised his eyebrows a couple of times, as if he couldn't wait. "Ever heard of solipsism?"

That stopped me in my tracks. "How do you know about that?"

He stopped and smiled at me. "You're not the only one who reads."

I started walking again, and so did he.

"I'm waiting for the point," I said.

"Solipsism says we can't know anything beyond ourselves. Everything we experience could be an illusion. All we really know for sure is that we" — he tapped his forehead — "exist. Somehow. Somewhere. But the world outside of us?"

"What's that got to do with me?"

"I think you're an illusion yourself. I'm not in there." He pointed at my head. "All I see is what you show me. And I think that's not the real you. It's merely what you want everybody to see."

I knew the concept. But that bit about me? "I'm not that complicated. What you see is what you get."

He shrugged. "Not buying it."

"I don't care. Your turn to answer the questions, Miles."

He did that thing where you point two fingers at your own eyes and then at the other person, me in this case, as if to remind me that he was watching me. I felt the strong urge to flip him off. "Fine. Extraordinary, Honolulu, six three, *Perfume*, and Kaleo."

"You're kidding," I said, and turned to look at him —

My foot caught on a root sticking out of the ground. I lost my balance and started falling, but Miles grabbed my arm and helped me steady myself.

"Thanks," I muttered.

He let go of my arm slowly, as though he was uncertain about something. "Which part am I supposed to be kidding about?"

"Kaleo being your favorite band. Who'd believe that?"

"If you don't want to believe me, fine, no problem," he said, and raised his hands in mock defeat, which made me chuckle. "Ha, you laughed. That means you can't hate me."

"Says who?"

"Me."

"Still hate you," I said, and tried to look as serious as I could.

The problem was just that, as much as I hated it, he wasn't quite as wrong as I wished he were. I didn't hate him. I just really disliked him, though my brain tried to make me like him, which surely had something to do with the fact that I liked his looks, as shallow as that was.

Get a grip! What was I thinking? This was still Miles. The same guy who from our very first proper interaction had let me know just what he thought of me. Called me pathetic.

I picked up the pace to get in front of him. He must have gotten the message because we passed the next hour mostly in silence, except for the few words we exchanged when we came across another banana tree. If that was everything we found for breakfast, lunch, and dinner, I already didn't look forward to it.

Finally, we saw the end of the jungle.

"That's not quite what I hoped we'd find," I said once we stepped into the sun.

We stood on rock formations, the edge of a cliff a couple feet away from us. Beyond that, there was only water as far as we could see. And down the coastline we found only more cliffs and the rumbling, gushing of waves crashing against stone.

My shoulders sagged. This was supposed to be different. We were supposed to find something to give us hope, not wash it away like a dead goldfish in the toilet.

"Maybe there's still something, someone, but

somewhere else? On the other side, to the right or left, we can't know for sure," Miles said, like he was trying not to lose his own hope, speaking almost more to himself than to me.

I took off my shoes and felt the warm stone beneath my feet; let it seep through my body and into my disappointed bones. Even though I was glad we'd managed to avoid the beast so far, walking for hours without even hearing it anywhere in the distance, we'd still failed in the grand scheme of things. We hadn't found anything but the other end of the island and a punch to the gut.

Crossing the few feet toward the edge, the ocean breeze caressing my face and body, I could almost taste the salt and tiny drops of water it carried. The water was quite a good distance below us. If you jumped into it, I was kind of sure you'd die, get carried and thrown against the stone wall by the waves, which weren't miles high but high enough to crack open your skull, and then your lifeless body would float atop the water while your mind and personality would cease to exist. I saw a maze of rocks sticking out of the water farther away from the island. Some were big and bulky, other slender, sharp and tall. Didn't look like a ship could easily navigate through there. It was as though everything on and around the island was designed to rip away any shards of hope we could cling to and leave behind nothing but despair and hopelessness.

"Hey," Miles said, his fingers curling around my left wrist. I looked back at him and thought I could see worry in his eyes, like he thought I might actually jump.

"I'm not suicidal, don't worry," I assured him, but he didn't let go. "But, do you know what *l'appel du vide* means?"

"The call of the void."

"Yes," I said and looked out at the ocean. So, he spoke French. What else? German? I was surprised, but at this point, I'd been surprised often enough that I was beginning to realize I didn't know Miles as well as I thought. "It's also used to describe that feeling you get when you stand atop a high building or a cliff like this and consider jumping down because it's the strongest choice you could make in that situation."

"Thanks for the lesson in psychology, but I'd still prefer it if you didn't stand so close to that edge," he said, and pulled me back.

I opened my mouth to argue, but his expression looked strained, and something flashed in his eyes. Something painful.

"We should probably head back," I said.

"I'm pretty sure, once we make it off this island, I'll never want to see a tropical place like this again."

"Not to be a downer, but didn't you say your favorite place was Honolulu? Definitely counts as place similar to this."

"I'd gladly give up ever going to Hawaii again if it'd mean getting off this island," he said, and shook his head. "There are enough pretty places in the world that don't have jungles and beasts."

There were a lot of things and places I wanted to see one day, many of which I was convinced I'd never actually get to experience other than through stories, movies, or pictures. The world had so much to offer, and I'd worked so hard to be where and who I was, I wasn't ready to even consider the possibility of my life ending this soon, and in a God-forsaken place like this.

We slipped back into the jungle. The air seemed to only turn warmer as we went, the sound of the wind moving through the leaves overhead turning a little louder, as well as the singing birds. Or maybe I was just listening to it more now. We deviated a little from the route we'd taken before—not much, but just enough to explore some more, to be sure.

"Name one thing that's on your bucket list," I said to end the silence that had temporarily taken over. It wasn't the game Miles had made us play, rather pure curiosity and maybe also just me wanting to actually get to know the person I was stranded with, at least a little.

"Good question," Miles said and thought about it for a moment. "I want to see Machu Picchu."

"Really? Doesn't seem like your thing." I tried to imagine Miles at Machu Picchu, an Inca city from the fifteenth century, a fascinating historical site high up in the mountains in Peru, but somehow it seemed too strange for my brain to make it happen.

"How did you say it? 'And you think you're competent enough to judge that'?" A smug smile appeared on his face. Well played.

"Throwing my own words back at me, classy," I said, and shook my head. "You always play this spoiled rich-boy type." I raised my eyebrows. "But I see through you."

"And what do you see?"

I thought about that. How he'd watched over me while I slept. Made breakfast. "Someone who cares more than he lets on."

"Of course I care." He looked straight at me as he said

it and frowned, as though he didn't quite understand my confusion.

"Somehow I have a really hard time imagining that."

"Your turn," he said, shrugging off my comment.

"I'd love to experience *hanami*." Amused, I watched him try to figure out what that might be.

"*Hanami*?"

"It's a Japanese tradition consisting of enjoying the blooming of cherry trees during spring," I explained. "Thousands of people gather to celebrate where cherry trees bloom, during the day and night. I've heard it's beautiful. I'd love to travel to the Nakijin Castle on the island of Okinawa during *hanami*."

There was a certain shade of surprise in Miles's eyes, like he was astonished by my answer, maybe able to see a part of me he'd never noticed before. I wondered if what he saw was positive or negative, if he was about to change his opinion of me, and if I should be thinking about any of this at all.

Just as Miles opened his mouth to say something, comment on what I'd said, the beast decided that it wasn't anything important and roared in the distance, loud and rolling like thunder, dark and sharp around the edges, sending a shiver down my spine. I groaned, even though it sounded more like a yelp or scream, or possibly a mix of all of them. The day had been going so well. We'd tried so hard to keep away from it, from the cockpit and the land around it, yet it had found us. I almost wanted to blame Miles for it, for making us talk, but this time it'd been me who started it. He only meant well, thought that it would help, and it had. We'd relaxed, or at least I had, my state of high alert going down to a more manageable and bearable level than before, thanks to him distracting me from my fears.

But that didn't matter anymore. Now the only thing that mattered was to run, fast and far, away from the beast. I looked toward Miles, quickly asked if he thought the sound had come from somewhere to the right as well. He nodded. We took off in the opposite direction while I hoped that we hadn't misheard it and that we wouldn't run into it instead. A tired part of me, probably the same one that stood on the cliff and contemplated jumping, wondered what exactly would happen if I just stopped running when it appeared.

Immediately I pushed that thought aside. I wouldn't give up that easily, even if there were moments where it almost seemed like a desirable option. It was an easy out, like admitting to failure, and I couldn't do that, had been conditioned into doing anything and everything I could to not fail. My father didn't tolerate failure.

"We won't be able to run all the way back to the beach," I said, my words breathless. "We need a place to hide."

"Easier said than done," Miles said, but nodded in agreement nonetheless. "Over there." He pointed toward something far in front of us, surrounded by bushes and shrubs. It was as good an option as any, better than trying to run a good couple of hours' worth of distance at this pace. Neither of us would be able to do that, at least, not after merely a few packets of crackers, some bananas, and not nearly enough water and sleep.

Without really knowing what it was, and if it would be a good enough place to hide in, we raced toward it and then jumped. It was a dip in the ground, a pit just deep enough that we could disappear into it, hopefully far down enough for the beast not to see us. I hit the ground a little harder than anticipated, knocking the air out of my lungs, the dirt cool against my skin.

I turned to check on Miles, to see if he was okay, but instead my eyes landed on a dead body.

CHAPTER FOURTEEN
THE ISLAND

Before I could even scream or curse, Miles's hand covered my mouth and his other arm wrapped around my middle, pulling me closer to him, away from the bodies. My mind was caught between worrying about the beast, wondering why there were fucking dead people in that pit with us, and Miles's surprise move.

"Quiet," he whispered close to my ear, the velvety texture of his voice sending a shiver down my spine. All I could do was nod, though it seemed like he didn't trust me enough to take his hand away. His chest was against my back, his heart beating hard. Could he feel mine beat just as hard?

We moved our heads almost simultaneously at the sound of the beast approaching and then breaking out of the tree line not too far away from us. Lying in the pit, we could look out over the edge just enough that maybe the beast wouldn't even spot us, think we disappeared somehow, and maybe it would just go away, leave us be.

It was the first time we'd ever seen it up close, and it certainly wasn't what I expected. I didn't quite know what I thought it would be, but a gigantic brown bear certainly wasn't it. How did a bear like that end up in a jungle on a damn tropical island? Didn't they live farther north?

I tried to turn my head just enough to look at Miles from the corner of my eye, wanting to ask if he saw it, too. His expression made my question unnecessary. His eyes were wide open, his lips parted in shock, and his face definitely a shade or two paler than it should be.

The bear looked right at us with such intensity and focus, it almost seemed impossible, considering we were like sixty feet or something away from it. Its eyes were big and round and awfully dark, nearly black. It seemed to create the illusion of two holes leading into the abyss of nothingness, yet somehow there was a wild type of fury in them as well, a bear on a mission I didn't want to be part of. And then it raised its giant head and roared once again. Miles flinched, his arm pulling me closer, even if just a fraction. My mind raced, wondering where we could go to escape it, where we could run, but to my surprise, the bear didn't come closer. I frowned and continued to stare at it, waited for the moment it would suddenly start moving again, ready to attack, but it didn't. It just stood there and stared right back at us.

The air practically vibrated with tension. My breathing was shallow, my heart hammering in my chest as though it wanted to rip right through my flesh and bones to run away and hide.

As slowly as I could, so it wouldn't notice, even though I was pretty sure it couldn't see us, I moved my hand and grabbed Miles's to pull it off my face. He seemed still too stunned by the bear to resist, his hand slack. "Why is it just standing there?" I finally asked, my voice barely a whisper. I wasn't even sure Miles heard.

But then he said, "It looks wary, or almost scared, no?"

"Why?"

He just barely shook his head. Fair enough. I had no idea, either, so I couldn't expect him to have an answer.

The bear started to move. It took a step or two to the right, then back to the left, raised its head and then lowered it back down like it was trying to see something. But it didn't move toward us, stayed at the same distance as though there was some invisible barrier between us that it couldn't cross.

And then, to my utter bafflement, the bear retreated. Slowly it turned around and disappeared into the jungle, leaving us behind in that hole. It had a perfect chance to catch and kill us, yet it hadn't even tried. I couldn't understand it at all. It didn't make sense.

But I didn't even care. We were still alive. And now we knew what it was. Sort of.

For a few more minutes we remained in the exact same position, waited to see if it would come back, change its mind, but it didn't. Everything around us was quiet again, as quiet as it ever got inside the jungle, and slowly the tension left my body.

Miles let go of me, and I moved away just enough, turned so my back was against the wall of the pit, putting as much distance between those bodies and me, tried my best to ignore them somehow. I just needed a moment to breathe, which wasn't easy considering the bodies smelled awful, even worse than the pilot had.

"A damn bear?" I whispered, worried that maybe it was still around, close enough to hear us, and that if it were to hear us, it would come back. And this time, it would kill us after all.

"I think it's safe to say that this is not good," Miles said, his tone dry, ignoring my question. I ripped my eyes away from the sky and instead looked at him, realizing that he was staring at the bodies lying in the pit along with us.

"Not good? Not *good*?" I shot him a look that I hoped would cause him infinite amounts of pain. It didn't of course. I sat up and backed away as much as possible, wanting to put more space between them and us. "These are fucking corpses!"

"I know," he said, his voice flat. He turned his head, moved closer to them and leaned a little forward so he could look at them more closely, while I really just wanted to get up and run away. But I couldn't do that, not yet. Whoever these people were, something about them was important, especially considering the bear hadn't been interested in getting anywhere near them.

Fear nagged at the edges of my consciousness, but I pushed it away, back into oblivion, because there was no space for it in that moment. I needed to be focused, alert, and as calm as I could be, had to pay attention. I shook my head just a little to throw off that feeling, bring something clearer back into my mind. I could do this, I had to do it, and I would do it. But, no matter what, this entire situation was absolute insanity. Suddenly, exploring the jungle didn't even seem so bad anymore. Anything to not be in that pit, to not have to look at those bodies a second longer.

After I buried the pilot I never wanted to see a dead body again. Damn it.

The four corpses were in two different states of decay. Two of them looked like they'd been around for quite a while, their skin resembling old rough leather, their teeth exposed and their gums black, but the other two seemed relatively fresh, if one could even call it that. There were three guys and one girl based on the fact that one of them was wearing a skirt, a tank top, and silver heart-shaped necklace with a few small pink stones forming an *I*. The guys seemed around Miles's height, give or take, the girl, though, much shorter than me. Their skin tones were hard to make out. Then again, for all I cared, they could've all been violet; it didn't change that they were dead and whoever put them into that pit could do the same to us. Nothing about them indicated where they came from, whether they were Americans like us or from somewhere completely different.

What happened to them?

"There are four of them, right? Two pairs, based on the state of their bodies?" I said, the realization painting even grimmer of a picture.

"And all of them have what I assume are bullet holes in their foreheads," Miles said and pointed at the body closest to him. I looked over all four of them again, and just like he said, all of them had identical circular holes in their foreheads. As far as I knew only bullets would do something like that.

"Someone killed them," I said absentmindedly, like a voiced realization.

"Never seen a bear with a gun before."

A bear with a gun. I wanted to laugh, but it came out strangled.

"This is seriously messed up," I said. "If not for those bullet holes, I'd think the bear was the worst danger on this island, but that's clearly not the case anymore, now, is it? Someone actually came here and shot them, or shot them and then brought them here, whatever."

"Let's also not forget that something about them kept the bear away," he reminded me, as though I could've forgotten that.

I got up and took a few steps back, took in all four bodies, tried to see if anything besides the bullet holes stuck out to me. Their positions were the same, all four lying on their backs, their arms parallel to their bodies, their eyes closed. It didn't look like any kind of animal had tried to take a bite from them, but also no one had been properly buried. As far as I was aware, burying bodies was something every culture did, so why hadn't whoever killed them bothered?

"Miles," I said, my eyes roaming over the entire pit, realization dropping in my mind like a ton of lead. "Have you noticed the size of this pit—that there is just enough space left for two more bodies?"

Miles got up from his spot and walked over to me. He looked at the pit and the bodies the same way I had and then quietly cursed under his breath. "Are you thinking what I'm thinking?" he said.

"Yeah." My skin tingled, electric, the way it did in the moments before I stepped into a match. "We aren't alone. At least, not the way we thought we were."

CHAPTER FIFTEEN
BERLIN

Telling Miles about Joe's message was a risky thing to do, I knew as much. There was a very real chance that this would blow up in my face, that I could be wrong and would then have to try and handle the consequences of my actions, but I had no other option left. This was it, the final one.

I had to trust Miles.

Everything within me screamed *no*, Joe's words — trust no one — echoing in my mind again and again like they had after I listened to his message the first time. But really, what else was I supposed to do? Besides, if I truly thought about it, Miles hadn't given me a single reason to doubt him since we'd landed in Berlin. I expected him to do something mean, at least one thing, just to remind me why I rightfully hated him, but he never did.

For all I knew, he was just as much of a victim of whatever was happening as I was, and he had a right to know this.

"Miles," I said and got up from the floor. He turned and looked at me questioningly. "Sit down. There's something I have to show you."

"Unless that something is two tickets home you somehow managed to book, or perfect replicas of our passports, I doubt this is important."

"Believe me, it is important." Something about my tone must've done the trick because he went and sat down on his bed just like I'd asked him to.

I pulled out my phone from my pocket and unlocked it, then switched to my voice messages. Before I could change my mind, I held my phone out toward him and waited for him to take it. He hesitated, looked at me, not quite convinced, but after another moment or two he took it.

"Press play."

And he did.

"Fiona, it's me." The now all too familiar pause stretched almost endlessly, even more than usual, giving Miles time to look at me again like he was about to ask me if I was trying to pull some kind of prank on him. I wished I were. "I don't have long. But you have to know. They're watching you. They're behind this." Another long pause. "Trust no one."

I'd listened to those words so many times I could've recited them in my sleep, described every pause, his accent and intonation, which syllables he emphasized and which he didn't. Those final words haunted my dreams and my every waking moment.

Miles pressed play once more, listened while I watched him. I looked at his face, at his eyes, and tried to read what he thought, gauging his reaction. There wasn't much for me to go by, nothing more than a light frown and his eyes shifting a bit as he listened, nothing really useful or helpful to me in any way.

Everything depended on his reaction to that message. This was where either he'd reveal his bluff, that he'd been pretending all along, or he'd feel the way I had when I first heard it, worried and confused. Showing it to him at all, sharing this with him and trying to trust that this wasn't the worst idea I'd had in a long time, was hard enough. Trusting, in general, was hard, trusting him even more, and after Joe's message, basically impossible.

But there we were, he with my phone in hand, listening to Joe's message for the third time.

"I had a feeling something about you was off, even more than usual," he said, his voice even and calm, "that there was something going on with you. I even wanted to ask you about it but figured that if it were relevant to our situation you'd say something, or you'd only tell me off once again, but you just continued pretending like everything was fine."

"Trust no one," I said. Was I really that bad of an actress, that bad at masking my true feelings? He'd looked through me so easily, seemingly without even trying much, even though I'd tried so hard to not let any of my worries show. I was both impressed and freaked out by that fact. If he was with the bad guys after all, that would mean he knew I knew something all along, meaning that I was even more screwed than I thought. *Please let it not be like that!* "I simply didn't know…"

Miles remained silent at first, then handed me back my phone and sighed a little. What was he thinking? Did he believe the message, or did he think it was just a joke, that I was overreacting or something?

"Who's the guy from the message?" he finally asked and looked at me again.

"A friend. I've known him for a while. He's this homeless guy from a park not too far from my place. I know it probably makes no sense, a guy like that leaving me a message like this. But I know he would never lie to me. I mean, what reason would he have to do it, anyway?"

"If this guy is homeless, how would he know anything? What if he's simply crazy, and that's why he left you that message?"

Joe did have an affinity for conspiracy theories, but he'd never go this far, never alarm me in such a way. It was one thing to try and convince me that we never landed on the moon, but something else entirely to make an international call to try and make me believe I was in danger even though I wasn't. Even he was *there* enough, even on his less *there* days, to not do something like that. He was my friend, and I trusted his words. He knew that, would never betray me this way.

"I don't know about you, but looking at all the shit that's happened so far in Berlin makes the message all the more believable, don't you think?" I moved farther onto my bed until I could rest my back against the wall. "I have no idea how Joe knows anything, how any of it is possible, but he obviously has to know somehow. The message isn't any more insane than anything else that's happened. He just tried to warn me so I'd be cautious, wouldn't accidentally get into more trouble than we kind of already are in."

"And you thought what he said also included me." I couldn't quite tell if he sounded disappointed, or offended, or like he didn't care, or maybe all those things combined somehow. His voice was still too calm and controlled. But his facial expression shifted slowly, turned almost a little mad, his eyes a little harder than they usually were.

"What else was I supposed to think? It's not like we are buddies in any sense of that word, so how was I supposed to know that it didn't, or that it did."

"See, I can understand where you're coming from. At least, kind of. But…" He trailed off and then sighed. "We've been wondering what the hell is happening for four days, tried time and time again to save our asses, and you took this long to show this to me? And sure, we might not be friends, but concluding that I was probably just here to fuck you over, that's a little harsh, don't you think?"

"As if you would've thought differently if our roles were reversed."

"Maybe not, or maybe I would have. That isn't the point. The point is that you withheld important information from me. I'm just as screwed as you are, can't get away from here, either, so did it really not cross your mind earlier to tell me? As if our current situation wasn't awful enough just yet, you were all about playing it cool and like everything was totally okay, even though all along you suspected I am an asshole just waiting to betray you."

"To be fair, you are kind of an asshole in many cases, just not this one." I tried to smile, at least somewhat, so he'd know I was just teasing, but his face remained hard.

But looking at his reaction, at his words, how raw and kind of mad they sounded, maybe even truly a little hurt, it was exactly what I had hoped and longed for. It told me he wasn't lying. He couldn't be. There was something much too honest in all of it to be a lie, some kind of trained response designed to make me think I had everything figured out, even though I didn't.

And sure, that could still be the case. Maybe he was supposed to make me believe that he was on my side to lull me into safety and make me careless. It was an option, but I didn't think the chances of it being true were high. Or maybe I just didn't want to believe that it could be the case. Based on everything we'd gone through, I just couldn't see how he could be evil enough to play me like this. He could be an arrogant jerk sometimes, but he wasn't a psychopath. I would keep my eyes open, stay on top of my game, focused, so that if things went south, I could save my skin.

There was also the chance that if it came to it, he'd turn me into a scapegoat if it meant he'd stay alive. He was just human, after all, just like me, but I hoped we would never get in a situation like that.

But, if he was saying the truth, it meant that, in this case, I had been the asshole. He said it perfectly; I'd jumped to conclusions and left him in the dark, even though he was drowning just as much as I was. In the end, I was glad I'd told him, that I didn't have to carry this almost burden of some sort with me, that I didn't have to keep a secret from him anymore. All cards were on the table, the both of us on the same page.

I was relieved, far more than I ever would've thought I would be because of anything to do with Miles, and a part of me felt like we were just a little less screwed. It was a stupid thing to think, of course, because our situation hadn't changed in any tangible way. We were still just as stuck in Berlin as two hours ago, but at least I knew I had someone to confide in now, that I didn't have to watch my back anymore when it came to him—at least not as much as I thought I had to—just everyone else.

"They're watching you," Miles said almost absentmindedly. "Isn't that what your friend said?" I nodded, wondering where this was going. "I don't want to alarm you, in case you haven't noticed, but I'm pretty sure I've seen the same two dudes pop up in several of the places we've been, and it's been too many times for it to be a coincidence."

I hadn't imagined it? I'd been convinced that I was just getting so paranoid that I made that up, those two men at Siemensstadt and then at the airport, but Miles had seen them, too.

"I've noticed them," I said, my heartbeat quickening.

"Considering what your friend said, his warning of *them* watching you, and *them* being behind this, I think we should figure out if it really is the same two guys, if they are following and watching us, and then who *they* actually are." A smile spread across Miles's face, one that told me he was more than ready to turn things around, to make them see that we weren't just pawns in their game, whatever game it was, and whichever rules applied.

"What are you thinking?"

His smile grew wider. "I think I'm tired of running. Let's make a plan."

CHAPTER SIXTEEN
THE ISLAND

"There's something I'd like to discuss, or rather, propose," Miles said once we returned to the beach a few hours later. The joy I still felt over a few mangos we found along the way was almost stupid, but unlike bananas, I loved mangos. Using flat rocks with kind of sharp edges to cut them hadn't been easy, but it worked. We sat down in the sand a few feet away from the ocean, the waves a little harsher than the previous evening. The sun was about to set, the sky painted in hues of red, orange, and yellow. The salty ocean air was a welcome change from the stench of death and the jungle.

"And what's that?" Absentmindedly I ran my fingers through my hair, loosening the knots that formed during the day, pulling out a few dry pieces of leaves and a small broken twig. At least it wasn't anything connected to the bodies.

"Looking at how awful our situation is, I think it's time

to, you know, officially put an end, or at least a pause, to our whole hating each other thing."

"What?" I asked, surprised, and looked at him. I expected to see a smile, some kind of expression that would indicate he was joking, that it was just some kind of shtick of his, but there was nothing. His expression was completely serious, his eyes focused.

"It's a known fact that we've never gotten along, and I'd like to change that, even though I find your sass toward me very entertaining. I'll be the first to admit it, getting you all riled up and annoyed is fun, but while we're here, it won't help us."

"So, you want to make some kind of temporary truce?"

To call me suspicious would be an understatement. But his friends weren't around, so he had no way or reason to try to trick me, no possibility of humiliating me for his amusement or someone else's. There was only the two of us, no phones, no cameras, no internet, and no social media.

Besides, he needed me. Even if this was only about him trying to get out of this alive, I couldn't really dismiss his help when I had the same problem. I needed him, too.

"Yes, that's exactly what I want," he said.

"Why?"

"What do you mean why? Isn't it obvious?"

It was obvious, of course it was, but I wanted to hear it from him, wanted him to work for it, and I was sure that if he lied, I'd know it. I said I could see through him, and I was beginning to believe I actually did. It was easy to spot it in his eyes, at least when I paid attention. I'd never bothered before, ignored most details about him, because I never had a reason to care, to try to look beyond, but now I did pay attention. When he spoke the truth, his eyes seemed clear somehow and had this honesty in them that I couldn't quite explain. They looked different when he lied.

"Indulge me."

"We're alone on a cursed island with a broken plane that might as well be just a movie prop, a giant bear playing guardian, a hole in the ground with four bodies and enough space for two more," he began. "I don't know about you, but I don't think any of this is good, and the longer we're here, the more we find out, the less I think anyone will come to save us. I could pretend none of this scares me, act like it doesn't keep me up at night with worry, but I don't think it makes much sense. So, looking at all that, instead of continuing to act the way we used to, to continue to be the two we used to be at school, I'd like to make peace with you. And really, if we'd try, I think there's a chance we could even be friends."

Miles and I being friends… It seemed as insane a concept as an actual hover board or a car in space. How would that work? How was I supposed to trust him, of all people, the personification of what you'd get if you Googled "arrogant egocentric rich boy"?

But hadn't we gotten along well so far? Agreeing to an actual truce instead of following the unspoken rule we'd followed since we arrived on the island, would that make so much of a difference? There had been so many chances for him to betray me, to throw me to the bear in an attempt to appease it, or let me stand too close to the edge of the cliff and possibly fall off of it accidentally, yet he hadn't done any of it. He pulled me away, had made an effort to distract us with his stupid game, and now he extended this peace offering.

I had to see things for what they were. The island was dangerous, a new threat seemingly waiting around every corner and hiding behind each tree cluster in the jungle. I was strong on my own, had titles and achievements to prove it, but the reality was that together, we were stronger, and we needed to be as strong as possible.

There was also the fact that I was worried about him, or at least about losing him. It was the last thing I wanted. I didn't know what I'd do if I had to stay behind on my own, whether I'd be strong enough to face the island and the forces behind it alone. Also, if I looked deeper, allowed myself to be honest, I could admit that I was starting to like him in a way I never thought I'd be able to. Two weeks prior I would've sooner cut off my own hand—after my competitive career was over—before I'd even consider giving Miles any kind of chance.

Maybe I had no other choice but to take a risk, a leap of faith, and accept. Being friends couldn't be much harder than hating him, or at least thinking that I did. I didn't dislike him anymore, which was nice but also worrisome. What if I was wrong? What if I put my faith in him just to get burned later down the line?

But I also couldn't deny that I was slowly getting to know a completely different side of him, one I never would've even suspected he possessed. Under all the layers of douchebag and money was someone who was funny, nice to talk to, who cared and was smart. Maybe he really was more than what I gave him credit for. Maybe there was more to him than met the eye. And maybe he thought the same about me.

There was only one way to find out.

"I'll accept," I said, and I swore his eyes lit up, even if only a fraction. "But only if we establish a set of rules we'll both follow."

"Rules?"

"Exactly."

"And what rules do you have in mind?"

"Rule number one," I said, but then paused for a moment, thought about it. "We need to stick together, no matter what."

"Okay."

"Rule number two: no games. We need to be able to trust each other if we want to survive this, because I really don't want to end the way the other four did." A cold shudder ran down my spine.

"I'm pretty sure they didn't, either," Miles said with a huff. "Pretty basic stuff so far. I guess I'll be able to follow them if I try hard enough."

I couldn't help but chuckle. "And the third and final rule: no dirty thoughts." Miles just looked at me blankly, obviously perplexed by my words. "Don't look at me like that. I've heard enough stories and gossip about you to have an idea of how you think and act."

"Have you ever considered that maybe those stories and gossip aren't true?"

"How would I be able to do that? I don't really know you, so all I've ever had to go by was you telling me I'm pathetic and the millions of stories of all of Miles Echo's conquests circulating through our school." For a moment he looked away, his facial expression strangely off. He seemed almost a bit sad, maybe, or disappointed? But that didn't make much sense. I was probably just interpreting it wrong.

"Then maybe we should go back to the beginning and get to know each other," he offered. To my surprise, he stretched out his hand toward me. I just looked at it and then at him, confused but also curious. What was this supposed to be? He continued to look at me and patiently waited. Finally, I gave in, took his hand, and we shook hands. It was one of the most bizarre moments since we landed on the island. "Hi, I'm Miles Echo, seventeen—well, eighteen in five weeks—from a small town near Miami, Florida, USA."

"You're ridiculous," I said with a laugh. He couldn't be serious. But he simply continued, a smile blooming on his face.

"I'm part American, French, and Lebanese. I'm a straight-A student, speak a couple of languages at a conversational level—"

"Which ones?" I asked, well aware that he wasn't done talking yet, but I was curious.

"French, Italian—"

"German," I murmured.

"Yes," he agreed, the single word sounding more surprised than I thought three letters could. "How'd you know?"

That was strange. I didn't actually know; I'd guessed and had gotten lucky. I shrugged as a way of answering, though I wondered when and how he had the energy and time to learn so many languages. Just looking at French gave me a headache.

"Anyway, I enjoy social media and documentaries

about space," Miles continued once he realized I didn't plan on saying anything more. "I can't stand shooter games and could never be a vet because seeing hurt and sick animals makes me too sad. If we survive this island, I'm the sole heir to the Echo fortune."

"So, you're basically like Paris Hilton or one of the Kardashians."

"That is such a mean thing to say. But I'd totally be Kylie if I had to choose."

I cocked my eyebrows at him and smiled while I tried my best not to laugh.

"Oh, and I also have a ragdoll cat named Felix."

"You have a cat?" For some reason I hadn't expect that.

"Yeah, he's big, fluffy, and a bit fat, but we're working on it. He kind of reminds me of you."

"Wow, thank you, you really know how to make a girl feel special."

He rolled his eyes. "Not in the fat sense. Just like you on first glance, he's all claws, but if you give him time and are friendly to him, he's the nicest cat you can imagine."

"What if I'm actually all claws and no cuddles, though?" I challenged.

"Then I doubt Melany would be your best friend."

I raised one eyebrow. "What if she's into it?"

"And you say I'm the one with the dirty mind," he said, and laughed. "Anyway, your turn."

"I'm not doing this." I raised my hand toward him in what I hoped would come across as a talk-to-the-hand gesture and looked out at the ocean. The last bits of sunlight were scattered across the surface.

"Come on, relax. It's not like I'm asking you to tell me

your social security number and deepest, darkest secrets. It's just some fun. Having fun is necessary for survival, too." He bumped his shoulder into mine playfully and smiled.

"Fucking fine." I rolled my eyes. This was so dumb. "I'm Fiona Jane Wolf, seventeen and the current Florida State lightweight kickboxing champion and got second place in Muay Thai. I'm simply American, no fancy combination of anything. Besides English, I'm fluent enough in Mandarin and Japanese to get by, though my father never fails to remind me that my accent is apparently the worst. I love reading and big dogs, though I've never been allowed to have one. If we make it back home in time, I have a chance at becoming the national kickboxing champion."

"See, that wasn't so bad, was it?"

"At least one of us thinks so."

"I've learned a lot of new things about you, so I would call this a success. Though, I probably have to confess something."

Was now the moment I'd regret all of it after all? This fast? I'd be very disappointed, but not really shocked. "That being?"

"I've actually watched one of your competitions before."

"You did *what*?" This certainly wasn't something I ever expected to hear from him. Why would he do something like that?

"Don't act so surprised, I'm pretty sure everyone in our class, even the entire school, did so at one point or another," he said, and lay down on the sand, propping himself up on his elbows.

"I seriously doubt that."

"It's true! I mean, I only saw the one fight, but Jesus.

I was scared just watching you. And it's not because the fight was at—"

"East End," I murmured.

He cocked his head. "Yeah. How'd you know which one?"

How *had* I known which one? "It's the one with the most views on YouTube."

He shrugged. "Well, it was the biggest fight of your career, at least according to the announcer, so no wonder. I can't speak for everyone, but at one point I simply got curious. You don't meet a champion of something like kickboxing every day, and surely don't share classrooms with one, so I Googled you."

"That's really creepy, even by your standards." He didn't have to know that I might've Googled his family that first week after joining our school because I wanted to know just who he was and why he thought he had the right to feel like the king of the world. I quickly learned that his father was almost something like the king of the world, pretty high up there on the Forbes 100 list.

"You're impressive," he said. "I'll give you that."

"I know."

"See, that's why…"

I waited for him to finish, but he just gave me that annoying smile. He knew he'd hooked me.

"Okay. That's why what?"

"If someone killed those people in the pit… If someone put us here, and if those same someones are coming back for us… Then we both need to be ready." He paused, let that hang there. "I want you to teach me how to fight."

CHAPTER SEVENTEEN
THE ISLAND

"Fiona? What are you doing?" a sleepy voice asked. I turned my head to see Miles watching me curiously from his seat, his eyes half hidden by his hair.

"Good morning," I said, my voice sweet and innocent. "Now that you're awake, let's get to work."

I handed Miles my improvised boxing bag made out of a seat cover, instructed him to change into something more exercise appropriate, and then go fill the bag with sand and hang it on a tree, ideally in the shade. Amused, he actually did what he was told, and then left. Once he was gone, I dug through my luggage and put on my kickboxing attire.

Before I left the plane, I took one of my shirts—I didn't really want to ruin any of them, but what had to be done had to be done—and cut it up with a metal part from the plane that had a sharp enough edge until I had four equal strips of fabric. Not as good as the real thing, but it would have to do.

Just like I had ordered him, Miles had hung up the bag on a strong, thick-looking branch hidden in the shadows of the tree.

"Good work."

He turned and looked me up and down.

"You seriously brought your actual kickboxing stuff with you?" he asked with a raised eyebrow.

Said attire consisted of a tight black sport bra with golden embroidery in a couple of places. The embroidery didn't really do anything; it just looked nice. My shorts were loose around my legs and made of a light and slightly shiny black material with similar embroidery. Both pieces had my last name on them, on the back of the bra and the side of my right leg. I only used this particular set for training. I had a bunch of sets specifically made for tournaments hanging in my closet made of much better materials and looking way more impressive than the relatively simple black and gold training one.

"I always do. In order to win state and national championships it's not enough to just show up. You need to train almost every day, which is usually what I do, regardless of where I am," I explained and inspected the bag some more. No sand was leaking out, so there was hope that it would survive being punched repeatedly.

I used to think it was ridiculous, as well, but my father gave me no choice, and over time I got used to it. Kickboxing was such an integral part of my life, most of the time I couldn't really imagine what it would look like without it, who I'd be or what I'd do if I weren't a fighter.

"If you say so," Miles said while I handed him two of the fabric strips. I wrapped each of mine around the knuckles of my hands. Once I was done, I helped him do his, since he had no idea what he was supposed to do. He watched my every move with equal parts intrigue and confusion.

"Welcome to Kickboxing 101," I said and tried to imitate my father's tone, stoic and calm with that certain authoritative ring to it. I couldn't quite get the intimidating part right, so I didn't even try. "Let's start with the most basic thing: form a fist." I watched as he did just that. I stepped closer to him, took his right hand in mine and pulled his thumb out and placed it on the outside of his fist. "If you punch someone or something with your thumb inside your fist, you could break it. Bad idea."

Next, I explained that he wasn't supposed to fully stretch out his arm because, depending on how hard the punched object or person was, it might lead to a broken elbow. I showed him how to properly execute an uppercut, jab, and right and left cross.

I was pleasantly surprised that he actually took this seriously, that he didn't make fun of me whenever I struggled to describe things that to me were so basic I did them without even thinking. Then again, we weren't doing this just for fun. He tried his best and asked questions or for clarification. Seeing him do these things so familiar to me, the way his body moved, it had a certain intrigue to it that was just a tiny bit distracting.

Kicks were a bit trickier. Many people didn't understand that you didn't kick out of your leg but rather out of your hip, that if your kick didn't meet an obstacle you would simply end up doing a three hundred sixty degree turn around your own axis. Kickboxing was much more than just mindless kicking and punching. It was like a strategic dance, an occasionally violent and bloody one, but still with a certain grace to it.

"You show potential," I said after he finished the last sequence I made him repeat a few times.

"Well, thank you," he answered and pretended to bow.

"Don't let it get to your head, I only said you have potential, doesn't mean you're any good or whatever," I clarified. "I could still take you down with five hits or less."

A mischievous expression spread across Miles's face, his lips pulled into a smirk, his eyes just a little squinted as he looked at me. I raised one eyebrow at him questioningly, wondering what kind of dumb idea he'd just come up with, because judging by that expression, it couldn't be anything good. Before I really knew what was happening, he closed the distance between us and then heaved me over his shoulder like it was nothing. I yelped in surprise.

"You really are lightweight," he commented and chuckled. I hadn't expected him to actually be strong enough to do this, but it was surprisingly nice that he could.

"What is this once it's done?" I asked, realizing that he was walking toward the water. *Oh no.* "Miles?" He pointedly ignored me and just continued walking. I tried to wiggle off of him, escape his evil plan, but before I could, he'd made it into the water, the waves crashing against his legs. "Don't you dare!"

And then I was in the water.

The shocking temperature difference took me by surprise, and I needed a moment to get my body to work, get up on my feet and stand up. I gasped for air, my hair sticking to my face, something between a laugh and a cough escaping me.

"You should've seen your face!" He laughed, his face bright and smiling, not like he was making fun of me in a mean way, just having fun, a good time. I'd show him a good damn time.

Somehow it ended in a game of who could splash the other with more water quicker, followed by me trying to escape and him chasing after me, grabbing me around the waist from behind and spinning me around in a fit of laughter once he caught me. It felt like such a mundane moment, something that reminded me of summer holidays, the sort of thing you'd do with best friends or a boyfriend, yet we'd barely just become friends. And we certainly weren't on holiday.

But maybe we could be more than this one day, a desire I didn't even know I might have until we stood there in the ocean, soaking wet and laughing, the sun shining in a perfect blue sky, sharing this moment amid tragedy.

CHAPTER EIGHTEEN
BERLIN

The next day we walked up the stairs out of the U-Bahn station at the Brandenburg Gate just after ten a.m. It was time to set our plan into motion, and this was the stage we'd chosen for it. As public as possible, the most touristy place in the entire city, with lots of people moving around, groups of foreigners, and young kids on some excursions. They all walked around with their DSLR cameras and phones ready to take pictures of everything they could see, or to take another selfie with the Brandenburg Gate in the background.

The plan for the day was relatively simple, at least in theory: see if we were truly being followed, and depending on the outcome of that, figure out who those men were and what their deal was.

Unter den Linden was the perfect place for us to try and get lost in the masses, but also to act as though we were just tourists like everyone else, a deception I hoped would lure those guys closer if they really were there, make them believe that we weren't aware that we were being followed. Once above ground, we looked around, my eyes wandering over the box-like souvenir shop with painted plates and all sorts of other cheap trinkets, and the red-carpet entrance to the five-star Hotel Adlon on the other side. Concrete pillars blocked off a road to our right, with two guards watching everyone who passed by, and a police van standing halfway down the street. I had no idea what could possibly be there, but it certainly looked like it was something important.

The first point on our list was to find a place to eat. Immediately going to the Brandenburg Gate was tempting, but it had to wait. So we followed the street and tried to find something that was open and didn't cost an arm and a leg, which seemed to be a very popular pricing option along that very street, judging by the fancy, modern aesthetic restaurants. Dunkin' Donuts and Starbucks had been options, too, but both were so full of people it probably would've taken half an hour or more to get to the front of the lines. Also, we had plenty of those back in the States, no need to stick to them while we were in Germany.

After straying off to a side road, we finally found a small bakery nestled between two other buildings that both seemed to be closed tax offices. It wasn't anything special, but their prices seemed much more fair than any of the other ones we'd seen, so we walked inside. A few tables and armchairs stood around the space, with the counter and display at the other end of the room, where two middle-aged women took orders and handled the cash register. There were a few people standing in line, but compared to the numbers we'd seen before, this was nothing.

Since I couldn't understand any of the signs—honestly, what the hell was a *Schrippe, Käsestulle,* or *Napfkuchen* supposed to be?—I let Miles take over ordering something while I found us a place to sit near the windows. A group of elderly women watched me from a few tables over, their expressions curious but almost a little scandalized, like they'd never seen someone who looked like me before. Or maybe they had, just not with someone like Miles. I'd tried to dress as inconspicuously as possible, but considering my general aesthetic, I still didn't blend in nearly as well as Miles did.

Ignoring them, I sat down and placed the tote we'd taken along with us, containing Miles's laptop, some notebook, one of my shirts, and a few other small things, on the windowsill next to me. Considering everything that happened so far, it seemed like a wise idea to take the most important and valuable things with us, just in case. At that point, I wouldn't have been surprised to find that the cleaning staff had gone through our stuff or something like that, though I hoped that wouldn't happen. Out of habit I pulled out my phone and checked if the bakery offered free wifi—it didn't—and then checked if my parents had called or texted, but they hadn't. The messages I'd sent out were sitting there unread, a fact I still couldn't get over. Usually at least my mom, or Melany, answered my texts within minutes, but now, nothing.

Once Miles came around with our food, I attentively listened to him explaining what all those names I could barely even decipher, let alone pronounce, were, along with how strange and odd the names themselves were. A *Berliner Pfannkuchen*, which he claimed translated to "Berlin pancake," wasn't actually a pancake but a type of German jelly doughnut with typically a plum or rose jam filling, while a *Schrippe* was a small bread roll, and a *Käsestulle*, which I thought sounded like something extravagant or unusual, was nothing more than a slice of bread, or bread roll, with cheese.

"Do you think it'll work?" I asked once we'd eaten almost all of our food.

"It has to," he said and leaned back in his chair. "I refuse to believe that they are smarter than us. We'll find out who they are, if they are really following us and will buy the act. We're just two teens having a look around Berlin's tourist hot spots, nothing to see here. I'm still not quite sure your plan to separate them and knock one of them out will work, but I guess time will tell."

I huffed a half laugh at his words. If only we could really just be there to go sightseeing instead of going through this hell. So far, those men had managed to follow us to a few places. Who knew if they'd do it again, or if they'd be good enough to not lose us in the crowds. All we could do was hope that they would believe that we were unaware of their presence, even though it definitely wasn't so.

The second part of the plan would be much harder, but I'd worry about it once the time came. For now, it was time to go see some stuff.

When they told me I'd been chosen for the internship in Berlin, I'd looked forward to seeing all these historical places I'd so far only heard or seen pictures of. I wanted to see this city that used to be literally divided by a wall, see what made it special, so different than our cities back home. Everything had a history here—buildings with centuries-old architecture, cobblestone paths that looked just the way they had a hundred or more years prior, the differences between East and West. All my excitement seemed so far away now, like it had never even been there in the first place, replaced by dread and worry.

Leaving the bakery behind, we walked along Unter den Linden once again, this time toward the Pariser Platz and the Brandenburg Gate. Even from afar it was imposing and captivating with its six columns and the greenish chariot pulled by four horses sitting on top of it, even more so with the clear sky as its backdrop, the sun shining brightly, an otherwise beautiful day despite how bleak our reality was. The space in front of the Gate was crowded with people taking pictures in groups or with selfie sticks, a boy walking along talking to his camera probably recording a vlog, a group of Japanese tourists trying to not lose each other. Their tour guide explained the history behind the Gate—it'd been built on the orders of some eighteenth-century king to represent peace, the citizens at the time only allowed to walk through the outermost passageways—so quickly I could barely keep up, his voice practically drowning in all the noises.

I watched as Miles pulled out his phone and snapped a picture of it like a proper tourist would, while a woman came up to me and asked if I could take a picture of her with her family. I nodded and did as she asked, waited for them to move together with the Gate behind them, then snapped a series of pictures in case any turned out blurry.

"We should take a picture together," Miles said after I handed the camera back to the woman and she walked off. His request surprised me. The Miles from a week or two ago would've never wanted to be in a picture with me.

"Fine," I said, mostly because it would only add more to our act, and it would be nice to have this moment caught on camera should we ever make it home. I doubted we'd still be something like friends once we left Berlin behind, but at least I'd have this picture as proof for Melany that I'd actually managed to get along with Miles without ripping off his head.

Looking at the picture, it wasn't half bad. Our faces blocked about half of the Gate, and Miles had one of his signature smiles on, charming and nice. He was one hell of a photogenic bastard, because of course he was. I wondered just how shocked our classmates would be if he were to post that picture on Instagram—not that it was an option, since both our apps decided to just not work anymore, like what the fuck—how many of them would wonder what it had taken for Miles to willingly do it, and how many of his thirsty followers would come for me, telling me to get away from him and other pretty things anonymous idiots usually say online.

"You have a pretty smile," Miles commented, his tone light, as though his statement was no big deal, before he put his phone away again.

"Are you sick?" I asked, because honestly, he had to be. Miles Echo, of all people, giving me a compliment? I was sure there was a joke hidden in there somewhere.

He shrugged. "Just saying the truth."

I wasn't sure if I believed him but forced myself to not poke any further and just accept his words. It felt nice to hear something like that from him, especially because it was him.

"Thanks."

We walked through the Gate, on to the other side, looked at the Reichstag and its glass dome from afar, and saw the Victory Column in the distance, with its glittering golden angel perched on top, but that was everything we managed to see before I noticed *them* in the crowd.

They stood just off to the side next to some kind of hot dog stand, pretending to look at the prices, but I could see them turn and look toward us again and again. They wore different clothes than before, looked like everyone else with their gray and light brown shirts and khaki pants, but I knew it was them without a doubt. I recognized the taller one's combed-back blond hair and the other one's buzz cut with some kind of line shaved in behind his ear—a scar, maybe, or a strange style choice. They were the same guys I'd seen in the lobby at our first hotel, then at Siemensstadt, and finally at the airport.

"They're here," I said to Miles, and watched as his expression soured immediately. It'd been nice to just pretend to spend a normal, even fun, day in Berlin. Until I'd spotted them, I'd almost forgotten they were probably around, that they watched and followed us, but that was no more.

My skin began to crawl under their watchful eyes, my heart beating quicker. I hated everything about this, the fact that we couldn't just have a nice time in Berlin, have our internship, collect memories, and go home. Instead we had to deal with all of this. Even getting beaten bloody and bruised and losing during a competition would've been a less bitter pill to swallow.

But now wasn't the time for me to get angry and contemplate just how unfair our situation was. I had to focus, continue following our plan.

Miles quietly cursed next to me but didn't turn. It was enough that I'd seen them. I hoped that maybe they thought I was looking at the building behind them, or the U.S. flag waving in the wind on top of the U.S. Embassy located at the end of the street to the right of the Brandenburg Gate.

"Let's go into the park," Miles said, the next part of our plan starting. I nodded.

We crossed the street and entered the park on the left, which according to a sign at the entrance was called Großer Tiergarten, which Miles said literally translated to "Big Animal Garden." It didn't really make any sense to me. This was a park and not a zoo, so why was it called that?

We went along the dirt and gravel paths leading through the park, walking past a statue showing a family of lions that reminded me just a bit too much of *that* scene in *The Lion King*. We passed a field of rock formations I didn't quite understand the purpose of and then crossed a small bridge over a creek that stretched through the park then flowed into a few lakes dotted with tiny islands.

At some point we came to a square with an artificial lake with little fountains along its middle and a monument on the other end. Groups of people sat on the benches spread out around the lake, kids ran around playing games, and a young woman tried to keep her dog from running after some bicycle. Curious, continuing our act, we walked over to the monument to see what it was. It was hexagonal with three larger sides that had statues of Mozart, Haydn, and Beethoven standing in shallow alcoves, golden swirls and shapes accentuating the effect, with three small angels at the top, holding up some kind of wreath. It was beautiful and kind of pompous. It was mainly made of white marble, after all, though I guessed that only seemed fitting.

While Miles took a picture of it, I tried to look around and see if our stalkers were still after us, or if maybe I'd been wrong. But of course I hadn't been. They were still there pretending to look at something, having a conversation. To everyone else around us they probably looked like two normal people taking a walk.

We continued on toward an area of the park that was a bit more dense with trees and shrubbery, and less with people, which would become the stage for the next part of our plan. Somehow, we wanted to catch one of them. How we'd go about it I wasn't sure, so we had to simply wing it.

Slowing down, we let them come closer, pretended to look at something and take some more pictures, luring them in. The two were of slightly different heights, though both still seemed shorter than Miles, and neither was so bulky or heavy looking that I'd have trouble with them. My preference was that the skinnier one would be the one to involuntarily stay while the other ran, but I doubted I'd get my wish granted.

It was now or never.

"Go," I said and nodded at Miles. And just like that, we took off in opposite directions, the only way I thought we'd be able to split the guys, force them to each follow one of us.

I tried my best to keep to denser areas, slip through between bushes, across paths that seemed basically deserted. Every once in a while, I turned my head just enough to check if the dude was following me, the chase was still on, and he was. I'd been lucky—the skinnier one had decided to follow me just like I wished he would. They likely assumed it would take a bigger guy to catch Miles, or whatever it was they planned. But if Miles stuck to our plan, the guy following him wouldn't get him.

Finally, I saw my chance, a place to hide and wait for the guy to run past me. It was an old, thick-barked tree surrounded by bushes and slightly taller unkempt grass. If I was fast enough, I could hide behind it without the guy seeing it happen. I only had one chance to get this right.

Controlling my breathing so I could hear what was around me, I stood with my back pressed against the tree and listened to the dude's approaching footsteps and wheezing. Just as he ran past, I stepped back out onto the path behind him.

"Hey, asshole," I called out to him, watched as he skidded to a halt and began to turn around. Quickly I closed the distance between us and, using the element of surprise, struck his jaw with a mad uppercut I hoped would be hard enough to knock him out just the way I planned it. I'd seen it happen enough in instructional videos that actually advised against this, but in that moment, I didn't care about the dude's health much.

My plan didn't quite work out like I hoped it would. The guy looked back at me a little shocked, maybe mad, I wasn't sure. Either way, he advanced at me, and before I knew it, I was full-on fighting him. That wasn't how it was supposed to go, but what had to be done had to be done. So I fought, gave the guy my best, made him work for this. In the end, using a moment of distraction when he looked off toward where some kid laughed, I struck him again with another uppercut, even stronger this time.

The guy fell to the ground onto his back, his head luckily landing on a softer patch of mossy grass, his eyes closed. I'd certainly have some bruises to show for this, and my fists hurt like a bitch, but I'd done it. I could only hope that Miles managed to make his part of the plan happen.

I pulled out my phone and called him, surprised that he actually picked up after just two beeps, and told him where I was, more or less. I didn't have much to go by, but it didn't take too long until he came around the corner out of breath.

"You okay?" I asked.

"Should've seen his face when he realized that we know, that they weren't as sneaky as they thought. I lost him in some seriously huge group of tourists slowly moving toward that Victory thing," he said instead of answering my question. "Doesn't mean we should waste any time."

Miles was right, the longer we were around him, the more likely it was that someone could notice. Taking a deep breath, I crouched down next to the guy. I worried that the dude would come to while I looked through his pockets but pushed that feeling aside and away from me. There was nothing he could do to me, so there was nothing to be remotely afraid of. I also tried not to think about how this entire scene was a crime, but then again, so was stalking minors, or anyone really, and it wasn't like we actually planned on stealing anything.

Of course, the dude had to have what I assumed would be his wallet in the right front pocket of his pants since that was just my luck. Awkwardly, and just wanting to get it over with, I pulled it out and handed it to Miles, since he'd be actually able to understand the documents that'd be in there. I knew that a German ID couldn't look much different than a U.S. one, but still.

I watched as he opened the relatively thin black leather wallet, and his face turned a shade paler within a heartbeat. Mine immediately skipped one, my mouth turning dry. That reaction couldn't mean anything good. Was he with Briola? Was his ID stolen? Did he not have one, and the wallet was simply empty, which would explain why it was so light?

"What is it?" I finally asked, simultaneously impatient and dreading his answer.

"*Zivilpolizei*," Miles said, and I just looked at him blankly, the word not sounding like any I knew and definitely German. Miles turned the wallet around so I could see it, and then repeated in English this time: "Non-uniformed police officer."

CHAPTER NINETEEN
THE ISLAND

"Have you noticed the clouds?" Miles asked the next day.

I frowned. The clouds? No, I definitely hadn't, at least not beyond noticing that there were more compared to the previous days, which had been mostly cloud free. The clouds seemed higher than usual today. They were wispy, some of them similar to the traces that planes left behind, but not quite, a bit more feathery, maybe.

"What about them?"

"Those clouds mean that the weather will change soon," he explained while I just looked at him. Where was he taking this knowledge from? Were cloud studies somehow something rich kids learned, or had I just really not paid proper attention at school and completely forgotten all about this? "We have, like, a day or two until rain will come, or even a storm. I'm not quite sure."

"Either you're really good at making up crap as you

go along, or this is something that's actually true. I'm not sure which I think is more likely."

"Didn't you learn about clouds and cloud formation at whatever school you were at before you came to us?" I shook my head. As far as I remembered, I certainly hadn't. "If I remember correctly, those are cirrus clouds, or something like that. Anyway, basically, if a storm of any kind is supposed to come, I don't think staying at the beach is a good idea. The plane has been fine to hide in so far, but I think we need something different, and away from the beach. Who knows how harsh and high the waves might become, you know. Plus, whoever put us on the island could come back whenever, and we'd be way too easily found in the plane, so seeking shelter elsewhere seems like the right thing to do, no?"

I was impressed, there was no other way of calling it. I knew he was smart, but I always just thought it was a question of studying well for a test and then he'd forget it all, the same way all of us did. It seemed like I was wrong. Maybe our skills did complement each other surprisingly well. I could run and fight, he could play weather forecaster.

"So, the plan is what, now? Walking around and hoping we'll find something?"

"Basically, yeah," he said with a shrug. As much as I appreciated that he thought ahead, he hadn't thought quite far enough, it seemed. Walking around aimlessly and hoping for the best wasn't necessarily a bad idea, but it could take hours and possibly bring no result whatsoever. But, now that I thought about it, I remembered something. He wasn't the only smart one around.

"Remember the 'call of the void' cliff?"

"Call of the void cliff?" He raised a brow. "Interesting name. And yes, I remember it."

"When we were there the first time, I thought I saw something, briefly, like water coming out of the cliffs farther down toward the ocean. We could look around there, see if there's anything that could help or work for us, and if there isn't, we'd at least have water," I explained. "I know, it might turn out to be nothing, but it's worth a try."

He nodded. "A steady source of drinking water would be nice."

Going through the jungle, taking the same route as we'd taken last time, would only lead us to the top of the cliff. Not ideal in this case, so I decided we'd take a different one. I just hoped I remembered the general direction well enough.

We walked down the beach, along the perimeter of the island instead of going across it, which was surprisingly much longer than I anticipated it would be, until the beach ended and transformed into a rising cliff and rock formation, with more rocks and stone plateaus closer to the water. Some of them were still wet or half covered by some slippery moss type thing, making me wonder if the water had receded since last night. I thought we could see more of our beach as we walked along it, but hadn't bothered to ask Miles about the beach, filed it up as unimportant side detail.

I led as confidently as I could, feeling surer as we went farther, though dearly hoping we wouldn't break our bones along the way. A few times Miles had to help me climb up some bigger rocks, or grab my arm to keep me from slipping and breaking my skull. I wasn't sure if I'd always been this clumsy, or if this just really wasn't my type of terrain, both likely options.

I could keep my balance perfectly in various positions for a long time, could walk perfectly straight while balancing a tray with porcelain on my head, but walking across slippery rocks? I was out.

Finally, after what felt like hours of staring at the cliff to our right as we went, I saw what I was looking for: a tiny waterfall emerged from a crack more or less halfway between the ocean and the top. "Over there," I said and pointed toward a pile of rocks that almost seemed like stairs if you squinted just a little. "I knew it." It was hard to see exactly where the water started, but as it fell it seemed to sparkle in the sunlight. In that moment I wished I could have snapped a picture of the view so I could remember it, show it to my parents or post it on Instagram. If only our phones weren't dead. On the island, social media and the internet seemed like such abstract things, like some kind of crazy luxury, so different than at home where both were merely a click and a swipe away.

Miles smiled at me, wide and bright. "Amazing! Not that I questioned your leading abilities at any point, of course."

I rolled my eyes and tried my best to not smile back but failed spectacularly. If asked, I smiled because I was proud of myself, not because I found his comment amusing, of course. "Let's get some cold water, shall we?"

Climbing along the rocks, jumping from one onto the other while being careful not to fall or slip, was hard work. We moved forward slowly with a lot of caution, even more than before, stopping periodically to assess the situation, the next steps, and which rocks seemed smartest to climb onto.

Pearls of sweat formed and ran down my forehead and

my back. I had the urge to furiously scratch myself—my body's natural response to sweat, which was one of the more annoying features it had going on—but I resisted. The closer we got to the cliff itself, the bigger the distances, and height differences, were between the rocks. Sometimes Miles went first, for obvious reasons, and helped me climb onto them once again. His hands were gigantic, I noticed at some point, a fact I'd ignored somehow until then. They felt smooth and showed no scars, whereas mine were full of them, especially around my knuckles.

Once we got to the cliff face, we saw something like a narrow ledge run up toward the waterfall and farther along. The ledge didn't run continuously, but the gaps didn't seem to be too wide, so getting over them shouldn't be a problem. With our backs against the wall, we inched forward with our goal in sight. The farther we got, the happier I was that I wasn't afraid of heights. One wrong step and I would've fallen and probably died, worst-case scenario, or at least broken a leg or an arm or both. Not very helpful when trying to survive.

We reached the water and pulled out our bottles from the tote I'd taken along, then filled them up. I'd never appreciated access to fresh water more than in that moment. It felt like some kind of magical balm going down my throat, my body immediately feeling much better. Now that we knew where to get it from, we wouldn't have to be so extremely frugal with it, which was a relief. Food and water issues solved. Covering long distances and training, both in high temperatures, in a state bordering on dehydration hadn't seemed a good idea all along, but thankfully, now that wouldn't be an issue.

At least one thing had worked out in our favor.

"I think there might be something like a cave farther along," Miles said while handing me the third filled bottle, which I quickly packed away. "Let's check it out."

I nodded and slowly followed him, but it didn't take long until he stopped again, abruptly enough that I almost smacked into his back.

"What's wrong?" I asked, confused and concerned.

"Snakes," he said. Immediately a shiver ran down my spine, my blood turning cold, my heart sinking.

I loved animals as much as the next person, but snakes were among the creatures I was terrified of. I'd heard enough horror stories of snakebites and deaths caused by them to never want to encounter any snake ever in my life. Looking at where we were, chances of those snakes being poisonous were much too high for my liking.

Quickly we retreated the way we'd come, back down the stairs and onto the stone plateau closest to them. It was as good a place to recollect and try to figure out what to do as any.

"As far as I could tell, there really is a cave, and it seems to be deep enough to be a good place for us to hide in."

"I'm sorry, but have you already forgotten the snakes guarding it? I don't know about you, but I'd very much like to not sleep next to them, or just get bitten when trying to walk past."

"So, there is something the great Fiona Wolf is afraid of after all," Miles teased and smirked, the bastard.

"I wouldn't call it fear. Rather, common fucking sense."

I thought the bear would be the worst thing on the island, our biggest threat besides whoever put us here in the first place, yet of course there had to be something else that was just as bad, smaller and way more quiet. Silent slithering killers. Disgusting. The farther we walked away from the cliff, the better I felt. Putting more distance between those creatures and us seemed like the only good solution, though it meant we'd have to find a different place.

"What are we supposed to do now?" I asked. "Back to your version of the plan, walking around and hoping for the best?"

"That cave is the best place, snakes or not. Thankfully, I know just how to get rid of them," Miles said, sounding way too satisfied with himself. Was this yet another random piece of info he simply knew because of course he did? "We need to make a fire. The most likely place to find a lighter or some matches is the cockpit."

"You can't be serious," I practically groaned. I'd been ready to never go back to that godforsaken plane piece, never get near the pilot's grave and the beast's territory again, yet Miles wanted us to march right back in there. Was he crazy?

"Would you rather try rubbing two sticks together?"

"No."

"Then the cockpit is our only option. I looked through our plane and the cargo area and didn't find anything we could use." He shrugged and steadily continued walking. He was set on following through with that plan, and I had no other choice but to come along and help him. We'd promised each other to stick together, and going near the bear alone just seemed like a dumb idea. I would know.

"Tell me, are you some kind of secret snake whisperer on top of everything else? How do you know that making a fire will scare them away?" I asked after we'd entered the jungle again. I could take the quiet and not talking while we were on the beach, but in the jungle, I sought the distraction, craved it, anything to keep myself from obsessively listening to everything around us.

"My brother told me about it a few years ago," he said, and I immediately looked up at him. It was as though someone had pressed a switch, the mood shifting the second the words passed his lips.

"I didn't know you had a brother."

"His name was Leon," Miles said and reached for that necklace I'd seen him wear. He pulled it out from under his shirt and then softly and kind of absentmindedly ran his fingers across the dog tags that hung on the silver chain. "He was seven years older than me."

"Was? You mean he's…"

"Yeah." The corners of his mouth that usually pointed upward now leaned downward, his eyes colored in with shades of sadness I'd never seen on him before. "He died four years ago."

"The dog tags…they're his, aren't they?" In a way, I already regretted asking, even though another part of me couldn't help but want to know more, like some asshole. At least I stayed on brand. I wanted to get to know Miles, get to know the things he cared about and who he really was, and this seemed like an important piece in the puzzle.

"Four, almost five, years ago, someone rang our door," Miles began and looked straight ahead, avoided meeting my eyes as though that would make it harder. I quietly walked next to him and listened to anything he was willing to tell me, these memories that were so clearly important to him but also hard to share. "My father went to open it while I watched from the stairs. Behind the door stood one of my brother's comrades, still dressed in his military attire. He handed my father Leon's tags and informed him about his death. He told us as much about his final days as he could, praised him highly for how good of a friend and comrade he was, how valued he was to their regiment, and how many lives were saved because of him, and that Leon didn't die for nothing."

"I'm sorry." Those words didn't seem nearly enough, but they were all I had.

"I still remember how, after our mother died and my father turned into the useless piece of shit that he is, Leon took care of me even though we were both still kids. One day, when I was like four or five, Leon and I went to the store to buy groceries. He let me look for most of the things, place them in our cart and, even though I wasn't nearly tall enough, place them in front of the cashier. When the lady said how much we needed to pay Leon pulled out the money, gave it to me and lifted me up so I could hand them to the lady."

Not only had he lost his brother, he also lost his mother? That explained why I'd never heard anything about her, only his father. I couldn't, and didn't even want to, imagine what it would be like if I lost my mom. She was my pillar, the one giving me strength whenever my father made me feel like I would simply never be good enough. She was the one who loved me unconditionally, always found a way to make me laugh and smile, with whom I could talk about everything. I'd be lost without her.

I tried to muster up a smile. "It sounds like Leon was

a really good brother."

"He was the best brother one could wish for." A pained expression crossed his face, his eyes filled with deep sadness. My heart squeezed painfully.

"What was his position in the army?" I asked, carefully, after a pause.

"Leon used to be something like an IT specialist," Miles told me. "He's always been amazing with computers. As far as I remember, he always used to work on them. He learned how to program in no time after our parents bought him his first computer. Later he was known for programming all sorts of stuff, even small games. He was like a programming genius, a god almost. That's also why the army recruited him the second he was done with high school.

"He also used to teach me little tricks, you know. Things like, how to hack into someone else's network or account, how to leave as few traces online as possible or how to access our father's account, taking money and erasing our traces."

"How is it possible that you manage to do all those things while having straight As at school and maintaining that playboy reputation that you have going on?" I asked, because was there anything he wasn't able to do, didn't know how to do? At least this explained how he knew what to do with the board computer of the plane. But there was so much more.

I had certainly underestimated him, had just seen him as this cocky rich boy, but he was so much more than that. I didn't know why that both did and didn't surprise me, though I was grateful and appreciated it a lot that he'd decided to share this with me, that he went into much more detail than I expected.

"That was also something Leon taught me. He showed me how to get into our school's system, how to access test results and end of term grades, how to change your number of missed days and detentions."

"So, what you're essentially telling me is that you cheated your way to the top of the list?"

"Of course not. I use my powers only for truth, justice, and fighting the tyranny of bad teachers."

Strangely enough, his words brought back a memory. "Wait," I said and grabbed his arm to stop him, make him actually look at me. "Last year in November we wrote a test in chemistry and I was one hundred percent sure I failed miserably, yet suddenly instead of getting an F, I had a C... That wasn't you, was it?"

He smirked, and I had my answer.

There was something in Miles's voice as he spoke about Leon, the sound of pain and loss, anger and despair caused by the obvious wish to have him back.

Something suddenly shifted in Miles, like something was about to break that had been sealed for years, like a dam holding back the waters that were his emotions and feelings for his brother.

"I miss him," Miles said in a pained tone that made my heart bleed. "Sometimes when I don't know what to do, I wish he was still here. I wish I could ask him for advice because I know he knew everything, always had an answer for all the questions in life. But, that's impossible. He will never come back, and I will never be able to ask him for advice again. It feels like since the day he died and we buried him, something inside me disappeared, like a part of me died with him. It's strange, and I can't really explain it."

A tear ran down Miles's cheek. They say boys shouldn't cry because it is a sign of weakness and, for reasons I didn't understand, society thought that boys shouldn't show their weaknesses, but I thought otherwise. I thought crying was a sign of strength, a sign of personality and the ability to really feel and care. Seeing Miles cry, *the* Miles who always acted as though he owned the entire world and nothing could bring him down, might have just made it on top of the list of the saddest things I'd ever seen.

I took a step toward him, closing the distance between us, and pulled him into a hug. I had no idea if it was the right thing to do, but it seemed like something that people did when they saw another cry. A moment later, I felt his arms around my back, his head resting on top of my shoulder, slightly leaning against my head. Behind his persona, the easy jokes and charming smiles, hid a boy with feelings like everybody else, a boy that missed his brother and surely his mother, a boy who was sad and misunderstood, a boy who was more than just good looks and money.

"This is the first time I've talked about Leon with anyone outside my family," Miles whispered near my ear, causing the hairs on my neck to stand up. "I feel like such a weakling for crying."

He was so smart yet so stupid sometimes. "If you were weak you would have given up the moment we realized just how damned we are on this island. It's okay to cry. Sometimes it feels good to just let it out. It helps deal with the things going on inside of us. That's basically why so many people have therapists. I mean, you pay people for listening to you talk about yourself and crying."

"Thank you."

I frowned, confused. "For what?"

"For not laughing."

"I would never laugh when someone tells me things like what you just told me."

I realized that that moment right there might have been the first time in three years that I'd gotten an actual proper look at the real Miles, that I really saw the person in him and not the act he always played at school. "Also, thank you for sharing all of this with me," I said and slowly pulled back. "It was easy to see how hard it was, yet you still did it."

"You said you didn't know me, so I thought this was the least I could do, share something about myself. I didn't expect it to be this, and that it would come with the whole crying part, but that's fine. Besides, it felt good to talk about it, in a way, and telling you about it felt like the right choice."

"Really?"

"Everyone else would've judged me for everything I said, for how Leon's death affected me even though I never showed it to anyone, but you didn't. You listened, and it just felt like you understood me."

His admission caught me off guard, but it also made me realize something. I'd always thought that his life was so perfect because he was rich and had seemingly everything, but maybe that wasn't everything. Maybe I still had things he didn't have and could never buy.

I'd hated him for the way he judged me, called me pathetic and acted like he was above me, but maybe in my own way I hadn't been any better. I judged him based on the superficial and never bothered to look any deeper. But now it was clear to me that he was so much more than met the eye, even more than I'd already thought.

Maybe my initial impression of him had been right after all. Maybe he was a good guy, and maybe the way he acted back in Florida was exactly that, an act. Based on what he said, that he never spoke about his brother and his death because he feared judgment even from those he called friends, it seemed like he struggled with being understood just like me. For different reasons, but still. People placed expectations on the both of us, and what else could we do but follow or fight them. There was no middle ground. We'd made our choices, and I hated him for the one he made, without bothering to wonder why.

We continued toward the cockpit, watching everything around us, until I thought I saw something off to our left between the trees. I stopped walking and, looking harder, could make out some kind of wooden structure, maybe, though I wasn't sure.

"Fiona?" Miles asked, his voice tainted by confusion.

"What the hell is that?" I asked.

He looked where I pointed, and then slowly turned back toward me. "Maybe it belongs to the people who put us here?"

There was, of course, the chance that it could belong to the enemy, but I still thought it could be worth checking out. Maybe we'd find some clues there, anything that could help us figure out why we were here, why there was a pit with dead people, and just what the hell was going on. "Let's check it out."

Slowly we approached it, avoiding making any noise at all, which wasn't nearly as easy in the wild as it was indoors. The ground was littered with things that made noises, like dry leaves and twigs.

"Is that a camp?" Miles asked, half surprised and half confused, and frowned.

The wooden structure looked like a small wooden tent like thing made of logs and twigs, leaves and stones. Inside it stood two airplane seats, and a small circle of stones rested a couple feet away from it. A bonfire maybe?

"Maybe the people before us lived here?" Miles asked and looked around. Considering the plane seats, that seemed likely, since they were like ours, just with dark brown leather instead of light. There were no traces of life around, no footprints, no fresh wood or supplies. Whichever pair lived here before us, it had definitely been a good while since they stopped and moved into the pit.

"I think you were right about the cave being our best option, since it doesn't seem like hiding in the jungle worked out particularly well for them."

I peeked into the wooden tent. A couple of plastic bottles lay farther in the back, all empty and dirty. Looking around some more, I hoped I'd find something, anything, that could help us, give us a clue about any of what was happening to us or what happened to them, but there was nothing. Whoever took them out had done a good job of erasing all their traces and leaving behind nothing useful.

"I think someone burned their clothes once they killed them."

"What?" I asked and crawled back out of the wooden tent to find Miles crouching next to the bonfire.

"There are pieces of burned fabric in here." He pulled a piece from the ashes. It looked like a black sleeve, or something that once used to be one. Now this was really starting to creep me out. Goose bumps appeared all over my arms, and I felt strangely cold, despite it being easily ninety degrees or more.

"The tent is empty," I said with a sigh.

"Nothing besides the burned clothes around outside, either," Miles said and stood up again.

"So much for finding some clues or actual answers."

I tried not to feel disappointed. This was far better than accidentally running right into the arms of the enemy, but it still wasn't what we needed. All we knew now was that the jungle, and any obvious place, wasn't a good enough spot to hide from the enemy. The cave really was our only option, a place they wouldn't easily find us. And even if they knew we were there, we'd notice them as they approached, and could try and get away.

"I wonder if this means they searched and found them, or if they were watching them and, by extension, watching us." A shiver ran down my spine at the mere thought of that, my skin crawling. It was one thing to know that people watched my fights, took countless pictures and videos, material they could analyze to criticize me later, but the thought of strangers secretly watching us after dumping us on this island…it was far worse. A whole universe of worse.

"Let's get out of here. This place is creeping me out," Miles said, but before we retreated, we looked around one more time, just to be sure that we hadn't missed anything. I was surprised they didn't rip down the camp so we wouldn't even find that. But maybe their plan was different. Maybe they thought we wouldn't even make it this far or something, the bear ripping us to pieces before we could discover this.

Leaving the camp behind, we returned to our previous route and continued toward the cockpit. Soon enough, we were close to the clearing, now too-familiar territory. We needed to focus on our next task, finding that stupid lighter or some matches, so I pushed all my thoughts, wondering, and worries about the camp, pit, and our enemies aside.

Slowly and as quietly as possible, we snuck the remaining distance toward the cockpit, listening to and watching everything around us, ready to bolt at any moment. I'd left my tote behind at the edge of the clearing to make an escape easier, plus I doubted the beast would care for it much anyway. There was only water in it, after all.

Thankfully, it seemed like the bear was taking a day off, maybe sleeping somewhere and relaxing after chasing us again and again the previous days. All I wished for was to find a lighter in the cockpit and get away without it noticing us.

"I'll look through the drawers and you the actual cockpit, okay?" I offered. Splitting the work seemed like a wise idea, one that would get us a result quicker than staying together to search.

"If you hear something, let me know, please."

"Don't worry, I remember my own rules," I joked, trying to lighten the mood. But I knew there was no way of achieving that as long as we were there. He shook his head and then walked off to get to the window to climb into the cockpit.

Quickly I moved over to the drawers, located to the right and left of the cockpit door from the side that led into where our part of the plane used to be, opened one after the other. I knew that usually those drawers would hold all sorts of things that planes needed, along with the food and drink supplies, maybe something useful for first aid or other emergencies, but the farther I went, the more I came to realize that there was nothing. Considering the fact that the entire plane, the cockpit and our part, were fake, I shouldn't have been so surprised. Why should they have bothered filling the drawers with useful things if they hoped the beast would kill us during an attempt at getting to the cockpit?

I cursed, and then cursed some more. This couldn't be happening. We'd been so close, had found a steady water source and a possible storm-appropriate shelter (though, of course, there had to be the snakes), but the plane was useless in our quest to win against them. We'd taken a step forward and then seven backward again.

"Did you find anything?" Miles asked a little while later. Looking at how empty his hands were, I knew that he hadn't found anything, either.

I shook my head no and sighed, my shoulders sagging. "Where else are we supposed to find a lighter?"

I knew the answer as soon as Miles looked at the ground behind me. The spot marked by a shallow grave.

"The pilot," I said, my heart sinking. "We need to check his pockets."

CHAPTER TWENTY
BERLIN

I'd considered many options for what Joe could've meant by *they are watching*, thought that maybe it was Briola just trying to mess with us somehow, but I never would've even come up with the idea that the police could be involved in this. I'd hoped those men were just two random guys, that maybe we just imagined that they were following us, just a funny coincidence and nothing more. But this was far bigger than I anticipated if it reached as far as the cops, who were supposed to protect and not stalk us.

"I've been trying to find an explanation for why the airport security guys had done what they did," Miles said. "Maybe that's the answer? Maybe they were somehow involved in all of this as well?"

"Since when is airport security connected to the actual police?"

"It isn't, but if the cops, then why not also the airport guys? Maybe they were just a small part of something far bigger that we can't see yet."

I laughed, not a big, loud laugh, just a small one, the absurdity of everything hitting me.

"You know, Joe is one of those people who love conspiracy theories, eats them up like crazy. It's ironic that it literally seems like we've landed in the middle of one happening as we speak. It's the most bizarre conspiracy possible. I mean, who and why would anyone do something like this, go through all this bullshit just to get us here? But Joe had somehow known things weren't right, had smelled it."

If we'd ever make it back home and I got the chance to talk to Joe again, I was sure he would listen to me when I told him about this. It was the sort of truly unbelievable story he was usually all about, every detail making it sound crazier. Yet it was all true this time. There was no trickery, no witty TV script guiding us, and no way for us to redo a scene or simply ask someone how this story would end.

Who knew, maybe this case would one day end up as material for a *BuzzFeed Unsolved* episode. Two teens flying to Berlin and never returning, a grand conspiracy, the police playing stalkers and airports trying to keep them from leaving. If this hadn't happened to me, I definitely would've loved that episode, but right now I hated everything about this.

There was literally an unconscious undercover police officer lying on the ground between us, for fuck's sake. How did we end up here, and why the two of us? Why was any of this happening? A grand plan or simply misfortune?

"At least now we know that Joe was right," I said and took a step back. "We really cannot trust anyone, not even the one type of authority that was designed to be trustworthy, to be your helper in need."

"Great kind of helpers," Miles said, his words dry and sarcastic. "But maybe this puts us at an advantage now. We know they're watching us, we know who they are and how they look, their names and everything. We know who we can't trust. Something about all of this has to be useful, help us somehow, give us the edge we've been missing so far."

"Maybe the reason why all of this is happening isn't important, just that we'll figure out a way through it."

Did we even stand any sort of chance, realistically? If the police were involved, could the two of us be smarter and stronger than them? Did we have another choice but to try, keep on trying even if our options were slowly but surely running out and I wasn't sure anymore how we could keep going? But we had to. We would make it through this.

"We should leave before someone notices us, or rather, before anyone sees us with him," Miles said.

"Let's go back to the motel and get our things. At least this time they can't follow, though who knows where the other dude is."

"Guess we'll see if he shows up again as we move through the city. Or maybe he'll come here, instead, to check on his partner and will lose us."

That seemed like too good of an option; I barely even wanted to consider it. But as we made our way back, moved from one public transport to the other, crossed streets and walked past shops, the second police guy never showed up. We'd looked, probably freaked out everyone around us with how we watched everything, but he wasn't there.

A tiny bit of hope bloomed in my chest. Maybe we'd gotten rid of them, both of them. Maybe we'd scared them, got them to retreat at least for a while, leave us alone. Maybe we finally showed them that we weren't as defenseless as they hoped. Surely they hadn't expected me to be able to K.O. a dude way taller and like twice as heavy as I was.

Then again, they were the police. They could access all kinds of info sources, knew all about who we were and where we came from. But still I'd proven that I was capable of exactly what the internet claimed I was, and that they shouldn't mess with us.

By the time we reached our motel, I almost felt like I could breathe a little easier now that this crawling, nasty feeling of being watched was gone, at least for now. At the same time, I was mildly crushed by the discovery we'd made, but I didn't want to focus on it, wanted to just enjoy this tiny break we were getting.

But I should've known that it was all just false hope, a false feeling of security, possibly exactly what they'd hoped I'd feel.

Just as we walked through the first set of doors that led into the motel, Miles grabbed my arm, and we stopped dead in our tracks. I looked at him, confused. But he didn't say anything, just continued looking ahead, his expression focused.

"...*die zwei sind siebzehn Jahre alt und werden seit ein paar Tagen vermisst. Das Mädchen hat blaue Haare, recht einfach zu entdecken. Haben Sie sie vielleicht gesehen?*" said a voice from farther into the lobby. I had no idea what that man was saying, but judging by Miles's abrupt halt and the frown on his face, it couldn't be anything good.

"It's him," Miles finally said, his voice nothing more than a whisper, before he started to slowly walk back toward the door, pulling me along with him. "The second guy."

My blood immediately ran cold. Why was he here?

"What did he say?" I asked once we were outside again, hiding behind a delivery van.

"He was asking the receptionist if he'd seen us. I heard him mention your hair." Self-consciously I touched my hair. I'd loved the color ever since I first decided to go for blue, but now that decision had turned into a giant disadvantage. We definitely would've been harder to spot if my hair were its natural color. "It's pretty, but not ideal for our current situation."

I just looked at him, caught off guard by his comment. I wanted to say something snarky, ask how long he'd thought that way about it, since he never said anything positive or not teasing about it before, but now wasn't the time.

"The guy is blocking our way in, and even if he leaves, we can't go back in there," Miles said, and then took a calming breath. "We have to go to plan B."

"All our things," I said, a bit too whiny for my own liking.

"You have all your important things, no?" I nodded. I hadn't taken much with me to Berlin to begin with, at least in terms of electronics and important things. The few valuables we had, we'd put into the tote on my shoulder. "Then it's just clothes, replaceable things."

For him most things were probably replaceable ones,

clothes just meaningless things. I was sure he could've easily taken no luggage with him and just bought an entire new wardrobe upon arrival, but for me, things were different. But he was right, we had no other choice. Even if Miles had gone in alone, the receptionist still would've recognized him, and we had no idea what would happen in that case. We couldn't afford him calling even more cops on us. And compared to our passports, this was a loss we could live with. It certainly made us more mobile and quicker, harder to spot even with my hair.

Plan B it was, then.

Peeking around the van, we checked if the area was clear—it was—and then made our way back to the nearest bus station we could find, two streets over. Inside, we looked at the public transport map of Berlin and tried to figure out the most convoluted route possible from the motel to the S-Bahnhof Neukölln on the other side of the city. There was a much easier way to get there than the one we took, but we hoped that this way the chances of those bastards tracking us down would be diminished at least a bit. There was a chance they could access the CCTV cameras across all the S- and U-Bahn stations, but moving around this much, and switching to buses where possible, would make their job definitely harder.

Sure, we could've made it even harder by leaving the city altogether—we'd actually briefly considered it—but if our parents or school got suspicious because we didn't call or text, why we didn't return home, they'd only look for us in Berlin. If we left the city, no one would ever be able to find us.

After what seemed like the longest hour and a half of

my life, we'd made it to Neukölln. Together with a sea of strangers, we were swept out of the train and up a set of stairs into a bigger hall. There was a store and two bakeries in it, a big set of doors to our left, a tunnel opposite to us, and another exit toward the right. We chose to go left through the doors and into the traffic of Berlin. The intersection was buzzing with pedestrians, cars, delivery vans, and buses. The smell of Chinese and Arabic food mixed with a distinct note of McDonald's floated through the air.

We found the hostel, which we'd previously seen advertised in one of the buses we'd taken, located in a relatively new building with a wine store next door. The hostel wasn't very big, looked like a three- or four-story high rectangular box quite close to the rails and the station.

Our idea was that maybe the police guys had found us because we'd kept close to the airport, relatively, and that maybe if we went to a district like Neukölln, which was practically halfway between both airports, they wouldn't figure it out nearly as fast. Maybe they never would. We started out in a luxury hotel—who would think to look for us in a cheap, shitty hostel? Berlin was a giant city with millions of citizens and thousands of tourists. There had to be tens or hundreds of girls of a similar build with colorful hair, some surely also blue. So good luck to those bastards finding us now.

Inside, we were met with the stench of alcohol, and laughter coming from a group of twenty-somethings. The reception area was small, with a middle-aged man sitting behind the desk. We quickly received a key to a room for four with the info that most likely we would have strangers staying with us in it. Sharing a room with strangers, even if they were just something like backpackers, was probably the least desirable thing I could think of, but we had no other choice. Who knew who those people would be, if they weren't more undercover cops or other stalking strangers sent out to look for us?

No, I couldn't even think that way or I would drive myself insane, not like I wasn't doing that already, but it would've only made it worse. I wasn't sure how our situation could've been any worse, but I certainly didn't want to find out.

Our room was on the third floor. The lighting was cold and dull. Two sets of iron bunk beds stood to the right and left, and a small window with milky glass rested between them. A shabby rug covered the floor. There was no bathroom. The walls were mostly bare except for a cheap-looking picture hanging on one of the walls.

"It'll have to do," Miles mumbled, more to himself than to me as we walked in.

"Do you think we'll ever get back home?" I asked after we'd split up into our respective beds, me in the top one and Miles below, to rest and think. The room was too quiet, suffocating, despite the fact that trains were passing through the station next door every few minutes — squeaking brakes, blaring warning signals and closing doors, trains moving away and people calling out to each other, ringing phones and honking cars.

"I hope so," he said, but he didn't sound too convinced by his own words. "In three weeks, when the internship should be over and your parents realize you didn't come home, they'll call the cops and make them look for you.

They'll file a missing person report for you. They will come and save you."

"If we make it, considering how everything went downhill since we got here."

"Of course we'll make it," he interrupted. "We'll find a way. I don't know how yet, but we will."

I heard the unspoken words from him. He'd talked about my parents coming to look for me, but when it came to his own parents? Nothing. I thought again of that brief reference he'd made to his father. I was lucky to have parents who cared about me so much.

"Your dad will worry about you, too," I said.

He stayed silent for a while, but eventually, halfheartedly, said: "Sure."

Maybe an hour later, Miles got up and left to find the public bathrooms. No strangers had come, and the room still belonged to only us. A headache had made its way into my brain. I let my hair free from the ponytail I had it in and started massaging my scalp.

Back when I was a kid, around ten or so, my mom always used to do this. Somehow her head massages always freed me of the headaches within minutes.

I closed my eyes and blocked out our new reality. I thought about home, thought about my bed and how it would feel like to lie down on it. How it would feel to be back in my life, the one I'd always known, back to version 1.0 of Fiona and Miles. Enemies, not teammates. I thought back far enough to remember the look on Miles's face when he came around a corner to find "asshole" written in red on his locker. The anger was painted across his face, fire burning in his eyes when he noticed me leaning against a wall on the other end of the hall with a smug smile on my face, my arms crossed in front of my chest, lipstick in hand.

I wanted to go back to that. I wanted to go back to hating Miles, to fighting with him because I refused to let him call me, or as much as see me as, pathetic, to make me feel like a peasant while he saw himself as king. But I couldn't. We were stuck in version 2.0.

My trip down memory lane got interrupted as the door to our room opened and smashed against the wall. My eyes immediately darted toward the door. Miles stumbled into the room looking like he'd come straight out of hell.

I jumped down from my bed and crossed the few steps toward him. He was slightly bent over, his face obscured by his hair, his arms hugging his middle.

"Oh my God, Miles," I said once he raised his head toward me. Blood dripped from his nose and there was a cut above his left eye. "What happened?" I led him to his bed and helped him sit down. He was limping slightly on his right leg. I reached up to my tote and pulled out the single shirt I'd taken with me just in case. I held his head as carefully as I could with my left hand while I had my shirt with the right, dabbing at the blood. Pain flickered through his eyes each time I touched him, erasing some of the red. I didn't care about my shirt, barely registered that it was now stained with actual human blood—

I looked away from the window, to my other side. At

Miles. I was sure there would be a bloody corpse. But no. No blood on his white button-down shirt that I could see. Which was good, but that didn't mean anything. Not when he wasn't moving—

What the hell?

I shook my head. The images had come out of nowhere, like my worst fear had punched me in the gut.

"There was this guy," Miles was saying. "He came in after me, watched me strangely, so I asked him what his problem was. I thought that he was alone, went as far as wondering if maybe he was one of them, working with the other two guys following us. Turns out he wasn't alone. They didn't like me asking why they were staring at me and stuff. Before I even really realized what was happening, they advanced toward me. I had no chance."

"What did they do, besides the obvious?" There was a hint of panic and fear in my voice, which I disliked but couldn't stop. New blood trickled out of the cut. As carefully as I could, I pressed a clean spot of the shirt against it. He pulled a pain-slashed grimace that hurt my heart despite our history.

"They took everything," Miles continued. His voice sounded broken, raspy and hushed, different than it usually did. I didn't like it. Didn't like any of it. "My phone, my wallet, my portion of the money, my credit cards, my ID, everything. It's all…gone." He looked away then, like he was ashamed.

I was speechless. What could I say in that moment? If only he knew how to fight—

"Let's start with the most basic thing: form a fist." I watched as he did just that. I stepped closer to him, took his

right hand into mine and pulled his thumb out and placed it on the outside of his fist.

I shook my head once again, and the image disappeared.

"We have to do something about your wounds," I finally said, trying to focus. "We need to stop the bleeding, disinfect the cuts, and put a bandage on them."

"I'm so sorry," he whispered.

"It's not your fault." He couldn't have done anything. Even I, with years of training and extensive skills, probably wouldn't have stood a chance against a group of guys, though I certainly would have tried.

"This feels like such a déjà vu," Miles said absent-mindedly.

I snapped to attention. "What're you talking about? A déjà vu of what?"

"I've been having these dreams or whatever lately," he said and flinched ever so slightly as I moved my hand a little. My heart felt like it slowed down with every word he said. "In the first one we were in a similar situation to this, me a wreck after we crashed on some island and you having to be the brave one."

"I'm always the brave one," I murmured. Like I was repeating something I'd heard before. "But this is crazy."

"Why?"

"Because I've had that dream, too. More of them every night, a crash and the jungle."

Miles eyes widened a little the more I spoke, his shock mirroring what I felt. This was impossible in every way.

"So we've been dreaming the same thing?" he asked, incredulous.

"Two people can't dream the exact same thing, can

they?" I was so confused. How was any of this possible? Though, after everything that happened in Berlin, the two of us dreaming the same thing seemed like the least shocking and definitely the most harmless thing of it all.

"And yet here we are."

It made no sense, none of it. There was no logical explanation for this no matter how I looked at it. But, there was at least one silver lining in it, a tiny one compared to all the awful things that were happening, but I took what I could get. Miles couldn't be making that up. There was no way for him to know that I'd been having those dreams, even less what they were about, which gave me the last and most powerful piece of evidence that he really was my ally and not my enemy. He could've pretended everything else, but not this.

"Déjà vu or not, we need to do something about your injuries," I said firmly. "Since you can't go get a first aid kit or something yourself, I will. It'll be quick and easy."

"Like hell you will," he argued, his voice sounding firmer now, though with an obvious strain in it, his hand wrapping around my free wrist. It was easy to see that arguing robbed him of any energy he had left, a fact that would hopefully work in my favor. Why did he have to be so stubborn? "You can't go, no. What if they attack you, too? No fucking way, Fiona."

Once he was sitting inside, I turned toward the jungle. Cracked my neck. Quietly groaned.

I so didn't sign up for any of this.

"*Just do it,*" he said. "*The quicker you go, the sooner you'll find the pilot, radio for help, and we'll be out of here. I'll be fine.*" Groan. "*Just get it done.*"

"You can't tell me what to do. Besides, on that island in our dreams you basically made me go into the jungle on my own and there was a bear in there, so really, how much worse can a quick pharmacy run really be?"

"You can't seriously compare real life to a dream," he said, looking straight at me, his eyes hard. "Are you really foolish enough to go out there and potentially get yourself into the same trouble? What will you do then? What will we do?"

I sighed lightly and pressed my lips into a straight line, silence filling the room around us for just a moment. "Miles, shut up, will you?" I finally said, my tone of voice emulating the way my father spoke when he forbade me from doing something or scolded me. It was a tone that left no room for arguing and sent a shiver down my spine despite the fact that I was the one who'd used it. "I have years of training under my belt, a ton of achievements to back up my argument, I know how to protect myself, okay? The safest place for you is right here."

Before he could try and argue any further, I twisted my arm out of his grip and then took his hand and raised it up to the shirt I held against his head. I made sure he was holding it, and then I got to my feet, took my wallet, and left. Using that dream as an argument was dumb, I knew it, but what else was I supposed to do?

Quickly I made my way downstairs, wondering if I should ask the receptionist if they had a first aid kit or if he could tell me where the closest pharmacy was. I didn't have much time, so the quicker I got what we needed, the better. Rounding a corner, I stopped dead in my tracks as my eyes landed on two figures that'd just come in through the door across the room. I could just make out their faces above the sea of tourists crowding the space and trying to check in, their suitcases practically blocking the way in and out.

I backed away and pressed my back against the wall, hoping and praying that they hadn't seen me.

This couldn't be happening. This wasn't possible. Despite how hard we tried, the hassle we'd gone through and the complicated route we'd taken, the place to stay we'd chosen that should've been the least obvious one, they'd still found us. I was tempted to look again, but I knew I couldn't. I was sure it was them even without it.

Any hope I'd had up until that moment shattered like a piece of glass, leaving behind a million broken shards.

CHAPTER TWENTY-ONE
THE ISLAND

"What makes you think the pilot has a lighter?"

"I remember the stench, the reek of death and the distinct smell of smoke, cigarette smoke," I said and wrinkled my nose at the memory, something I would never forget no matter how much I tried.

"So, you're basically suggesting that we dig him up and look through his pockets in hopes of finding a lighter?" Miles looked like he more than just hoped that I wasn't suggesting that. I wished I wasn't.

Before I could change my mind, I took his wrist and pulled him away from the cockpit. "I hate this plan as much as you do, but we don't have another choice."

We looked through the metal pieces lying around until we found two that seemed like they could act as shovels. It was either the metal or our hands, the latter an option I didn't want to consider for a second time.

I led the way to the shallow grave. If I hadn't been the

one who'd dug it, I wouldn't even notice that it was there.
Somehow that made me feel bad, though not as bad as
the fact that we had to exhume him and raid his pockets.
All these things we had to do that I never thought I would
be capable of. I wished I didn't have to do them, wished
that there was an easy escape route, like a safe word that
would call the entire thing off, but of course there wasn't.
This wasn't a game.

It had been a few days since I buried the pilot, which
meant that his body would now be even further into the
decaying process. He would smell way worse than last
time. We didn't have anything to shield us from the stench,
my stomach turning at the mere thought. The only thing
I could hope was that it would be over quick.

Digging the pilot up was the easy part of our plan, the
most tiring, but still easier. Together it took us surely only
half as much time to do the job than it took me on my own.
Once we reached him and saw him lying in his pilot suit,
covered in dirt, his skin bloated and awfully discolored,
my stomach flipped once more. I'd already seen him, and
four other corpses, but the sight was still just as harrowing.

"One of us needs to look in his pockets," I said and
looked at Miles. For a moment, all I saw on his face was
disgust, but then it was replaced by determination.

"I will," he said, his voice strong. "You should stand
guard in case the damn bear decides to show itself again."

"Are you sure?"

He nodded.

I walked away, just a few feet, not too far, so he
could get it over with. Listening to the jungle around us,
searching for any indication that the bear was coming

or as much as nearby, my hand reaching absentmindedly for my bracelet, I still watched Miles take a deep breath with closed eyes. Once they were open again, he leaned forward and started to pat down the pilot.

I wanted to look away, and I did if only for a moment, letting my eyes wander over the edge of the clearing, but I didn't see anything. After that, I couldn't resist, I looked back toward Miles, watched as he worked, if you could even call it that.

Judging by the angle, it seemed like Miles had gone for the pockets on his chest first, the easiest ones, but quickly he let out some mildly annoyed noise telling me that he found nothing at all. Next, he moved down toward the front pockets of his pants. The left one was empty but there seemed to be something in the right one. Miles looked up for a moment, his eyes meeting mine as if he was searching for reassurance or something. I nodded at him and he nodded back. He leaned forward again and slowly reached into the pocket. A moment later he pulled something out of it, something silver that reflected the light of the sun, though I couldn't quite make out what it was.

"A flask?" Miles asked, confused, and turned the flask over in his hand. "Our pilot was a drunk? Way to make your passengers feel safe."

"Remember, though, the plane never flew." I walked over to him and took the flask. It was heavy, entirely made of silver without any engravings or marks, just a polished surface. I could feel and hear liquid sloshing from one side to the other when I moved it. I opened it and held the flask under my nose to smell what was inside. "Definitely filled with alcohol, maybe even hard liquor."

"It'll be helpful when we try to light a fire," Miles commented. "But that's not what we've been looking for."

"No," I agreed, and put the flask into one of my pockets.

With collective force, we turned the man over so that Miles could check his back pockets. His body felt disgusting and the smell was starting to reach an unbearable level. Quickly I went back to my spot a few feet away, looked around the area once more, but still saw nothing except for some kind of bird taking flight across the clearing.

"Score!" Miles exclaimed.

I turned to see, afraid to get my hopes up that it was the lighter, but I also couldn't imagine it being anything else.

My heart made a happy triple flip when I noticed the red plastic lighter in his hand. I jumped and screamed, unable to contain my excitement.

"Completely full, too," Miles said. "For once, luck is on our—"

The bear's roar and thunderous approach killed the otherwise peaceful quiet around us. I knew it; I simply knew it. We'd been too lucky already today, even with the snakes. We'd made it across the jungle while talking without the beast noticing us. It had simply been a question of time until it would come, our private nightmare racing toward us on all fours. We were so stupid. Why did we have to be so loud?

Just as I was about to suggest that we should run, leave the grave as it was, despite how awful of a thing that was to do, since we had what we needed, I noticed Miles look at the ground. His head turned left and right, his eyes roaming, searching for something, though I had no idea what.

"What do you think you're doing?" I asked, alarmed, the beast roaring once more, even closer than before. We were running out of time, quickly.

"I have a theory." He walked a few steps and then picked up a thick-looking stick off of the ground, held it up and inspected it, finally giving it an approving nod.

Had he lost his mind? "Unless you are a hundred percent sure this theory will work—"

"I'm not."

"—then I suggest getting the fuck out of here."

The sound of breaking branches and shrubbery turned louder, nature giving way to the bear. I turned my head at the sound, and just then it emerged into the clearing. The cockpit was blocking part of it, but I could still see its furry body, a massive leg and paw. I moved backward slowly, yelling at myself in my head to run, run, run, but I wouldn't. Not without Miles. We made a rule—stick together.

Miles had taken off his shirt and wrapped it around the stick, the flask open in his hand. He poured a bit of its contents over his shirt and then handed the flask to me. With trembling fingers, I took it and screwed it shut again. Did he really think a measly torch would be enough to stop that gigantic bear? Snakes were one thing, small and nasty, but this, this was something else entirely.

The flame reflected and danced across his eyes, an almost devilish smirk taking over Miles's face. He moved forward, the torch held up high, and stood in front of me like a shield.

I didn't have time to consider why he would do that, though, because just then the bear came around the cockpit—death approaching us on fast, clawed paws—but when it spotted the fire, it stopped. It raised its head high, stood on its hind legs and roared loud, louder than ever before, the anger clear in the sound. All the hairs on my body stood up, my heart stopping for a moment, and my stomach dropped, a scream getting stuck in my throat. I prepared for it to advance, rip us to pieces one by one, but it didn't.

It returned back down to all fours and stared at us, snarling. Time seemed to slow down, almost stop, until, to my surprise and indescribable relief, the bear turned and walked off.

My body deflated once the animal was out of sight, disappearing the same way it had come, and I sank to my knees. I cursed and cursed, thankful Miles's theory had been right, but also angry with him for being reckless enough to do this, to not even ask if I was okay with it first. Part of me wanted to yell at him for it, but another knew he'd saved our asses and proven that we now had something that could keep the beast away from us.

Fire, the solution against snakes and bears. So simple… *too* simple?

I'd figure it out later. For now, I was just happy to be alive.

"You're such an asshole," I said, laughing as I did.

"You're welcome." He sounded confident and happy, maybe even a little proud.

"Next time you decide to risk our lives to test a theory, tell me what you're planning to do so I can run and not be involved in any damned way." I slowly picked myself up off of the ground and then looked at him, trying to give him what I hoped was a mean side-eye. But judging by his much too amused expression, it hadn't worked.

"You have to admit that was exhilarating." He'd lost his mind; it was the only explanation. Or maybe he was just so high on adrenaline and dead-body fumes that he didn't get that we could've just died.

"Like a car crash," I deadpanned.

"Come on, Fiona," he said and put his arm over my shoulder, "look at the bright side. We're still very much alive, and now it knows we're not to be messed with."

I shook my head. "I can't believe that actually worked." I wouldn't even have considered fire as an option, yet he had. Maybe it was also part of whatever Leon had taught him, *beasts hate fire, little brother,* or whatever.

"Team humans, one; bear, zero." The happy smile on his face, radiant and filled with relief and pride, was enough to keep me from pointing out how it was more like one to three or something. Miles raised his free hand for a high five. I couldn't help but give in, smiling. I was just impossibly happy that we were still alive.

"Let's go back before it changes its mind and maybe brings back some buddies."

Miles didn't argue; instead, we crossed the clearing to retrieve our water from where I'd left it. By the time we'd found it, the torch was already dwindling down, the flame not even a fourth of its original size, so Miles used some dirt, as carefully as possible, to extinguish the torch. No need to waste it while it was light outside and we weren't even close to the cave. I could barely believe we'd found a way to keep the beast away, to get the snakes away from our cave. It was impossible. Even though it looked like we would just drown in all the bad luck and everything working against us, we finally had some success.

Something about all of this—the pit, the camp, how easy the bear got scared and just left—it just didn't seem right. The fire trick shouldn't have worked, yet it had. Why hadn't the bear still tried to come closer, and why had it stayed so far away from the pit?

Quickly I pushed the nagging voices aside again. Not now.

With smiles on our faces, we made our way back, stopping by some mango trees to collect a few so we could take them with us to the cave, since we simply didn't have any left at the plane and it was only a question of time until we'd get hungry.

"Tomorrow, when we have our cave and everything set, we'll go fishing," Miles said, and I just huffed a laugh. Miles fishing? The spoiled rich kid gutting and scaling? I was looking forward to seeing that particular train wreck.

CHAPTER TWENTY-TWO
THE ISLAND

We spent the rest of the day milling around our part of the plane, deciding what we wanted to take with us and how to accomplish that. First, I looked for my book, which I ended up finding underneath one of the seats. It was a gift, and it didn't feel right to leave it. Then I pulled up my suitcase and separated my clothes into two piles—wearable and definitely not—the former unfortunately much smaller than the latter. I'd known it would be warm in Germany, it was summer after all, but we weren't supposed to go there for fun, but to represent our school, learn stuff, which required more office-appropriate type clothes. For our first meeting with Briola, I planned on wearing black skinny jeans, a white button-down, and my favorite jacket with the studded shoulders that my father hated. I hadn't taken along much that was thin or short enough that I wouldn't sweat through it in a minute.

In the end, all I had to choose from were a select

few shirts, though most of them were black, some pants, and a dress I wanted to take along simply because. It wasn't an island or a summer dress, but whatever. From the bottom of my suitcase I dug out the backpack my mom had recommended I'd take along and tried to fit all my things into it as neatly as possible, along with my toiletries and underwear. I didn't even want to imagine what a giant pain in the ass it would be if I got my period while we were on a deserted island.

"We should see if we can take the cushioning off the seats," I suggested some time later. "Would make for more comfortable beds than sleeping on the ground."

So we did just that. It wasn't difficult, with the cushioning not properly attached, anyway, like the manufacturing was rushed. If the plane never flew and was never meant to, I guess it didn't have to go through a quality check. The cushions weren't heavy, either, just a bit bulky, making them a bit awkward to carry, but we made do by putting them into our net. It was just big enough to hold all of them. I laughed as Miles threw the net over his shoulder and pretended to be Santa with a bagful of slightly unconventional presents.

Lastly, we gathered a few sticks for torches. It was an easy enough task, though walking even just a few feet into the jungle while the sun was setting seemed dangerous. We'd never seen the beast this close to the beach, and there was a chance it wouldn't show after we'd scared it earlier that day, but I was still wary and still listened, though mainly I could only hear the ocean and the wind.

Once we'd gotten to the plane, I took my scarf and used a piece of sharp metal to cut it into strips that we could tie around the sticks. The only thing left to do was put some alcohol on, and then lighting the torches would be easy. If Miles was right about the snakes, they stood no chance against us.

After the night had long begun, and we'd eaten a few more bananas and mangos, it was time to move.

In the end, each of us had a backpack full of our stuff, Miles had the net and torches, and I had the tote with our empty bottles. It wasn't much but would allow us to move quicker. Without saying much, we left the plane behind and began our walk along the beach. The sky was partially covered by clouds, but the silver moonlight illuminated our path, bright enough for us to have no issue at all. The ocean had retreated a little farther, and the wind picked up a bit.

From time to time, I looked over my shoulder back at the plane, watched as it grew smaller and smaller with every step we took. I felt simultaneously happy and almost a little strange to leave it. Happy because we would finally get away from this glaring reminder of what happened—or rather, *didn't*, somehow—this metal contraption that was nothing more than a prop, yet had given us shelter for the past few days and nights. Strange because leaving it felt almost like admitting the fact that the likelihood of anyone coming to save us was basically none. It felt like we were giving up hope of rescue, were settling ourselves to survive far longer on the island than I'd thought we'd have to.

But, at the end of the day, we knew someone was behind all of this, that we hadn't actually crashed, that someone orchestrated this entire thing. Looking at the camp we'd found, the fact that it was in the middle of the jungle, a place you'd think would be hidden enough to keep them safe, yet they still ended up dead. That meant the plane would have kept us safe even less. Thinking about it, staying in it longer would've been like sitting on a silver platter and just asking to be found and killed. If someone watched us, though I still refused to really think about it, they'd know we were in the cave, but getting there was harder, for us but also for them. The rocks out in the ocean would keep a ship away so they'd have to come by foot, the ledge leading to the cave giving us an advantage. We'd have a warning, time to figure out a way to escape or make some kind of fight plan.

Staying in the plane would've been easier, more comfortable, but it wouldn't have been the right decision. The cave was.

"Can I ask you something?" I said. I knew staying silent was probably safer, would allow us to stay more alert, but it felt too deafening.

"Sure."

"Did you ever learn to play an instrument?" It was the most random question I could think of, one that seemed at least a little less dumb than asking for his favorite color or anything like that.

"I once considered learning to play the piano but gave up on the idea about three minutes into a YouTube tutorial," Miles said with a huff. "Seemed way too complicated and too much work to learn. I'd rather listen to someone who can already do it way better than I'd ever be able to, anyway."

"I thought you would've," I admitted.

"Why's that?"

"Playing the piano or violin or whatever, I don't know, just seems like a rich people thing. Usually all the rich people in movies do it."

"I hate to disappoint, but not everything they do in the movies is factual."

"Wait, so Darth Vader isn't real?" I asked, faking surprise and shock. He laughed.

"Any other rich people stereotypes you'd like to have debunked or proven?"

"You have a pool, right?" I asked. "Wait, it's Florida, so of course you do."

"Two, actually. And a whirlpool."

"Five cars?"

"Just four."

"Well, damn, Miles, and here I thought you were a proper rich person, but how could you be with just four cars?"

"I know, I struggle with that fact every day." He tried to look sad, but his attempt crumbled, and he grinned shamelessly instead.

"How about a butler?"

"You mean like Lurch?" At that I just stared at him. Somehow I hadn't expected him to be the sort of person who would watch or even as much as know about *The Addams Family*. He was full of surprises. "I think we used to have one, but then my father fired him for whatever reason some years ago."

"Got too expensive, huh?"

"You're awful," Miles said and laughed.

"Right back at you."

Once we'd made it onto the ledge that led to the cave, Miles pulled out the flask and poured just enough of its contents onto one of our torches. He handed me the flask, so I screwed it shut while he took the lighter and lit the torch on fire.

I stood back and watched, held our net, while Miles moved toward the cave and did whatever it was he was doing to scare the snakes away. I didn't even want to look too closely, didn't want to see any of those nasty creatures slither away. I just wanted to know that they were gone, hated that I knew they'd been there in the first place.

"It's done," Miles finally announced after he walked back out of the cave onto the ledge and waved toward me.

"You sure?" I asked.

"One hundred percent."

The cave was wide, reaching a dozen or more feet into the cliff. Though, as far as I could see, it got narrower toward the back. The walls were jagged and the ceiling relatively high, high enough for Miles to stand upright with a straight back. It offered much more space than the plane had, and was cooler, a welcome change from the heat of the beach.

It would do; it had to. We'd gone through so much trouble to get there it would've been dumb to reconsider the decision after all.

Tired, we placed our stuff farther back in the cave and then pulled the cushioning out of the net, building two too-small beds on the cave floor. It was better than sleeping on the stone, so I wasn't about to complain.

Somehow, we'd made it.

CHAPTER TWENTY-THREE
BERLIN

I raced back to our room, skipping the elevator and taking the stairs at the other end of the hallway instead. Every second counted, every fraction of a moment I wasted was a risk to our safety. I needed to get Miles, and then we needed to get out of the hostel immediately, somehow without them noticing. I had no idea how to accomplish that, but I needed to work on one problem at a time.

I practically fell through the door to our room, the door itself smacking loudly against the wall. Miles raised his head off of his pillow and looked toward the door.

"Fiona?" he asked, unsure.

"We need to go," I said between two gasps. Quickly I moved across the room, grabbed my tote off my bed, and put it over my shoulder. "And we need to do it now."

Miles looked more than confused, maybe even a little panicked, his eyes wide. "Why?"

"They're here."

His eyes widened even more, a pain-slashed flinch running across his face a moment later. He must've moved it a little too much, the strain irritating his injury. I wanted to help him somehow, make sure his injury was cared for, but it was either that or get away from the hostel. Both were impossible.

"Can you walk?" I asked, concerned. I knew I could run, but he was the problem, the question mark. I didn't know how good he was at suppressing and ignoring pain, or if he'd be able to move at all.

I held out my hand to him, helped him get up, but as much as he tried, he could barely take a step on his own without swaying. This was bad, the worst way for all of these events to come together, everything happening at the same time, one affecting the other. Our time was running out, and I had no idea how much of it was left, how much longer it would take before those men made it to the guy at the desk and he would tell them that, yes, he'd seen the girl with blue hair and her tall companion, told them our room number and got to us.

"Lean on me," I told Miles, and he did. It was awkward, considering our height difference, but it would have to do. We were slow, much slower than we would've been if he could walk on his own, but this was all we had to work with, and it would have to do.

Avoiding the elevator, we went for the stairs. Getting down all those flights was a painfully slow process filled with hisses and gasps from Miles. I wished I could've spared him, but I couldn't. If everything we went through hadn't been enough to get those bastards off our back, I doubted any distraction I could come up with in a few seconds would've done the trick, either.

Leaving was our only option, though, unlike the last few times, we didn't have a definite destination in mind. I'd have to improvise on the go.

Looking around the corner, I surveyed the lobby, tried to spot the cops. Luckily the new arrivals were still crowding the space, standing around, talking, laughing, trying to get stuff done. Their suitcases blocked most of the area, but I could see a semi-easy path for us to get out. A moment later, I spotted our friendly stalkers, still dressed the same way they had been hours earlier, the two of them trying to fight their way past a group of guys laughing at something on one of their phones. The two had their backs toward us.

It was risky—they could turn around any second, spot us, since I had no way of hiding my hair, or we could be too slow—but we had no other choice. We had to go, and we had to do it now.

Pulling Miles along with me I was painfully aware of just how bad we must've looked, him leaning on me, limping along, with small traces of blood on his face I'd missed, and me looking worried, my eyes carefully watching everything happening around us. I probably looked insane, paranoid, but maybe the people around us would simply think we were drunk or something. Or maybe they were so caught up in their own shit they wouldn't notice us at all.

Somehow, we'd made it outside. As far as I'd seen, the cops hadn't noticed us, were too occupied doing whatever. Maybe we'd at least have some kind of advantage, maybe no one had seen us, so when asked, they wouldn't know.

Maybe we'd manage to get away.

"You okay?" I asked Miles as we walked down the street away from the hostel.

"Splendid," he said, his voice a little hoarse yet a bit less weak than before. He could walk a little better, more easily, as though he'd grown used to the pain enough to walk through it. I knew that feeling too well, had been there a million times before, pushed through injuries and pain like they weren't even there, knew I had no other option — certainly not upsetting my father with the admission to what he considered weakness.

I looked over my shoulder again and again as we walked, made sure that the air was still clear, that the cops hadn't followed. And for a while it seemed like maybe luck was on our side, like maybe we'd done it.

But that would've simply been too easy.

They walked out of the hostel. I watched, hoped that they wouldn't notice us, that we were far enough away that we'd blend in, but of course we didn't. One of them looked right at me, right into my eyes, and then pointed, said something to his friend. We'd been found out, spotted, the air turning electric and my mind kicking into overdrive.

What could I do?

How could we get away quickly?

The answer was a bus coming down the street toward us. I had no idea where it was going, all I cared about was making it to the bus stop, just a little farther, and getting in. We could make them believe that we'd take it somewhere, but really, we'd get off on the next station and then walk.

Maybe I should've figured out a plan that would've meant less walking for Miles, for his poor hurt body, but

I knew this was the only way. If I'd seen a taxi, I might've tried to get us into it, but the bus was the only thing that was there. So we got on it.

I watched the cops run toward the bus, but thankfully the bus driver didn't seem to have noticed them, just closed the doors and drove off. The people around us gave us odd looks, raised brows and some looks of disgust and revulsion, but I ignored them. They could stick their opinions where the sun didn't shine. I dared them to figure out how to act in our situation with only seconds to decide and make plans.

We got off at the next station and continued on foot.

Slowly, the air started to cool. The sun was setting, the streetlights turning on as time went by. We followed random streets and kept away from the main ones. One led us under a train bridge then over a river, past a postal outpost and a gigantic construction site, along a tree-lined alley past a cigarette factory and into a more industrial-looking district. Most of the buildings didn't really look like they were in active use; understandable, since it was the middle of the night. A few cars passed us, but barely any pedestrians.

The cops didn't show. I looked around us, behind us, checked, but I couldn't spot them anywhere.

After we passed yet another bridge, this one next to a coffee factory with a gigantic poster and the smell of freshly brewed coffee floating through the air, we stopped in front of two glass signs talking about the Berlin Wall, which said that the wall followed the paved road along the water. We descended the steps to the asphalt path. It was surrounded by tall trees, shrubs, and grass. I had no idea where the path led, where we were exactly, but it wasn't like we had any clear idea of what to do. Miles leaned against me more and more while my own legs grew more and more tired and demanded a break. I wanted to curl up in a ball of pity and despair, dissolve and disappear.

But I wouldn't do that. No way.

Another bridge came into sight. *What's up with all the bridges?* It was a highway bridge going over our path and the river to our right. There was loads of space under it, and so, even without words, we decided to seek shelter beneath it.

We climbed over the metal fence separating the path from a stretch of earth leading to the edge of the water. We decided to hide out behind the fence in hopes that strangers walking down the path at night wouldn't notice us. We sat with our backs against the fence and our faces toward the lights of some factories across the river, a giant LED billboard illuminating everything around it.

"How did they find us?" Miles asked quietly after I checked the cut on his face. It'd stopped bleeding.

"I don't know," was my shitty answer. "Maybe because of the CCTV cameras. Maybe there were more of them than we thought. Maybe the one I knocked out got up and followed us after all. I have no idea."

There were a million possibilities, and I didn't want to think about them anymore. I was tired, wanted to sleep, wanted to escape our reality, take a break for just a minute, but that wasn't an option. All I could hope for was that the cops wouldn't think of looking here. There were no CCTV cameras anywhere even close to us; no one had even really been around to tell them they'd seen us. This was a far better hiding place than the hostel, even though it was a million times less comfortable. But if it meant we'd stay safe overnight, I was willing to do it.

Chilly wind swept past us and made me shiver. I pulled my jacket closer around me, wrapped my arms around my middle. I felt cold no matter what I tried. I had a feeling this would turn out to be the worst night of my life. How could it get any worse than this? All that was missing was rain, which I hoped wouldn't come.

"You cold?" Miles said. I'd thought he was already asleep.

"Yeah," I admitted. To my surprise, Miles pulled me close, his arm around me while my head rested on his shoulder. I could feel a hint of warmth coming from him, not much, but at least a bit. With a bit of luck, we wouldn't freeze to death out here.

It made me think of Joe, of the nights he'd spent sleeping on his bench in the park. How did he do that? I guessed it wasn't like he had much of a choice. I looked down at my wrist where the bracelet he'd given me rested. I wished I could rewind time and go back to my last conversation with him, the ease with which we talked, the relaxed atmosphere. But all that came up in my mind now when I thought of him was his message to me, the weight of how right he'd been sitting like an elephant on my chest.

"Miles?"

"Yeah?"

"Can I ask you something?" No sleep was in sight, so I figured that maybe talking would make us more tired, and I was desperate for any kind of distraction, something to keep me from thinking about the cops.

"Sure."

"What's the deal with you and your father?"

"There isn't much to say about him," he said after a long pause. "He's a self-absorbed idiot, an even bigger one since my mother died. He doesn't care about anything or anyone besides himself." I didn't know his mother was dead. He'd never spoken about trying to reach her since this whole thing started, but the idea that she might be dead never crossed my mind.

"I'm sorry. About your mother, I mean."

"Thanks," he said, quietly. "It's been a while since it happened, but I wish she were still here, you know?"

"Yeah, I know." And the truth was, I'd never felt bad for him, never even considered the possibility of doing so. My parents and I had problems—their current disappearance least of all—but they had always been there for me. My mom was my anchor. I couldn't imagine life without her. "How is it possible that your father actually doesn't mind you spending loads of money?"

He never answered.

There were other rich kids in our class, our school, but I never understood how it all worked. My own family wasn't exactly destitute, not like we used to be, but we were still far from rich. Even my place in our school was only possible because of the scholarship. I'd never known what it was like to have so much money that you didn't care what something cost.

Except now, hearing the emptiness in Miles's voice when he talked about his parents, I realized I had things he didn't. Things that money could never buy.

CHAPTER TWENTY-FOUR
THE ISLAND

"You still want to go fishing?" I asked, rolling my shoulders and trying to get my muscles to wake up.

"Sure, it'll be fun." He smiled encouragingly, his expression dangerously close to something that looked like pleading puppy eyes. "Just think about how, if we actually catch any, we can have ourselves a nice dinner later tonight that isn't just fruit."

That did sound nice, a change after the same old same old these last few days. Also, part of me was really curious how exactly Miles planned on catching those fish and turning them into food. He didn't seem like the type who'd know the first thing about how to do either.

"Fine," I finally said, his eyes seemingly lighting up as I did.

With the net, lighter, tote, and the torch, we made our way down to the water and then along the stone plateaus and rocks. There was a spot not far from our cave that looked like a stone beach enclosed between two cliffs. Following the stones, you could get to the jungle or walk into the water. Hundreds of fish swam around there—my theory was that there was a reef somewhere nearby, but we didn't check—so Miles wanted to try to fish there.

"So, are you going to help me or just stand around?" Miles asked, net in hand.

"Seeing as you were so keen on fishing, I'll let you have the honors while I go find coconuts," I said. "There is a tree nearby if I remember correctly. And then maybe also some firewood."

"Stay close enough so we can hear each other, at least if one of us screams or something."

"Are you scared something might happen to me?" I asked him, teasingly.

"Obviously."

While Miles tried to figure out how exactly he planned on catching any fish, I moved inland. I climbed from rock to rock until I reached the tiny bit of sand that connected the stone beach with the jungle.

First, I collected some wood for a fire, a nicely mind-numbing task. It was a pleasant day. The sky was still marked by wispy clouds, far more of them now than yesterday, the temperature warm. There was a nice breeze, stronger than the previous day's, indicating that what Miles had said was probably right. A storm was slowly approaching.

My hair was losing its color thanks to the ocean and the sun. The strong turquoise was fading and revealing the true color. It'd been years since I saw it last, at least for more than a few minutes between stripping an old color and applying the new one.

Once I had a big pile of wood stacked up at the beach, I started my second task. I tried to remember where, exactly, that coconut tree was. Walking to the right, I found nothing, so I turned around and wandered to the left.

Now that I thought about it, the fact that coconuts even grew on the island—didn't that mean we weren't anywhere even close to Europe? It was just another weird thing to add to our steadily growing list of things that didn't fit together, that painted our entire situation in even darker colors. If the plane never flew, how did we really get here, and where the hell even were we? What was the point of all of this? Was Briola behind this? No, that seemed unlikely. It would've been too obvious, considering how many people knew we'd go on this trip. But who else then?

Finally, I spotted the coconut tree. It wasn't as tall as the other trees around it. Loads of coconuts crowded its branches, green and ready to be picked. Walking closer to it I noticed a few coconuts lying on the ground. I guessed that solved at least one of my problems. What a lucky girl I was.

I picked them up and returned to the stone beach so that I could see Miles, watch him as he failed, and laugh at him.

"Any luck yet?" I called out to him after I sat down on a bigger rock. It probably wasn't my brightest idea to yell, but it was too late now. We'd be fine.

He cursed and almost slipped the second I called out to him. With a slightly angry, or maybe frustrated, look on his face, he turned around. "Not yet," he called back. "You?"

"Not yet."

Looking at my pile, I wondered how I was supposed to get them open, and if it was even possible to do it nicely and not in a messy and totally inefficient way. I guessed my only option was try and repeat until I managed to do it. There were more than enough of them around.

After way more time than it would have taken me if I had a laptop, wifi, and YouTube tutorials, I found a way to get those coconuts open without spilling all the juice. I placed the nut between two bigger rocks, put a smaller cylindrical stone on it, then smashed down a bigger, heavier rock onto the stone until it cracked open the skin and shell and thus created an opening. It was a tiring procedure, which caused me to sweat, but I didn't care. At least I could say I managed to open a coconut entirely on my own without any help, which had to count for something.

"Aha!" Miles called out. I turned to see him raise the net with two fish trapped inside of it into the air like a trophy. "I got it!"

"I'm proud of you!" I couldn't help but smile a little to myself. Maybe we were not entirely failures when it came to surviving in nature, or maybe that was just my hopes speaking, wishing we would make it and get home somehow. Wishing that someone might come and take us away, take us home. But considering the pit of death, the abandoned camp, and the plane that never flew, I'd say our chances were slim to none, leaning more toward none.

But today wasn't about that.

While I sat farther back in our cave and tried to cut our fruit into squares—not easy when you lacked a proper knife, cutting board, and plates—Miles tried to set up a way to grill the fish over our fire. So far, two of his constructions caught fire. Lucky number three?

On the beach I had found two relatively flat stones we could use as plates. I tried to arrange the cut-up mangos, papayas and passion fruit—ten points to me for finding them—nicely on our stone plates, wanting to mimic the way food got served in five-star restaurants, and wondered why I was putting so much effort into this. It was only a meal. But somehow it felt special, different, like something big was coming, I just didn't know what.

Once I was done, I carried the plates over to Miles so he could place the fish on them once they were cooked. Then I returned to the cave and crouched down next to my pile of clothes. Somewhere at the bottom of it, I found my dress.

I looked over my shoulder at Miles. His back was toward me, his head slightly turned toward his right, and he poked around in the fire with a stick. I turned away, pulled my shirt over my head, and then put on the dress. Next, I slipped out of my shorts. The fabric of the dress was light, frilly, and way more girly than my usual ones. It wasn't even black, but almost royal blue. It complemented my hair nicely. At least, it did while it was still turquoise. It was sleeveless, had a V-shaped neckline, and fell about an inch above my knees.

I considered putting on some makeup as well, but

quickly decided against it since it would melt off of my face in like ten minutes and I'd look like a hot mess. Not an option, even if that was normally Miles's type.

Which was maybe something I should have considered before I put on this stupid dress.

"Almost done," he called out.

"Me, too," I said.

He turned around to look at me. His eyes widened, barely noticeably. I braced myself for laughter or a snide comment, but neither happened.

"Wow," he finally said. "You look… You look good."

"You blushing?" I asked.

Even if someone wasn't, just saying that they were almost always made them blush. And on cue, a flash of red burst onto his cheeks.

"Could you watch the fish for a second?"

"Sure," I said, forcing myself not to laugh.

He got up and disappeared into our cave. I knelt down next to the fire, watched the flames, and turned the fish from side to side every once in a while. How exactly he'd managed to roughly fillet them, if you could even call it that, was honestly a mystery to me. I wondered what Miles was doing, wanted to turn my head and have a look, but didn't.

Miles reappeared next to me. I got up to give him space to get the fish off of his grilling contraption. As I stepped aside, I finally looked at him. His raven hair was a mess atop his head making him look like he just rolled out of bed, a tiny smile rested on his lips and his eyes seemed as golden as ever. He'd changed his clothes, just like I had, and now wore a white dress shirt with the two top buttons undone and black pants that made me wonder how he wasn't boiling in them. He looked good; there was no other way to put it.

With our plates of fruit and fish, we sat down on the edge of our balcony, our legs hanging off of it.

"The fish is really good," I said between bites. "Well done."

"Thanks," he said, proudly, and smiled.

After we were done, Miles lent me a hand so I could get up. I walked back into our cave and used my coconut method to open two. Once that was done I dug up the flask we found with the pilot and poured a little of it into each of the coconuts. Cocktails were not really something we could make, so that was as good as it got.

"Unfortunately, I couldn't find any straws or tiny umbrellas," I said once I was back at the edge of the balcony. Miles turned around and chuckled when I handed him his coconut.

"Are you trying to get us drunk?" he asked after I sat back down next to him.

"Maybe." I smirked. He lightly shook his head.

To my own surprise, my mix was quite tasty, despite the fact that I was not that big of a fan of alcohol.

"I have two questions," Miles said at some point.

"Shoot."

"Question number one: why do you have a triskelion tattoo on your back?" I frowned at his question. I didn't think he noticed it, didn't think he cared because he hadn't brought it up sooner. "Did you watch too much *Teen Wolf* or something?"

"I could ask you the same, seeing as you know that they are mentioned in the show," I pointed out smugly.

"I...might have watched an episode or two."

"An episode or two, sure," I teased and nudged his shoulder with mine. "I have it tattooed as a reminder. I know, how cliché."

"A reminder of what?" He actually sounded curious, not acted but real, honest curiosity.

"Each one of the spirals stands for something else," I explained. "Different cultures see something different in them. For me, personally, they stand for the past, present and future. With the tattoo I remind myself to learn out of the past, apply it to the present and benefit from it in the future. Each action has an effect on your life, and I want to remind myself to make the best out of it. Though, it also applies to the three higher trainings, as my father explained once. There's discipline, meditation, and wisdom. All equally important."

"That is much deeper than I thought your answer would be," Miles said and looked surprised. "I'm impressed."

"Why? Did you think I'm some shallow idiot with a tattoo inspired by a TV show because she finds the actor who has it sexy?"

"No," he said. "I don't think you're shallow, nor do I think you are an idiot. I think you're incredibly smart. You just don't always show it. You act like you're all tough and don't care about what others think, but I think you care much more than you let on, and I don't mean that in a bad way."

"Is that supposed to be a compliment?" I asked, slightly confused. Sometimes he had this slightly weird way of talking that made it really hard to determine whether he meant what he said in a positive or negative way.

"Yes, that was supposed to be a compliment," he said.

"What's the second question?" I couldn't get over the fact that he wanted to know anything about me. After the way he'd treated me the past three years, this seemed like a miracle.

He took a longer sip from his coconut and then asked: "Why do you have so many scars on your hands? What happened?" His expression changed from amusement to something that almost looked like worry. Was he worried that someone might have hurt me and that was why I had those scars? Was that something Miles Echo was capable of?

"It's kind of a fucked-up story." He looked at me, equal parts confused, curious, and what I thought might've been concern. "I cannot believe I'm really going to tell you this." I hesitated. I'd never told anybody about my past, at least, not much and not in any great detail.

"Hey, you don't have to if you don't want to." He smiled at me, a smile that said, "it's okay."

I took a deep breath, a sip of my drink, and looked toward the horizon. "My family has never been wealthy, nothing compared to your family," I began. "It wasn't until about three years ago that my mother finally struck luck and scored a well-paying job. I grew up in New York City, in Chinatown actually. On my street, we were one of the only non-Asian families. Once it was time for me to attend kindergarten, my parents didn't have the money to send me to a fancy one, so I went to the one only a couple of houses away from the building we lived in. It was led by a man in his early fifties and his much younger wife."

Every once in a while, I looked over at Miles to catch

his reaction, to see if he found my story amusing, if he was about to laugh at me for being so far below him. But he didn't. He listened attentively, like I was telling the most fascinating story he ever heard.

"What made the kindergarten different than the one you surely went to is that instead of having playtime, finger painting, and other similar activities, we learned the basics of kickboxing," I said and smiled at the thought and memory of little me trying to figure out the easiest of kicks or punches.

"Wait, you started kickboxing in kindergarten?" he asked, surprised.

"I did." I nodded with a proud smile. Putting it that way, I realized just how many years had passed, and for just how long I'd been doing it. "Private schools were not really something my family could afford, so I went to a public school with my friends. I trained, learned, and grew up with them. At least until a certain point. My father actually has a past in kickboxing and Muay Thai himself, so once it became clear that I have an affinity for it, showed enough potential that people started to claim I could make it international one day, my father decided to take over my training." That wasn't entirely true. He'd taken over when he'd fired my previous trainer for not going hard enough on me. "Fun, right, being coached by someone who's related to you, who knows and cares about you? In my case, not at all."

"I didn't know your father was a kickboxer as well."

"Never made it big. Got some kind of career ending injury, and that was it. But I remember in our old apartment there was this wall basically dedicated to him with old competition pictures, the few titles and medals he did win, you know, that kind of stuff. As a kid, I found it amazing. I wanted to be like him. So, when he took over my coaching, I thought that maybe that would finally bring us closer, since I'd never really been close with him."

"Same," Miles said with a huff and raised his hand.

"My father has very strict methods of training, extremely high expectations, that sort of thing," I continued and sighed a little. It was almost strange to talk with someone about this, even more so with someone outside my family. I'd barely even told Melany about any of it, just scratched the surface. Mom always just said that my father had the best intentions, that he was simply bad at expressing how much I meant to him, while my grandma claimed I was supposed to do as I was told. If my father said those were the right methods, I was to believe it and follow it. So I did. "So, wanting to please my father, become the sort of daughter he wanted me to be, the fighter he claimed to see within me, who's probably just the fighter he wished he could've been but never got the chance to, my friends and I did some crazy shit, resulting in some of those scars.

"One of them has a brother, Cong, about ten years older than us. He always used to tell us about the crazy things he and his kickboxing mates did while growing up. So, of course, we wanted to be tougher, more hardcore than our opponents. We decided that pain made us weak, just like my father had told me numerous times, and so we wanted to learn how to take as much pain as possible. Looking back at it now, I know we were utterly stupid beyond measure, but back then we thought we were amazing."

"Do I even want to know how you achieved that level

of hardcore?" Miles asked, slightly unsure.

"You asked, so now you have to live with the answer." I pulled a smug face. "We did all sorts of crazy things. We tried walking on burning hot coals, punching walls — which, by the way, is where the scars on my knuckles come from — punching each other in the stomach, and even insane things like cutting each other. Everything just to learn to accept pain, to use it as strength and not as weakness, so we could beat our opponents."

While I told him about the wall punching, he reached out and carefully took my left hand into his and looked at it a little closer and let his thumb softly caress the skin and the scars. I never thought he had a gentle side at all.

"And those cuts on your stomach? Are they also from the cutting?" he asked.

"Cong and his friends created this system which basically consisted of literally cutting out tiny strips of your skin on your stomach to show how much pain you're able to take," I explained while I saw Miles pull a grimace and lightly wince at my words. "I know, it's totally stupid and idiotic, and my father went berserk when he saw it. I'd seen him furious, but that had been something else. If I could go back in time, I would punch myself in the face for doing all of it, but back then I felt invincible, won competition after competition, the only thing that managed to get my father off my back again after pulling that number. Once he saw how much stronger it had made me, he didn't seem so appalled anymore. Figures. I'd been sucked into this river, became part of it. It took me until we moved away to realize how dangerous some of the things we did were."

"What do five cuts mean?"

"They don't mean anything." I sighed. "But, back when I got them, they meant a great deal to me. Most of my friends could only take three or four, but I managed five. It made me feel powerful, strong as a mountain, especially because I was the only girl in our group."

"If it wasn't so crazy, and somewhat sick, I would say I'm deeply impressed," Miles admitted. I looked at him and into his eyes. There was something about his eyes that drew me in. They say that eyes are the windows to our souls. I wondered what Miles saw when he looked into mine.

"So, that's where all my scars come from," I said and looked away toward the setting sun. The sky stood in flames and reflected off of the infinite ocean, a perfect painting, a million-dollar photo. "How crazy do you think I am?"

At first he didn't say anything, just remained perfectly silent. I waited for him to get up and leave, but he didn't.

Finally he looked at me and said: "I don't think you are crazy at all. I think you are extraordinary, passionate, and smart, smarter than any girl I've ever known. And you look beautiful, especially in that dress, with your hair that's been every color of the rainbow."

His words took me by surprise. They were nothing like what I thought he'd say. I looked up into those eyes that seemed infinite, that told me his words were honest, true, not just part of a game he might've been playing. But could that be? Was that possible? Could Miles Echo really like *me*?

We certainly had our differences in the past, a lot of them, but since we woke up on the island I'd gotten to know a completely different side of him, the real him and not the arrogant snob he played at school. He wasn't anything like what I thought; instead, he was genuinely nice, funny, and caring. Even if being stuck on the island sucked, and everything else sucked, being in this together wasn't nearly as awful as I thought it would be.

I enjoyed his company, and I actually liked him, a realization that took me by surprise, maybe even more than I wanted to admit to myself. There was something in the way he looked at me, showed genuine interest in the things I told him, the fact that he somehow wasn't afraid to be vulnerable in front of me, that made me wonder *what if*. What if I gave him a chance, if I gave in to these feelings? I was pretty sure we weren't the people we used to be before all of this happened, and maybe that didn't erase the past, but maybe everything he'd done for me, for our survival, was enough to make me willing to give him a second chance.

I gathered all the strength and courage I could find inside of me and said: "Kiss me." The second the words passed my lips, doubt flooded my mind, and I wanted to run and hide. My heart raced like a wild horse.

He put his coconut aside without breaking our stare. His hand found its way to my cheek while his eyes softened like liquid honey. Our faces came closer until our lips met in the most delicate kiss. His lips were soft, inviting. I'd been kissed before but never had a kiss that felt like this. A kiss as soft as the wings of a butterfly, so careful, gentle, sweet, and beautiful. Somewhere in the background I heard the splash of water—my coconut.

The moment our lips parted, I longed for more; a

hunger awoke that demanded to be satisfied. There was a smile on his face, a genuine one that brightened up his face and eyes.

"You know, usually things like this born out of situations like ours don't last," I whispered once I found the ability to speak again.

"Considering we might die tomorrow, I think that's something we shouldn't worry about right now," he said, his voice husky. "I won't let them hurt you."

His words seemed silly considering the pit of death, the beast, and our lack of weapons, but at the same time they warmed my heart and made it bleed in a joyful way.

"Mr. Echo, is this the alcohol speaking?"

"Do you want it to be the alcohol?" he asked and looked unsure. Seeing things like vulnerability, and even the briefest moment of doubt, on him was still strange.

"No." I meant it. I didn't want these feelings to be caused by alcohol. I wanted them to be real, even though I was slightly afraid to feel them.

"I promise this is not just some game," Miles said and placed two fingers underneath my chin, tilted my head up, made me look up at him. "This is me kissing you because I want to. Besides, we promised each other to be honest."

I grabbed his collar and pulled him toward me. We kissed again, but this time the kiss wasn't shy. It was a kiss worth dying for.

CHAPTER TWENTY-FIVE
THE ISLAND

"**Y**ou've hated me for three years. How come you suddenly changed your mind?"

We still sat in the same place while the moon shone down its silver light and the fire crackled behind us. Miles had his arm around me and my head rested on his shoulder. This was definitely a position I never thought I would find myself in, never thought I would like, but I did.

"I know I could give you some bullshit answer, but that wouldn't be fair, especially after you were so honest with me about your past," he said, and then placed a kiss on the side of my head. "But the truth is that I suck at feelings. I know that sounds stupid, but it's true."

"Guess that makes two of us," I said.

"Three years ago, when you joined our class, I knew you were different, and I don't mean that to sound cheesy or to make you like me. But there was something about you that immediately caught my attention, like you just had this sort of commanding aura around you I'd never seen on a girl before." A silly smile appeared on his face. "Then I heard about who you were—I mean, we all kind of did—and I was even more intrigued."

"And then you went on to become the president of the Fiona Sucks Club. How's that fit into the story?" I asked, genuinely curious because I couldn't really see how he could go from being intrigued to hating me just like that, especially since I'd never done anything to him until our enemy thing really started. "I mean, do you even remember what the first thing was you ever said to me?"

"I called you pathetic," he said, voice colored by shame that I didn't expect to hear. I was surprised that he remembered this, that I wasn't the only one, because I'd been the one that was hurt by his words. "I'm awfully sorry about that, by the way."

"And it took you three years to figure that out and tell me?"

"No. I knew I'd said the entirely wrong thing the second I said it. I was so used to talking to my friends that way that it hadn't even crossed my mind that you wouldn't see it as just some stupid shit you say because everyone knows you're not being serious, until I saw your face fall." He sighed heavily. "I tried to fix the situation, but the longer I talked, the more I knew I'd fucked up. So I turned and walked away before I could do any more damage. Later that day I told my best friend about it, asked him for advice, and he said I should just leave it, that chances were you'd think I was weird, or you'd think I'm just the brooding type and that I'm hot like we were in some *Twilight* type book or whatever. Being fourteen and clueless, I believed him."

"I was convinced you were making fun of me," I admitted. "You sounded almost amused as you spoke, so I assumed you thought I was an idiot, and that you were making fun of me because silly Fiona needed to be saved like some damsel in distress."

"We all know you're anything but a damsel, let's be real. You're like the strongest person I've ever known."

"Yet you treated me like I was some kind of peasant unworthy of even talking to you. Remember that time I asked if you could help Melany with chemistry and you told me no then laughed at my reaction?"

"It was meant as a joke, and it's not like you were any better."

"So it's my fault?"

"What? No!" He shook his head and took my hand while I just looked at him doubtfully. "That's not what I meant."

This entire conversation was all sorts of bizarre, and I hated the fact that maybe he wasn't completely wrong. I hadn't been much better than him, and to a certain degree the animosity that built between us was my fault. Partly. I'd been so hung up on the fact that he'd called me pathetic that everything else stopped mattering to me. If I'd listened and actually thought about what he said, stopped him from walking away to ask him about it, maybe all of it could've been avoided. But then again, he was just as much at fault as I was. He could've not listened to his friend's obviously unqualified advice and apologized sooner.

"What I'm trying to say is that I'm sorry for having called you pathetic, that I know I shouldn't have done it, that I should have apologized, but I let myself be influenced by my friends who only saw your family's financial status instead of you as a person and concluded that you weren't someone worth being friends with, and then…things turned out the way they did." Even though I'd known that was exactly what most people in our school thought about me, the poor girl only there on a scholarship, and they looked down on me for it, actually hearing Miles confirm my thoughts still sucked. "I know my words can't fix what I did in the past, but I hope that I can show you in the future that I'm not who I used to be at fourteen, and that I really do like you and don't think you're pathetic, not even for a second."

"Then I suppose I should apologize for writing 'asshole' on your locker, hmm?"

"Absolutely not," he said decisively. "I deserved that. And every other time you flipped me off or whatever."

For years I'd been convinced that he hated me for who I was, for just being some "pathetic" little thing with no money who had no place in our school, that he looked down on me from that first interaction onward—and now it turned out that wasn't true, at least not the way I thought it was. We'd disliked each other based on a misunderstanding, three years passing without either of us trying to get to the bottom of it. Instead, we just rolled with it. Melany always told me I was right for feeling upset and calling him out on his behavior, but we'd only known my side of the story.

And now I laughed.

"What's so funny?" Miles asked after a moment, sounding genuinely confused.

"I just thought about how, if we'd gotten our shit

together sooner, we could've been friends these past few years. Or, if you'd let your mind run a little further, I might've gotten to kiss you without having to end up on a deserted island first."

"You mean like this?" He kissed my cheek. I couldn't help but smile.

"More like this," I said, and leaned in to kiss him properly. He pulled me a little closer and kissed me back.

After the kiss he looked at me, his eyes hopeful. "Does that mean you forgive me?"

I usually wasn't the forgiving type, with others or myself, but seeing that hopefulness in his eyes, hearing that honesty and remorse in his apology, I could make an exception. Ever since we woke up on the island, he'd proven again and again that he wasn't the person I'd thought. He helped me, was nice to me, and he even came up with the idea for this evening. He'd made a genuine effort to show me that he wasn't a bad person, and that he cared. He'd even helped me before we landed on the island, but I didn't know about that until he told me. And maybe all of that couldn't erase the hurt I'd felt three years ago, but I could see he really was sorry, that he wouldn't do it again, and just this once I was willing to forgive.

"Yes, but if you ever say something like that to me again, I will punch you."

"I swear I won't, never again," he said, looking me straight in the eye. "Thank you."

I leaned against him, his arms around me, and just let myself breathe for a moment. I was happy to finally know his side of the story, that we finally talked about it, and I was glad that the things between us were the way they were right in that moment. I liked him and being able to act upon it, knowing we were on the same page and that if things had been a bit different we could've been here sooner, it felt…nice. Surprising, even.

"There's actually something I always wondered," he said after a while. "Something about you that I could never really figure out."

"Besides the rainbow hair?"

"Well, it clearly violates our school rules and none of our teachers ever said anything, and that totally confused me, but that's not it."

"My mom made up some story about the hair being part of my brand and how my sponsors liked it because it gave me some kind of uniqueness factor. Somehow the school actually bought it. Anyway, you were saying?"

"Despite being such a strong person, someone who just went and won competitions in a sport that demands so much of you, you seemed unable to stand up to any of our teachers whenever they gave you shit, even when the thing they were giving you shit for wasn't your fault or even about you. How can you beat your opponents black and blue, yet our teachers seem too much? I could never figure it out."

I bit my lip, my mind a storm, as I tried to decide what to do. I'd already told him so much, would telling him this make that big of a difference? Yes, it would. It would make the biggest difference, would mean discussing something I barely even knew how to discuss with myself, tried to not think about at all if possible. I didn't know if anyone had to deal with things like this, or if Miles would even be able to understand it. He'd mentioned not having a good relationship with his father, taking his money basically without permission, which just all seemed so strange to me. I'd always thought he must have a good relationship with him, hence the fact that he allowed him to spend all that cash and do whatever he pleased, but now I knew that wasn't the case.

He'd opened up to me about his brother, about the loss he'd dealt with alone for so long, had mentioned his mother. So if he could be this honest, maybe I could, too. Maybe he would be the one person who'd understand me, when I didn't even understand me, who wouldn't just push my words aside as unimportant or trivial. Maybe he could help me figure out the very thing that I hadn't been able to.

"My father isn't what you'd consider a loving father by any stretch of the imagination," I said, my voice a little shaky no matter how much I tried to keep it steady. Why was this so hard? I'd fought in state competitions; compared to that, a simple conversation shouldn't have been this hard to do. "As I said, he's strict when it comes to my training, but also in general. He's controlling and demanding to a ridiculous extent. Since I was a kid, he's always taught me how I needed to be strong, basically had to if I wanted or not, how any sign of weakness is a flaw that needs to be eradicated, how I could only win if I pulled myself together and did it without allowing myself to feel fear or worry of any kind. He never bothered to ask why I was scared, why I worried, not once across all those years. For a long time, I thought that he said and did all of that because he genuinely wanted me to be this special someone he and the people around me always claimed I had the potential to be. I thought he meant well, but then

I realized that wasn't it."

As I spoke Miles pulled me a little closer, lightly caressed my hand in a comforting manner, the gesture so affectionate I barely knew what to make of it, so I just kept talking.

"He wasn't demanding of me so I'd grow. No, he was demanding because he refused for me to fail, to lose *any* match, because he thought it would make *him* look bad," I continued. "He didn't care about me the way I always thought he did; he cared about his image and how my achievements and shortcomings reflected on him, my every win raising his status among the coaches, my every loss making him look like he hadn't done his job well. Over the years I've learned not to disappoint, displease, or anger him, and learned the price of failure."

"Are you implying what I think you are?" Miles asked, sounding hard, almost mad in a way I didn't quite understand.

"It doesn't matter."

"How can it not matter?" The shock and disbelief were palpable in his voice. I'd never heard him sound that way. "He was mentally abusing you, at least it sounds that way, and that is seriously messed up. Has he ever done more than that? Did he ever physically hurt you?"

"It doesn't fucking matter," I said and looked at him, hoping my expression would get him to drop that particular line of questioning. I wasn't ready to talk about that. When you fail, punishment follows, that was simply how it was, though I didn't expect him to understand that. "Think of him as you like, but he managed to make me unafraid in ways most people aren't, even if his methods might not have been the most conventional ones. I conquered my fear of pain, of opponents that appeared stronger than I thought I could ever be, of most things that used to scare me. But then when it comes to our teachers, for example, it's like I just can't. My father helped me become so strong, yet for some reason I just completely freeze around them, and I just really don't understand why. It doesn't make any sense. I shouldn't be afraid of them, because why should I be?"

I watched his face, tried to decipher from his expression, his eyes, what he was thinking, but I wasn't sure if what I saw was judgment, concern, anger, disbelief, or something completely different. Maybe he was trying to understand what I'd told him, maybe he was failing to do so, our differences too great for him to be able to as much as imagine what my life was like, the fact that it was probably nothing like he thought it was.

"Have you ever considered that it isn't that he was unable to make you strong enough, or unafraid enough, but rather that he is the reason why you are afraid of our teachers and such in the first place?" he finally asked, his voice sounding far more cautious now.

"Don't be ridiculous," I said. My father despised fear of any kind, so what use would it be for me to fear teachers, let alone that he'd be the reason why? I hated his punishments. Any person would, which was why they were punishments. But that didn't mean I was afraid of him. He was my father after all, so I had no reason to be. Maybe I'd been wrong; this was an issue Miles wouldn't be able to help me with and I had to solve on my own. "It's simply a character flaw I have to get over eventually, or not."

Miles looked torn, like he wanted to say something more, possibly argue against me. He even opened his mouth to speak but then closed it again and looked off toward the horizon. I wondered what he was thinking about, why it was so hard for him to see that I was right. But maybe he didn't need to understand it. It didn't matter, at least not now.

"I know it doesn't mean much, but I hope that one day you'll be able to see yourself as the strong and fierce girl that I see every time I look at you," he said. "And, also, thank you."

"For what?"

"For giving me a second chance, sharing all of these things about your father. For trusting me enough to do that, despite how I've acted until we ended up on the island. You'd think we're still kids playing in the sandbox with our mothers claiming that me pulling your hair is just my way of showing you that I *like* you or something."

"How lucky you are that I am not opposed to a little hair-pulling," I teased, more than ready for this moment of talking about much too real topics and emotions to be over.

"Fiona," he practically groaned and leaned forward, letting his head drop until it rested against my shoulder, his hair hiding his face, while I burst out laughing.

Maybe we would be okay.

CHAPTER TWENTY-SIX
THE ISLAND

The first day of gloomy weather arrived a couple days after the kiss, a little later than Miles had predicted it would.

During the morning, the wind picked up, and the waves turned harsher and crashed against our cliff with more force than they normally did. The sky was white and gray, turning grayer as the day progressed.

We decided to stay in our cave just in case it started pouring and became almost impossible to get back. Now that the water was going crazy, walking across the rocks and plateaus was a very risky idea to consider.

Luckily, we had quite a pile of fruit stored in our cave so that we wouldn't go without food the whole day. The thing was just that there wasn't much we could do inside, with no video or board games, no movies or shows to watch, no internet to browse. All we had was each other, not that I particularly minded right now.

"I never knew your hair was actually blond," Miles commented while twirling a strand of it around his finger. The act alone made me smile. It wasn't anything special, yet it still felt nice, silly. We sat on our bed—even thinking that still sounded unbelievable to me—which we'd made out of all the cushioning we'd gotten to the cave the first time, and some more that we'd managed to rip from the plane yesterday. Our backs were against the cave wall and our legs stretched out in front of us. His were much longer than mine, and his skin a few shades darker.

"Did you think my hair was naturally a rainbow?"

"As awesome as that would be, I know that it's not a thing, yet." I watched his lips move as he spoke, a mesmerizing view, I now realized. "But I thought black would be more your color."

"I had it black a few years ago. Though it's gotten darker already, it used to be almost platinum colored. Having blond hair definitely made my dyeing endeavors much easier."

Funny enough, I was born with pitch-black hair that quickly switched to the opposite end of the hair color spectrum. As a kid, many said that I looked like an angel with my light hair and cute chubby little cheeks, but I got fed up with the look pretty early on. I wasn't an angel, and I would never be one. Over the years, lots of people told me that, thanks to my obsession with dyeing my hair, I would end up bald by the time I was forty. I didn't care, because I'd be damned if I wouldn't rock that bald head, anyway.

"It suits you," he said and put on that smile of his, a smile that was almost a smirk.

I leaned in and kissed him. It still felt surreal each time it happened, like my mind was unable to process that it was really happening, and my center of emotions was still trying to work out my feelings for him. All I knew was that I enjoyed kissing him. I loved the feeling I got when it happened, loved the way his lips felt on mine and how gentle yet passionate he was and how he didn't push anything.

After a small lunch, I decided to take a nap.

Feeling his fingertips lightly caress my shoulders and back was comforting. It let me know that he was there, that I could fall asleep and be okay, that nothing would happen, and I was safe.

When I woke up, Miles was still leaning against the wall, though now he had a black notebook in his hands.

"I didn't know you have a diary," I said, and he jerked in surprise.

"I didn't know you were awake," he said after taking a deep breath. "And no, I'm not writing a diary. It's just a notebook I use when I don't want to forget something, or when I think of something I want to do, you know?"

"Sounds interesting." I turned onto my side, watched him as he skimmed through the pages with a look of concentration. I was pretty sure I'd seen him flip through that notebook at some point earlier on after the crash that never happened, but I hadn't asked him about it then. Finally he stopped at a page, and his face suddenly lost its color just as the rain began to fall outside.

He stared at the page in front of him intently. Immediately I was nervous and anxious as to what it might be that he found in there. I sat up without taking my eyes off of him.

"Are you okay?" I asked, cautiously.

"I'm not sure," he said slowly. Each word almost stood on its own, a one-word sentence filled with endless silences in between.

"Miles?"

"Listen to this," he said but stayed silent for another moment while I began to worry more than I probably should have—or at least, I hoped there was no actual need for it. The longer he stayed silent, the more I realized that maybe I should be panicking, that I should worry.

Miles cleared his throat. *"We just arrived in our hotel in Berlin. The flight was all right, nothing special, slept through most of it. The hotel seems way too expensive for something rented for summer interns, but then again, I'm used to better. Anyway, turns out we got a double room with just one bed. Fiona is not amused and just stormed out of the room to go and complain at the reception desk. It's hilarious to watch her get angry, turn into a fury. I'm just waiting for her hair to turn into snakes, blue ones. Though, that angry frown on her forehead looks kind of cute, not that I would tell her. Even if I did she wouldn't believe me. The bed itself is quite comfy, and I'm curious whether Fiona will manage to get another room or if she'll have to accept the fact that she has to share a bed with me. I can hear steps echoing from the hallway."* His voice came out shakier with each new sentence. "That's it." He looked from the pages, and our eyes met. I saw panic in them, panic mirroring my own.

"How?" I muttered. My thoughts began to race, turned into a storm similar to the one outside our cave. My mind turned into deep waters with sky-high waves building up and crashing down. I didn't understand it; it made no sense at all.

Before Miles could say another word, I crawled over to my suitcase and started digging through it. Finally I found what I'd been looking for—my hoodie, the one I'd had with me in the plane. I pulled it out and looked through the pockets. In one of them, I felt something plastic that I was pretty sure had not been in there before, and thus definitely didn't belong to me. Maybe I should've looked through those damn pockets more thoroughly the first time, but how was I supposed to know that maybe some kind of clue would be hidden in one?

"Fuck," I said. I pulled out a slim plastic card with a hotel name on it, the word "Berlin" prominently printed in all caps below it, along with some swirly design with the Berlin bear in the middle. I moved over to Miles, sitting down next to him. Curious, he took the card from me.

"A hotel key card?" he said examining it. "How is this even possible?"

"I...don't know." My mind suddenly turned from storm to blank white page. It made no sense, even less than that the plane that never flew.

Thunder cracked and rumbled outside, startling me, and my heart rate rose even further. Lightning cut through the sky. Miles put his arm around my shoulders.

"Nothing can happen to us in here," he said reassuringly. "It's only a storm, nothing that can harm us."

I turned the plastic key card around in my hand and tried to make sense of it, but there was nothing that could explain it. Nothing that would explain how this key card ended up in my pocket or where the entry in Miles's notebook came from.

"The key card and your entry, they are both from Berlin," I said. "But we've never been there. We fell asleep in the plane and woke up on this island. So…what's going on?"

"I don't know. I really don't." He looked through the entry once more. He turned to a different page. His handwriting was the same in both the Berlin entry and the older ones. "This is insane. How did I not notice this last time? When I got into the plane's system, I remember checking the time and date, the only thing that was actually working. There is no way we could have made a detour to Berlin. There was no time for that. It just doesn't fit."

I glanced outside just as another bolt of lightning slashed through the sky, illuminated the clouds, and disappeared a heartbeat later. The thunder roared even louder. But then, just before I was going to say something, I noticed that another sound had joined the symphony, a sound that didn't belong, like a single person singing off-key in a choir.

"Do you hear that?" I asked, frowning.

"What?"

"I don't know, there's something, like a sound that doesn't fit." I tried to listen to the storm and figure it out. But there were too many noises that made filtering out a single one way too difficult.

"Are you sure it's not just the storm?"

"Yes, I'm sure it's something else." I got up and walked toward the entrance of our cave.

My eyes were glued to the sky, the dark clouds and the pouring rain. At first I couldn't see anything out of the ordinary, nothing that seemed odd, until—

A blinking light, then two. At first I thought it was more lightning, but it wasn't white, but rather something like red or orange. What the…?

There was some kind of dark, black shape with blinking lights. "Miles!" I heard Miles get up and come over to me, and I pointed toward the shape. It was definitely moving toward us. "What is that?"

"A helicopter?" Miles asked in disbelief.

He was right; it was a helicopter, a black one with two blinking red lights to either side of it. The odd sound was its rotor.

"Maybe they're coming to save us?" Miles said with hope in his voice.

"What if it's the people who put us here in the first place and who are now coming to kill us?" I asked.

"There's only one way to find out." Miles walked past me and toward our secondary path that led up and onto the cliff.

Quickly I caught up with him, grabbed his arm. "This is the opposite of being careful!" I argued. "We can't just go up there and reveal our location, especially not if they really are the bad guys. Do you want to end up in that fucking pit?"

"No, but we can't just hide. We have to check. I mean, what if they're the good guys coming to save us, and they'll just leave if they don't find us fast enough? What would we do then?"

"And what if they aren't?"

"Then we'll deal with that," he said. "One step at a time."

Before I could argue anymore, or find another way

to stop him, he slipped from my grasp and was already a good few feet away from me, climbing up our cliff.

Reluctantly, I followed him, afraid to stay behind, afraid to let him go alone. Just as we were halfway up the cliff, the helicopter flew above our heads and over the island, its sound louder now, more distorted. I noticed it wasn't flying steadily but swaying from side to side like the pilot was barely about to keep it under control.

Miles reached the top first and helped me up. The wind was much harsher up here and sent my hair flying in a wild mess all around my head, blinding me in the process.

Stopping in our tracks, we watched as a dark figure jumped out of the helicopter, a parachute opening a moment later while the helicopter continued its flight and disappeared out of sight as quickly as it had appeared. Silently we watched the parachute slowly descend toward the jungle and then disappear between the trees.

We scrambled into the jungle toward where the parachute was likely to have landed. Navigating the jungle in the semi-darkness and rain wasn't easy, but after a couple of minutes we finally spotted a dark figure a good dozen or more feet away from us. He was dressed all in black and tried to fight himself free of the ropes of his parachute in which he seemed to be trapped.

Miles and I crept a little closer to look at him, see more details and decide what to do next. We hid behind a half wall of bushes.

"What should we do?" Miles asked quietly, looking at me for a moment before turning back toward the stranger.

"I think, if we'd want to talk to him, figure out if he's on our side or against us, now's the best time," I said, my eyes glued to the man, the ropes still trapping him in place. "If he tries anything, I can just knock him out."

For a moment he considered my words, his eyes still on the stranger, then he finally lightly nodded. "Okay."

This was likely a really bad idea, I could feel it, but we had to try. Maybe he was our way out of this mess. Maybe he was here to find us and bring us home. All of this seemed too crazy, impossibly so, but something good had to happen to us sometime.

The man, whoever he might have been, looked like he was in his thirties. His hair was black and short. He looked Asian, though I couldn't pinpoint if he was Chinese or Japanese, maybe Vietnamese, I didn't know.

Slowly we stepped out from behind the bushes and walked toward him, our steps cautious, our eyes never leaving the stranger. It took him a moment to realize that we were there, his arms finally stilling, his hands still holding on to two of the ropes that had wound around his legs in tight tangles.

"Thank goodness," the stranger said, his tone relieved, as he spotted us coming closer. "Could you help me?"

"Who are you?" I asked instead, the two of us stopping a few steps out of reach from him just to be sure.

"My name is Dong Ji and I'm here to help you." I desperately wanted that to be true but left my face unmoved, nothing showing my feelings. The chances of him actually saying the truth were rather less than ideal, even though I wished differently. "I was sent here as part of a rescue mission to find you and get you home. Please, could you help me? I'll explain everything else later."

"How can we be sure you're not going to kill us the

second those ropes are off?" Miles asked, his arms crossed in front of his chest and the skepticism evident in his voice.

"What reason would I have to kill you? I've risked my life to get here, especially in this weather. What sense would it make if I were here to kill you? Please, I promise I'm here to help! Besides, there are two of you, and I'm alone."

Miles and I exchanged a look, silently evaluated what we should do, but in the end, even if it was potentially a really stupid idea, we agreed to help Ji. There was a fifty-fifty chance that he said the truth, and I really wanted that fifty percent to be the right one, for this nightmare to be over. If the other fifty percent were right, Ji had said it himself—there were two of us against him.

Slowly, with combined efforts, we managed to get Ji out of his ropes. The parachute caught in the branches above our heads shielded us from the rain, at least somewhat, which made everything a tiny bit easier. As we worked, Ji told us about how he was supposed to land on the island and then find us so he could help us get back home, leave the island. It sounded so good, finally going home, something I'd dreamed of since day one. Ji seemed nice, calm in the way he spoke, and nothing about him seemed to point toward danger, toward something evil.

"A boat will come at some point to get us," Ji said as he pulled up his backpack while we stood and watched from a bit of a distance, still not quite sure if trusting him really was a good idea. After everything we'd been through, could anyone fault us? Slowly he rummaged through the backpack, as though searching for something.

It sounded like it would take a while for that boat to

come, but if it was the case, why didn't he have any supplies with him? Why did they send him alone? Something about this entire situation just didn't seem right, like he wasn't telling us the whole truth.

"Have you found the targets?" a voice asked from the inside of his backpack, the voice distorted but just clear enough for us to make out the words, my blood immediately turning cold. "Do you need more time to eliminate them?" Time seemed to stand still, the air filled with nothing but the sound of the storm and the beating of my heart in my ears, my eyes making contact with Ji.

I held my breath as the three of us just stood there, my thoughts simultaneously racing faster than seemed possible and not moving at all. I tried to figure out what to do, what to say, what to even think. Ji looked at us, his eyes slowly wandering back and forth, his hand still buried deep within his backpack, the voice not saying any more. The damage was done, Ji's cover blown.

Then everything seemed to happen all at once, us taking a step back as Ji pulled out a gun from his backpack and pointed it at us. I didn't think. Only acted.

Before Ji could flinch or pull the trigger, I advanced toward him and threw my leg into a high kick, my foot meeting his hand hard enough for him to drop the gun. Unfortunately, luck wasn't on our side, because I very quickly realized that Ji, just like me, had training in martial arts or combat techniques, his moves too fluid and clean, his strength greater than mine.

I ducked as his fist swung toward my face, my own right one making contact with his side, stealing part of the air from his lung, a groan coming from him. It was a lucky jab, only making him angry instead of weakening him.

Everything seemed to turn into a blur, my body moving as though on autopilot, my training helping me, my mind focused, my footwork surprisingly good on this slippery grass and uneven dirt. I put up a hard fight, my father's voice echoing in my mind—failure not acceptable, punishment would await me if I'd lose. I knew this time our lives were on the line, a much steeper price than any other. But Ji was too good, leaving me mostly trying to block his moves and avoid any critical hits.

I tried another kick, but he stepped backward, avoiding contact skillfully, a devilish grin on his face like he could smell that I wasn't as skilled as him, a fact I could barely swallow. But then, suddenly he was falling. His body hit the ground, and I expected him to move, roll over, jump back up, but instead he just lay there. Cautiously I stepped toward him, waited to see if he would react. He didn't. I took another step and then one more until I stood right by him, looking down on his face, but it was as though he was caught in a picture, his eyes wide and unblinking, his mouth lightly open. My gaze shifted to his chest, wanting to see if it was moving, and to my horror I realized that it wasn't.

Ji wasn't breathing, wasn't moving, wasn't doing anything at all.

Ji was dead, the rock beneath his head slowly turning crimson.

CHAPTER TWENTY-SEVEN
BERLIN

Slowly, even though it seemed impossible given how uncomfortable our position was, I drifted toward sleep. I could barely wait for the sweet release into a state in which I didn't have to think about everything that was happening, could catch just a tiny break and relax. I moved a little closer toward Miles without even opening my eyes and felt myself slipping, falling, the sounds around us turning quieter despite the highway being literally right above us.

But just there at the edge of my consciousness was a noise. There were a lot of noises, but that noise…it didn't belong. It wasn't loud, was almost drowned out by the rumbling highway, but it still caught my attention. The sleep I'd almost slipped into was forgotten, my tiredness took a seat, and instead, my mind switched back into high alert.

It could be nothing, but it could also be something.

Even if I wanted to, I wouldn't be able to ignore it. I had to check what it was.

I opened my eyes and tried to move, just enough so I could look over the barrier behind us, check the two sides of the pathway. I was sure I'd heard a branch snap or something like that, a noise another person must've made, or an animal. Looking toward the left, it took me a moment, but there in the white light of the billboard illuminating the path, I saw a person walking toward us.

But it wasn't just any person.

No way. This couldn't be happening. It couldn't be—

CHAPTER TWENTY-EIGHT
THE ISLAND

Wordlessly, we raided Ji of everything he had with him. Trying to look anywhere but at his face, we took his backpack and his gun. As we worked, the rain slowly stopped, though the sky remained dark, leaving the possibility that it could rain again soon.

Miles offered to drag Ji away, hide his body somewhere in between some bushes and out of view. I didn't trust my voice, so I merely nodded and refused to watch him do it, to even so much as look in Ji's direction while I knew he was still there. Instead, I pulled my legs up close to me and put my head in my hands. While we'd taken Ji's things, the adrenaline still circulating through my system, my mind occupied, I'd managed to not think about what actually happened. But now I couldn't stop.

I couldn't believe what I'd done, couldn't stop thinking about it once I started. It was like a movie snippet crashing through my mind, tormenting me, replaying over and over again. No matter how much I tried to push it away, I couldn't do it. It'd been my fault. He was dead because of me, because I killed him. My body began to shiver, though I didn't feel cold on the outside, but rather on the inside.

"What have I done?" I muttered quietly, nothing more than a whisper, the words barely passing my lips. "I broke it, the one rule we vowed never to break. Oh God, what have I done? I killed him, I really did."

Tears streamed down my cheeks and a deep sob shuddered my body. I could feel my control, the very one usually made of steel, drift away out of reach, like water slipping away through my fingers. My mind changed from panic to nothing and back to panic with every passing second. I couldn't finish a single thought before it was gone again, replaced by another. The world turned blurry, out of focus, nothing mattered anymore, the damage done, irreversible.

If my father ever found out what I'd done, I didn't even want to consider the consequences, didn't want to imagine his anger and disappointment, didn't want to imagine what he'd say or do.

"Fiona, hey," Miles said softly, calmly, though with the faintest note of confusion and worry. I hadn't even noticed that he was back. "What are you talking about? What rule?"

"Never to use our abilities t-to ha-a-rm another person, only as me-ea-ns of self-defense or during ring fights," I stuttered. It was hard to speak because I couldn't stop sobbing and crying like a baby. I was the embodiment of everything my father loathed in that moment, showing weakness so openly, crying, embarrassing myself.

"Fiona, hey, look at me," Miles said gently. I raised my head, but my eyes stayed cast downward. He took my face into his hands, swiped away my tears with his thumbs. His touch was ever gentle, slow and soft. Miles's voice was so calm, sounded so appealing, it forced me to finally look up at him, into those infinite eyes of his. "Don't beat yourself up about this. You've done nothing wrong."

His words made me wonder, frown in confusion, because they didn't make any sense at all. "How can you say that?"

"Because it was an accident," he told me. I saw no fear, no lies, in his eyes. "You didn't mean to kill him. You were just defending us. And Ji didn't come in peace. He came to kill us the way they killed the others. What you did was save us. You *saved* us from landing in that pit just like the four before us. And you stood up for us, for yourself, just like I always said you were able to, even though he was a male authority figure, kinda."

I could hear his words, I knew what they meant, but it was like my brain was filled with a thick mist that I could hardly see through. All my thoughts moved slowly, so painfully slowly.

"But I still killed him!"

"What are you talking about? You didn't kill him, Fiona. He stumbled and fell while he tried to dodge your kick. You had nothing to do with it. You tried to save us. What you did was noble, and his death isn't on you."

"But…"

"No but," he interrupted before I could say any more. "You saw danger, and you reacted. You risked your own life to save the both of us. That he fell and broke his skull, it was an accident, no one's fault but his, if even that. What matters is that we are still alive, that we are unharmed. You're okay, right?"

I had no idea if I was okay, physically or mentally. I was sure I'd have a few bruises to show for this, but they weren't anything I hadn't dealt with before. I shrugged. Thinking was still hard, my thoughts racing, my emotions all over the place, but I still tried to consider what Miles had said. Was it true, or possible, that Ji had simply fallen by mistake, that there was no blood on my hands after all? Could it be, or was Miles just saying it to make me feel better?

Whoever Ji really was, he hadn't come to help us. He'd come to kill us. He had a gun, and he'd threatened us. I'd had no other choice but to act, right?

It took me another handful of minutes to fully calm down, to regain control, but I managed to do it with Miles's help. He told me everything was all right; that what I'd done was right, that I hadn't done anything wrong because it was either him or us. And to be honest, as harsh as it probably sounded, I valued Miles's life, and mine, over that of a killer. I didn't break my father's rule because I acted to defend us, him and me, two lives in exchange for one. It didn't make it fair, but we were innocent and he was the evil in this equation.

It didn't change the fact that I attacked him, that I broke a rule I swore never to break, but did I have another choice? No. I did what I had to do, so maybe it was okay. Maybe I would be okay, hadn't brought disgrace on myself. I saved us, just like any other person would do.

*N*o way. This couldn't be happening. It couldn't be real.
     *"Miles." I spoke as quietly as possible and shook
him just enough to wake him, careful not to hurt him. "Miles,
wake up."*

*Slowly his eyes blinked open and he looked around,
confused, as though he couldn't remember where he was.
He turned his head back toward me, his eyes oddly empty
but also endlessly tired.*

"Fiona, what's—"

"They're here. They found us again. We need to go."

"*H*ow about we look through the backpack?" Miles
offered with an encouraging smile. "Maybe there's
something useful in there."

"I'd really dig some answers right about now," I said
with a huff, my mood a little better. I was trying, doing my
best, and I appreciated Miles's effort to take my mind off
of what happened. "Like who he worked for, who brought
him here, and who wants us dead."

I doubted his backpack would contain a work contract
or a pretty little memo written on a sticky note that
would spell all the answers out for us, but there had to
be something. Miles got up and fetched the backpack, sat
down opposite to me cross legged, and then reached inside.

"Does that thing work?" I asked while I watched Miles

turn Ji's phone or radio, whatever it was, around in his hand. It was chunky and matte black with a few keys and a small screen. Miles pressed a couple of the buttons, touched the screen, but nothing seemed to happen.

"I guess he must've done something to disable it," he said with a sigh. That was just our luck. Disappointing, but nothing we could do about it. Really, I shouldn't have been so surprised; it only made sense for Ji to kill any chance for us to escape when he wasn't sure if he'd make it. "Would've been too easy, wouldn't it? Dead end." With that, Miles placed the thing on the ground next to him and returned to the backpack.

It was large and black, similar to those that hikers use, with enough space for both his parachute and whatever else he had with him. Miles looked it over, then turned the backpack upside down, and shook it so everything fell out onto the space between us.

There was a black shirt, a tiny med-kit, goggles like those you'd wear for diving, three pairs of black rubber gloves, and two cylindrical, transparent tubes that could fit in the palm of your hand.

I inspected them a little closer. They seemed to be made of plastic, and a small strip of paper was glued to each of them.

"What the…?" I said and showed Miles the tubes. Each of them was marked with our name, gender, and age. Miles looked from the tubes up to me.

"I told you that he wasn't here to help us," he said and continued looking through the stuff. I put the tubes aside and picked up something that looked like a black hair dryer. There were only two buttons on its hilt: one to turn it on and one to turn it off. Feeling brave I turned the thing on and pointed it at my forearm, which could've been a truly stupid idea.

Suddenly, I didn't see my skin anymore. Instead I saw all the veins running though my arm, the strings and muscles. My eyes widened in response, and my breathing hitched briefly. I'd never seen something like this. It wasn't a portable x-ray or anything I could name. It didn't show me my bones, just what lay underneath my skin.

"Now that's freaky," Miles said when he noticed what I was doing. "I wonder what that's for."

"I'm not sure I want to know," I said and turned off the gun thing. My arm went back to normal, to the way I preferred seeing it. I ran my hand over the patch of skin that had been translucent a second ago. It felt completely normal. The entire scene sent a chill down my spine. This was every shade of bizarre.

While I put the gun thing back into the backpack, Miles pulled out a folded piece of paper from under the pile. I watched him as he unfolded it.

"I think I know what that gun is for, and I'm pretty sure you won't like it," he said and turned the paper around so I could have a look.

Assignment: Search, destroy, retrieve.
Danger Warning: Before you start your assignment apply safety measures to protect your body.
1) Find female host Wolf and male host Echo.
2) Eliminate hosts Wolf and Echo.
→ Preferred method of elimination: shot at the head, either through the back or forehead.

3) Once the hosts are eliminated, use scanner to find the implant in each host's neck.

4) Make incision in the appropriate place.

5) Find implant and store it in the vial marked with the respective name. Do not get them mixed up.

6) Seal vial tight.

7) Discard host Wolf and Echo.

8) Before you leave the island, take off safety measures and dispose of them into the appropriate airtight box.

The further I read, the more the blood in my veins began to freeze. Not only was Ji here to kill us, he even had a manual telling him how to do it, like instructions for how to boot up a laptop or set up your smartphone. This was insane, but what was even more insane, and alarming at the same time, was the danger warning and the talk about implants.

"Did you notice the logo at the top?" Miles said.

I shook my head. I was too caught up with the instructions on how to kill us to notice anything else.

"It's the same logo, the same name, as the company in Berlin that we were supposed to work for   Briola Bio Tech."

"They put us here," I said as realization hit me. "Offering the internship was only a way to get fresh meat, wasn't it? Choosing the two of us based on some fucked-up criteria? To do what, experiment on us?"

"Wait, rewind…implants. What implants?" Miles asked, his voice shaded in by panic.

Instead of answering, I grabbed the gun thing and got up. Quickly I walked around and kneeled behind him, my hand on the back of his head to tip it forward and expose his neck.

"What are you doing?"

"The instructions were talking about an implant in our necks, right? I want to know if it's true, or if this is just another piece of bullshit they're trying to sell us like the plane."

My hands lightly trembled, and I pleaded to any higher power I could think of that it was all just a farce, that maybe, somehow, we were trapped in some psychological experiment, that I wouldn't find anything. I knew the chances probably weren't high, but I still hoped. I clicked the gun on and pulled down Miles's collar, exposing the entire expanse of his neck.

It seemed like it was all we did, run and run and run some more. But no matter where we ran or hid, they always found us. I'd been so sure that this was a place they wouldn't ever think of, especially in a city this big, but I'd been wrong.

Why did I have to be wrong?

I sucked in a sharp breath and then cursed as I watched his skin turn translucent the way mine had. And just in the middle of it all I could see this implant the instructions talked about. I didn't know much about human anatomy

and the human skeleton, but I was a hundred percent
certain that a pill-sized thing didn't naturally belong in
a human neck.

"What is it?" Miles asked, his voice now clearly alarmed.
I couldn't blame him.

"I found it," I said, my eyes still glued to what I was
seeing. Somehow I willed myself to turn the gun back off,
to stop looking. Closing my eyes, I leaned forward until
my forehead rested against his shoulder blade and moved
my hand that previously held his head onto his neck, his
skin warm against my fingers. "You should check mine."

I didn't want to know if that implant was really there,
the mere idea making my skin crawl with the force of a
thousand spiders, but we had to find out. We exchanged
places and I held my breath as Miles checked my neck. The
way he sucked in a breath, harsh and quick, was enough
for me to know that it was there.

"What are we going to do?"

"Cut mine out." He couldn't be serious, could he?
"Fiona, I'm not kidding. Get it out!"

"Are you insane?" I asked and turned around to look at
him. His expression was serious, but he had to be joking, right?

"We have to find out what they are, and that's the only
way to do it."

"I can't just cut open your neck," I argued.

"I can take it."

"That is so not the point." I couldn't believe him. Maybe
I was still asleep, was only dreaming that all of this was
happening. I hadn't minded punching Ji, but purposefully
hurting Miles, literally cutting his neck open, no way. "I
can't do that."

"Yes, yes you can," he said, his voice unwavering. "And you will. It's the only way, and I'm even volunteering to go first. I trust you."

"I can't hurt you."

"Even if I give you the permission to do it? See it as payback for all the times I hurt you," he offered, and in that moment, I wanted to punch him. It was a nice gesture of him, offering to be the one being cut, but that didn't change anything. It was insane, and I had no idea how to do something like that.

"It's going to hurt, a lot," I said, my voice so much fainter than his.

"If you could take someone cutting away your skin, I'm sure I can take this."

"This isn't some kind of contest to see which of us is more hardcore than the other, Miles."

At that he reached out and took my hand, squeezed it a little. There was the smallest of smiles on his face; his eyes looking into mine were clear and honest, not backing down. I didn't see any doubt in them, didn't see any indication that he was still thinking about this. His mind was made up, I realized. No matter what I said, he wouldn't change it.

Leaning in, I kissed him. This was the dumbest idea he could've had, but the fact that he volunteered to take the pain first, to let me literally cut him open, it said a lot about him, about just how much he trusted me. He kissed me back, deepened the kiss for just a moment, like a man drowning and desperate for air, before he pulled away.

"You're stalling," he teased with a small smirk.

"Busted."

I got up and fetched the med-kit, as well as the hunting knife I'd seen between the other things that had fallen out, and one of the pairs of rubber gloves. With all those things in hand, I moved behind Miles again, kneeled, and then opened the med-kit to see if what I needed was in there. Thankfully I found some bandages—probably too small, but they would have to do—and some antiseptic I could use to disinfect the knife as well as Miles's skin and then the cut later on to make sure nothing would get infected.

"Are you sure?" I asked after I checked the location of the implant again.

"Yes," he said without a moment of hesitation.

The blade broke skin, blood pearling around it, and he hissed very audibly. I tried to work as quickly as I could, while still being precise and effective to avoid having to redo it, hurt him only more. The implant was really close to the skin, so once the cut was done it was fairly easy to get it out. With bloody rubber fingers I dumped the implant in the labeled vial and handed it to Miles, trying my best to ignore how much his hand was trembling.

"Almost done," I said and wiped away the blood before disinfecting the area again and trying my best to put the bandages on.

"Wasn't so bad," Miles said and tried to sound like he meant it. I didn't believe him for a second, but the sight of the implant outside of his body was oddly reassuring. We had no idea what those implants did, but if Briola put them there, the same bastards that had placed us on the island to begin with, I was sure it was better to not run around with them. Even more so considering the safety warning that had come with the instructions.

Suddenly, just as I was about to tell Miles that it was my turn now, I heard loud rustling from somewhere in the jungle not too far from us. The bear—it had to be, the sound too harsh to be anything or anyone else. With everything that had happened, I'd completely forgotten about it, though now that I thought about it, we'd been exceptionally lucky that it had taken it so long to realize that we were just sitting there as though on a silver platter.

"The bear," I said and jumped up onto my feet, more than ready to bolt.

"What?" Miles asked, looking up at me. There was something off about his expression, like he was confused somehow. Was it possible that he simply didn't hear it? He hadn't lost any substantial amount of blood, but who knew how it affected him.

"The bear, I can hear it coming," I said, my voice sounding far more alarmed than I intended. "Come on, we need to go!" Just as I said it, the bear roared in the distance, the sound already too close for my liking. "Miles!"

Finally, he moved, stood up, and we threw the stuff back into the backpack. Taking my implant out would have to wait until we made it back to our cave. Now we had to go, and we had to do it quickly. Like this day hadn't been awful enough, of course the bear had to show itself as well.

We ran, fast, away, off in the opposite direction from where the roaring had come, the thunderous sound of the bear closing in. My heart raced, my breathing turning labored, my body exhausted from everything that happened, all the emotions it had to process, but still I ran, pushed my body to go farther and farther.

At some point Miles slowed down, and my mind immediately jumped into an even greater state of alert and panic. Was he not feeling well? Had the cut taken more out of him than he let on? What would we do if he couldn't continue?

"Fiona!" he called out from a few feet behind me. I hadn't even realized our distance had become this great, the sound of his voice only adding to my worry. It sounded too calm, maybe surprised, shocked somehow. I had no idea. None of it made sense. "Fiona, stop!"

To my surprise, I actually did.

I turned toward him, my heart beating practically in my ears, the need to run like a force within me, pushing, pulling. But I stood there and looked back at him. What was wrong?

"We need to go!" I repeated as the beast roared once more. I flinched, but he didn't. He didn't react at all to the sound.

"It's not real," he said.

"Have you completely lost your mind?" This was it. Miles had finally lost his mind for good. Maybe the pain had been too much after all, had robbed him of any kind of logical thinking somehow. I didn't know if it was possible, but something had to be wrong with him. "How can it not be real if I can hear it?"

"Believe me, it's not real!"

My eyes widened, and I took a step back as I noticed the bear between the trees off in the distance behind Miles, coming closer, racing toward us. "How can it not be real if I can fucking see it?"

"I swear it isn't real," he said calmly, and actually smiled.

What? How? This couldn't be, none of this. "I can't hear or see it. Trust me."

I took another step backward as I listened to him, tried to understand his words. He asked me to trust him, but how could I when I saw the bear behind him? How could he claim he didn't see or hear it? But wasn't this what we'd sworn, our rules, trusting each other and sticking together, that we'd be honest with each other. He'd told me so much about himself, as had I, and he hadn't given me any sort of reason to doubt him, doubt his words, but this, this just seemed insane in every sort of way.

The fear I had such complete control over before we'd woken up on the island overflowed, an unstoppable wave taking hold my entire body. I wanted to scream, to cry, to run, but my body felt frozen, paralyzed right in that place, my eyes switching between Miles and the bear. I could see it, its giant eyes and flared nose, its brown fur and clawed paws, open mouth and sharp teeth ready to rip me into pieces.

If Miles was wrong, the only thing I could hope for was that death would come quick and painless, as much as possible, at least.

The bear passed Miles, and he didn't take his eyes off of me, his hair didn't move, though it should have, considering the size of the bear and its speed. He just continued to look at me, unflinching, a smile on him, trustful and affectionate, the grandest display of belief in my own strength I'd ever seen on another person.

I could do this.

So I looked at the bear, watched as it came closer, grew bigger and bigger, got faster. I refused to flinch, to close my eyes, to make any kind of sound. Instead I just stood there, looked at it challengingly, ready to see what would happen.

The beast jumped, its claws out and teeth bared, but just as I expected its weight to throw me to the ground, for pain to break in on me, neither of those things happened. Instead the bear turned into smoke, swirls of black and gray surrounding me, slowly dissolving. The bear I'd seen a second ago disappeared right in front of my eyes.

This entire time, it hadn't been real.

CHAPTER TWENTY-NINE
THE ISLAND

"How?" I asked, perplexed, staring ahead of me where the bear had been just a moment ago before it turned into literal smoke and disappeared. I still couldn't wrap my head around it. The bear we'd feared this entire time, that had turned every trip into the jungle into literal hell, hadn't been real the entire time. How was that even possible?

"I think it could have something to do with the implants," he said, coming toward me. Of course. It was so obvious. "Once you took mine out, poof, the bear was gone. I saw the fear in your eyes, I knew it was approaching but nothing. The bear wasn't real."

I only blinked, swallowed the lump in my throat, tried to figure out something to say, but there was nothing. My mind turned blank. My body shook with adrenaline, with the emotional roller-coaster I'd just survived, and no words wanted to come. It had all happened so fast,

I couldn't keep up.

Miles closed the distance between us and pulled me into a hug, his arms around me, his warmth enveloping me. He was real, at least. I could feel and smell him, a reassuring fact. For a moment I'd thought that maybe he would turn out to just be smoke as well, even though I'd touched him many times, so I knew he was real. Slowly I relaxed, the tension easing away. I wrapped my arms around him, pulled him closer, and just breathed.

"You trusted me," Miles said, quietly. "And you looked fear in the eye, showed how strong you are. I knew you could do it."

"I thought about you," I admitted. "What you said."

"That's cute."

"I want that implant out," I said instead of commenting. I was semi-sure I was calm enough to do something besides hold on to him, that I could face whatever would come next, whatever those damn implants stood for. If they were really what had made the bear happen, I wanted it out, just to be sure it wouldn't appear again somehow.

We took a moment to look for a small clearing, a patch with a bit more light so Miles could better see what he was doing. While he unpacked the things he'd need, I put my hair up into a bun so he could access my neck and braced myself for what was about to happen. It would suck, a lot, but it would be worth it.

"Ready?" Miles asked and placed a kiss on the junction of my right shoulder and neck. A shiver ran down my spine, and I could practically feel him smiling for just a moment against my skin.

"As ready as I'll ever be." I took a deep breath, let my

eyes fall shut.

It wasn't as bad as I anticipated it would be, not much worse than my tattoo had been, most of my ring fights, or most of the dumb stuff I'd done with my friends. It wasn't pleasant in any kind of way, but it wasn't something painful enough that I wouldn't be able to take it. Instead of thinking about the pain I tried to focus on my breathing, calm in and out, and tried to block out everything else.

"Done," Miles announced far quicker than I thought. I raised my hand to my neck, felt the bandage that covered the cut, and felt comforted. Realistically, I didn't feel any different than I had before, but knowing that this foreign object was gone from my body still tricked me into feeling like something had changed somehow. It was almost like a shade of freedom, even though we were still just as trapped on the island as before.

I helped Miles pack away the med-kit and knife in the backpack. Who would've thought that something like this would ever be something we'd have to do, take implants out of each other's bodies, spill our blood because of some company that decided they wanted to have a little fun, put us on an island and see what would happen. I hoped they were fucking entertained enough.

"What do you think these are for?" Miles asked while holding his implant between his thumb and pointer. "Besides inducing the beast, that is."

"My first guess would be that it's a tracker," I said while looking at mine. They weren't much bigger than those pills with small beads inside of them, but I guessed they were still big enough to have some kind of tech in them. "Maybe the others had those implants, too, and that's how

Briola found the camp in the jungle."

"Sounds like a possibility, yeah. Trackers come in all sorts of sizes." The outer layer of the capsule was dark, which made it basically impossible to see if there was anything inside. "I think the best way to go about this would be to simply open one and check."

While Miles fiddled around with the capsule and tried to figure out how to open it, if there even was a way to do it, I inspected the outside of mine a little further. The surface was completely smooth, and there didn't appear to be any markings or words. Except—

"Wait!" I suddenly said and raised my hand at him. He immediately stopped, and the capsule almost fell from his hand.

"What?"

"Changed my mind, don't think opening them is a good idea," I said and looked closer at the four signs embossed on one end of my capsule.

"Why?"

I leaned over and showed him. They were tiny, barely visible, and just readable enough for me to decipher what they said. Immediately he looked at his, looked for the signs and found them a moment later in almost the exact same place. "Do you know what it means?" he asked.

I nodded. "These four signs are *hànzì*, Chinese characters for biohazard."

"If these things have a biohazard warning on them, and the instructions Ji had with him had a danger warning, what the fuck is in them and why were they implanted into our necks?" Miles asked.

These were the crucial questions: what was in these

implants? "Maybe it's some kind of virus? I mean, they do tests with new diseases or mutated ones all the time in places of this world no one seems to care about, so why not take us as lab rats?"

It was such a bizarre thought. I'd seen myself as many things across my life, but I'd never thought I'd end up in a place like this. I knew that sometimes people volunteered for human trials of new medication in exchange for money, but this, us on the island, it was something entirely different. There had to be something we didn't see, or maybe there wasn't, and we were simply screwed.

The latter seemed way too likely.

"Maybe." Miles looked away. "Or maybe, if there really is a virus involved, we took them out before the virus, or whatever it is, could spread and hook itself into every inch of us."

I wanted to believe his words, wanted to make myself believe that maybe we were not as good as dead just yet, that there was a chance for us to survive all this, but the grim reality was that we would probably die out here.

"Either way, we should put them into those vials just to be sure," I said and reached into the backpack. Seeing the label with my name on it took my breath away even the second time around, showed the gravity of this entire thing only more.

After we put the implants away, we packed our things and slowly made our way back toward the cliff. It was only a question of time until the sun set and it would likely start raining again. We had to get back to the cave before our way down would be too dangerous.

"As crazy as all of this is, I'm strangely intrigued by the

whole bear aspect," Miles said, his words catching me by surprise. "I don't know about you, but I've never heard of any kind of implants or pills or whatever that would cause that realistic of a hallucination."

"I'm not a drug person—I mean my father would kill me if I'd even get close to any—but I'm sure some of them could cause something like this. You hear it in the news sometimes, someone having so intense a drug trip that they thought they were being chased by something or had an imaginary friend telling them what to do."

"Maybe, but I don't think those trips work quite like this. And also, if it were so, what would be the chances of us seeing the exact same thing at the same time?"

"Basically none." That was another thing I couldn't understand. I could buy into the idea of the implants containing some kind of drugs, but us experiencing the same things at the same time, that seemed impossible. Yet it had happened somehow.

"So maybe it is some kind of really freaky virus type of thing that's causing vivid hallucinations, both visual and auditory, after all."

"What if these also had something to do with the fact that I can remember the moment we crashed, yet we know that didn't actually happen. If they could conjure up the bear, maybe they could also fake that memory?" I'd never heard of any kind of virus or technology or anything that would be able to do something like that. Faking memories—it sounded like some kind of freaky futuristic idea scientists loved to theorize and Hollywood made movies about, but could it happen in real life? "Is something like that even possible?"

This wasn't the Matrix, wasn't some kind of VR simulation we were involuntarily participating in—the graphics would be way too good for it to be true—it was real life, or some truly, strangely morphed version of real life.

"Before this I would've said no, but now…" He shrugged, but then something washed over his face, some kind of idea or realization maybe. "Speaking of which, if the crash didn't happen, and the memory really was fake, why did I feel so awful after we woke up?"

"Maybe it was some kind of side effect, your body struggling to adjust to the implant and virus while mine was okay. Maybe it's also why we were fine with the food we found, the relatively small amount of it, and how we were never *that* hungry or thirsty." Even as I said it, it sounded absurd, the entire thing did. "Also, remember your notebook and the key card? What was that about? Did the implant make you sleepwalk and write that entry yourself or something?

"At this point I wouldn't put it past Briola's abilities."

"Or, who knows, maybe we were in Berlin, but they erased our memory of it, replaced it with the crash?"

"I don't think so," he said and shook his head. "When I tried to get the computer board to work, I was on my laptop and I looked at the date. It was the day after we took off in Miami, so how would we take a trip to Berlin in that short a time?"

"Like they wouldn't be smart enough to simply set the date back on your laptop."

"It's password protected."

"So is our school's system and your father's bank account, and you didn't seem to have issues with getting past those," I pointed out. "So, if you can do that, I'm sure a bio tech company can crack your password with ease."

"Touché," he said and huffed a little laugh. "I've always liked watching documentaries about crazy cases and conspiracies like this, but I never actually wanted to be part of one."

"Ditto. But, I think there is one overarching thing in all of this that's even more important than the implants, what they do, and how they work," I finally said as a weight settled onto my shoulders, one I'd been aware of for a while but had tried my best to ignore.

"Being?"

"This wasn't all just some kind of accident. They know our names, our ages. Everything that happened, the bear, the helicopter flying Ji in, the instructions, the damn implants, it's all been done deliberately, following some kind of plan. What kind of bullshit is this, seriously? Why would Briola do any of this, and what is this for?"

Even as I spoke, the thoughts arranging themselves in my mind accordingly, I could barely comprehend the things I said. We'd known something was off the moment Miles said the plane wasn't real, but this was so much bigger than I ever dared consider. Before us, Briola had four other people here, killed them, then they took us, implanted us with whatever, and hired someone to come and kill us as well. They were the force steering this entire thing, the one that chose us, a force we stood no chance against.

"That means it was them who killed our pilot, no?" Miles said with a sigh. "And we never found the flight attendant...what was her name—"

"Stephany?"

"Yes. We never found her, either, so she was probably in on the entire thing."

"I knew something about this entire thing was off when I arrived at the airport, and even more when she led us to that damn private jet. That didn't make any sense to me from the start. Guess it's easier to take us from a jet than a commercial plane under the watchful eyes of like six hundred other passengers."

All of it had been planned, painstakingly so. Every time we'd felt like we had the upper hand, it'd all just been fake safety. We'd never been in control of anything since we landed on the island, since we got onto that plane, maybe even before that. Who knew how big and far reaching this was.

"If they've gone this far, is there anything that'll stop them from going even further, finding a way to kill us despite Ji failing to do so?"

"Looking at the other four, chances are none at all."

It was as though a giant rock sat on my chest, squeezed the air out of my lungs, squished my heart hard enough that every beat seemed to hurt, take more effort than it should. We'd fought so hard to stay alive, to figure out what was happening, and now we had, but it was nothing like what I expected it would be.

"This is so much worse than I thought or imagined," Miles continued. "Every possible escape or outcome I can think of just leads to a dead end or the two of us dead. Who knows, maybe those implants had some virus in them after all, and that shit will end us, or Briola will do it, or, I don't know, they'll just leave us here and we'll die sooner or later."

It was such a tempting little thing, reaching out and taking the cold hand that hopelessness was holding out toward us, toward me. It would've been so easy to give in to this void slowly opening up before us, dive into the darkness and get swallowed by nothingness, fall into this state of "nothing matters anymore and no matter what we do it's all useless anyway." But just because it was easy, because it was so tempting, did that mean it was the right thing to do? Was the easy solution always, ever, the right one?

The other solution was much harder; believing and holding on to it seemed as impossible as climbing Mount Everest without any expertise and equipment, but just because it was hard, did it mean it wasn't worth a try? Just because my opponents had won whatever competition bouts came before me, seemed like the favorites for the titles, had it ever meant I shouldn't try?

No.

I always tried, wanted to stand my ground, wanted to prove that I could do it regardless of how unlikely it seemed. And so many times I'd managed to succeed—I'd won State even though my opponent had stood unbeaten for two years in a row, was seemingly stronger and better than me. Yet, I'd taken that title from her. Coming from nothing and aiming for everything had been basically my entire life, working toward something I knew I could do if I tried hard enough, if I followed my father's training regimen and believed in my own abilities.

So, if I could do all that, why shouldn't the two of us be able to do this, survive somehow?

"If you believe you might lose," I said, recalling my father's words, "it will happen. You'll psyche yourself out. If we give in to this idea, this thought that we are screwed and stand no chance, the same will happen. We can't do that."

"What are you suggesting we do instead?" Miles asked.

"The next time they show up—and I'm sure they will, since we're still very much alive—I suggest we show them they've chosen the wrong teens to fuck with."

CHAPTER THIRTY
THE ISLAND

The next morning, we decided to go back into the jungle to see if maybe there was something in the area where Ji landed that we hadn't noticed yesterday.

I wasn't quite sure how I felt about going there again, about getting close to Ji's dead body even after Miles had moved him, but I knew it was a good idea. Maybe there was something we'd missed that would help us, maybe something that fell from his pocket or had fallen out of the helicopter along with him. I didn't know what I hoped we'd find—no, that was a lie. I hoped we'd maybe find another radio or whatever to try to contact the outside world. Actually, I hoped we'd find anything at all.

Even though I'd seen the beast vanish, I still slipped back into listening to the jungle around us, still somehow expected to hear it roar in the distance, rush toward us. But it never happened. It hadn't been real, not even for a second. It was still hard to just accept that, to walk around the jungle without a bit of worry on my mind, without my body on high alert, ready to bolt.

We'd been on the island for nine days, yet every time I was still surprised by how much easier it seemed to navigate the area. There were no street signs, no paths, nothing really there to help us, yet somehow I recognized certain things, could find places we'd been to previously. I never thought I'd be able to do it in real life, despite being able to do it with ease in video games. Maybe those had been helpful in a way.

"This is where the bear chased us yesterday, no?" Miles asked, pulling me out of my thoughts. I looked around and I remembered those trees; one of them had the strangest crooked branch I'd seen in the jungle so far, so it had to be the right one.

"There should be traces here—of the bear, I mean, if it were real," I said, my eyes cast toward the ground as I took a few steps.

"But there's nothing."

We looked around for a while, walked along the way where I was pretty sure I'd seen the bear come through, but, just as Miles said, there was nothing at all. No claw marks, no broken branches, no footprints in the dirt. Absolutely nothing.

"How didn't we notice this before?" I wondered.

"We didn't have a reason to." Miles shrugged. "Also, we were too freaked out to even consider it, or at least I was."

"To be honest I'm still freaked out."

It wasn't the same freaked out as before. Now that the bear was gone, what I truly feared and was freaked out by were the forces that stood behind all of this, the power they held, and the fact that this was their island. I tried to fight against this fear for so long, but after what happened yesterday, I wanted to allow myself to feel it at least a little. Maybe it was useful somehow; maybe I needed to feel fear to be brave? Also, who knew if Briola had any other surprises hidden on the island, which honestly seemed like a good enough argument to me to feel some degree of fear.

"At least now we have a gun, so we're not as defenseless as they hoped we'd be," Miles said, a cocky smile on his face, and took my hand.

"Because we're both such good shooters, hmm?" I pointed out. "And if you tell me you actually know how to handle a gun because your father took you hunting or to a shooting range or something, I'll smack your gorgeous, rich face."

"Well, thank you," Miles said, clearly trying not to laugh, and squeezed my hand. "As much as my father is a firm believer in the value of expensive steaks and meats, he isn't into hunting. And even if he were, he'd never take me along, not that I would've wanted him to."

It took us another couple of minutes to find our way back to Ji's landing site, his parachute still tangled in the branches of some trees, the strings dangling from it like thin vines, a few broken off branches littering the ground beneath it. I pointedly avoided looking toward the bushes where I knew Miles had hidden Ji's body. Instead, we split off and searched the area in a wide circle. But no matter how well I looked, how many times I walked across the same patches of dirt and searched through the clusters of bushes and tall grass nearby, I didn't find anything at all.

"Nothing," Miles said, to which I just nodded. "What

a waste of time."

"At least we know for sure," I offered. "We can say we tried everything."

"I guess so."

I'd always done a good enough job at not getting my hopes up, but this time I failed, could see that both our moods took a plunge after this. We'd figured out so much, but we were still in the same place we were before we knew all of it, still didn't have a way to get away, to contact the outside world. All we had was the knowledge of who was using us but no idea how to stop them or escape from them.

Since the weather was better than it had been yesterday, the storm having turned out not nearly as bad as we expected it to be, we decided to stop and eat. Maybe given enough time we'd come up with something. We had to.

We'd found a clearing somewhere halfway between our cliff and Ji's spot. It wasn't much, just a few feet by a few feet of tree-free space covered by grass and moss, soft and nice enough for us to sit on. Thanks to Ji's hunting knife, we could cut the mangos we'd found on the way into neat slices, much nicer than anything we'd managed to do with what we had before.

At some point Miles reached for our backpack and, to my surprise, pulled out his notebook. "I didn't even realize you brought that along," I said and watched him flip through it.

"I don't know, I thought we could look at the entry again, look through the whole thing," he said with a shrug. "Maybe I missed something the first time around, maybe there is something else in there, some kind of clue, perhaps."

"Can I?" I nodded toward it. I doubted he'd let me look through it, hand over something as valuable and personal as that, but asking never hurt anyone. Without saying anything, he actually handed it to me, a tiny, almost shy smile on his lips.

Carefully I opened it to the first page, which didn't have much on it besides *Property of Miles E. B. Echo* written in his neat handwriting in the middle of it. "What does E. B. stand for?"

"Edward Bahir. I can understand why they chose the Arabic one, since my father is three quarters Lebanese and all, but my mother wasn't British. She was French." He shrugged.

"Miles Edward Bahir Echo," I said marveling over how it all rolled off my tongue. I couldn't get over the gorgeous smile that spread across his face as I did. He leaned in for a quick kiss.

Even though I would've gladly spent the next hour just making out, I forced my attention back to the notebook in my lap. I flipped through the pages, all of them almost entirely covered in his handwriting, some passages crossed out, others circled in or marked with big exclamation marks. Only a handful of pages had dates on them, mostly from anywhere between last week and two years ago. As much as I wanted to, I didn't stop to properly read any of them, just a sentence or two at most. From what I could gather he wrote about everything and anything, some passages going on about some teacher, others about soccer practice, his friends, some parties, rants about bad songs or albums, relatively mundane things.

None of it stood out. None of it was connected to our situation, nothing besides the Berlin entry.

But then my eyes landed on a passage, just a few lines, written in a different handwriting with a purple glitter gel pen that stood out amid the sea of royal blue and black. The first few words were written in Cyrillic, and just below the entry itself were two initials, N. I.

"Natasha Ivanova?" I asked. She was the only Russian girl I could remember ever having been in our class. Miles nodded, his expression turning ever so slightly sad. "What does it say, the Russian part, I mean?"

"Каждый кузнец своего счастья—every person is the blacksmith of their own destiny, or happiness, however you prefer," he said, his pronunciation of the actual Russian sounding butchered even to me, and I didn't speak the language. "She wrote that like three weeks before her suicide. I'd told her about how I was worried I could never live up to what people thought and expected of me, that I had no idea what I really wanted to do with my life, so she took my notebook and wrote that. Unlike you, she didn't ask."

It'd been so long since I even last thought about Natasha. I'd never been friends with her, and we only shared one class across two years, but I remembered the day the news of her death made all the local papers—she did belong to one of the wealthiest families in our town, her mother the owner of some European luxury car dealership and her father some business mogul—and reached our school. My heart felt heavy thinking back to it. I'd seen her brother a few days before we left, and he still looked just as awful as he did months ago, not that I was surprised. How do you even recover from something like that?

On the other hand, I heard that their younger sister, Anastasia, won another medal at some competition. She probably already had more of them than I did and would possibly ever get, depending on how the entire island situation would end.

"Well, her words still apply," I said, trying to sound positive. "We might be royally fucked, but we can still try our best to not end up dead. To remain in control of our own destiny."

"Considering we've made it this far, I'd say we're doing a mighty fine job of that."

In the end, the notebook turned out to be just another dead end. It held no answers for us, just that single entry that we couldn't explain, and that held no clues at all. It'd been worth a try, and if I was honest with myself, I'd known it wouldn't really be able to help us even before I asked for permission to look through it. What had I expected, that someone wrote down the answers to all our problems on the last few pages and magically we'd know how to get home? It wouldn't be that easy, but I knew we were strong enough to somehow get through this.

Putting the notebook aside, I leaned over to Miles and kissed him.

We stayed in that clearing for a while, tried to forget everything that happened around us for just a little while, forget that we were in danger and trapped on an island. It was just the two of us in that moment, in that clearing, and nothing else mattered. Not our past, our future, our current reality.

Over time, our kisses turned more passionate, feverish, desperate almost, like we were running out of time but still wanted to cherish every second somehow. I'd never expected this trip to lead us here, for us to realize that we did like each other and could have a chance with the other. It was as though my body melted to his touch, my hands trembling ever so slightly as I caressed the bare expanses of his skin across his arms, shoulders, and chest, warm and smooth, flawless almost, a contrast so impossible to mine. His gentleness almost stole my breath, his fingers lightly tracing all my scars, his kisses seeming to show his awe at each and every one of them, of what I'd done to get where I was, to accomplish the things I had.

It wasn't anything like I expected this would go, not that I'd ever spent much time dwelling upon it in general, yet no setting I'd ever envisioned was quite like this. On an island in the middle of nowhere surrounded by an unexplored jungle, just the two of us and no one else. At least the one reassuring fact was that there was no one there to tell us not to, or to catch us, or walk in on the entire thing. We could do as we pleased, take our time and not worry about anything at all besides each other.

It was a beautiful moment, and if I could've, I might have chosen that one to live in forever, hold on to it for as long as I could.

"Fiona, I think I might be losing my mind, but I swear I can see a ship on the horizon," Miles said after we'd emerged from the jungle sometime later. We were about a mile away from where the beach and the cliffs met, but we could see out to the ocean far and clear.

"What?" I asked, surprised, looking at him and then the horizon.

He raised his arm and pointed toward where he thought

the ship was. I tried to find it but I could only see the open ocean in its entire turquoise glory and the rocks farther out in the water. But then I saw it, a white and gray speck floating atop the water, rising and sinking on the incoming waves. Immediately panic shot through me, even more as I noticed a black ship, a smaller one, departing from the white one and moving toward the island. A sinking feeling took over my body and mind.

"Miles, you're not losing your mind. I see it, too."

CHAPTER THIRTY-ONE
THE ISLAND

I turned my head toward him. Our eyes met, mirroring each other's expressions with a mix of panic, horror, and hope, though I was trying to squash the hope because there was no hope on this island. "Do you think this is the boat Ji mentioned? The people he was supposed to meet after getting rid of us?"

"I'm pretty sure they gave up on Ji the second he killed that radio of his or whatever."

"Maybe, but what if they didn't and that's them?"

"What are we supposed to do?" he asked instead of answering my question.

"We can't go back into our cave. They might see us climb down, and then we'll be easy prey."

Miles looked at me again and, just at that moment, I saw his expression change. Fear turned into determination, hate, and bravery. He reached into our backpack and pulled out Ji's shiny black gun. I didn't even notice that he'd taken it along.

"You said we can't make it easy for them, that we can't just give up, that we need to fight," he began while looking down at the gun in his hands, mesmerized. "Now is our chance to show them they decided to take the wrong pair of teens."

I looked into his eyes. He really wanted to fight. He didn't want to hide any more, and neither did I.

"Let's hunt those who want to hunt us," I said, determined, and cracked the fingers of my right balled up fist. I was born a fighter, and I was determined to die a fighter.

We left our things and then slipped into the jungle, deep enough so they wouldn't see us but we could still check where they were, check how much time was left until they landed on our island. The birds were singing loudly, their songs happy and cheerful. I almost felt the need to punch at least one to make them stop. This wasn't the right time for cheerful chirping, but rather for battle music, heavy drums and music filled with anger.

As the black ship came closer, I realized it wasn't a proper ship but more of a small boat the size of a lifeboat or something, though I still didn't know how many were inside. It looked like they planned on landing at our beach near our burned-out plane, not more than two miles away from us if I had to guess. Led by fury and adrenaline, we dove farther into the jungle, past trees and vines, jumping over bushes and dips in the ground.

Only a couple of minutes later, we were close to the beach. We watched as a single man dressed all in black pulled his boat onto the shore. A plan formed in my mind.

I didn't know if he was one of the bad guys, one of the people Ji mentioned, or maybe part of the rescue party we'd hoped for so long. All I knew was that we couldn't risk it. Treating him as part of the bad guys was easier, a defense against hope, and also a way to be prepared for a fight instead of thinking he was a good guy and potentially getting killed by letting our guards down. Just from looking at him, there was no indicator of anything, nothing that could've told us if he was good or bad, but we'd been through that with Ji before.

"We have to split up," I whispered toward Miles.

"Why? What are you thinking?" Miles asked without taking his eyes off of our maybe killer.

"You distract him, and I'll knock him down so we can force him to tell us everything. Before reinforcements from the bigger ship can reach the beach, he might tell us why we're here, why *us*, and what might have been in those implants."

"Good plan," he agreed and pulled out the gun again. He hesitated for a brief moment before he looked up from the gun in his hand to my eyes. "See you on the other side."

Quickly Miles leaned in for a kiss, nothing but the faintest brush of his lips against mine before he turned around and walked off.

My heart was still beating all over the place while the feeling of his lips on mine still lingered. I shook my head to clear my mind, willing my feet to move. There was a reason why we were here, why we had a plan, needed to act. I remembered my assignment and the man on the beach still occupied with his boat.

Miles emerged from the jungle and onto the beach

with the gun raised in front of him, pointing it at the stranger. He seemed oblivious until Miles was close and said something to him. The stranger's head whipped around. A moment later he raised his hands while Miles kept the gun pointed at him from a few feet away.

Now it was my turn.

After taking a deep breath, calming and centering myself, I broke into a run like a bullet racing toward its target. The world around me blurred; only the stranger was clear and focused, sharp like the edge of a knife. I wanted to roar a mighty battle cry.

Just as I reached him, I kicked the back of his knees. His legs gave in, and I jumped on his back. Together we went down like a toppled tower.

"Surprise, asshole," I said, my mouth close to the stranger's ear.

I grabbed his arms and twisted them up on his back, and then, after I got up, I turned him around to look into the eyes of the man who came to kill us. But just as he landed on his back, his face toward me, eyes looking straight into mine, my heart stopped, and my stomach dropped.

"Joe?"

CHAPTER THIRTY-TWO
THE ISLAND

After saying his name, I was rendered completely speechless. It couldn't be Joe, there was no way. But as I stared into his eyes, their color so brown they almost seemed black, there was no doubting it. It was his face, the laugh lines around his eyes and wrinkles around his mouth and across his forehead like maps giving away his age, his skin only a few shades lighter than his eyes. His bald head he once told me he'd inherited from his father, who'd also lost his hair at a very young age, and the same small scar I'd seen on his jaw so many times while I watched him play chess, which he claimed was a battle scar from a cat that simply didn't like him.

It was him. Joe the homeless man, Joe who shouldn't be here.

How the fuck did he fit into all of this? What was he doing here? No matter how I thought about it, I couldn't understand the situation. Part of me yelled, *He's a traitor!*

He's part of this! But the other refused to believe it. Confusion mixed with anger inside my blood, my mind buzzing, my thoughts racing, but none of them giving me any answers.

I staggered back a few steps, wanting to put a little bit of space between Joe and me. In a blink of an eye Miles walked over to me. He put one arm around my waist and held my arm with the other like he wanted to steady me, feared I might faint or something. Who knew, maybe I would because this moment felt like overkill, like too much for my mind to process.

"He can't be here," I whispered more to myself than anyone else.

"You know him?" Miles asked, his voice low, his mouth close to my ear. I leaned into him a little more, though my eyes never left Joe. He slowly sat up and then just looked back at us.

"He's a homeless guy I know from back home. I sometimes gave him my books, and we played chess." I closed my eyes to hold back another wave of emotion.

"My name is Joseph Carver," he said suddenly. The name, the dark, raspy voice that made him sound like a smoker even though he wasn't one, all of it fit. "And I'm not actually homeless, I just pretended to be to keep an eye on you."

"That's called stalking and is illegal," Miles said drily.

"Why are you here? And how? Who are you really if you're not the man I thought you were?" I asked, my voice shaky, making me feel embarrassed. My father would give me an earful for sounding and behaving so weak.

"I am not your enemy, Fiona. I'm not here to harm

either of you, I swear." I wanted to believe him so badly, but how was I supposed to do that if everything I'd known about him apparently was just lies? "I used to work for the FBI." Nonsense. "I worked as an agent for over two decades, to be exact. I met my wife there, we got married and had a daughter called Ivy. But then my wife passed away, and it was only the two of us, until Ivy disappeared."

Joe an FBI agent? A father who lost his daughter? *Right, sure, cool story, bro.* But was it possibly true? Was he telling the truth this time, for the first time, or was it just another trick? As fake as the bear? I watched his eyes as he spoke and noticed that there was a subtle shakiness in his voice as his daughter came up. Maybe he was telling the truth. I feared believing him and regretting it the moment he shot Miles and me.

"After Ivy disappeared, I tried everything to find her," Joe said. "I tried to get my boss and my coworkers to help me. I was going insane, made mistakes at work. I was a mess but how could I not have been one? It wasn't like my dog ran away and I could just get over it. It was my daughter for fuck's sake, but they didn't care."

There was hurt in his voice, the hurt of a man who'd lost everything.

"Finally, one day, my boss called me into his office, and I was sure he would tell me he'd help me, but instead he told me to pack my things because I was fired," Joe said with a heavy sigh. "At first I didn't know what to do, until I woke up one morning and decided to continue looking for her on my own. I hadn't been an agent for so many years for nothing, hadn't acquired skills and contacts for nothing. I couldn't rely on official channels anymore, but there are always ways to bypass the system."

"And that's how you found Fiona?" Miles asked.

"I got a hold on different documents and communications from unknown sources that indicated that two American teenagers were supposed to be taken under false pretenses and flown out of the country," Joe said. "At first, I didn't know which teenagers, since no names were mentioned in any of the documents, but then I found some more. I followed paths and found a few more details, though most of it was coded and restricted, impossible to crack, though I tried everything I could. It talked about a boy and a girl, who both would be age seventeen when everything happened. I found the boy's initials, M.E., and then I found the girl's initials, F.W., and part of a picture. There was no way in hell I could find out what name M.E. stood for, so I went with the picture, and soon enough, there you were, Fiona."

I felt sicker the longer I listened to him. Everything we feared about Briola having chosen us, having placed us in their little game against our will, it was all true. Even though we'd known that already, hearing it all again from another person, being told the size of this entire operation, the secrecy around it, it made it seem so much heavier, so much realer.

"You okay?" Miles asked quietly, almost in a whisper. I didn't notice how much I was leaning on him. I blinked and tried to straighten up a bit, lean on him less, but it was harder than I wanted to admit.

Pull yourself together, coward!

I couldn't show how much of an effect Joe's words had on me. *Your enemy can use your moments of weakness against you.* For years I learned how to appear strong and composed even during moments of weakness and fear, and I had to do just that right now once more.

I took a deep breath and stood up straight again, let go of Miles's arm and crossed mine in front of my chest.

"One day you finally mentioned the school trip to Berlin," Joe continued, "mentioned the company name, and that's when I knew that I'd definitely found the right girl. I'd worried that I'd been wrong all along, even though all details pointed to you, so once I knew it was definitely you, I had to do something."

"Guess that didn't work out too well, since she still ended up here," Miles said, his tone tainted by anger. He didn't argue both our fates, just mine, as though I was the only one who mattered. Like he hadn't been screwed over just as badly.

"The bracelet I gave you, and the book," Joe said, ignoring Miles's remark. Just as he mentioned it, I looked down at my wrist where the bracelet still rested. I'd never taken it off, and the book was buried among my things inside our cave. "Both have tiny trackers built into them that can send GPS signals. They connected themselves to an antenna somewhere on the island, and that's how I knew you were here."

"So, to recap, you're a former FBI agent whose daughter disappeared so he stalked a teenage girl whom he knew would be abducted, along with another teen, and you decided to wait until she was gone to actually do something about it?" I said, the story sounding impossibly absurd as I said it. "Let's pretend for a second that you're telling the truth—"

"I *am* telling you the truth."

"Why did you care if I was the girl? Why do you care if I'm alive? Why did any of this matter to you? You didn't know me, and we're not related in any way."

"I know this sounds crazy, but I cared. Still do," Joe said, slowly moving in an attempt to get up. In the corner of my eye, I saw Miles tense up in response.

"Why?"

"Because I think the same thing that happened to the two of you might have happened to my daughter." His words were heavy, loaded with emotions, and laced with infinite pain.

There was no way in hell he could be a good enough actor to deliver those words in such a manner, say them in a way that almost felt like a knife cutting across my skin. He was telling us the truth, I was sure of it. His words didn't sound rehearsed, didn't seem scripted, but like those of a man who lost everything and was just trying to make it up to his daughter, and surely his wife.

"We found four dead bodies on this island," I said. Something at the pit of my stomach told me that he'd been right, that just like Miles and me, Ivy had been on this island, but unlike the two of us, she hadn't survived. "One of them was a girl with a heart necklace with an 'I' on it."

Something broke in his eyes at my words. Whatever lies he might be telling, his pain was real.

"Can you take me to them?"

CHAPTER THIRTY-THREE
THE ISLAND

We made Joe walk in front of us as we slipped through the jungle toward the pit of death. No one spoke, though Miles took my hand. I wanted to ask him what he thought of the entire thing, what he thought of Joe and the story he told us, but the time wasn't right yet.

We stood watching as Joe crossed the last steps toward the pit. He fell to his knees and began to sob. My heart ached for him. That wasn't acting, it wasn't a show put on to trick us. His entire body shook while I felt cold. I'd seen the piece of hope in his eyes, the piece that hoped the dead girl wasn't his daughter, that hoped she was still out there somewhere, alive and well. But that piece died like a flame, leaving behind nothing but pitch-black empty space.

"We should talk," Miles whispered, and I nodded.

I turned around to look at Joe once more. He was still sobbing. His grieving would probably take a while.

Miles led me away, not far so we could still see Joe,

but enough that he wouldn't be able to hear us. My mind was running haywire with everything Joe said.

"What are you thinking?" I asked.

"I don't know if I believe him," he said and leaned against a tree. Every once in a while, he looked toward Joe as though to make sure he was still there. I did the same. "I mean, that whole FBI story and the way he found you seems a bit dubious, doesn't it?"

"It does sound pretty crazy," I admitted. "But then again, it wasn't any crazier than the story of us being dumped on an island with a fake plane, bear hallucinations, a pit filled with dead teens, and a helicopter dropping off a killer."

"Still, I don't know. Something about him is weird. Why didn't his boss want to help him after his daughter disappeared if he worked for the FBI? I don't know. I'm not sure if I trust this guy."

"He's not lying. At least not about this. They murdered his daughter." I looked at the figure hunched over next to the pit. "I mean, you heard him wailing. Do you really think he'd be that good?"

"He did manage to convince you that he's homeless."

"It can't be hard to pretend that, easy to find some shitty clothes and sit on a bench every few weeks or so. But giving a performance like this... I really don't think he's making this up."

Miles looked at me and then at Joe. I could see the gears spinning in his mind.

"What if you're wrong?" he finally asked, turning his head back toward me, his eyes meeting mine.

"Let's just hope I'm not," I said, not my strongest of answers, but it was all I had. I'd already been involved in the death of one man, even if it was an accident and self-defense, and I refused to be responsible for another. I couldn't break my father's rule.

"After he allowed for you to end up here, you're willing to believe him?"

"He also didn't stop them from taking you," I reminded him. This wasn't just about me. I wasn't the only one that mattered. He did, too. "Besides, even if he's lying, even if he's not on our side, we need to get off this island. More than that, we need answers."

I sent a collective prayer to anyone I could think of, even some superheroes just to be sure, pleading for me not to be wrong. I had to be right because if I wasn't, the stakes were too high against us. I hated this, all of it, but there was no escaping it, no way of postponing any of this. This wasn't some school assignment I could talk myself out of.

I raised my hands toward Miles's face, put them lightly against his cheeks and looked him in the eyes. "Do you trust me?"

His words coming out of my mouth.

He put his hands on my waist and pulled me a little closer. "You'll lead, I'll follow. Besides, we need answers."

Joe stood a few feet away from the pit as we returned. He'd stopped sobbing and shaking. He tried to smile, but it was really some sort of strangled grimace.

"What have you decided? Do you believe me?" he asked.

Please don't let me be wrong.

"Yes," I said.

I really hoped I wouldn't have to kill him.

"It seems like I've been right all along. The people that took you also took my daughter," Joe said, half to us and half to himself. "I have no idea why they did it or who they are, but they are responsible for this."

I wanted to say "It's okay," because that was the reflex answer engrained in us, but it wasn't okay. None of this was, would never be.

Miles asked the most important question of all: "So, what now?"

"I have a satellite phone in my backpack in my boat on the beach," Joe said, and I felt my heart drop. A phone? A working phone? Why had I been so dumb and asked him to leave that backpack? "I have a friend who still works at the FBI. We made a deal that if I'm right about this, if I manage to find you, that friend will help me get you back home."

I turned my head to look at Miles, my mouth hanging open in shock. A light, unsure smile tugged up one corner of his mouth, and his eyes were wide.

"Then what are we waiting for? Let's go!" Freedom was so close.

Miles held my hand as we walked back to the beach, a small smile on his face. If Joe would get us off the island it would be a miracle, a real-life wonder.

"Since I never managed to find an answer, what does M.E. stand for?" Joe asked Miles with a genuine smile. He actually seemed curious. Maybe he was the man I knew after all, at least parts of him.

"Miles Echo."

He nodded in understanding. "It's good to finally meet

you, and to see that the both of you are okay," Joe said. He seemed to hold up pretty well. Maybe a part of him had always known that Ivy was dead, maybe he was happy he found us before the same could happen. We didn't mean as much as Ivy, but maybe our lives still mattered to him. He used to be an FBI agent, after all.

"As okay as can be."

"Right. I can't imagine what you two have been through."

I squeezed Miles's hand lightly and smiled. This was good, this would be good, it simply had to be. The world had to be on our side for once, after everything we'd been through.

But just as we walked onto the beach, Joe cursed. It didn't take me too long to see the reason why. The ship, the bigger one, was gone.

"And what will we do now?" Miles asked while I still felt unable to.

"We still have my boat; we can take that and try making it to the mainland. Kenya isn't too far away," Joe said while scratching his jaw. "I should've known that paid people cannot be trusted."

"Meaning what?" I asked. Also…Kenya?

"Meaning that the men I hired to get me here were simple people, a bunch of fishermen I met at the port," he explained. "When we disappeared into the jungle, they must've thought they could leave."

"Fantastic," I said, sarcastically.

Joe took a deep breath and then sighed. "Okay, how about this," he said. "I'll call my friend, then you can go and get whatever you want to take with you, and after that, we'll leave. The weather is clear, and the ocean seems fine, so we should be okay."

That didn't sound too reassuring, the fact that we *should* be fine, but it was light-years better than "we will die here, and everything sucks."

"Fine," I said, and nodded.

Joe nodded back and then walked over to his boat, fetched his backpack, and finally pulled his black satellite phone out of it.

Miles and I sat down in the sand while we watched and listened to Joe call the person.

Joe said, "I found them. They're alive. They're okay." After a pause, he said, "Yeah. My daughter, too." Another pause. "No."

"Speakerphone," I said. "Now."

Joe glanced at us, then pressed a button that turned on the speakerphone.

"Okay, listen," the person on the other side of the line was saying. Whoever they were, their voice was distorted to a point where I couldn't even make out if it was a woman or a guy talking. "Bring them to these coordinates. We can't afford to come to the island. Not when the others could be watching."

"I don't have enough fuel to get that far out," Joe said. "What do you want us to do? Paddle?"

"If you want to get back, then yes," the other person said, "you'll paddle."

Joe confirmed we would meet at those coordinates, then hung up and turned to us. "Get your things."

Miles and I exchanged a look.

It was more than we could've ever hoped for.

Good or bad, we were finally leaving the island.

CHAPTER THIRTY-FOUR
GONE

Armed with our backpack filled with the few things we wanted to take with us off of the island—our gun, a few pieces of clothing, Miles's laptop and notebook, our phones, and even the implants in their vials—and a change of clothes and water, we helped Joe push the boat off of the beach and into the water.

It felt almost odd to wear something more normal, something that was more me than everything I wore on the island. Sure, half-wet jeans were annoying, but wearing them still felt amazing. Seeing Miles in pants that weren't ruined by my mediocre cutting skills and a shirt that wasn't white or completely worn out was interesting, too.

Joe was right; the ocean was fine while we sailed toward the horizon. Whoever those people were, they definitely went through a lot of hassle to get us onto that island, that much was clear.

The sun began to set, the sky changing color from

clear blue to flaming red and orange with streaks of pink and violet. I wasn't too sure about the idea of being out on the open ocean in a boat at night, but I wasn't about to complain. The fact that we were on a boat at all was already the event of the year for me.

Before the island disappeared, I looked back at it one last time, told it just how much I wouldn't miss it in my mind, and then flipped it off because I could. There was no place on earth that I hated more than that island.

"Can you believe this?" Miles asked, his voice relatively quiet, though still loud enough so I could hear it over the sound of the engine. "We actually left the island."

"We did, didn't we?" I said and smiled at him. I still couldn't believe it. "One step closer to being home."

"It'll be weird to not have you around twenty-four-seven." Considering our history, both the recent and old one, it still seemed so impossible. Me from before the trip would've never believed me if I told her this would happen, ever.

And there was a bigger problem. We'd turned to each other on the island because we had no one else. But if we were off the island? If we were back in the real world? Would Miles really choose me?

"Don't look forward to getting away from me too much," I said and winked at him, hoping it showed the confidence I wanted to feel. Fake it till you make it.

I'd never been out in the ocean before, never been on a cruise ship or anything like that, so it was an interesting feeling to do it now, especially in a relatively small boat like this, the three of us taking up most of the space. The thought of just how deep the water beneath us was made me a bit queasy. Even though I could swim perfectly fine, I had no idea what kind of sea creatures could be roaming the deep water below us.

"Hey, Joe, I have a question," Miles said a while later, moving a little closer toward him.

"What is it?" Joe asked without taking his eyes off of the horizon.

"You said you were tracking Fiona via that GPS thing, right?" Joe nodded. "Were we ever in Berlin before the island?"

We'd theorized that maybe we'd been there and Briola simply erased our memories, but I wasn't sure if I wanted Joe to say yes, to confirm what we thought. Then again, if he said no, that wouldn't make any more sense, either, would still leave the entry and hotel key card a mystery we had no inkling how to solve.

"No," Joe said. "After the airport there was a break, and then you popped up across the map over on the island in the middle of the ocean. No other locations between that."

Even though it was the answer I honestly expected, it still left so many unanswered questions. If we'd never really been in Berlin, where did the key card and the diary entry come from? Did someone else write it, imitating Miles's handwriting well enough that even he believed it was his? And what was the purpose of it? What did Briola hope to achieve with that? Confuse us? If so, they'd certainly managed to do that just fine.

As Joe had said, we ran out of fuel shortly after the sun went down. So we switched to paddling, Joe on one side, and me and Miles taking turns on the other. The boat was much slower than cruising with the engine on full speed, but at least we were moving. It was tiring as hell, but after everything I much preferred this to being stuck on the island.

Joe's giant flashlight held up pretty well as our only means to see what was ahead of us, though there really wasn't much to see besides an endless stretch of water and more water. Thankfully Joe had his satellite phone and its navigation feature to guide us. Without it, I had no idea how we would've blindly managed to get anywhere besides lost.

But then, suddenly, there was something to see, a light quite a distance ahead of us, barely moving. At first I was convinced it was merely a star or the moonlight reflecting off of the waves, but the light was steady and soon joined by a second one.

"Is that a ship up ahead?" I asked Joe and Miles, hoping I wasn't seeing things that weren't actually there.

"Possibly," Joe said. "This is much closer than the coordinates my contact gave me."

If movies have taught me anything, either that ship would shoot us on sight, kidnap one of us, or actually be what Joe said it might. We'd come this far, so getting shot now would be way too ironic.

To our surprise, the two lights moved toward us after a while, like they noticed us coming in their direction and decided to make the process a bit quicker. The ship was much larger than our little boat. It looked like a fishing boat, though a relatively new one, similar to the ones I'd seen in some documentary Melany's dad claimed we needed to watch.

Someone on board turned on a bigger spotlight and

directed it right at us. I raised my arm and tried to shield my eyes from the blindingly bright light. After our journey through the relative darkness, that spotlight almost felt like looking directly into the sun.

"Carver?" someone from the ship called out, a deep male voice. It took me a moment to realize that it wasn't some foreign word I didn't know but simply Joe's last name. Were these his people after all?

"Lido?" Joe called back with a smile on his face while Miles and I exchanged a look.

"It's them," the voice called out to someone we couldn't see, his voice sounding friendly and almost a tiny bit cheerful. A moment later the spotlight was turned off while an array of much less aggressive lights was turned on aboard. Two people, a man and a woman, stood next to each other and waved us toward something a few feet away from them, a metal ladder, as it turned out.

What devil rode me to go first was beyond me, but if this really was Joe's people, which it very much seemed like it was, there was no reason for me to be afraid.

The metal was cool against my hands, my arms and legs tired and barely able to heave me up, but I slowly climbed higher and higher. The man—Lido?—lent me a hand as I climbed over the railing. He was a big guy, definitely taller than Miles, with bulky muscles, a shaved head and dark eyes, his clothes all black, a button-up shirt with the sleeves rolled up to his elbows and slacks. He seemed at least a decade or more older than us.

The woman, on the other hand, had barely shoulder-length hair of a plain, dull shade of blond, silver-framed glasses rested on her nose, and her eyes were a deep shade of blue and her lips thin. A few wrinkles in the form of laugh lines marked her face, but she looked rather young, despite the fact that she was probably around the same age as Joe. Her clothes mirrored Lido's, though hers were light gray and black instead of only black. All in all, she seemed small—her frame petite, though with a touch of chubbiness—was forgettable and plain, not quite what I imaged an FBI agent to look like.

"Thanks," I said, looking up at Lido. I didn't really want to take my eyes off of them, but I still turned around and watched Miles climb up.

Just like he'd done with me, Lido helped Miles come on board while the woman instructed Joe how to securely attach our boat to the ship. I didn't listen much, though I did look down toward Joe every once in a while to make sure he was still there.

"It's going to be okay," I said to Miles, quietly, stepping a little closer to him. He looked tense, nervous maybe, and I wasn't surprised. I was nervous, too. I didn't know what to think or what to expect. The thought that this was possibly the end of our struggle, our rescue party, was almost too good to be true.

"Come on in then, no need to stand outside," Lido said and waved us toward the door leading inside. Quietly, though exchanging a few brief words with Joe that I couldn't hear, they led us into something that looked like a living room with two sofas and a table surrounded by chairs standing on the other end of the room. There was a small TV secured to the wall opposite the sofas and a simple lamp hung from the ceiling. It'd been so long since I'd last seen a sofa.

"So, you are Fiona Wolf and Miles Echo?" Lido asked once we sat down on the sofas.

"Yes," I said, unsure what to expect.

Lido and the woman reached into the pockets of their slacks, and I instinctively flinched. Whatever I expected them to pull out, it wasn't what I assumed were their FBI badges. That hadn't occurred to me, not even for a second. No matter how much I wanted to relax, to welcome the idea of everything being finally truly okay, our experience with Ji still made me wary.

"I'm Special Agent James Lido, and that's Special Agent Nikita McCarty," Lido said while both of them held their open badges out toward us.

Reluctantly I looked a little closer at them. I'd never seen such badges before, so it wasn't like I'd be able to differentiate between a fake and a real one. Both had their names, pictures, signatures, and everything on them. They seemed legit, my body and mind relaxing a little at that realization. Besides, Joe knew these people, so if Joe could trust them, why shouldn't we?

"I know we agreed to meet you farther out, but we couldn't take the chance you wouldn't make it that far," McCarty explained. "We're overjoyed to have found you alive and well. You were very lucky, and I cannot even imagine how horrible it must've been to go through everything you did." She didn't even know the half of it, though telling them about exactly what we saw, the bodies and everything, was the last thing I wanted to do now.

But as I listened to McCarty, I couldn't shake the feeling that she somehow felt familiar, like maybe I'd seen her before or something, but no matter how much

I tried to figure it out, I couldn't pinpoint when or where. Then again, maybe my tired mind was just playing tricks on me. Maybe I was just so suspicious of everything and everyone that I was starting to actually be paranoid. But McCarty seemed nice, her voice friendly and welcoming somehow.

"Thank you," I finally said. Despite it all I was grateful to be off the island, to be this much closer to getting home, to have survived that entire mess.

"Who's the captain?" Joe asked a moment later.

"He should be here in a moment," Lido said. "Very friendly guy, joined the mission the second we asked for someone who was in the area and could handle a boat."

As though on cue, the door opened and two people, a man and a woman, came inside. The man was tall, at least Miles's height or maybe even taller, with shoulder-length black hair. His eyes were an oddly familiar shade of brown. He wore the same black clothes as Lido, though he definitely lacked his bulky frame, despite being muscular as well. The woman was slender and tall, her hair up in a neat platinum-blond bun, her clothes a crisp white shirt and gray slacks.

"You must be the ones we've been looking for," the man said. "This is Gail Ford, my assistant, and I am Leon Echo, your captain."

CHAPTER THIRTY-FIVE
GONE

What the actual fuck?

Leon Echo, Miles's older brother, was dead.

I turned to Miles. The color visibly drained from his face. His eyes grew a little bigger, and his mouth was slightly open. I couldn't even fathom what was going on inside his head, what he was thinking and feeling.

Looking back at the man claiming to be Leon, I couldn't get past their resemblance. I knew he looked familiar even before he spoke, but now all the details screamed at me, flashing in bright colors. Their eyes had a similar shape, their color nearly identical, and their stance and frame were so alike although Leon was more muscular. His hair was also longer, but it was the same mess, the same obsidian shade. Despite their age gap, one could clearly see that they were related.

"Leon," Miles finally said. His tone almost broke my heart in two. The little boy inside of him, the one that lost his brother, was torn between believing and doubting, happiness and shock. It was written across his eyes, his face, and tainted his voice. "Is it really you?"

I caught the confused expression on Joe's face in the corner of my eye. If I knew how, I would've charades-style mimed him the piece of information he was missing, but I couldn't and didn't. Besides, how do you explain "this is my boyfriend's dead brother"?

Hold on, *boyfriend*? Where had *that* thought come from?

Focusing on Leon, I watched his face, the way the easy smile faltered and he looked confused by Miles's reaction and question. He blinked then looked over toward Gail, who ever so subtly mouthed something, a word or phrase I couldn't read, before turning back toward Miles. As though a coin had dropped in his mind, Leon's smile grew, and he said: "Brother?"

This entire scene hadn't taken more than four seconds, if even, and looking at Miles's smile I was sure he hadn't picked up on any of it, but I sure as hell had. Was it really possible that Leon hadn't recognized him, that he needed some kind of cue from Gail to know how to react? No, that couldn't be, could it? Sure, Miles wasn't the kid he was when they'd last seen each other, but they looked so alike, there was no way for him to not realize it. It was bizarre, and suspicious.

Miles got up and walked over to him while I had to stop myself from grabbing his arm and holding him back. As much as I wanted Miles to be happy, this seemed too good. A missing brother back from the grave? How was this even possible? Had the army lied to Miles and his father?

"It's so good to see you again," Leon said, sounding almost genuine. While they spoke, Lido, McCarty, and Gail walked over to the side of the room, watching everything from a distance. While I still couldn't figure McCarty out, I somehow really didn't like the vibes I was getting from Gail. She hadn't really done anything, hadn't even said a word, yet something about her rubbed me the wrong way.

"Leon is Miles's brother?" Joe asked me quietly, leaning toward me.

"Miles's *dead* older brother."

"Really? Doesn't look dead to me."

He certainly wasn't dead, but how? If I tried hard enough, I could come up with some farfetched and impossible explanation for what happened to us on the island, but there was no way to revive a human who died during war. Dead was dead. I didn't like any of it, the entire scene seeming wrong. If they knew who we were because of Joe, that meant Leon must've seen or at least heard Miles's name. It would've made him realize their connection sooner, even if only because of their shared last name, yet it hadn't, or at least it seemed that way, I so didn't look forward to sharing my thoughts with Miles.

I shifted my gaze to McCarty, Gail, and Lido, who had sat down at the table.

"How is it possible that McCarty seems familiar to me?" I finally asked Joe, using the moment we still had to talk just between the two of us.

"You've seen her before. You must have," Joe said, sounding as though my question was strange and his answer pointing out the obvious. "She's been around when I pretended to be homeless, came by to visit or just watched from afar."

Before I could say anything to that, or ask further questions, Miles returned to the sofa and I pushed the whole McCarty thing aside. I moved back to Miles, watched his face and eyes. Happiness and shock was written across them, his hands lightly trembling. Carefully I reached out and took one of them into mine, a gesture I hoped would maybe calm him down or something.

Miles looked at me briefly, an almost insecure smile on his face, while I squeezed his hand. He ran his thumb across my skin as Leon began to speak, telling us the story of what happened to him all those years ago. Above all, the story of how he didn't actually die.

"It's the craziest story, and far too long to explain it all in detail," he said, his tone reminiscent but also maybe just a tad too light considering the subject matter. "Basically, I was on a mission with my troop, was supposed to support them from afar via hacked CCTV cameras, that sort of thing. But our cover was blown, and I got taken hostage, found myself in the middle of some kind of plot we had no idea about. Finally, they told me I had two choices: either do as they said and live or be the reason my entire family died. It wasn't until almost a year later, when the FBI rescued me and took me in, that I even found out what happened, that they made my troop and family believe I was dead. I wanted to contact you, Miles, let you know I was okay, I really did, but I couldn't. The FBI didn't know if my former captors would try to get some kind of revenge for their rescuing me, so I had to remain hidden and dead."

The three of us listened attentively, but the further Leon got with his story, the less I believed any of it. Everything he said, it sounded straight-up like he'd watched one too many action movies and tried to sell us a mashup plot as true story. And even if there was just the smallest amount of truth to it, would sending one tiny message really make that big of a difference, cause that much danger? If Leon taught Miles how to hack, I was sure he could've figured out how to send Miles an encrypted message to spare him living for years with the thought that his brother died for our country. I so badly wanted for Leon's words to be true, just like Joe's, but I just couldn't believe them.

Leon spoke completely freely, naturally, and there was happiness in his voice each time he pointed out how grateful he was that he finally found Miles again, that Miles finally knew what happened, and that he was okay, but that happiness felt like acid on my skin. It was too good, too wonderful to be true.

Once Leon was done with his story, he asked us how we managed to get by on the island, what happened while we were there. Miles kept it brief, which I was thankful for, only giving them the bullet-point version of the past days, leaving out certain details like the implants and the Berlin notebook entry. I could see McCarty cover her mouth with her hand in shock at the whole dead teens part and Lido lightly shake his head. Leon's eyes widened just a tad. Whatever they thought we'd gone through, the real events had been much worse. I'd probably see all those corpses in my nightmares until I died.

"It's such a lucky coincidence that I took this job, but the most important thing is that everything is okay now, that you two are safe and don't have to worry about anything anymore. Trust me," Leon said, smiling. "Fate has funny ways sometimes, doesn't it?"

Coincidence and fate, my ass.

After everything that happened to Miles and me, I didn't believe in coincidences anymore, didn't believe in fate's funny ways. Something about Leon and Gail smelled fishy ten miles against the wind, his strange behavior and now this crazy hostage story. I refused to believe any of his words, my guts screaming in protest. I so badly wanted to believe it for Miles, wanted to give him this happiness, wanted nothing more for him than to have his brother back, the one he loved and missed so much over the years, but I just couldn't do it. I wanted to protect him, and everything about Leon told me I had to be cautious, wary of his every move, every word he spoke.

I couldn't lose Miles, not after everything.

"Please, make yourself at home," Leon said, standing up. "A room with enough space for all three of you to catch some sleep is ready just down the hallway. If you need anything, just let one of us know and we'll get you whatever it is." With those words, and another over the top friendly and happy smile, Leon turned and left with Gail on his heels.

While Joe stayed behind to talk to Lido and McCarty, Miles and I found our way to our room. All the way there, and even inside as we sat down together on the lower bunk of one of the two bunk beds, I tried to figure out how to start the discussion we had to have. I tried to form sentences in my mind, tried to figure out how to voice my worries to Miles, but I was afraid of it, afraid he might think I wanted to stand between him and his brother. I didn't care about Leon; I cared about Miles.

I knew all those people, these agents, were here to help us, save us from whatever fate had waited for us on the island, all thanks to Joe, but somehow it just didn't feel right. Maybe I was paranoid, my level of suspicion bordering on sheer ungratefulness, but I simply wanted us to be okay, to make it out of this alive. I was afraid of accepting all of this at face value just to wake up at some point and realize that I'd made a mistake that would get us killed after all. Could anyone blame me for it?

"I can't believe this," Miles said, more to himself than to me. "Leon is alive. And he is here, oh my God."

My heart ached at his words, and I hated myself for feeling so differently about his brother than he did. But he was too shocked by the revelation and too emotionally invested to see through the fog, realize that it was all just smoke and mirrors. I hated this.

"Miles," I said, my voice almost shaking. "We need to talk."

He turned toward me, looked into my eyes, and it made all of this only so much worse. "What is it?"

How do you tell someone you think their brother is a liar without making them hate you? "I know this is amazing. Leon is alive, it's wonderful, and I know it makes you happy, but...I just, I don't know, Miles." Why was this so hard? Why did my tongue suddenly feel ten sizes too big?

"What are you saying?"

I forced the words out of my mouth. "Something about Leon seems off is what I'm saying."

"What? Are you kidding me?" There it was, everything I feared—a defensive stance and this look he gave me like

I'd done something wrong. He moved a bit away from me, barely noticeable yet it felt like a chasm opened up between us. "All these people and Leon are here because of us. Come on, he is my brother."

"Your brother who you thought was *dead* for years."

"But he isn't dead. Don't you see how amazing that is? Leon was alive the whole time," Miles argued. Leon was the light, and Miles the moth drawn to it. I stood between them, powerless to stop Miles from getting burned. "Listen. I'm not saying it doesn't raise questions. We'll keep our eyes open, okay?"

"And what if that isn't enough? He didn't even try to find a way to contact you, consciously deciding to just let you suffer. If he did this once, what makes you think he wouldn't do it again? How can you act like it's all forgiven and forgotten?"

Even as I spoke, I knew my words would never be enough. His expression became more guarded than I'd seen it in days. I just couldn't understand him, his unwillingness to even consider my arguments and doubts. He just wanted his brother so badly that he was willing to buy into the game.

I could sit there next to him and watch, wait, and hope that nothing would happen, that he'd be right and I wrong, or I could try and find out what was really happening here.

I'd never been known for being too patient.

CHAPTER THIRTY-SIX
GONE

Once Miles fell asleep, I listened to his steady breathing, making sure he really was sleeping. Part of me just wanted to let it go, accept Leon's words and look past his behavior, accept that this was our rescue party and that everything was okay, that we were safe, but a far stronger part knew I couldn't. Ji seemed fine at first, too, but in the end, he was just a killer, so who could say Leon wasn't the same? What if this was what they counted on, Miles blindly believing him and getting me to do it, too, hoping that I wouldn't question anything, too happy to be off the island, and would trust Miles's opinion? Then again, what if I was just being paranoid, if Miles really was right, if Leon's words were true?

Footsteps came down the hallway, the sound of thick rubber soles against metal echoing through the quiet, and finally halted just outside our door. I closed my eyes and pretended to be asleep, forced my breathing to slow down, to seem calm and quiet as the door softly opened. The seconds seemed to stretch into hours, days, millions of years, until it closed again. Whoever that was, they definitely had been sent to check on us. I had no idea what that meant, but I sure as hell would find out.

While the steps turned quieter, retreating down the hallway, I slid out of bed and out of the room. The idea of being caught terrified me, but I pushed the thought and the fear aside the way I'd been taught.

I walked down the hallway like a ghost, listening to the sounds around me. My footsteps were quiet and light on the dark metal flooring, a skill acquired through years of training. Just ahead of me, I saw what I could only assume was Lido's tall, bulky frame, taking the next hallway right and walking like a man on a mission. *What are you doing, Agent Lido?*

Finally he came to a halt, opened a door, and went inside, the door slowly closing behind him. In a split-second decision, I rushed toward it and stopped it before it could close. I could only hope that he wouldn't walk back to check, that he didn't even notice that the door was still ajar, just enough for me to peek inside.

Leon and Gail stood together in what looked like the captain's bridge of the ship, the windows in front of them overlooking the front of the ship and the ocean stretching out around us toward the horizon, the space below them lined with what looked like control panels and the steering wheel. At least Joe was nowhere to be seen, and McCarty stood a few steps away from them, looking down at some table in front of her.

"And?" Leon asked, his voice different from the one

he'd used with us before, more controlled and stoic. *And what, Leon?* I leaned against the wall with my ear as close to the door as could be while I listened to their conversation, feeling colder and colder the longer I did.

"Everything is going as planned," Lido said. "The cargo is sleeping, unaware of anything."

"You were very convincing," Gail said, amused, and lightly clapped someone on the back. "Then again, I had no doubt in you."

"Once we get there, we'll be able to return them to their owner, fulfill our assignment just as planned."

"Very good," Leon said, his tone a disgusting shade of pleased. "And here I thought it'd be harder. Well, they are just kids after all, and Miles seems just as gullible as the papers make him out to be. A shame, really, for him at least. Good for us, though. They're willing to believe anything to get home." Leon's words almost made me gag, his voice like the sound of nails against a blackboard. He was a traitor after all; all of them were. Miles was wrong, and I was right. We were nothing besides cargo, part of an assignment. And whatever feelings Leon faked toward Miles, they were just that, illusions and lies.

Horrified, I stood there, my heart slamming against my rib cage, my mind suddenly blank. What was I supposed to do now? Miles wouldn't believe me. *I* didn't even want to believe me. Cargo, they called us. Not even people, just objects that needed to be returned to their rightful owner.

Who did they even think they were that they could talk about us like this, treat us like we were nothing and no one? And how was it possible that Leon took a minute to even recognize Miles in the first place, then was so happy to see him, and now he talked about him like he didn't give two cents about him and was more than aware of who the both of us were, especially Miles? Why was he basing his assessment of Miles's behavior on some kind of paperwork instead of his own memories? How did any of this fit together?

Just as I started to back away, slowly and quietly, an arm grabbed me around my waist and a hand covered my mouth to keep me from screaming. Panicked, I wanted to break free, at the same time feeling terrified that I'd been caught and everything that could mean.

"It's me," a familiar voice whispered barely audibly next to my ear. *Miles*. Immediately I stopped fighting while he let me go. He'd followed me, but did he hear what Leon and the others had said, too?

Slowly we retreated back to our room, me closing the door behind us quietly to avoid anyone coming to check on us. The last thing we needed was for the agents to grow suspicious of us the way we were of them. Who knew, maybe they'd lock us away in our room under false pretenses or something.

"It's your brother."

"I heard," Miles said, his tone sad, with a shade of disappointment mixed into it. He'd been right, keeping our eyes open made the difference, though surely not the way Miles had hoped, or even I. "I really thought…" He sighed heavily. "But after what you said, I couldn't stop thinking about it, wondering if maybe you were right." I stepped closer to him and pulled him into a hug like it would allow me to share some of his pain, take some of it and make this easier for him, though I knew that it was impossible. "Whoever he might be, this isn't my brother, at least not the one I remember."

"I'm so sorry."

"It's fine…well, it's not, actually, but it doesn't matter," he said and pulled away just enough that he could look at me. "If Leon is lying, if we are just an assignment, what are we supposed to do now? Can we still trust Joe if he knows these people?"

There was something in the way he looked at me, his eyes seemingly searching mine like he hoped I'd be able to lead us, and that I knew what I was doing. I knew I could trust my intuition, but could I get us out of this mess alive? I certainly would try my best, but would that be enough?

"Joe is okay, I really do trust him, plus he wasn't there. According to what he told us, he didn't come here with Leon and the others, and only McCarty is his friend," I said trying to sort through all the thoughts racing through my mind. "She didn't say anything, just stood there off to the side and listened, so maybe she's okay as well?"

Enemy, friend, ally, liar, why had the lines turned so damn blurry?

"Our time is limited," I said, my mind racing. "We have no idea where we are headed or how long until we get there. We needed to find Joe, tell him what we heard, and make a plan to get the hell off this ship as soon as possible."

After a bit of looking around, we finally found Joe on deck, leaning against the railing, looking out on the water. There wasn't much to see besides darkness, stars, and the moon reflecting off the waves, though it was surprisingly loud. The latter was definitely a useful fact, since it would drown out our voices, lowering as much as possible the chances of anyone overhearing us.

"Everything okay?" Joe asked as we approached him, his brows drawn together.

"We are royally fucked, so no, nothing's okay," I said.

"What happened?"

"Leon happened, and the others. This entire thing is all lies, nothing but an act, even possibly that friend of yours." I took a deep breath, trying to steady my voice. "I heard Leon talking with Gail, McCarty, and Lido. This is all part of an assignment and not a rescue party, at least, not the way we would like it to be."

"Are you sure?" Joe asked. He didn't sound surprised or shocked, at least, not as much as I expected him to. Maybe he had the same worries as me but didn't let it show.

"They called us cargo, not even humans. Delivered to an *owner* like we're dogs that ran away," I said, my hands balling into fists. "We need to get off this ship as soon as possible, before they figure out we know something or get us wherever they are supposed to deliver us to."

"I see," Joe said and lightly nodded. "Okay. The two of you should go back to your room so they won't get suspicious, get your things, and in an hour, we'll meet here again, yes?"

"And what will you do?" Miles asked.

"I will watch, maybe go in and talk to them, act natural. Maybe I'll overhear more, something that could help. Who knows, maybe you heard something out of context and everything isn't as bad as it seems, just a misunderstanding."

"Don't try me," I warned. How dare he claim something like that? I knew what I had heard!

"And if what you heard is true, we'll get out of here using one of the safety rafts of the ship. I have enough old contacts that I'm sure we'll manage to get back to safety. I said I was going to help you, and I intend on keeping my word."

"I think he's right," Miles said while I stared at Joe. "He used to be an agent. He knows what he's doing, don't you think?"

I didn't say anything, just sighed. As much as I would've liked to do something, be active, act, a part of me knew that both of them were right. Joe creeping around was far less suspicious than the two of us, since we were the targets, not him.

Without further discussion, Miles and I retreated back inside. I rounded the corner into the hallway that led to our room, but a retreating figure caught my eye. Grabbing Miles's arm, I stopped dead in my tracks, him coming to a halt next to me, eyes wide with surprise and confusion. I pulled him back around the corner and then whispered: "McCarty."

He nodded back at me and then turned his head like he was trying to listen more into the space around us. I did the same, listened to McCarty's quick steps disappearing farther into the ship. It'd been such a close call. Who knew what would've happened if we ran into her.

We waited until the hallways were quiet again and then rushed into our room. As I closed the door behind us, Miles fell back into his bunk. We had an hour to kill and

I already hated every minute of it. I itched to get off the ship. Following Miles's lead, I climbed into the top bunk, falling onto the unpleasant, stiff, and somewhat scratchy sheets. A weird sound caught my attention, something that sounded like crinkling paper.

Confused I sat up, looked back at my sheets but saw nothing. Curious, I grabbed the blanket and pulled it aside, checked if there was something hidden underneath it. Two pages lay there, now slightly wrinkled, the top one with my own mug shot looking back at me. Where the hell did they come from? A gasp escaped me as I took the entire thing in, at first convinced that maybe somehow it was just my eyes and mind playing a trick on me, another one of Briola's dirty tricks. But as I reached out and grabbed the pages, they were really there.

"Are you okay?" Miles asked, his voice lightly confused or maybe concerned, I wasn't sure.

"No." It was all I managed to say before I slid off of my bed and jumped back down, my eyes meeting Miles's a second later. I had no idea what those pages were, my fear almost too great to look at them closer.

"What's that?"

"I don't know," I said, honestly. Reluctantly I handed him the second page, the one with his picture on it. My hand trembled, my heart beating harder, faster. I tried to swallow the lump that suddenly formed in my throat but couldn't seem to do it.

"Shit," Miles said.

Willing myself to raise my hand, to look down on the page, I read what was written on it. The top held the Briola Bio Tech logo, just like had been on Ji's instructions, and below it on the left was my picture, the same one as on my ID and passport. Next to it on the right was my basic information like my name, date and place of birth, address, height and eye color, even my blood type.

My hand trembled even more when I reached the last few lines on the page, which came before what seemed to be like a basic description of my personality and behavior:

Father: Anthony Wolf
Mother: Allesia Mayson
Contact person and seller: Carla Wolf
Value: two million dollars (SOLD)

What the actual fuck?

"Fiona?" I heard Miles ask but found myself unable to react in any way. I hadn't even realized that I started to cry until the words in front of me blurred too much for me to read them, until wet patches formed on the paper, my eyes stinging.

Contact person and seller: Carla Wolf

Lies, it had to be, but there it was clearly, the name of a woman I'd never heard of listed as my mother. And the woman I thought was my mother. The woman I'd thought I could trust above all others. She was listed as the seller.

This was it, the final nail to the coffin. Everything until now I could deal with, but this? This was it, the one thing that crossed the line so far that I wasn't sure if I could ever recover. I felt like something within me was this close to shattering, the pieces scattering everywhere, disappearing out of sight.

"Fiona, talk to me."

"Look at this," was all I managed to say, my voice strangled and unsteady.

I handed him my paper, let it go as quickly as I could, as though it were poisonous. It might as well have been. In the same motion, he handed me his, though I wasn't sure if he did it so I could read it or just hold it. Against my better judgment, I still looked at it, my eyes scanning the page down to the same lines that had me in tears, the words blurry but just readable enough.

Father: Minsar Echo
Mother: Victoire Elise Echo (DECEASED)
Brother: Leon James Saqr Echo
Contact person and seller: Minsar Echo
Value: one million three hundred and fifty thousand dollars (SOLD)

Miles's information wasn't any better than mine—the fact that his own father had sold him to this madness—but somehow the only thing I felt inside of me was pain and hurt. Not only had my mother sold me, on top of that, she wasn't even my mother. I couldn't believe it.

"You're worth more than me," Miles said, his voice sounding as though he was trying to somehow find something amusing about this, even though nothing was. "See, I told you, you are worth more than you give yourself credit for."

"This isn't funny," I said, new tears blurring my vision once again. My words seemed to have their intended effect because a moment later he pulled me into a tight hug, holding me as I cried.

The one person I thought I could rely on, who loved me unconditionally, turned out to be a fraud, nothing but an actress pretending to love me, cherish me, just so she could give me away for money. Two million dollars, no wonder. Who would say no to having that instead of a daughter that wasn't even yours.

Every time she told me she loved me, was happy to have me, was that nothing but bullshit? Did I really not mean anything to the woman that pretended to be my mother? It hurt so bad I felt as though someone had set my insides on fire and thrown my body into a pit of broken glass.

"No, it's not funny; you're right," he agreed. "What is all of this about if we were worth just that much money. And why?"

"I can't believe she would do something like this to me," I said instead of answering or even thinking about his question. "I don't even know who she is."

"Who?"

"My mother or Carla or whoever the hell she is." Another wave of tears overcame me, my throat closing, and my body shaking.

"You didn't know," Miles said, a statement and not a question.

"I don't know who this Allesia person is. I've never heard of her. Carla is the only mother I've ever known, but now? All these years, all those lies."

Miles pulled me even closer, his arms enveloping my body perfectly, and in that moment all I wanted was to just melt into him so I wouldn't have to think about any of this for a second longer. Briola wasn't only about to take away my future, but now they'd even taken my past, my family.

"All these years she took care of me, loved me and helped me through all my problems, and all of it for what? So she could cash in two million at the end? Why would anyone do something like this? And your father! He lost one son and decided to sell away the other? How could they do something like this?"

"I'm so sorry you had to find out about your mom like this," he said and lightly kissed the side of my head. "I know how much it hurts to lose someone, though I won't even pretend I can imagine how much this must hurt. Usually I'd never say something like this, but damn, your mom is a bitch." I laughed, wet and mangled.

"I'm sorry your father is a dick."

"Believe me, I know." How was it possible that he was taking this so calmly, trying to be funny, consoling me when this wasn't just about me? His father had sold him off just as much as my mo — no, no, no, no — Carla did me. "But if anything, I'm surprised he didn't get Briola to come and get me sooner. Would've saved him a good sum of money."

"Why are you so calm?" I asked and leaned back enough to look up at him.

"Because I've always known that my father doesn't give a shit about me. Maybe this was why — because it wouldn't have made sense to care if Briola would take us anyway. Or maybe he already didn't care before that. He was a bastard before this, and he's an even bigger one now."

I wanted to cry even more. For me, for him, for everything he had to go through with losing his mother, his brother, and the way his father treated him. More tears pooled in my eyes, stung, and threatened to spill over.

Pull yourself together!

All of this was absolutely ludicrous, every single piece of this puzzle that somehow only grew bigger and more complex the more we found out, instead of getting smaller and clearer. This wasn't some kind of made-up dystopian alternate reality. It was the real world, where selling and buying teens was fucking illegal, but somehow Briola was getting away with it.

I couldn't fall apart now, even though I could feel myself standing right on the edge. It was such a tempting idea, to just fall apart and give up, let Briola do whatever the hell they wanted, but that was bullshit. We'd made it this far, had gotten off the island, were so close to making it, I couldn't give up now. Everything within me hurt, my heart bleeding and feeling like it was a second away from being ripped into hundreds of little pieces, but I knew I was stronger than this. I had to be.

Wasn't this what Briola wanted, to play with and break us, use us for their plans? They tried to do it with the plane, the bear, the implants, Ji attempting to kill us, that damn notebook entry, and even Miles's damn brother. They tried so hard, yet we were still here, still standing, breathing, so very much alive. I couldn't give them this, couldn't give them the satisfaction of having defeated us just like this. My entire life was nothing but lies. Carla nothing but a billion empty words and meaningless gestures, but despite that, it was in part thanks to her that I was who I was. She and my father had made me this way, made me strong, a fighter, a champion, a survivor. If that truly was why Briola wanted me, why my father trained me, why I was worth such an outrageous amount of money, the least I could do was prove that I was worth that money, right?

The fight isn't lost until it's over. We'd see who would have the last laugh if we'd just disappeared, no agents, no siblings, nothing.

"Let's get our things, meet Joe, and get out of here," I finally said and tried to pull away, but Miles held on to me, his eyes watching me like he wasn't sure what he thought about my words and sudden change of mood.

"Will you be okay?" he asked.

"Honestly? I don't know. But what I do know is that I will mourn my loss, will mourn the lie I lived, but now isn't the right time for it. Now we need to make sure that we get off this ship and survive."

"Okay." He nodded and then moved one of his arms away from my back and instead raised his hand to my face. Lightly he put his hand on my cheek, his thumb wiping away the stray tear that dared to escape my eye against my best efforts. "Despite all of this, everything your parents have done, I want you to remember that I'm still on your side. And maybe she lied whenever she told you she cared about you, but I truly do mean it."

Slowly, as though giving me time to decide if I wanted it or not, he leaned in and kissed me, and I kissed him back, melted against him. This wasn't anything passionate, wasn't the sort of big kiss that in movies would come with fireworks or some grand piece of music. No. It was the opposite, gentle and soft, slow and so genuine, the type of kiss that spoke a million words in complete silence, an admission and acceptance. Everything around us was falling apart by the minute, everything we once thought had turned into dust, but we still had each other.

"As much as that was a clear ten out of ten," I said once our kiss ended, "we really need to go."

"I know," he said, breathless, and I wished we could just stay in that moment for a little longer, ignore everything outside this room, ignore the papers, the agents, Briola, and everything else. But we couldn't.

It was time to go, and I truly couldn't wait to leave this ship behind.

We grabbed our backpack, stuffed our papers into it, and then peeked out into the hallway, listened for footsteps, but there were none. The air was clear, at least for now. As quietly as we could, we walked down the hallways and back onto the deck. I looked over my shoulder again and again, expecting one of them to appear just around the corner, to see us with our things. I didn't know what they would do if that happened, and I wanted to avoid finding it out.

"Guess now we need to wait," I said once we made it to the spot where we were supposed to meet up with Joe. He wasn't there yet, nowhere in sight. The longer we stood there, the higher the chances of one of them noticing us.

Less than five minutes later, I spotted Joe slowly walking toward us with something in his hands, maybe bags or something, I wasn't quite sure. I was so ready to leave, to get away from this nightmare.

"There's one more thing," Miles began, his tone unsure, "that I want you to know before we leave."

"What is it?" I asked, his words setting off all sorts of bells in my mind.

"I…" He closed his eyes for just a moment like he was trying to calm himself. Why was he so nervous? I really couldn't take any more bad news. "I love you."

My heart skipped a beat, and all my thoughts turned into thin air, my mind blank.

I blinked. "What?"

"I have no idea what will happen next, where this journey will take us, so I...I just wanted you to know that."

Standing up on my tiptoes I kissed him. I was speechless, could barely comprehend that he actually just said that, that out of all the people there were, somehow Miles Echo loved *me*. I looked at him, unable to keep the smile off of my face, even less so once he smiled back at me, a smile so gorgeous it made my knees weak.

"That was such a sweet display, really," a new voice suddenly said, Leon appearing close to us, seemingly out of nowhere. When did he get here? "But unfortunately, I cannot let you leave."

CHAPTER THIRTY-SEVEN
GONE

Time suddenly stopped, all four of us frozen into place, three pairs of eyes directed toward Leon, who looked torn somehow. I couldn't help but frown as the expression in his eyes shifted back and forth between nothing at all and something desperate, fighting a losing battle. His words echoed through my mind, my heart sinking. We'd taken too long, our chance had slipped away through our fingers once again, the realization nearly ripping my heart into two.

"Leon," Miles said, his voice more controlled than I expected it to sound. "You don't have to do this."

"I'm trying," Leon said, his words making no sense whatsoever. How could he claim to be trying not to force us to stay if that was exactly what he was trying to do? What the hell was going on? "I really am trying to stop, but I…can't. They won't let me."

I'd known that something was wrong with Leon, clearly,

but this was worse than anything I thought of before. Had he lost his mind somehow in the past few hours? Or was he always crazy? Also, who didn't let him do what? It simply made no sense at all.

"Who? What are you talking about?"

"I..." Leon tried but trailed off just as Gail appeared next to him, her eyes moving across Miles and me, then toward Joe, and finally back to Leon. Within a blink of an eye her hand appeared next to his arm, holding something, a syringe maybe, judging by the needle plunged into his flesh, though it looked more like a tattoo gun somehow.

"Now, now, Leon, no more of that," she said to him, though her eyes were on us, her expression almost predatory, sending a shiver down my spine. "You have an assignment to fulfill, a purpose for being on this ship. Remember where your place is."

While Gail spoke, her words cold and calculated, Leon's entire demeanor changed again, morphed into whatever it had been before he started to stammer weird nonsense to us. His eyes turned hard again, his jaw set and face almost perfectly expressionless before it shifted into something a little more relaxed.

Was this what Leon was trying to tell us, that he was being controlled by the agents somehow through whatever Gail had injected him? But how was that possible if Gail was his assistant, thus Leon being her superior? It made no sense whatsoever. But it proved me right in thinking that something was most certainly off about Gail, her eyes harsh as she looked at us, lacking any empathy, any positive emotion I could name. It was easy to see that in her eyes the two of us really were just cargo, part of an assignment and not two defenseless teens.

As I watched Gail, watched every move of her body, every twitch of a muscle I could see, trying to figure out what her next step might be, I could feel Miles shift around me as though trying to place himself in front of me somehow. If it weren't such a stupid and reckless thing to do I'd be touched, but right at that moment, all I wanted was to push him aside, yell at him to not be stupid. But really, I didn't do anything, let it happen, hoped that I would come up with some kind of solution to our problem, a way out of the situation we were in, in time.

In the corner of my field of vision, I noticed movement, Leon reaching for something, his arm and hand moving quickly, fluidly, followed by a flash of silver catching the light. A *knife*. My body froze.

Gail's face transformed into a menacing grimace, a smile so vile it made my stomach clench, just as Leon raised his hand, pulled back his arm, and threw the knife right at Miles, at his own brother in cold blood.

This was it, the end of the road, the moment one of us would end up dead just like we'd feared for so long. Miles killed by his own brother. My throat almost ripped in two by a fearful cry, panic flooding my blood like ice water. I felt like I watched everything happen in slow motion, everything turning blurry, distorted, leaving me powerless, my body refusing to respond, to do anything, knowing there was nothing I could do.

Suddenly it was over, two bodies crashing onto the floor with a loud *thump*. But that wasn't right... How could it be two? I was almost too afraid to look, forced myself to do it, more scared than ever before to see Miles lying at my feet dead with a knife in his chest.

Miles looked up at me with his eyes blown wide and a body shielding him. In a split-second reaction, Joe had pushed Miles aside and taken the knife instead of him, the blood rapidly seeping out of the wound and tainting his shirt deep red, the stain growing by the second.

Joe had given his life to save Miles. Joe, the man who pretended to be homeless to find a way to help me, to watch over me, the man who talked to me like I was an equal instead of a clueless child, who treated me the way a father should. It wasn't fair.

I looked up at Leon and Gail, time stopping while my mind raced. How could they, how could Leon, or rather how could Gail, and why? Suddenly I felt like we were back on the island, like I was looking at Ji facing the same problem again, but this time, my body refused to move. What Leon had done was so much worse, he'd killed a man who'd done nothing wrong, who simply wanted justice, and I wanted to make him pay for it, avenge my friend who'd sacrificed himself for a boy he didn't even know.

But I couldn't.

Ji was a stranger, but Leon and Gail, they were authority figures, the ones in control, who held all the power. I'd fought so many fights, won competitions and practice fights, but fighting Leon? He was bigger, older, ex-military, and above all, a male authority. Every fiber of my being screamed *no, you can't, you're not allowed*, but I had to do something. Miles and I had to get off this ship, try to get home even though I didn't even know what that meant anymore, and Leon and Gail were what stood in our way.

When I looked the bear in the eye, it felt like standing up to this threat that equaled authority in a way, but this was different. Leon and Gail were real, wouldn't just turn into smoke. They would fight back, and they could kill us. I'd lost almost everything, and Miles was all I had left now. It was clear that Leon wouldn't hesitate to take his life. And if he was willing to kill his own brother, he'd very much do the same with me in the blink of an eye.

I couldn't let any of that happen.

All my life I was taught that fear was something I wasn't allowed to feel, that I had to be brave, that I had to fight and I had to win. Weakness wasn't an option; losing wasn't an option, no matter what. But maybe I needed to feel fear, the entire spectrum of it, to do this, maybe it would be what would make me brave enough to understand my issue and do this.

So I let it happen.

I opened the gate and invited fear in, welcomed it, let it seize my body, but only for a moment. Its cold claws dug into every cell of me, a ringing in my ears threatening to shatter my eardrums, a fist around my heart like steel, an immovable force turning my body into stone. I never understood why I was afraid of authority, why male ones specifically had such power over me, but then Miles mentioned something on the island and it made me think. Now as I looked at Leon, fear coursing through my body, it was like I was seeing a mirror image of my father, even though Leon looked nothing like him.

Without consciously knowing it, my father was the monster I'd been afraid of all my life, the one that made me afraid subconsciously, even though he made me believe that all kinds of fear were unacceptable. So many times, I wanted to tell him what I thought, that I couldn't go on, that I wanted to stop, wanted to beg and plead, but I never could. He wouldn't accept something like that, every act of mine he deemed out of line was followed by a punishment.

Maybe I'd never get the chance to talk to him again, tell him that I finally knew what the side effects were to the way he treated me, to make him understand what he truly had done to me, but I could do this. I could stand up to Leon even if it was the last damn thing I would do.

If I could do this, I would be able to break out of the cycle, could break out of this mold my father forced me into.

I took a deep breath…

Dad, you've taught me to be afraid of you and people like you, to show respect, be meek and follow every order, but I'm done with that.

…and slowly let the air back out. My body eased and relaxed as I did, my mind clearing and focusing, zeroing in on the enemy and task at hand.

Breaking out of my stupor, I advanced toward Leon, Gail jumping aside with a surprised yelp escaping her. Although Leon was taller than me, heavier, his reaction time was more than pathetic, be it because of the stuff Gail had injected him or simply because he was a bad fighter — something that made little sense to me considering his military background — but at that moment I was thankful for it.

Leon tried his best to counter my every move, every trick I tried to pull, but it didn't take long for me to analyze him, his style, locate his weakness. His footwork was about as pathetic as his reaction time, a flaw I was all too happy to use to my advantage, moving around him, pretending to attack just to have him react without actually doing anything. Getting him into a position where he'd think my every move was just a bluff and let his guard falter just enough, just for a second, that time more than enough for me to attack, take him down with relative ease, my body rejoicing in the familiar movement.

In the corner of my eye I noticed Miles pick himself up off the floor and move toward Gail. I had no idea what skills she had, what background in martial arts or military type combat, so I could only hope the things I taught Miles on the island would be enough that he could at least defend himself against her. In a best-case scenario he'd be able to take her out, but I didn't want to get my hopes up.

Knocking Leon out once he was down turned out to be easy, his body remaining on the floor after that one precise blow, and I jumped back onto my feet. *One down, one more to go.* As much hate as I felt for Leon, the fact that he betrayed Miles in a way no brother should, and the fact that he killed Joe, I knew that the one pulling the strings was Gail. Whoever she was, she deserved every little ounce of pain I could give her. I didn't know if she was the one standing at the top of the food chain at Briola, though I had my doubts, and I really didn't care. It seemed like she was the one in control of everything happening on the ship, controlling Leon, and probably also the other agents. She deserved this.

For just a second, I smiled almost fondly at the way Miles tried to get Gail with a slightly sloppy right hook.

He was doing his best, and judging by the grimace she pulled, it still hurt even if it didn't look pretty.

"Miles," I said and walked over to him, hoping that would be enough for him to understand that I wanted him to let me handle it. He dodged a straight jab from Gail, used the momentum to step aside and making way for me.

Taking her down, her body writhing beneath mine on the cold metal floor, her arms pinned down by my hands, it had almost been too easy.

"I have no idea who you think you are, what makes you think you have the right to put us through this hell, and at this point I don't even care anymore," I hissed at her, my anger slowly seeping away from me, the will to run slowly taking over again. As much as I wanted to punish her for what she'd done, I knew that sooner or later Lido would show up, and that was something we most definitely had to avoid. "The only thing that matters right now is the fact that we are leaving, and if you have one ounce of sanity left, you better not fucking follow us."

At that I let her go, jumped back onto my feet, and grabbed Miles who, while I'd been a bit occupied, had gathered the bags Joe had carried, along with our backpack, and watched everything happen. I could see the question in his eyes, but was relieved that he didn't ask, that he spared me from having to lie and pretend like I was okay, because I truly had no idea how I really felt.

We moved toward the rafts quickly, tried to figure out how to get them free from where they were secured to the ship. Every few seconds, I'd looked back at Gail to make sure that she was still down, that Leon was still out cold, my heart squeezing painfully whenever my eyes wandered over Joe's dead, lifeless body, the blood pooling around him on the floor.

"It's almost over," Miles whispered next to me just as he managed to get the rope of the raft free, a small smile slipping onto his lips. Maybe we would make it this time, maybe this would finally be it. The idea was too good to be true. I pushed it away immediately. "Let's go home."

"You're not going anywhere," Gail said, suddenly back on her feet, using my second of distraction, my second of victory to try and take back control over the situation. I wanted to curse, to scream, to cry, but instead I just looked at her, horrified, my eyes widening only so much more as she pulled out a gun and raised it at us.

Was this it, the moment when we really would die? Would Joe's sacrifice be pointless? There was nothing left that I could have possibly done, that much I knew. Trying to attack her again would just get me shot faster, but maybe if she shot me, that would give Miles the time he needed to flee, to survive, to make it and tell our story.

As though he could read my mind, Miles took my hand and held on to it with almost an iron grip, a silent way to keep me from doing something reckless. Damn him and damn me for not trying anyway.

I flinched and braced myself for whatever it would feel like to be shot, as the loud sound of a gun going off shattered the air around us, the sound louder than the engines and my beating heart. But I felt nothing, no pain, no blood. My eyes darted at Miles, tried to see if he'd been hit, but I couldn't see anything. I just found the same confused expression in his eyes as our eyes met.

There, not far away from Gail, stood McCarty, her own

gun raised, the smoke still rising from it while a red patch formed on Gail's white shirt, turning it the same awful shade as Joe's, though somehow it seemed even more vivid and saturated against the white. Her mouth fell open in surprise, her gun falling to the ground as it slipped from her hand, her entire body following a second later like a sack of potatoes, lifeless, motionless.

CHAPTER THIRTY-EIGHT
GONE

Who was friend, who was enemy? Did this mean McCarty really was on our side? She had to be, right? What other reason would she have to shoot Gail than to show us exactly that?

McCarty raised her gun into the air, her finger moving away from the trigger, her hands up as though in surrender. "I'm on your side," she said, answering my unvoiced question, her voice clear, calm.

It was all too much at once. Leon turning out to be a puppet controlled by Gail, Joe dying to save us, or rather to save Miles, and now McCarty shooting Gail. My emotions were all over the place, sadness and anger mixing with fear and relief, with panic and the almost animalistic need to run, hide, and flee.

"We have to go," I said, instead of asking McCarty any clarifying questions, instead of saying anything else that raced through my mind, those words the most pressing and important ones. There were a thousand things I needed to ask her, a million answers I wanted from her, because this meant she was the one who could actually give them to us, but I knew that now wasn't the time. It had to wait at least until we were off the ship.

"We don't have much time until Lido comes out to check on what's taking so long," McCarty said as she walked toward us, pushing her gun back into the holster secured to her belt, clipping the safety strap over it, another sign that she really meant what she said, I could only assume.

"What about Leon? We can't just leave him," Miles argued, and my jaw nearly hit the floor.

"Are you crazy?" I asked, incredulous. "He's under their control, and I don't know about you, but I don't want to watch him try to kill you a second time."

"He's still my brother."

"Miles, I know he is, but that would be madness. We can't risk it!"

"It'll wear off," McCarty interjected. Immediately both our heads turned toward her, frowns taking over both of our faces. "The injection he received from Gail, it'll wear off, and he'll go back to normal."

Miles turned toward me, his expression almost triumphant, a small smile, the kind that made me weak, something he knew all too well. I sighed, resigned, and finally nodded. I still thought it was a bad idea, even if McCarty was telling the truth. Who knew if Leon was a good guy when not under Gail's influence? Something must've led him toward them in the first place, and who knew if that something wasn't evil, too, wouldn't try to manipulate us somehow.

With McCarty's help we managed to get Leon and our supplies into the boat, climb into it, the space just enough for all of us to fit, and slip away without Lido noticing, or at least I hoped so. I felt guilty for leaving Joe behind, even if he was dead and there was nothing I could do about it. It still felt wrong to leave him with Lido and the people he worked for. But it didn't matter. I didn't have time or the mental capacity to dwell on it, everything else taking up all the brainpower I had.

There were so many questions in my mind, so many things that barely made any sense, the hurt of Carla's betrayal still raw, something that would stick with me for longer than I was willing to admit to myself. Silently I watched the ship slowly get smaller as we made our way in the opposite direction, into the darkness. Once we were far enough away, McCarty turned on a lamp she'd grabbed off of the ship so we could see each other and at least something of where we were going, not that there was much to see. I didn't know if we had some kind of destination, if McCarty had a plan, and in that moment, it barely mattered, anyway. Gail was dead, and we had made it off of that God-forsaken ship.

I expected to feel bad about Gail's death, the way I felt guilty after Ji died, but found that I didn't. It was either her or us, and right then and still right now, I preferred her dead on the floor instead of Miles and me.

Quietly I moved closer to Miles, the simple gesture earning me a small smile from him, before resting my head against his shoulder. He helped me to relax and after everything that happened I was in desperate need of it. My body was screaming at me, tired and drained both mentally and physically, running on reserves I didn't know I had. Miles took my hand into his, the gesture comforting and calming, exactly what I needed.

"Who are you really?" Miles asked after a while, raising his eyes from his unconscious brother lying at our feet and toward McCarty. "If you're not with them, then…?"

"My name really is Nikita McCarty, and I am an FBI agent, that wasn't a lie. My badge is real, but I'm a double-agent," she said calmly, her eyes flicking from the horizon toward us and back. "I am happy to see that the two of you are alive and well, that I got there before Gail could do more damage than she'd already caused. I am deeply sorry for what you two had to go through, I really am."

"We're just happy that we're off that ship and away from them," Miles said. Somehow, even though I knew that, in theory, everything could finally be okay now—that maybe, just maybe, we were done, the nightmare over—I still struggled with even thinking it. There were so many times I'd given in to the illusion of safety, just to be forcefully ripped out of it again, that I was almost afraid to do it again.

Even if this was the moment we would finally reach the good ending of this journey, there was so much left uncertain. Carla wasn't my mother, had sold me off to these people, and my father surely was in on it, too, which meant that I couldn't go home. And really, neither could Miles. But if we couldn't go home, where would we go and what would we do? What would happen to us, what future waited for us on the other side?

And even after making it off the ship, would Briola

really give up on investments they'd spent more than three million dollars on?

"This really is it, I promise you," McCarty said, genuinely, with a smile. "I am ashamed of my actions, of the fact that I didn't believe Joe when his daughter disappeared and he tried to tell me what he found out about you, Miss Wolf. Maybe if I had, everything would've gone differently. That's why I volunteered for this operation, snuck into that part of the agency wanting to find out more, the things Joe wouldn't be able to access no matter how hard he tried. I knew something was going on, Joe telling me about the things he found, and I just had to know for myself. I hoped that it would all turn out to be false information but we all know it wasn't."

"Joe saved our lives even if that meant he had to die in the process," I said, even though we all knew that. "He's a hero."

"That he is, most definitely. Knowing Joe, he did it for you because he couldn't do it for Ivy. It was his way to atone for what happened. He couldn't save Ivy, but at least he could save you."

I forever owed my life to Joe, and I knew that somehow I would make his sacrifice worth it. I didn't know how, quite yet, but sooner or later I would figure it out.

The memory of Joe, the fact that he truly was gone, brought back the sadness I'd tried so hard to push away. I didn't want to cry, not again, but in that moment, I didn't have any strength to stop it. I'd already cried so much that night that I wondered how much more I could cry before I ran out of tears.

"Sorry," I said while Miles put his arm around my

shoulder and pulled me even closer toward him.

"No need to apologize," McCarty said, sympathetically. "I cannot even imagine how hard this must've been for you, the trauma of losing a friend in such a way. Crying is more than a natural reaction to it."

"Someone slipped us documents containing information about us, about who sold us to Briola," I said instead of commenting on McCarty's words, trying my best to keep my voice from shaking. Someone on that ship had to be on our side and, looking at what happened, it only made sense that it would be her. "Was that you?"

"I needed a way to show you that Lido and especially Gail were not to be trusted, and that seemed like the easiest way to do it, to show you that this was all part of a scheme to make you believe they were here to save you when really they simply wanted to hand you over to Briola," she explained.

It clicked in my mind then, and I wondered how I'd been too dense to realize it sooner. We'd seen her walk down that hallway away from our room after she left the papers, something so obvious I had no idea how I hadn't put one and one together sooner.

"So, our parents really did sell us?"

"Yes," she said with a nod. "I'm really sorry. I cannot fathom how you must feel because of it, seeing it so bluntly on paper, but I thought it would help if you knew."

"What is all of this about really? Why did Briola go through all this trouble with us?" Miles asked.

"It's all part of a top-secret project," McCarty said and then sighed. "There's a ship not too far away from here. That ship is filled with my people, agents I have trained and who are trustworthy. I promise once we get there, one of them will explain everything to you, the purpose behind Briola's actions, in a manner that I wouldn't be able to. I had people look into it after Joe reached out for my help, but personally, I didn't go into too many details, although I probably should have. Regardless of why all of it happened, the only thing that truly does matter right now is that everything is over and that you are safe now."

What kind of madman would contrive a top-secret project that not only required millions of dollars but also cost literal lives of minors? And what kind of project involved implants and fake bears, what purpose did that serve, what did it prove or test? If the FBI knew something about this, just how much bigger was this than we thought?

Neither of us said any more, so McCarty used the moment to reach for something she'd hidden in her bag, a transponder device of some sort, as far as I could see. She pushed a button on the side, and a small green light appeared at the top. Slowly she typed something in and then waited, a voice coming through a moment later.

We listened as she talked to someone on the other end, starting off by saying her own name and then some number, along with asking for voice verification. The voice confirmed what she said, and she proceeded by letting the other person know that we were coming and asking for location clarification. Once she was done with her relatively short conversation, she typed something into the device again and slightly adjusted our direction to the right.

"Do you know how long it'll take until Leon is back to normal?" Miles asked after a while, breaking the silence.

He was still unconscious, and I wondered how long it would stay that way, and what he'd do if he woke up before the injection wore off.

"A few hours, a day, maximum," McCarty said after thinking about it. "As far as I've seen, it won't leave any permanent damage. He'll be okay."

Seemingly satisfied with that answer, Miles just nodded and remained silent.

I didn't know how long it took until a light appeared on the horizon, a white ship coming into view bearing no name, flag or signs. It seemed so much bigger than the one we'd come from. I'd never been happier to see people dressed in military attire and the same black and gray suits that McCarty and Lido had worn.

With a little help, we secured the boat to their ship and managed to get on board, two of the FBI-attired guys climbing back onto the raft to get Leon and bring him inside. Catching Miles's expression, McCarty informed him that one of the medically trained agents would look him over to make sure I hadn't done any lasting damage in my angry eagerness. Miles nodded, earning a smile from McCarty.

"Follow me. I'll show you to your room and explain what happens next," she said and motioned for us to come along. Taking everything in, the clean floors and the agents moving about, we walked behind her through the door into the ship, down a flight of steep stairs into the belly of the ship, where the flooring was light parquet instead of simple metal, the interior painted in shades of white and brown, the lighting a warm yellow instead of cold, clinical white.

McCarty opened a door down the hallway, and we

walked into a small bedroom, the furniture sparse but still seeming like a dream to me. After we'd spent so much time on the island, in our cave, even the simple beds with thin mattresses and sheets seemed like a blessing, an unimaginable luxury. Another door led to a bathroom, McCarty informing us that a fresh change of clothing, along with toothbrushes and other toiletries were there for us so we would feel welcome and see that this really was the end of the road, that we really were safe.

Never in my life did I appreciate bland toothpaste, slightly scratchy towels, and clean clothes as much as right then. It felt amazing, impossible in every way. It *was* something I'd dreamed about when we were on the island. Looking at myself in the mirror, ignoring the tired circles under my eyes and the few slowly forming bruises scattered across my body from the strikes that Leon had landed, I actually looked almost normal again. My hair was nothing like what it was before this nightmare, the blue faded out, leaving almost only blond hair behind, along with darker roots.

I smiled as I looked at Miles's reflection next to mine, his hair in dire need of a cut falling into his eyes, but besides that, just like me, he looked almost like himself again. We weren't who we used to be before all of this, but that was unimportant. The only important thing in all of this was that we had made it through that nightmare alive. Together.

Before we'd talk to them, listen to why we ended up on the island and what would happen next, there was one thing I felt needed to be said. It was something Miles already had, yet I didn't, even though we both knew it was true. I watched that beautiful smile grow on his face as I said, "I love you, Miles Echo."

My life was a lie. But sometimes truths were built on lies. I knew that now. And Miles had his brother back, something I was sure he'd never even dared dream of.

Ten minutes later McCarty returned to our room with two manila folders in her hands. Quietly we sat down, Miles and I on one bed and McCarty on the other one, and waited for her to speak.

"As I promised before, I think now would be a good time to talk about what has happened to you," she said. "Unfortunately, we don't yet know all the details, haven't managed to decode all the information, but what we do know is this: Briola Bio Tech has acquired you for a top-secret and highly illegal human trial. They'd flown you out and left you on the island so no one would find out. We also know that you've been chosen based on talents and traits, specific ones that fit into their scheme."

"My titles," I said. I suspected as much on the other ship. That it must've been why my father went so hard on me for all those years, and now I had my confirmation. Maybe his efforts to make me afraid of authority also had something to do with this, some kind of plan to make me more compliant despite my strength?

McCarty nodded. "It's the most likely answer, since your mental and physical strength were highlighted in all the documents concerning you. As for Mr. Echo, intelligence but also gullibility and a possible mental weakness, though the latter two were usually marked as uncertain."

I looked over at Miles as McCarty spoke about him, noticed how his jaw clenched almost unnoticeably at her words but otherwise his expression didn't change. I wondered who even came up with either of those things, though the gullibility part matched with what Leon said on the ship.

"Could the trial have something to do with the implants?" Miles asked instead of commenting.

McCarty frowned. "Implants?"

"Briola implanted us with something, though we're not quite sure what. Maybe your people could try and figure it out?" I didn't know if telling her about them, and even handing them over, was a good idea. McCarty had shot Gail, helped us get off the ship and brought us answers, but could we really, truly believe her? I was pretty sure that the answer was yes, but a tiny part of me would remain on the fence until we made it back to the States.

"I'd gladly have someone do that, though knowing about them at all will already be very helpful in our efforts to find out what exactly happened to you and Ivy." Miles got up and retrieved our backpack, reached inside and pulled out our two vials. Just looking at them made me simultaneously angry and sick. McCarty inspected them curiously, held one of them up against the ceiling lamp, and then slipped them into the pocket of her jacket. "As soon as we have something, I will let you know."

"What do our friends and school think happened to us?" I asked. Up until this moment I never even considered that, never wondered what Melany might've been told had happened to me, why I never called or emailed her. I felt bad for it.

"They think you died when your plane crashed only a few hours after takeoff and went up in flames, leaving nothing behind," McCarty said. "You received closed casket funerals and your school even commissioned a memorial plate in the entrance."

It was sad, and less than ideal, the fact that I could never see any of my friends again, our past lives gone, nonexistent now, but... "If everyone thinks we're dead and our parents are the ones who sold us, what will happen to us now? We obviously can't go home."

At that, McCarty held out the two manila envelopes toward us. "In those you will find everything you need to know about your new identities along with new IDs, drivers' licenses, passports, and birth certificates. Two agents have been ordered to take over the undercover job of playing your parents until your respective eighteenth birthdays. A small house has been quickly prepared for you, which will be rented for a year, when the agents will leave and you will be completely freed. Of course, occasionally someone will come by and check on you, make sure you are all right and well. Unfortunately, or maybe not, you two are not going back to Florida. As an additional layer of safety, your new lives have been arranged in California. It's similar to witness protection, but not the same program."

Curious, I reached into the envelope and pulled out my new driver's license. In the corner of my eye I saw Miles do the same. It looked different from my old one, but the name was what really caught my eye. Fiona Wolf was no more. Kellie Jackson stared blankly back at me, the girl I would now be, free and alive.

"I know this is a lot for you to take in, so please take your time, go through your folders and acquaint yourself with your new lives," McCarty said and stood up. "Once we get to Toamasina, we will board a plane back to the United States. Until then, please try to relax, and if you have any more questions, please do not hesitate to ask any of us. Also, should Leon wake up and be in a state suitable for visitors, one of us will come and get you."

With that, McCarty smiled once again at us and then left the room, the door closing quietly behind her. I looked back at the driver's license in my hand, the new me, my eyes scanning the words, all this new info I now had to learn about myself. My birthday used to be in late fall, and now it was in spring, my address in a different city and state, the word California prominent on the top above my picture, the layout and color scheme of the entire thing completely different from my old one.

The only things that hadn't changed were my height and eye color. Everything else was different.

"Oscar Lyel, what kind of name is that?" Miles chuckled and held his license out toward me. I took it from him and handed him mine. No matter how much I tried to say his new name in my mind, it didn't fit, not the way his real name fit him, but we'd get used to it just like I would get used to mine.

"Nice to meet you, Oscar. I'm Kellie." Miles shook his head as he took my hand and shook it, a smile pulling up the corners of his mouth. It was silly, but I didn't care.

It'd been so long since we had a reason to smile, actually smile, and laugh.

There were still things I didn't understand, like the notebook entry, how that fit into any of it, what really happened to Leon that he ended up as Gail's puppet, and if McCarty's explanation of Briola's actions really was the truth, but for now, what was important was the fact that we were okay. Briola tried to use us and tried so hard to silence us, yet against all odds, we'd still come out on top. And even if things went south on us again in the end, we would be able to face it together.

"It's finally over, isn't it?" Miles asked, pulling me into a hug, our position slightly awkward, both our folders falling onto the floor as I tried to move around to make it a bit more comfortable. In the end I climbed onto his lap, straddling him. "We're all right. We're alive. We're together, and we are finally going home."

EPILOGUE

Slowly breaking through the stupor and state of temporary unconsciousness, Gail blinked her eyes open, her chest a little sore from where the bullet had hit her bulletproof vest, her head pounding from having hit the floor. Leaning on her elbows, she looked across the deck, noting the missing boat and Joe's body lying right where she remembered it. Taking it slow, Gail sat up and then got to her feet, rolling her shoulders and her neck to wake up her muscles, which had gone stiff from lying on the cold flooring for so long.

With a few steps she crossed the distance to Joe and pulled out the fake knife, the blade elongating as she took it out and then threw it aside, the blade and hilt sticky with fake blood. Reaching into one of her pockets, she took out a vial and her syringe, pushing the vial into it before pushing the needle into Joe's arm just to be sure that the effect was still there. Once done, Gail stood up and walked toward the front of the ship and the door to get back inside, leaving Joe behind.

"You okay?" Lido asked as she walked into the room. Lido sat at the console watching the radar and a few other pieces of equipment just like he'd been instructed. The only answer he received was a quick nod.

"Go and take care of Joe," she finally said and watched as the man silently left the room. Gail pulled up her laptop she'd stored away in one of the cupboards, put in on the closest table, and opened it. It took a moment until it was started up and ready for use.

Gail waited, time moving slowly. It didn't take too long until a video call request appeared on her screen, the ring sounding way louder than it truly was in the otherwise quiet room. After she clicked Accept Call, the window transformed and expanded, the connection stabilizing enough for McCarty to look back at her.

"Did they believe you?" Gail asked.

McCarty smiled before she spoke. "They're convinced they're safe now. They saw me kill you. They'll believe anything I tell them."

"Do you have the implants?"

"Affirmative."

"Proceed as planned: find out if they know about Berlin, and if so, how much."

ACKNOWLEDGMENTS

I'm not really good with words, *she says after writing ninety-nine thousand words*, but I'll try to put my feelings into words. Saying thank you will never really be enough to express what I truly feel, those two words seemingly too simple, so how about writing them in every language I know without having to consult the internet:

Thank you. Dziękuje. Спасибо. Danke. Grazie. Gracias. Merci.

From first idea to finished novel it took around seven years. It was a long road, but thanks to my mom I didn't have to travel it alone. Thank you for always being on my side, for encouraging me to give this idea a try, to go deeper, look further, and explore every aspect of the story and the characters. You've always believed in me, even when I didn't believe in myself, and somehow you knew I could do it. If it weren't for you, I wouldn't have given *Echoes* that final fateful try, would've shelved it instead, so thank you for giving me that push I needed.

Thank you so much to my two brilliant editors, Stephen Morgan and Lydia Sharp, without whom *Echoes* never would've evolved into what it is now. Thank you, Stephen, for giving this story a chance, for believing in Miles and

Fiona, for not getting annoyed at my mile long emails, questions, and worries, for the things you've taught me that made me a better writer, and just everything you've done for me along the way. A big thank you also to Lydia for poking holes in plot points that needed that tiny bit more to be perfect, for scenes to come alive and for the characters to be even more complex, for seeing what the story could truly be with a little more work. I'm forever grateful for the hard work you've both done.

Thank you to every single person at Entangled that was involved with this story, the various stages of editing, proofreading, and reading it in general and giving your honest feedback, Melissa Montovani who did an amazing job at spreading the word, and the incredibly skilled Art Department for the beautiful cover. Without all of you, this never would have turned into a story that people would be able to buy and read, or even know about. You're amazing and I am so grateful.

Thank you to Mia Siegert for being a wonderful friend and critique partner, for helping me tackle the ridiculous word count of my revisions, for being a cheerleader, and the first person to ever officially blurb something I wrote. Here's to years more of friendship and story telling.

Another big thank you also goes to my best friend, Anthony Z. Davis, for listening to countless hours of whining or me going on and on about some scene or chapter, helping me out whenever I was stuck, reminding and encouraging me to not give up, or just cracking a joke whenever I needed to laugh or a little pick me up. I'll never be able to express how much all of it means to me.

Thank you also to my sister from another mister, Delasi, for being an amazing friend and listening to me going on and on about writing, and not giving up on me despite the many times I was too absorbed by writing to text you back for days.

It was a lot of fun to set part of the story in Berlin, all these places I know so well and could just revisit whenever I needed to check some detail, so thank you, Berlin, I guess? You were the perfect stage for this story, though it's a shame Miles and Fiona, and my readers, didn't get to see more of you.

And last, but most certainly not least, I want to thank YOU, dear reader. Thank you for picking up *Echoes*, giving it a try and spending precious hours on reading about Fiona and Miles's journey. It means a lot to me, and I truly hope you enjoyed reading it as much as I enjoyed writing it.

GRAB THE ENTANGLED TEEN RELEASES READERS ARE TALKING ABOUT!

PROJECT PROMETHEUS
BY ADEN POLYDOROS

An Assassin Fall novel

The Academy stole everything from Hades, their perfect assassin. Now, he simply wants revenge. Tyler and Shannon once killed for The Academy, but instead they're tracking and hunting down its scientists. Shannon will do whatever it takes to protect Tyler, even if it means teaming up with Hades, a former rival. They all need answers, even if it means returning to the organization where it all started.

HIDING LIES
BY JULIE CROSS

An Eleanor Ames novel

Eleanor Ames looks like a typical high school student, but on the inside, she's a reformed con artist. Her best chance at breaking free from her past lies in one last con that coincides with a school trip to New York. Even her teen FBI agent boyfriend thinks the risk is too high. But when deadly secrets start to spill, Ellie will do anything to protect those she loves, even if it costs her life.

LIES THAT BIND
BY DIANA RODRIGUEZ WALLACH

An Anastasia Phoenix novel

Reeling from the truths uncovered while searching for her sister, Anastasia Phoenix is ready to call it quits with spies. But before she can leave her parents' crimes behind her, tragedy strikes. No one is safe, not while Department D exists. Now, with help from her friends, Anastasia embarks on a dangerous plan to bring down the criminal empire. But soon she realizes the true danger might be coming from someone closer than she expects...

PRETTY DEAD GIRLS
BY MONICA MURPHY

In Cape Bonita, wicked lies are hidden just beneath the surface. But all it takes is one tragedy for them to be exposed. The most popular girls in school are turning up dead, and Penelope Malone is terrified she's next. All the victims have been linked to Penelope—and to a boy from her physics class. The one with the rumored dark past and a brooding stare that cuts right through her. There's something he isn't telling her. But there's something she's not telling him, either. Everyone has secrets, and theirs might get them killed.